(Un) Sound Mind

A Novel By Richard Amico

Published by 57th Street Press

Copyright © 2014 Authored By Richard Amico

ISBN: 0692255052
ISBN 13: 9780692255056
Library of Congress Control Number: 2014948446
57th Street Press, New York, NY and White Haven, PA

This is a work of fiction. Names, characters, businesses, places, events and incidents are either the products of the author's imagination or used in a fictitious manner. Any resemblance to actual persons, living or dead, or actual events is purely coincidental.

Printed in the United States of America

RICHARD AMICO

(UN) SOUND MIND

57th Street Press

Part 1

All men whilst they are awake are in one common world,
but each of them, when he is asleep, is in a world of his own.
—Plutarch

1

Red, orange, and yellow leaves ripped from their branches by the cold October wind cascaded onto the churning waters of the Lehigh River in northeastern Pennsylvania. The old railroad tracks passing through Lehigh Gorge showed their age. It had been over one hundred years since the road crew hammered the last spike into the creosote-soaked ties. The ties, under the weight of thousands of passing freight cars over the years, had sunk deep into the shale-and-gravel beds. The heavy rails and steel spikes were overgrown with a scaly coat of thick rust. Except, that is, for the very top surface of the rails, now worn smooth and shiny by the wheels of a single freight train that passed this way each night traveling west. Like clockwork, at eleven thirty, the diesel engine reached Tunnel Road and blew its whistle before entering the railroad crossing. Everyone in the area knew that the two-mile-long train would be rumbling and clattering through for the next seven loud minutes.

Not more than one mile from those tracks, in a brick-and-frame house on a suburban cul-de-sac, Franklin Jameson sat in his bedroom waiting for the echoing chorus of freight cars to pass before getting into bed. "Three, four, five…No," he whispered, trying to resist the temptation to count them, each rumble and clack representing a single car. He had lived in this house for more than two years, yet he could not bring himself to retire until the train had passed and peace and quiet were once again restored to the neighborhood.

When the whistle blew at the next crossing, the final one within his hearing, and the din of the last few cars faded into the distance, Franklin began to prepare for bed. "A place for everything and everything in its place," he murmured. He believed it so strongly that failure to observe even the smallest part of his nighttime routine would result in worry that would keep him awake for hours.

First, Franklin adjusted the thermostat, cool but not cold. Sleep did not come to one who shivered or sweated. The shades were pulled down and the shutters closed so that the moon in its travels from window to window wouldn't distract him. He lined up his emergency crackers and his bottle of spring water on his nightstand. Hunger was one of the enemies of insomniacs. Then he arranged his nasal spray, tissue box, flashlight, antacid tablets, and current reading material into straight rows, all within easy reach. He nodded.

Next Franklin placed his cane in the old umbrella stand alongside his bed. He removed his glasses and placed them on the nightstand near his half-empty cup of chamomile tea. He reached out and turned off his brass reading lamp and inhaled deeply, savoring the slightly floral scent of newly laundered bed linens. It was Monday. He always made up his bed with clean linens on Monday. He loved the fresh, cool feel of crisp sheets against his skin as he slipped into bed. Then it was time to close his eyes and begin his attempt to drift off to sleep.

On some nights, it was deep breathing that accomplished the task. Long, slow breaths helped him relax. Franklin filled his lungs with air and gently exhaled—in and out, in and out. The rhythmic breathing was hypnotic. It usually cleared his mind, but not tonight. In a few days, he would be traveling to New York to meet Myra, and the anticipation of seeing her again after so long was making him nervous. He rolled onto his back and then on his side again and gently punched his pillow a few times. He reached out for the switch to turn on his reading lamp, changed his mind, and pulled his hand back. The more he feared not sleeping, the longer sleep eluded him. Some nights, no matter how tired he was, no matter how comfortable his surroundings were, no matter how long he waited, sleep just did not come.

Franklin remembered better times, before his divorce, when sleep was a comfort, a time to rejuvenate his body and clear away the echoes of the day. Preparing for sleep was different then. He would listen to Myra's chatter about her day and even occasionally interject events from his own. Franklin often thought about those nights together. Not that their relationship had been close and loving—maybe in the beginning it was, but it soon eroded into a pairing of convenience. Well, convenient to him maybe. Myra obviously hadn't found it so.

Wednesday should be an interesting day. He hadn't seen Myra in more than three years, and he had to admit that he was both excited and apprehensive. Myra had moved to Colorado after their not-so-amicable divorce and had lived in Boulder ever since. No word for three years, and then a call saying she would be in town visiting a friend in New York and wanted to meet for coffee somewhere nearby to catch up on each other's lives. *What did she really want?* he wondered. He began to picture her as she was when they last saw each other. *Was she still the talkative young woman he'd married sixteen, no, almost seventeen years ago? Was she still slender and shapely? She was quite a knockout back then. The last three years had to have changed some of that. Did she still dress impeccably? She did like nice things. Maybe that was it. Maybe she's gone through all the money from the divorce settlement, and she's come back for more. Well, that's not going to happen. Was she still as exasperating to deal with as she was back then? That was probably a given.*

They had arranged to meet at a small coffee shop in Manhattan. Obviously when she said "nearby," she meant nearby her location, but that was a concession he was happy to make. He hadn't been in Manhattan for several years. *It could be fun*, he thought, *browsing through book stores and shops once the reunion was over.* He might even find time to visit a museum.

Now there seemed to be no way he would get any sleep tonight.

He sighed and scratched his head as he stared at the far wall, waiting for his eyes to become accustomed to the hall night-light. As they adjusted, he began to make out shadows on the walls and floor, each shadow begging his imagination to give it purpose. It was a welcome distraction. He tried to recognize familiar shapes of objects as he would with cloud formations in a summer sky. If he couldn't sleep, he could at least amuse himself. A shadow on the bedroom wall from the Parsons table in the hallway looked like a steamship sailing into the room. The two piles of books on the table gave the shadow of the ship smokestacks and an upper deck.

Now, he pretended that his bed was Manhattan Island, and his tall chest of drawers was the New Jersey Palisades rising high above the Hudson River. The ship was now steaming down the river into New York Harbor, and then out to sea. He was beginning to enjoy this. Maybe the ship's destination was Bermuda. Franklin could almost smell the ocean and hear the slapping of the waves against the ship's prow as he began to drift off. His eyes began to close, and he entered into that twilight state of mildly altered consciousness, the predecessor of restful sleep.

Then there was a creaking sound that roused and disturbed him. He tried to ignore it, only half opening his eyes, not wanting to lose the progress he had made toward sleep. Then another sound. *It was probably just the furnace kicking on*, he thought, *but what if it wasn't?* He fought hard not to give in to paranoia. In the last three years, since he had begun sleeping alone, every unexpected noise unnerved him. This time, as usual, his fears won out, and he turned his head, ever so slowly, toward the open doorway to the bedroom. He wasn't sure, but he thought he sensed some movement. Franklin felt a chill even through the covers, and his body stiffened. His fingers tightened, squeezing the end of the comforter. He listened, not daring to move.

First, he noticed a new shadow inching its way along the wall. The vague shadow haltingly advanced and grew until it appeared to reach from floor to ceiling. His glasses were on his nightstand, but he didn't dare reach for them. He tried to focus his eyes to give form to this shadow as he had the ship, and it began to take shape. It looked like the shadow of Poseidon, Greek god of the sea, standing in the water towering over the steamship. He shifted his eyes to the hall doorway to try to determine what was casting the shadow. Then he trembled as it became clear. The shadow was made by a man—a man standing in his bedroom doorway.

He was dressed in a loose-fitting dark-blue shirt buttoned to the neck, and he wore baggy gray pants. His old ragged gym shoes made no sound as he walked into the room. Franklin put his hand over his mouth to stifle a gasp when he saw the man's face. It appeared distorted with grotesquely deformed features. His nose was bent, his ears were flattened against his head, and his lips were pulled back in a sneer. He walked toward Franklin through the doorway and crossed to his dresser. He came closer with each step. Now that he was close, Franklin saw his face much more clearly. It was a stocking; the man was wearing a nylon stocking pulled over his head. At first Franklin felt some relief that this wasn't some sort of monster, but that was little consolation. He still quaked at the realization that there actually was a burglar in his room.

Franklin lay very still in his bed, barely breathing. The man opened each dresser drawer in turn and then closed it after he examined its contents. He took something from one of the drawers, a small rectangular object, and placed it in his pocket.

Franklin stared at the nightstand out of the corner of his eye. The bottom drawer held his handgun. He had never wanted to own a gun of any kind, but his dentist—and friend—Dr. Hyrum Green, had convinced him to buy the small .38-caliber stainless-steel Taurus revolver. There had been several burglaries reported in the newspapers over the last year, but never in this neighborhood. Not until now, at least. Franklin hadn't opened that drawer since he'd placed the gun in it almost a year ago. He didn't even like to touch it. The gun was loaded, of course. Hyrum had said, "What good would a handgun be if it wasn't loaded? It's here to keep you safe." Franklin would have felt a lot safer now if he knew it was empty. The burglar couldn't know that the gun was in the drawer, but if he inadvertently found it…

Franklin believed that his only chance to survive this home invasion unscathed was to stop the intruder before he reached the nightstand and thus the gun. His heart began to race, pounding in his chest; the arteries in his neck pulsed.

The burglar opened drawer after drawer until it was only a matter of seconds before he reached the nightstand.

Franklin kept his head. He waited, motionless, pretending to be asleep until the burglar either tired of his fruitless search and left—the most desirable outcome—or moved close enough for Franklin to reach. He'd never been a violent man, or even very athletic. His disability, a weakness in his left leg and arm, put him at a disadvantage, but this was a drastic situation, and every now and then a man must summon his courage and rise to the occasion.

Franklin mustered all his daring and leaped to his feet with a yell. He closed his eyes, clenching his fists, and swung his right arm as hard as he could at the prowler. He braced for the impact, but his fist just swished through the air. On the verge of panic, Franklin cocked his arm again to deliver a better-aimed punch, but before he could strike, the burglar picked up a chair and held it over his head. Franklin fell to one knee, raising his arms in front of his face to protect himself from the blow he knew was imminent. The burglar, however, didn't hit him. Instead he threw the chair, with great force, at a window and then leaped out through the splintered frame and falling glass.

Franklin was stunned. Something was very wrong. Although he'd seen the chair fly through the window and heard the crash of the glass, he knew it couldn't be. There were no windows on that wall of his bedroom.

He switched on the light and put on his glasses. Franklin took his cane from the umbrella stand, planted it in the carpet between his bare feet, and pulled himself erect. The room echoed the sound of his heavy breathing. The chill of cold perspiration stuck his drenched T-shirt to his chest and made him shiver. All else was normal and quiet.

With the light on, he saw that there was no broken window, no smashed chair, and he now knew that there had been no burglar.

It all seemed so palpable and so convincing in every way. He could almost smell the day-old sweat from the man's stained shirt and feel the heat that radiated from his body. He sat back down on the side of his bed and lifted his teacup to his lips; the tea was cold, but he drank it down anyway.

An hour later, Franklin was lying in bed, still staring at the ceiling. Normally a dream fades after just a few minutes, but this dream was still vivid. Every detail was as real now as when it had happened, or at least when he dreamed it had happened. Franklin was too tired to think about this now. He would think about it tomorrow when he was better rested. But as he again prepared for sleep, one thought kept nagging at him. At the end of the dream, he was standing in his bedroom, awake, but try as he might, he couldn't remember the point at which he had awakened. Was he awake when he jumped out of bed? No, he couldn't have been awake then, because he still saw the intruder at that time. Did he wake after the window was broken and the intruder jumped out? Maybe, but why had he been standing at all? Had he begun to walk in his sleep? And how did he jump up from bed without his cane? It was a mystery.

***

Over the next few nights, Franklin's nightmares became even more disturbing. He dreamed of wolves chasing him and awoke in the corner of his room panting, his heart pounding. On other nights people would appear in his room as he tried to fall asleep. On one occasion he opened his eyes and saw an odd silhouette begin to take form on top of his dresser. As he fine-tuned the image, a small figure of a man took shape, sitting cross-legged and wearing a three-pointed yellow, orange, and gold hat. Franklin blinked several times, but the image remained. It was a dwarf wearing a jester's costume. The little man sat playing a flute, yet Franklin couldn't hear the music. He was captivated by the apparition. He wondered what tune the little guy was playing as he puffed his cheeks and fingered the instrument. The tune seemed blithe and the jester frolicsome as he bobbed his head from side to side. But soon the jester turned toward Franklin, looked directly into his eyes, and stopped playing. Mirth and revelry gave way to a look of indignation and malevolence.

"Go away!" he shouted, and the jester vanished. Franklin was sitting up in bed waving his arm in the direction of the now-departed specter. He touched the cool sheets of the bed, then touched his face. *I'm awake,* he thought, *but how long have I been awake?*

He pinched his arm to be sure. Was he losing control of his mind? Tomorrow he would have to find someone to talk to. Someone who could help him understand what all this meant. But tonight he'd sit with the lights on, hoping that morning would come quickly.

2

How does one judge success as a clinical psychologist? Dr. Ruth Klein must have asked herself that question at least once a month. Ruth, now forty-two years of age, had been in practice for almost eight years. Clients came and clients went. Some stayed in treatment for years while others moved on within months. But was she really helping any of them? Were they truly better off for having spent their time and their money pouring out their thoughts and emotions to her, a person who felt that her own personal problems may be as considerable as theirs?

Ruth sat alone hunched over her antique Queen Anne desk, leafing through notes from recent patient sessions. She reached up and tilted the shade from her desk lamp to deflect some of the glare bouncing back from the pages. Her neck throbbed, and she could hear a crackling noise as she twisted her head from side to side. She had been reviewing notes for what seemed like hours. Time always stood still when a crisis of confidence dominated her thoughts.

Ruth massaged the back of her neck with both hands and ran her fingers through her short auburn hair, lifting it from her neck. Then she shook her head to settle it back down. She tilted her glasses up over her hair to the top of her head and rubbed her eyes. When she opened them, they flashed toward the full-length mirror on the inside of the open closet door. For just a brief moment, she saw her mother looking back at her in her reflection. The color of Ruth's hair and her hazel eyes were gifts from her mother. "Well, at least I didn't inherit your freckles," she said out loud. "Or your feeble sense of responsibility."

Ruth was raised in Tacoma, Washington, principally by her dad. Her mother had left them both when Ruth was eleven years old, just about the time when she needed her mother most. Her father had tried his best to be both father and mother to her but placed more emphasis on sports than on tea sets. He never remarried and did the best he could to raise a normal young woman.

Ruth's family life, compared with that of her friends, felt anything but normal, and her unusual physical stature only added to her problems.

"Hey, beanpole," Jake Brandon would shout. "Don't let the wind blow you away." Jake was one of many boys in middle school who'd found joy emphasizing anything that would make someone feel self-conscious. Not that she needed much help in that area. At thirteen, Ruth was already over six feet tall and gangly. Her arms and legs seemed to grow at a much faster rate than her ability to coordinate their movement.

That all changed in high school. After mastering control of her ample extremities and filling out her frame to more womanly proportions, she played varsity basketball and helped the Olympia Lady Dragonflies win the 1986 high school state championship. Although her academic grades were outstanding, it was her basketball skills that won her scholarship to the University of Washington to play for the Washington Huskies. It almost made tripping over those awkward feet for several years worthwhile.

Ruth checked her schedule for her next patient. Sylvia Radcliffe should be here soon; the woman was always on time. Sylvia's faithfulness to her schedule and her high energy level, almost to the point of being manic, were exhausting to watch. Ruth glanced at the small gold-and-rosewood clock on the corner of her desk for confirmation and then looked out the window at the long shadows cast by the oak tree, filtering the light from the lamppost in front of her office. It was just 5:45 p.m. and nearly dark already.

Sylvia worked as an assistant manager at Stanton's Fine Gems. She left work sharply at five each weekday evening. On Tuesday, today, she would order a salad at the Maplewood Diner, eat her dinner quickly, and arrive exactly five minutes early for her six o'clock session with Dr. Klein.

Ruth envied Sylvia's discipline, even if Sylvia was a little compulsive about it. *It's too bad obsessive compulsive disorder isn't contagious. I'd take a month's worth and get caught up on my life.* Ruth scanned her personal planner and grimaced at the number of items crossed out, moved, or written over.

Most of Ruth's patient sessions were scheduled during the evening primarily to accommodate their work hours. This agenda, however, did benefit Ruth as well, since it provided time in the morning, early afternoon, and late evening for routine domestic chores and enough time to perform at least a minimum of parenting responsibilities for her eleven-year-old daughter, Emma. Unfortunately the demands of maintaining a clinical psychology practice and managing her household eroded much of the *quality* from the quality time she tried to make available for her daughter.

Ruth was dedicated to her career, but these short days and long, cold nights, as winter approached, seemed to strip away some of her motivation and enthusiasm. "Let's concentrate," she said as she crushed a sheet of paper into a tight ball and tossed a foul shot at the wastepaper basket near the couch on the far side of the office. She stood frozen with her right hand over her head and watched the paper ball bounce off the rim of the basket and roll along the floor near the coffee table. "That makes the day perfect!"

Ruth rubbed her hands together to warm them and to help focus her thoughts. She opened the manila folder titled, "Radcliffe, Sylvia, November 19, 2011, Session Summary," and stacked it on top of a loosely assembled pile of folders and papers filled with handwritten notes. She adjusted her glasses, picked up her small handheld dictation recorder, pressed the talk button, and stared at the notes in the file. She began to read the patient overview: Sylvia Radcliffe began therapy in September 2008. She was born in 1971 and has been divorced for the last four years. She has issues with family members and feels that her life is unfulfilling and pointless. "Join the club," she murmured under her breath, then immediately erased the accidental recording. She smiled and shook her head.

Ruth looked back at her desk clock. Her father gave it to her when she opened her practice eight years ago. "You're going to have to learn to be on time," he had said, "or your patients will feel you have more problems than they do. I was going to give you an alarm clock, but this one was prettier." She smiled a tender but sad smile. "Note to self," she said into the recorder. "Call your father."

A knock on the door startled her. She immediately closed Sylvia's file and gathered the conglomeration of papers and folders on her desk and pushed them together into a ragged pile. She then stuffed them into the open lower drawer of her file cabinet. Ruth stood and looked into the mirror on the closet door. She frowned at her towering six-foot-one-inch height. Ruth looked at her feet, and a slight squeak escaped from her lips. She kicked her fuzzy pink slippers off, one at a time, into her closet and slipped on her plain black flat shoes. She adjusted her skirt, checked and smoothed her hair, and turned, shutting the closet door with her left foot. She then kicked the file drawer closed with her right and said in a serious, slightly deeper than usual voice, "Come in."

***

A slender woman about five feet six inches tall, wearing a navy-blue pant-suit, the jacket straining at its button enclosing her ample breasts, entered the room in a hurry and sat with perfect posture on the couch. She tossed her head and pushed her long black hair back off her shoulders. "What a week I've had," she exclaimed. Sylvia reached down, picked up the ball of wadded paper from the floor near the couch, and turned it over several times in her hands.

"It's so hard to get good cleaning help," Ruth said as she reached over and took the paper ball, raised her arm in the direction of the wastepaper basket, paused, and then placed the paper in her pocket.

Sylvia slouched back on the couch and placed both hands on her head. "I need to get control of my life," she said. "My boyfriend still hasn't called me. I can't believe I let him talk me into getting a tattoo. I'll probably get blood poisoning or some other infection." Dr. Ruth Klein lifted her notepad and secretly wrote: *Here we go!*

Sylvia began, "Last Friday my mother came to visit and stayed until yesterday. You know how I feel about my mother. I guess I owe her something for raising me, but I wanted her to leave almost as soon as she arrived."

At that point, Ruth postulated that Sylvia needed some new material. She had complained about her mother either making disparaging remarks that demoralized her or asking her for money in almost every session for the last two years. *At least she has a mother.* Ruth wondered what her own mother was like now. Had she grown old alone? Did she have a new family? Were there half brothers or sisters Ruth had never met? *For Christ's sake, she hasn't even seen her own granddaughter. She probably didn't even know I was married and divorced. She missed the first eleven years of Emma's childhood. She probably wouldn't recognize me on the street if we met, much less recognize her granddaughter.*

As a child, Ruth would fantasize about her mother's return. Ruth would open the front door, and her mother would be standing on the steps with her suitcase in one hand and a tearstained handkerchief in the other. She would apologize for having left and beg Ruth for forgiveness. After remaining indignant and scornful for an appropriate amount of time, Ruth would run to her. Her mother would drop to one knee, hug Ruth, and swear never to leave her again. But that never happened. Instead Ruth grew into a young woman struggling to catch up on life's lessons missed in a male-oriented, single-parent household. From puberty through dating and her eventual marriage, she'd learned to face the passages of youth without the gentle guiding hand of a loving mother. Sometimes she thought she'd really married Tom because her father adored the guy. *So much for Dad's ability to judge character.* Tom and Ruth had five good years together, but Ruth was dedicated to her career, and Tom's lack of wanting one further weakened a relationship that was not strong enough to survive their differences. She wondered about Tom. *It's been—*

"So I hid all the liquor bottles before she came and told her I didn't have any. Did I do the right thing, Dr. Klein?"

Oh God! Where are we? "Do you think you did the right thing?" Ruth asked. *Very psychoanalytical, Ruth,* she said to herself as she glanced at the recorder to ensure that it was still running.

"I hate her!" Sylvia said, dabbing her eyes with a tissue and trying not to completely smear what was left of her eyeliner.

"I doubt that that's true," Ruth said, glad for the pronouncement, which gave her an opportunity for a comment. "Have you tried to think about the good experiences you had with your mother while growing up?"

Sylvia looked squarely into Ruth's eyes and said, "There weren't any."

"You've talked at length about recent experiences with your mother, but you never told me much about your youth. You're a successful businesswoman. You must have developed at least some of your character from lessons learned at your mother's knee."

Sylvia bit her lip and looked across the room. Several boxes on the table under the window caught her attention. "Do you treat a lot of children?" she asked. The boxes were brightly colored with plastic windows displaying their contents. A bright-red truck with flame decals on its side shone through one box. Another boasted a set of wooden blocks with pictures of animals and large capital letters on each one. Sylvia walked to the stack of toys and retrieved the one that had been the focus of her attention. She picked it up and held it out to Dr. Klein.

"Where are the rest of Barbie's accessories?" she asked. Ruth looked up from her notes, noticing for the first time that Sylvia had left her spot on the couch.

"Those are toys for the Red Cross drive. They're all supposed to be new packaged toys, but my daughter insisted on donating her Barbie doll to a less-fortunate child," she said with a roll of her eyes. "I'm not sure the Red Cross will take it, but I promised her I'd try."

Sylvia held up the doll by its waist. "Barbie's been around for a long time. Do you mind if I hold her while we talk?" Ruth nodded as Sylvia returned to the couch, cradling the doll in her arms. "It's been so long since I've seen her. Her name was Alice."

Sylvia seemed unusually subdued, causing Ruth to ask, "Did your mother buy Alice for you when you were a child?"

"Not a chance," Sylvia said, suddenly focusing back on the session. "She thought that dolls were a waste of money. Why buy the kid a doll when you could buy five drinks with the same ten bucks?" Ruth waited for Sylvia to continue.

"When I was eight years old, I really wanted this doll. Barbie was tall and pretty with long hair. She had lots of clothes, and everybody liked her. She even had a boyfriend." Sylvia held up the doll and adjusted its hair. She bent the doll's limbs into a sitting position and placed her on the edge of the coffee table so that the doll was leaning back comfortably, listening to the story.

There was a gleam in Sylvia's eyes as she went on. "One night my mother came home, drunk as usual, and passed out on the living room sofa. I tiptoed to her purse and found a ten-dollar bill inside. I really didn't need to tiptoe; once she passed out, she was out for hours. There was little chance she would remember how much money she had left at the end of a night of drinking, so I took it. I felt a little guilty about taking the money, but I really wanted the doll.

"I felt so grown up standing in the department store holding the box with the doll and its wardrobe in my hands and the ten-dollar bill in my pocket. I saw a stack of bags with the store's name on them, and I took one and put my doll in it. I guess I didn't realize that it was customary to buy the doll before putting it in the bag. Well, anyway..." She leaned forward. Ruth's eyes brightened, responding to the newfound excitement in Sylvia's voice.

"'Excuse me,' I said to this tall saleswoman with a face like a prune, and I held up my bag with my new doll." Sylvia stopped talking and stared at the floor.

"Please go on," Ruth said. "It's a wonderful story."

"Well, I guess I wasn't a very experienced shopper," she said with a chuckle. "I was so proud of myself for just being there, so I said, 'This is going to be my new best friend. Her name is Alice.' The saleswoman tried to ignore me, but you know how bratty kids can be. I tugged on her dress until she finally looked down. I guess I really pissed her off, because she said, 'Please stop bothering me and go find your mother.'"

Ruth laughed at Sylvia's imitation of the saleswoman's haughty tone.

"When I told her my mother wasn't in the store, she said, 'Well, why don't you take your new friend and go home?' Then she rushed off to help some lady who was trying on a big flowered hat. I really didn't know what to do, so I just tucked the bag with Alice under my arm and went home. I wanted to pay for the doll, but she really didn't give me a chance. I probably should have just left the money on the counter."

"I wouldn't beat myself up over it," Ruth said. "You were a small child, and you intended to pay for the doll, even if it was with 'borrowed' money. The important thing is that you knew that taking the money from your mother's purse was wrong. I think it was a valuable lesson learned—a character-building lesson for an eight-year-old child."

Sylvia thought of telling Ruth about her mother's interpretation of the incident. Of course her mother didn't have all the facts. Sylvia had told her mother that she was playing with the doll, not that she wanted to buy it—not with money stolen from her purse, anyway. She said she didn't realize that she still had the doll until she was halfway home.

Her mother seemed to be proud of the fact that she had taken the doll. Her reaction was classic Henrietta Radcliffe. She'd said, "It's not your fault. If people can't pay close attention to their belongings, they deserve to lose them." It was a lesson well learned by an eight-year-old at her mother's knee, but not the same lesson Ruth was describing.

After Sylvia left, Ruth organized her notes, labeled the memory card from the recorder, and filed it away to be reviewed sometime before Sylvia's next session. Ruth felt that they had experienced a minor breakthrough for both of them. Sylvia had never talked about her childhood before. There was much more work to be done, but Sylvia was finally opening up to her and revealing her true emotions. And for Ruth, a patient whose therapy had been going nowhere now showed signs of progress. Ruth was confident that she had finally broken through and reached the real Sylvia Radcliffe. Although Ruth never judged a book by its cover, she gave a great deal of weight to the summary on the panel of the dust jacket. She knew as much about Sylvia as Sylvia wanted her to know. The details of Sylvia's life, however, differed greatly from the CliffsNotes version she had presented in therapy.

***

Sylvia Radcliffe was born Laura Sylvia Carpenter. Her first year of life was spent in a three-story walk-up apartment that smelled of cigar smoke and bourbon near Fifth Street in South Philadelphia. Her cradle was the middle drawer of an old scratched dresser her mother, Henrietta Carpenter, bought from the Salvation Army for seven dollars. Sylvia never knew her real father. At that point in Henrietta's life, men came and went, literally. It wasn't Henrietta's finest hour.

When Laura was two years old, her mother, dispirited by the meagerness of her surroundings and the pressure of current financial circumstances, married Joshua Radcliffe.

Joshua felt that marrying Henrietta was the right thing to do since she was six months pregnant with his child at the time. He knew all about her past life of barhopping and frequent sexual indiscretions, but he was sure that his influence, and the good Lord, would change all that.

The marriage lasted for only one year. Soon Henrietta Radcliffe was back on her own with little more than she'd had a year ago and an extra mouth to feed. She decided, after much introspection, to turn to her mother for help. She began to call Laura Sylvia in honor of her mother, or maybe it was an attempt to influence her to help support the children, but it was to no avail. Within weeks the old woman passed away, leaving Henrietta less than one hundred dollars after the funeral expenses were paid. Henrietta never forgave her mother for failing to provide for her in her youth; it seemed to be a family trait.

Henrietta kept the name Radcliffe after the divorce. Maybe she kept it as a reminder of a better time, when life was easier and someone cared about her. Maybe she was just too lazy to change it back to Carpenter. When her children were old enough to be enrolled in school, they were enrolled as Sylvia and Emily Radcliffe.

Sylvia Radcliffe grew into an attractive woman. She was smart and cunning. She appeared to be a warm, loving person, but she knew how to focus her efforts to improve her life and let no one stand in her way. By the age of thirty-seven, she had married and divorced, continued her education with two years of computer science at a community college, and secured a job as a sales associate at Stanton's Fine Gems.

It was at Stanton's that she developed her fascination, almost an obsession, for fine jewelry, and through her love of the jewelry she sold, and her skill at selling, she rose from the rank of sales associate to assistant manager of jewelry sales in just two years.

* * *

"I've got a Chinese chicken salad with extra snow peas and bean sprouts and an iced tea," said the deliveryman.

Sylvia Radcliffe put up her hand and beckoned him to her office. The tall young man smiled, turned his hat around so that the peak was facing forward, puffed up his chest, and walked to her door. He bent forward with a flourish to place the bag on her desk in what seemed to be almost a bow. Delivering Sylvia's lunch was always the high point of his day. She wasn't a big tipper, but she always gave him a wide smile and fodder for his fantasies before she sent him on his way.

Sylvia closed her door and spread a napkin open on her desk. Lunch was a time to catch up on personal business in the privacy of her office. It was time for an update. She opened the computer file containing a mailing list of customers and their purchases for the last four years. This data was being sent to a market research firm to help determine buying habits compared to local demographics. It was all very boring and probably would yield nothing useful for the store. It was, however, very useful to Sylvia and her partner, Mortimer Banks. She removed a small flash drive from her purse and plugged it into the USB receptacle on her computer.

Sylvia carefully planned every mission before she met with Mort to give him his instructions. She studied store receipts to find just the right piece of jewelry to steal. She would select a ring, a watch, a necklace, or some other fine piece, not too recently sold, which was of high value, or contained at least one stone that was of the size and quality she loved, but not distinctive enough to make the gem easily identifiable as stolen and thus difficult to resell.

Sylvia performed her "due diligence" on hundreds of prospective marks. She gathered all the available information about the purchaser from the store computers. She copied the buyer's credit information, home address, and place of business. Then, she usually worked from a public computer in a library or on occasion just drove around a neighborhood until she found an unsecure Wi-Fi access and worked from her laptop in her car.

She searched the Internet social networking pages to discover how many members were in the mark's family and any other useful information unwittingly offered online. She made anonymous calls to the mark's employer to determine work schedules to determine the most likely time that the home or apartment would be empty. Once she even made a call to the target's home, claiming to be a political poll taker and fitted questions into the survey that would give her the information she needed. It was easy to find out the things she wanted to know.

Sylvia developed a schedule for each job that would allow Mortimer to retrieve the prize with a minimum of risk. People who bought expensive jewelry usually owned other valuable objects as well. Mort's assignment was to "appropriate" anything of high value so that the single piece of jewelry would not appear to be the objective of the heist.

Sylvia highlighted the name "James Farnsworth" on the store database. He seemed to be a valued customer who was worth a more in-depth look. Of course he hadn't made a purchase in over a year, but in 2010 he bought a Patek Philippe series twenty ladies' wristwatch in eighteen-karat white gold. It was a fine choice and a bargain at only eighty-three thousand dollars. The sales slip showed a gift card addressed to Debora. If that was his wife's name, they were in business.

Sylvia knew that Mort could sell the watch for about half that value, and once they split the profit, she would probably be left with less than twenty thousand dollars. It was highway robbery, but the market for purloined jewelry was limited. Still, it wasn't bad for a few days' work.

After leaving Stanton's tonight, she would search the social networks to check Farnsworth's marital status. Assuming he had a wife named Debora, and assuming she was the recipient of the watch, the next step would be to determine the best time for the robbery.

If James Farnsworth or Debora had a Facebook account, it would be like striking gold. *Why do people make it so easy?* she thought. There always was the chance that the watch would not be in the house, but the wealth of the family was such that Mort could probably find enough other loot to make the trip profitable. This looked like a good prospect.

Sylvia turned toward the window in her office door to see if she was being watched and downloaded the details of both the sale and the buyer to her flash drive. Then she ejected the drive and slipped it back into her purse.

3

Franklin stood just inside the doorway of the coffee shop and looked down the row of tables. He listened to the sizzling of the eggs on the open grill and closed his eyes to savor the aroma of the bacon popping as it crisped in its own fat. It sounded like rain dancing on a woodland pond.

"Excuse me, honey," a white-uniformed waitress said as she swiveled her hips past him with three plates of the breakfast special lined up on one arm and an orange-capped pot of decaf coffee in the opposite hand. "Just sit anywhere you want." She hurried down the aisle before Franklin could reply. In seconds the waitress was lost in the crowd of patrons coming and going among the clatter of dishes and the sound of muffled conversation. Franklin walked between the rows of wood-grain laminate tables and chairs with red vinyl seat cushions. He stood for a few seconds and turned from side to side, scanning the room.

Even from the back of her head he knew it was her. Her hair—that long black hair—still shone as it fell around her shoulders. He took a deep breath and held it, trying to quiet the pounding in his chest. Three years, and he was still moved by the sight of her. Myra slowly stirred her coffee, clinking the spoon against the side of the cup. Franklin remembered how exasperated he had become and how he shouted at her each time that sound had interrupted the reading of his morning paper. Today it was a welcome sound.

"You got here early." He walked around the table to face her and hooked the Derby handle of his cane onto the back of a chair.

"I've changed the way I do a lot of things," she said. Myra reached up, took his hand, and pulled him down into his seat. She placed her elbows on the table and held her cup up to her lips. "I've already ordered; I hope you don't mind."

"That's fine; I'm just having coffee anyway." He turned the cup at his place setting right side up and poured from the coffee carafe already on the table. Franklin didn't recall her eyes being so bright, or her smile so wide. The last time he saw her she was leaving the courthouse with her lawyer. She smiled then too, but it was the smile of victory. Now she had a warmer smile. *Maybe three years apart had changed her. Maybe she came back because she's sorry about the way we—*

"What can I get'cha, honey?" the waitress asked, appearing out of nowhere.

Franklin shook his head. "I'm not having—"

"He'll have two poached eggs on rye toast," Myra interrupted. "You know you don't do well without a good breakfast."

Franklin smiled and nodded to the waitress. She looked at Franklin, then at Myra, and said, "Does he want orange juice with that?" Franklin touched the waitress's hand to attract her attention and then shook his head. The waitress smiled at him, then turned to Myra, exhaled loudly, and walked away.

"Still the same Myra," he said.

"Still the same Franklin?" she asked. "I've missed you. Are you still trading stocks, or whatever those arbitrage things were?"

"No." Franklin laughed. "Actually, I retired two years ago."

"Retired at forty-five—that must be nice," she said.

On the sidewalk outside the coffee shop, a man in a scarred brown leather bomber jacket with a brown lamb's-wool collar peered through the window, shading his eyes from the glare of the late-morning sun. Franklin looked up at him, and the man looked away as though he had been caught eavesdropping. *This guy could be waiting to rob someone as soon as they leave the restaurant.* Franklin rubbed the back of his neck. He became paranoid every time he came to Manhattan. *It's the middle of the morning. No one is dumb enough to commit a robbery in a crowd near high noon,* he told himself.

"What hotel are you staying in?" Franklin asked. He focused on her eyes to keep her from turning to see where his attention had wandered.

"Oh, no, I'm staying with a friend in Queens. I'm helping her through some problems she's having."

"What kind of problems?"

Franklin shifted his eyes to the window and watched the man in the leather jacket pacing back and forth in front of the coffee shop, his hands stuffed in his pockets and his breath making frosty plumes in front of him. A last glance at the window, and the man slipped out of view toward the corner of the street. Franklin focused his attention back to Myra, glad that the distraction was finally gone.

"Look, Franklin, she's having a difficult time. She just went through a divorce, and you know how rough that can be. I gave her more help than I could afford, but it wasn't enough. She's going to lose her apartment if she doesn't come up with twenty thousand dollars to pay back taxes and late mortgage payments. I thought you could help out. It's not for her. You could lend me the money to get us out of debt, and then when we sell the apartment, I could pay you back. That is, if you want the money back."

"Us, you said get *us* out of debt," Franklin said, watching her begin to squirm in her chair.

"Well, yes, she's agreed to sign half of the apartment over to me if you give me the money. It's a good investment."

Franklin's mind quickly began to line up the facts. *The housing market was poor, but not that poor in New York. Half of any New York apartment for twenty thousand dollars was a rare opportunity. Now if her girlfriend truly had received title to the apartment in the divorce, and she actually did sign half over to Myra...*

His evaluation of the possibilities was interrupted by the ring of Myra's cell phone.

Myra looked at the number on the screen. "It's my friend, Tiffany. She's the one I'm talking about. I'll call her back later."

"No, no, she may be having a crisis. You take this opportunity to talk to her while I go to the men's room. It was a long bus ride from Pennsylvania."

Franklin smiled, placed his napkin on the table, unhooked his cane, and walked toward the side of the restaurant. Myra nodded and said, "Hello, Tiffany, where are you?"

Franklin satisfied himself that she was well engrossed in her call and then circled around the coffee shop until he reached the front door. He leaned out, looking toward the corner, being careful not to lean so far that he could be easily seen.

Sure enough, he spotted the man in the brown bomber jacket facing away from him, leaning on a mailbox, but clearly holding a cell phone to his ear.

Franklin rushed back to the table, grabbed the telephone from Myra's hand, and listened. "Just get a check from this jerk, and let's get out of here before he catches on. I'm afraid he might have seen me through the window."

"That's right, Tiffany," Franklin said. "You should have stayed farther away. She's much better at ripping people off all by herself."

"Drop dead!" the man replied.

"No, *you* drop dead," Franklin said. He tossed the phone into Myra's lap, threw a twenty-dollar bill on the table, and said, "You can drop dead too!"

Franklin walked out the door, swinging it wide as heads turned to watch him leave.

***

That evening Franklin sat in front of his television. His eyes glazed over as the evening news anchorwoman talked about a politician that had been arrested for embezzling funds and a house fire that was burning out of control somewhere in the area.

Franklin sat in his favorite chair, a large tan leather recliner. He picked up the framed picture of Myra from the end table and turned it to the wall. Any bonds linking them together had been finally severed. He wasn't responsible for her future any longer.

He thumbed through an old photo album that he kept on the coffee table. He stopped at a picture of Myra standing in the kitchen of their first home. She was holding up a casserole and smiling. "What a fraud," he said out loud. She looked like Margaret Anderson from *Father Knows Best*. Myra never was the good wife waiting for her husband to come home with dinner on the table, ready to share conversation about her day. No, Myra was usually out when he came home from work. Her pots were more wall ornaments than cooking utensils. She never understood what he did for a living and didn't much care, as long as the money kept coming in.

He turned another page and stopped at a picture of a nineteen-year-old Myra and himself standing on the shore of Lake Oneida. The photo was thick and protruded from its sleeve. He slid the picture out of the plastic. The left side of the picture had been folded back so that one-third was hidden. Franklin unfolded the photograph. The third person in the picture, the one behind the fold, was his old friend, Dennis. Franklin nodded at the picture several times, refolded it so he and Dennis stood together, with Myra's image folded behind, and arranged it back in its sleeve. He placed the open album on the coffee table, yawned, picked up the remote, and shut off the television. He sat alone in the silence for several minutes.

Franklin had been living alone now for about three years, and until the recent disturbing dreams, he'd never really felt alone or vulnerable. Now he walked through the house and checked the windows and doors before going up to bed. In his room, he lifted the comforter and dropped to one knee to look under the king-size bed.

"This is ridiculous," he said out loud, but he walked to the closet and gave that a look also.

Again, sleep did not come quickly. Each time he closed his eyes, Myra appeared, her hand outstretched.

4

Franklin switched his cane to his left hand and pulled the heavy front door of 29 Office Park Place open with his right. The shadow from the door rippled across the building directory. His eye followed the shadow to a small sign now illuminated by the afternoon sun.

The sign on the bulletin board read:

> Dr. Ruth Klein, Clinical Psychologist, focusing on the evaluation, prevention, diagnosis, and treatment of mental health issues. Dr. Klein uses psychotherapy and other counseling skills to improve both emotional and mental health.

Had providence just directed him to this sign? He wasn't a religious man, but if some omniscient being was pointing a finger of light to guide him to a source of advice and comfort in his hour of need, could he refuse the help?

Franklin walked down the corridor to room 118, the office of Dr. Ruth Klein, and stood in front of the closed office door. He put his hand on the doorknob and froze. Should he or should he not walk in and make an appointment? What would he say?

Hi, my name is Franklin Jameson, and I think I'm losing my mind.

Or maybe, *Hi, I'm a forty-five-year-old man who is afraid to go to sleep because I see poltergeists almost every night.*

Franklin released the doorknob and looked down the hall toward his dentist's office, his intended destination for a 1:00 p.m. cleaning appointment. He turned back to the psychologist's door, this time with more conviction. He knew he should walk right into Dr. Klein's office and make the appointment. It was the smart thing to do, the right thing to do, and he would do it now if it wasn't so late. *Yes, that was it; he would do it now, but there just wasn't enough time.* Franklin hurried down the hall to his dentist's office.

He was generally cynical about all medical and dental checkups. He believed that even if nothing was wrong, and there usually wasn't, most doctors or dentists would still try to find something to generate a bigger bill, but when visiting Dr. Green's office, he was less skeptical. Dr. Green was a friend. He was always amiable and good-natured, he played sixties music throughout his office, and his dental hygienist, Michelle, was cute. He recalled how, on his last visit, she had wrapped her arms around his head as she scraped and picked at his teeth, seemingly lost in her work, and either knowingly or not, had pressed her breast against his ear. It made Franklin a strong advocate of regular oral hygiene. Several weeks ago he had met Michelle in a shopping mall and asked her to join him for a cup of coffee. He thought that had gone quite well, and he hoped to ask her out on a more formal date during this visit.

Franklin sat in the waiting room listening to "I Want to Hold Your Hand" by the Beatles and fantasizing about an erotic episode of dental foreplay with Michelle when a slender man in a smock and a face mask hanging below his chin called Franklin's name. "Hi, I'm Lars. Michelle is out today, so I will be performing your cleaning." Franklin slowly rose from his seat and followed Lars to the examining room. The sound system in the background appropriately played "You Can't Always Get What You Want" by the Rolling Stones.

When Lars completed his task, he told Franklin to rinse and spit and said Dr. Green would be in shortly to examine his teeth and gums. Franklin sat happily drumming his fingers to the music as he waited for the next blast from the past.

"Franklin, you look like crap," said Dr. Green, joking as he entered the room. He offered Franklin his hand. Hyrum Green stood six feet tall. The remainder of a deep suntan was just beginning to fade. His eyes danced as he smiled, and he seemed genuinely happy to see his friend.

"My sleep has been off for a few nights. What's your excuse?" Franklin chided with a smile. Hyrum Green had been Franklin's dentist since before Franklin's first implant. He trusted him.

"We missed you at the card party last week. I had to take someone else's money," said Hyrum as he pulled on his rubber gloves. "Elaine misses you too; no one else seems to like her artichoke dip." He raised his face mask to cover a look of repugnance.

Franklin leaned back and opened his mouth. He had found it diffi- cult to maintain his relationship with other couples since Myra had gone. And he now felt himself drifting away from one of his few remaining friends. "So what are you doing next weekend? You should come for a visit," Hyrum said while stretching Franklin's cheeks and examining his gums. Franklin made an unintelligible noise and rolled his eyes as the sound system played "Respect" by Aretha Franklin.

After Hyrum removed both hands from Franklin's mouth, Franklin restored some of his dignity by wiping the drool from his chin. He asked, "Did you chase your pretty dental hygienist around the office until she quit?"

"No, she seems to be having some personal problems at home. I gave her some time off." Franklin was disappointed to hear that Michelle was unavailable, but maybe he could use this information to solve a dif- ferent problem. He could find out more about the psychologist, Dr. Klein. Franklin seized the opportunity.

"Maybe she can use some help. I noticed there's a psychologist in the building. Do you know anything about her?" he asked, feeling proud of himself for being so crafty.

Hyrum smiled. "Smart lady and not bad looking." He paused, and they both looked up at the ceiling speaker as it burst forth with "California Dreamin" by the Mamas and the Papas.

Hyrum continued, "I've wanted to get to know her, but she always seems busy. She works mostly in the evenings, so she arrives just as I'm closing the office. I had to stay late one night last week, and I noticed she had some pretty good-looking patients."

Franklin decided that it was time to take action, but he still wasn't comfortable walking into her office. With a renewed sense of conviction, he wrapped up his conversation with Hyrum, made his next appointment, and headed for the door. As he was leaving, he heard the first refrains of "The Letter" by the Box Tops. *That's it—it's the coward's way out, but that's it.* Franklin removed a pen from his pocket and copied the name and address of the psychologist onto the back of his appointment card. As he again passed in front of his dentist's office on his way out of the building, he slightly opened the door to hear the song that was now playing. It was "Subterranean Homesick Blues" by Bob Dylan. He stopped and thought about it for a moment, then said out loud, "I got nothing," and strolled out of the building.

That evening Franklin sat at his desk in his home office and drummed on his mouse pad with a pencil as he tried to decide how to best approach writing a letter to Dr. Klein. Should he describe the details of his problem? Should he keep it on the lighter side, maybe start with a joke? No, he wanted to be taken seriously. He settled down at the keyboard of his computer and started to type, still not comfortable exposing his problems and the extent of his emotional concern, but committed to getting this done now.

5

Ten days later, the wheels of Franklin's car bounced over the same speed bump in the parking lot three times before he finally found a parking spot wide enough so that his car doors wouldn't be dinged.

He stepped out onto the asphalt and sniffed the air. The fragrance of french fries filled his nostrils. He could almost taste them. The familiar arches of a McDonald's restaurant stood just across the lot. He checked his wristwatch; he had just six minutes before his appointment with Dr. Klein. Franklin looked at the line of customers visible through the window of the brightly lit restaurant. It looked like at least a fifteen-minute wait. He considered being late for his appointment. After all, hunger always put him in a cantankerous mood, and he would need to be open and calm if any progress was to be made in therapy. He would actually be doing Dr. Klein a favor by arriving well fed. Or, he could blow off the appointment, reschedule it for another day— but then what about tonight? He would have to try to sleep sooner or later, and the thought of another night of ghostly visitors coming and going through his bedroom firmed his resolve. He was committed.

His eye wandered to a man standing at about the midway point in the restaurant line. He was wearing a hooded sweatshirt under a yellow plaid jacket. He was lean, yet his shoulders were broad. He was tall—about six feet. There was something very familiar about the look of him. Maybe it was the confidence with which he moved, or how he held his head high even though his hands were stuffed in his pockets. Franklin waited for the man to turn so he could get a better look at his face. He craned his neck, but the shadow of the man's hood cloaked his features.

Franklin could almost swear it looked like his old friend, Dennis Cleaver. Franklin and Dennis had been fast friends since they were toddlers growing up in Binghamton, New York. He hadn't seen Dennis since he left Binghamton more than twenty-five years ago. It couldn't be. He had just looked at a picture of Dennis yesterday. The coincidence of running into him in this small town in Pennsylvania today would be too great. Twenty-five years was a long time. Dennis probably looked very different by now. Franklin shook his head and turned away. *Mind playing tricks again.* He placed his hand on his rumbling stomach and cursed the evening rush-hour traffic that had delayed him. Then he walked toward the office building.

As he approached, a slender woman with long black hair came bounding down the front stairs, her hair and bosom gently bouncing with her youthful gait. As his eyes met hers, he smiled a broad smile, almost a grin. She returned his smile but in an affected, smug way, then immediately averted her eyes. It was more of a smirk than a smile, and Franklin did his best not to be offended. It was the same rebuff he received from other attractive women he encountered on the street. He tried not to take it personally. He was going to have to try his smile in a mirror and see what it was that was turning them off. He turned and watched her walk to her car.

"Have a nice day," he shouted. Her hips moved with a rhythmic motion that was mesmerizing. He didn't know her, but he certainly would have liked to. *Knock it off,* he told himself. He had more important things to do.

Franklin carefully climbed the stone stairs, holding his cane in his left hand and the black wrought-iron railing for support with his right. When he reached the door, he turned for one last look at the long-legged beauty. Too late. She was already in her car, a tan Mercedes-Benz. She drove out of the lot and passed the restaurant. The man from the fast-food line, the one in the hood and jacket, had left the restaurant and was now standing on the sidewalk, also watching the woman's car. He turned back to face Franklin and then stepped into the shadow of the restaurant and was gone. Franklin stood looking at the spot where the man had stood, and then again he shook his head.

He turned, opened the front door, and started down the long corridor to Dr. Klein's office.

Dr. Klein had responded to Franklin's letter of introduction almost immediately. She had called and then sent forms to be completed and returned. The entire process, including the scheduling of this appointment, had taken less than ten days. Franklin had requested the first available session, but now that he was here, his hands were beginning to shake.

Franklin was a very private person. Dr. Klein had sounded accommodating and supportive on the telephone, but he was still apprehensive. He fought back the urge to turn and run away. He hadn't told anyone about his dreams. Now he was about to discuss his innermost fears and secrets with a complete stranger. What if he was going insane? He paused, then steeled himself to the task at hand and turned the doorknob.

Ruth Klein's waiting room was small but elegant. The walls, painted in a soothing shade of pale green, were adorned with framed and matted photographs of covered bridges, waterfalls, and forest scenes. The contemporary sofa and two armchairs were upholstered with soft earthtone fabrics. The furniture was chic yet comfortable-looking. It was a pleasant environment. The kind of room that could help dispel some of the anxiety a new patient might experience prior to a therapy session—particularly this new patient.

Franklin sat on the firm, well-contoured sofa. He leaned forward and squinted to see the titles on some of the books lined up in the case on the far wall. They were arranged by size and color rather than subject matter. He hoped Dr. Klein was as good a psychologist as she was a decorator.

Franklin randomly picked up a magazine from the end table near the sofa. The door to the inner office opened almost immediately. There stood Ruth Klein, all six feet one inch of her. Franklin had had no idea that she was so tall. *Don't comment, and whatever you do, don't grin.*

"Mr. Jameson, I'm Dr. Ruth Klein. Please come in," she said as she offered her hand. Franklin leaned his cane against the bookcase and shook her hand; he hoped she didn't notice that his palm was sweating. He grabbed his cane and entered the office without realizing that he was still holding the magazine rolled into a tight tube in his left hand and was tapping it on the wall and furniture as he walked to the couch. He took a seat. He had shaved very carefully this morning, put on clean jeans, and even washed his gym shoes. He wanted to make a good impression. His hair, however, looked as though he had been caught in a windstorm, and dark circles under his eyes attested to his recent sleepless nights.

On his left, Franklin saw a small wastepaper basket half-filled with tissues and an empty tissue box on the end table. *The last patient must have had quite an emotional session,* he thought. He wondered if it had been the woman with the long black hair in the parking lot who had given him the cold shoulder. If so, he had no pity for her.

Franklin had rehearsed his opening remarks several times in the car. He wanted to ensure that he would remain in control of his emotions as he spoke, but now that he was here, his mind was a blank. Maybe he should ask her to refill the tissue box.

***

"Mr. Jameson?"

Franklin was jolted out of his reverie and looked up.

"I understand from your letter that you would like to discuss a dream that—"

"Several dreams," he interrupted.

"Several dreams," she continued, unfazed, "that have been troubling you?"

"Yes, I think one session should do it." He tried to laugh. "They were short dreams."

We have a comedian, Ruth thought. "Do you dream often, Mr. Jameson?" she asked.

"I probably don't dream more than the average person. I had some unusual childhood dreams, more fantasies than dreams, but doesn't every child? For most of my life, I think my dreams have been normal. That is, until recently, when I started having really strange experiences." He fidgeted with the rolled-up magazine, tapping it rhythmically on the coffee table.

"Go on," said Dr. Klein as she reached over and placed her hand on the magazine, silencing it.

Franklin unrolled it and placed it on the table. "Sorry." He took a deep breath and began again. "It's not so much the content of the dreams but—I'm not sure how to explain it."

Ruth Klein remained silent and leaned back in her chair.

Franklin continued, "My dreams are very realistic, and some of them are nightmarish, but that's not the problem, at least not all of the problem."

He picked up the empty tissue box, turned it over several times in his hands, and then placed it back on the table.

"The real problem is I'm having a hard time knowing when a dream ends and when it doesn't. Is that normal?"

Ruth watched him absent-mindedly wind his watch for a long moment. She wrote a short note on her pad: *Mr. Jameson seems extremely distressed about his dreams—fragile—tread carefully.*

"Mr. Jameson, maybe—"

"Franklin," he interrupted, looking up with a jerk of his head. "Call me Franklin."

"Franklin," Ruth repeated. "Maybe you should start by telling me more about yourself. Something about your youth—I see you grew up in New York." *This guy is wound tighter than his watch.*

"Most of my life story is in the forms I returned to you in the mail last week. My birthplace, my age, my education…"

"Maybe you could tell me about your childhood. Did you enjoy growing up in…" she looked down at the notepad on her lap, "Binghamton?"

Franklin adjusted his sleeves. "It was a good place to grow up, lots of trees, good schools."

"What about your family? Do they still live in Binghamton?"

Franklin leaned forward. "My father was really strict, and I don't think he liked me much when I was a kid. It seemed like I was always being punished for something. Maybe I deserved it. My mother always took my side. Anyway, we became closer as I got older. He's dead now. My mother still lives in Binghamton."

"I'm sorry about your dad," Ruth said. "Was his passing recent?"

"No, he's been gone for more than ten years. I've been over it for a long time."

"What about your childhood friends? I would imagine one develops close friendships growing up in a small town."

Franklin suddenly folded his arms across his chest and crossed his legs as well. He spoke in short, staccato bursts.

"I had one close friend when I was a kid, but we grew apart, different interests. We haven't seen each other since I left Binghamton." Franklin looked around the room, avoiding Ruth's eyes.

Ruth observed his defensive posture and made a note to come back to his childhood later, when he might be more relaxed. She changed the subject. "Maybe you could describe one of your dreams for me."

Franklin nodded several times and began, "I dreamed that a burglar was in my house. Sleep hasn't come easy lately. Maybe I'm just afraid to sleep. Anyway, I saw this burglar in a stocking mask, and he was coming right for the bed. At first I tried to pretend I was sleeping. Maybe he would just take what he wanted and leave, but he was coming right toward me." Franklin decided to leave out the part about fearing that the burglar would accidentally find his handgun. He didn't want Dr. Klein to know he owned a gun. She might think he was violent.

He went on. "When he approached the bed, I jumped up to defend myself, and when I tried to hit him, I guess my hand passed right through him. At first I thought I just missed, but that wasn't it. I couldn't hit him because he wasn't there. I finally realized that I must be dreaming when he threw the chair through…" Franklin stood up and made a motion as though he were throwing a chair. Ruth flinched, then smiled awkwardly and motioned for him to continue.

"He threw the chair through the window and jumped out. I was standing there, shaking, but I tried to defend myself," Franklin said. He waited for a comment.

"That was very brave of you," Ruth said. Franklin's chest swelled slightly as he waved off the compliment. Ruth made a notation on her notepad, then continued, "You said you attempted to strike him. Did you dream that you stood to strike him, or were you actually out of bed?"

"That's the problem," Franklin said, intertwining his fingers and holding them in front of him as though he were praying. "I thought I woke up when he came into the room, but that couldn't be, because he wasn't there. I didn't really wake up until after he left through the window. I was sure I woke up when I first saw him, and then again a few minutes later. How could I feel sure that I woke up twice from the same dream?"

She wrote several notes on her notepad, focused her eyes on his, and asked again, "When you realized that you had finally awakened, the second time, were you actually out of bed?"

Franklin nodded. "Is that important?"

"Not necessarily, but it helps me understand what's happening. There is a mechanism in the body that paralyzes the skeletal muscles while you sleep so that you don't act out your dreams. Does anyone in your family suffer from somnambulism?"

"What?"

"Sleepwalking."

"No, not that I'm aware of."

"Well, that's good, because most people who walk in their sleep have inherited the trait from one or both parents. Now, in this dream did you ever experience a feeling that something was out of place?"

"Yes, the burglar. He was in my house."

Ruth Klein smiled briefly. "Anything else besides the burglar?"

"No…wait, now that you mention it, he took a box from my dresser drawer. It was very small—plastic, I think. I didn't remember what he had taken until just now."

"What was in the box?"

"I don't know; I don't have a box in my dresser drawer."

"Mr. Jameson—"

"Franklin!" he said, more emphatically this time.

"Franklin," she repeated with as much emphasis. "There is a sleep condition, very appropriately called 'false awakening.' Are you familiar with it?"

He shook his head.

"A false awakening is one in which the subject thinks he has awakened from a dream, but is in fact still asleep. Sometimes the experience is so realistic that until the dreamer really wakes up, he doesn't realize that what has occurred was hallucinatory."

Franklin's face contorted as he tried to assimilate her explanation.

"Are you saying I'm having hallucinations?" he asked in a trembling voice.

"Not necessarily. Occasional false awakening dreams are not that uncommon." She placed a comforting hand on his shoulder.

"How many false awakening dreams have you had?"

"Three or four in the last month—is that too many?" He now found it difficult to swallow and ran his finger inside his shirt collar.

Ruth poured a glass of water from the pitcher on the coffee table, handed it to Franklin, and said, "In some respects, yes; they're usually pretty rare. The fact that you have had several in a short period of time could be an indication of a sleep disorder." Ruth glanced at her watch and said, "I'd like to hear about another dream before our time is up."

First a flash of headlights and then the roar of an engine and the piercing squeal of brakes hijacked Franklin's attention to the open window. He stared, almost bewitched by the garbage truck moving down the street. Franklin's ears pricked up at the whine of its hopper each time the truck paused in front of a building. The trash handlers in soiled, dark-green overalls hastened to keep up. They raced behind, dumping and banging cans of trash onto the hopper. Then the engine blew choking clouds of black smoke as it once again hauled the heavy vehicle to its next stop.

Ruth watched Franklin's head suddenly shift to the left, his gaze now drawn to the bus stop at the far corner. He seemed to be staring at the bench inside the three-sided glass enclosure, a windbreak for the bus passengers.

Franklin was mesmerized by a single figure he saw sitting on the bench. It was the same man he had seen outside the fast-food restaurant. Was he waiting for Franklin to finish his session and come out to meet him? Franklin still couldn't make out his face under the hood, yet his posture, the distinctive tilt of the head, the way his feet rested solidly on the concrete sidewalk all presented an air of confidence that Franklin found remarkably familiar.

The garbage truck proceeded past the bus stop, obscuring Franklin's view. He leaned forward to try to keep from losing sight of the man.

Ruth rose and walked to the window. She twisted the rod on the vertical blinds, blanking out the street. Leaving the blinds open had been a rookie mistake, and she shook her head as she wondered where her own concentration had gone.

"Wait," Franklin cried, limping to the window and parting the blinds with his hands. He tilted his head and stared at the street as the truck moved out of his line of sight.

"Is something wrong?" Ruth asked. She looked through the space in the blinds held open by Franklin's hands. He seemed to be staring at the empty bus stop bench.

"No," Franklin said, walking back to the couch. "I thought I saw someone I knew on the bench across the street, but I guess I was mistaken."

Ruth parted the blinds and looked left and right. No one was in view, other than the sanitation workers. She let the blinds close and returned to her seat. She studied his demeanor. He fidgeted with his cuffs, his eyes still focused on the closed blinds. After a momentary pause, he turned to Ruth and said, "I'm a little tired. Could we talk about another dream some other time?" He wanted to ask if Dr. Klein had seen the man in the hood, but if she hadn't…

"I think we're going to need to do some work to find out what the root cause of your dreams might be. I'd like to hear more about your early years with your family and friends. Your sleep problems could be related to some past experience or trauma. It may take some time. I suggest that we schedule regular weekly appointments."

Franklin thought for a minute about agreeing to be treated by a psychologist. The realization that he was going to be in therapy struck him for the first time. He didn't like the stigma of being a mental patient, but maybe treatment was the only way he could end these dreams and sleep soundly again.

"Do you really think this is going to take more than one or two more sessions?" he asked.

One or two more years maybe, she thought, but said, "It's really up to you."

Franklin agreed.

Ruth watched Franklin hobble toward the door, leaning heavily on his cane. This was a troubled man who exhibited more than enough symptoms of psychological problems to warrant treatment. Ruth sat at her desk and began to transcribe her notes of the session. Then she had a thought. She walked back to the window and carefully pulled one panel of the vertical blinds aside so that she could see out but hopefully no one could see her.

Within a few seconds, Franklin appeared on the street. Surprisingly, he was walking across to the bus stop rather than to the parking lot. The buses ran infrequently at this time of night, and few of her patients depended on them. Ruth decided to watch him for a few minutes while he waited. He approached the bench in the enclosure, his back toward Ruth's window. He stood for a long moment, apparently not moving. Ruth leaned forward, squinting, and observed subtle jerks of his head and occasional hand gestures. "He's talking to himself," she said out loud. "Why is he talking to himself? His problems are more serious than I thought. Normal people don't talk…" Ruth stopped talking and returned to her desk and her notes.

A few seconds later, the number eighteen bus pulled into the bus stop. The driver opened the door and waited, but the man with the cane didn't attempt to board. He just crossed back to the adjacent parking lot. The bus driver shook his head, closed the doors, and drove on.

6

The moon rose above the horizon, lighting the night sky. It was the hunter's moon—large, bright, and full—the brightest of the year. Shadows appeared on the ground, all radiating out from the mystical light that legend claimed guided Native American hunters on their quest to fill their larder with game before the winter snows. A gust of cold autumn wind whistled through the pine trees. Summer was gone.

"All the crazies will be out tonight," Officer Dugan said. "Every time there's a full moon, crime goes up twenty percent."

"That's a myth," his partner said as he drove the squad car through the upscale suburban Pennsylvania housing development. Each home was set back on an acre of well-landscaped lawn with manicured shrubbery. The police officers navigated the quiet streets looking for anything that seemed out of place on this quiet October night. The neighborhood had been plagued by robberies during the past year, but the police were always too late, and the thief never left a single clue.

"Studies show that all that stuff about the moon having an effect on people's behavior is a load of bunk," said Officer Riddle. "It's an urban legend; nobody believes that stuff anymore."

Out of the corner of his eye, Officer Dugan caught sight, in his side-view mirror, of what looked like a bear with large red feet riding a bicycle. The bear appeared to be carrying another small animal lying across the handlebars.

"That sounds great, Riddle, but could you pull over? I think we have an urban legend trying to wave us down."

The police car screeched to a stop, and Officer Dugan watched as the bear on the bicycle waved a large paw and raced toward their car. Within seconds the bear had shape-shifted into a man with a dark beard wearing a ladies' mink coat with several other furs balled up on the handlebars.

"Help, officers," he yelled. "My house is being robbed. I saved my wife's coats, but he's still in there."

Officer Dugan stepped out of the car and opened the door to the backseat. "Is your wife or anyone else in the house?" he asked as he ushered the man into the car and rested the bicycle on its side at the curb.

"Don't forget the other coats," the man cried as he ignored Dugan's question and pointed at the ball of fur across the handlebars. "My wife would kill me if I didn't save her furs." Dugan tossed the furs into the backseat with the man, who was now pointing back in the direction from which they had come. "Turn around," he demanded. "It's the house with the fieldstone front two blocks down. I was in the shower when I saw this man in a stocking mask pass the bathroom door. He ran when he saw me, but I don't know if he's still in the house. I just grabbed my wife's coats and slippers and ran out."

Officer Riddle called in their location as he stopped in front of the victim's house with all the lights on the police car flashing. The first floor of the house was dark, and the front door was wide open.

"Take the back, Riddle," Dugan said as he drew his weapon. "Is anyone else in the house?" he asked for the second time.

"I, I don't think so," the man said.

"You don't think so?" Dugan repeated. The man gazed toward his next-door neighbor's house. Dugan followed his line of sight and saw a woman with wet hair wrapped in a large bath towel. She disappeared through the front door.

"No," the man said. "No one else is in the house."

Dugan looked at the man, then shook his head. "Stay in the car," he said, and ran to the open front door.

Dugan pulled his flashlight from the nylon holder on his utility belt, held it under his weapon, and scanned the darkened entryway. He poked his head in and out quickly, and then slowly worked his way into the room. The beam of light bounced around the living room, moving rapidly from corner to corner, exposing any space large enough for a man to hide.

Dugan paused and tilted his head to listen for any sound that might betray the burglar's presence. A subtle creak of a floorboard, barely discernible to his ear, came from the next room. Dugan held his weapon out in front of him. He raised his arm and tilted his head down to wipe the sweat from his upper lip on the sleeve of his uniform shirt. He took three slow, deep breaths to calm himself. This was the first time Dugan's weapon had been out of its holster in an actual on-duty situation since he left the police academy ten years ago. He swallowed. His throat was dry and scratchy. Dugan pulled his hands in close to his chest, pointing his gun up at the ceiling as he flattened out against the wall leading to the kitchen doorway. He readied himself to burst through the door. He silently mouthed the words: "One." He licked his dry lips. "Two." He took a deep breath. "Three." Dugan charged through the doorway, gun first, yelling, "Police—don't move! Don't move or you're dead!"

"Don't shoot! It's Riddle, it's Riddle!" the officer shouted in a frantic, high-pitched voice.

Dugan raised his gun and slumped back against the wall. "What are you doing here? I almost shot you, you dumb shit."

"I'm sorry. The back door was open," Riddle said. "He must have gone out before we got here. I thought it was over."

Dugan holstered his gun and put his hand on Riddle's shoulder. They stood side by side, Dugan's hand massaging the base of Riddle's neck, and Riddle patting Dugan on the back.

"Let's call it in," Dugan said. "Yeah, we're done here." Neither man looked the other in the eye. Both exhaled deeply as they walked to the car.

***

The vertical posts from the guardrail of the interstate blended into a blur as Mortimer Banks sped down the highway, now several miles from the scene of the robbery. He flipped his cell phone open and pushed speed-dial three. He shouted into the phone, his voice quivering with anger.

"You were wrong! He was home. What kind of half-assed information are you giving me?"

"Take it easy, Mort," Sylvia said. "His wife is out of town, and he plays cards on Wednesday night. No one should have been home. What happened?"

"The wife was gone all right, but this guy and his neighbor were washing each other's backs in the shower when I came in. You were wrong. The house wasn't empty." Mort swerved across two lanes of the empty highway as he shook his fist in the air.

"I'm sorry, it won't happen again." After a long pause, she said, "How did we do?"

Mort took a deep breath. "The watch was there, just like you said." His voice was calmer now that he had gotten the rant out of his system. "I picked up a few rings, not worth much, and a cheap bracelet. The watch was the only thing worth taking." Mort snapped his phone closed and tossed it on the passenger seat. He reached into his pocket and dumped the contents of a small blue velvet bag onto the car's console. Mort smiled as he groped through the pile of jewelry and fished out a diamond tennis bracelet. He held it up in front of him. Forty matched diamonds set in a yellow-gold bracelet sparkled in turn, reflecting the light from the lampposts that flashed by the windows.

Mort made some mental calculations, waving his finger in the air as he computed the amount of profit he should receive from the bracelet and the rings. Keeping most of the profit for himself had become the rule rather than the exception. After all, he took all the risk, and what Sylvia didn't know wouldn't hurt him.

Mort and Sylvia had been working together for about a year—ever since he'd violated parole. He had amassed a fair amount of money over the year and now thought seriously of moving on. Sooner or later someone was going to realize that at least one item in each theft had been bought at Stanton's, and once they made that connection, Sylvia would be caught. He didn't intend to be within miles of this town when that happened. This partnership had to come to an end, and after tonight's screw-up, the sooner it ended the better.

7

The second Ruth Klein opened the door from her inner office, Franklin leaped from his place in the armchair by the window and charged forward, cane thumping on the rug. "You'll never guess what happened," he said. Just then his cane caught in the rug, and he lunged forward. Ruth raised both hands chest high in front of her to shield herself from his advance and stepped back into the doorway. He stopped short only inches from her.

"Sorry," Franklin said, regaining his balance. "I'm just so excited."

"I can tell," Ruth said. She backed into the inner office and directed him toward the sofa with a wave of her arm. Instead, Franklin ambled to the window and parted the blinds. He looked left and right before releasing the blinds and walking to the couch.

"What are you afraid of? Is someone following you?"

"Yes…No…I'm not sure."

Ruth pulled on the cord to open the vertical blinds and searched the street for any suspicious passersby. "What did he look like? It *was* a he, wasn't it?"

"It's like you knew this was going to happen the last time I was here. You asked about him, and then he showed up." Ruth watched as Franklin turned in small circles as he spoke, shifting his weight from foot to foot to minimize the pressure on his weak leg.

"Slow down and tell me," Ruth said with a nervous laugh, feeling the contagion of Franklin's concern but not wanting to exacerbate it.

"The last time I was here I was looking out your window; you remember that."

"Yes, I do. There was a garbage truck collecting trash from the tavern across the street. I apologize for the distraction," Ruth said. "I'll keep the blinds closed in the future."

Franklin waved a dismissive gesture. "Well, I thought I saw him before I came in. He was looking at a woman driving away, and then I saw him again..."

"Franklin, slow down. I'm not following."

"He came back," Franklin said, now pacing back and forth between the coffee table and the sofa. "I hadn't heard from him in over twenty years, and now I see him almost everywhere I go."

Ruth stepped forward and caught his shoulder on the third lap past her chair and settled him into his seat.

"Who came back, Franklin?" she asked. "Before I get too dizzy to stand."

"Dennis—Dennis Cleaver, my childhood friend. You remember? I told you in our last session that he and I had grown apart. Well, there's more to the story than that, but I can tell you that later."

Franklin popped up from the sofa, and Ruth just as quickly guided him back down with gentle pressure on his shoulder and a smile.

"How did he find you?" Ruth asked as she settled back in her chair and picked up her notepad.

"I don't know," Franklin said, attempting to rise out of his seat. Ruth stiffened her arm and pointed back at Franklin's place on the sofa. He sat back down and said, "OK, I'm OK, I'm fine now."

"I hope so. You know I can't prescribe sedatives. If I could, I would."

"It's OK," Franklin said. "I don't need a sedative."

"The sedative wasn't for you!" she said, laughing. "Tell me about your friend Dennis." This was the second time that Franklin had come unglued in her office, and both times Dennis had been the reason for his emotional reaction.

"Well, he just stopped coming around all of a sudden when we were about nineteen. We seemed to have different interests. It was my fault. That was when I met Myra, and I just didn't have enough time for friends. Well, that's not true either. You see, Myra didn't like Dennis. She made me choose between her and my friend."

"That doesn't sound fair. Couldn't you find room in your life for both?"

"I could have, but Myra forced me to choose."

"And you chose Myra over Dennis."

"You have to understand. I was nineteen. I guess my hormones did the choosing for me."

"Understandable, but how did Dennis take the decision?"

"Not so well, and the fact that he saved my life made me feel even worse."

"Wait, Dennis saved your life? Tell me about that."

"It's a long story." Franklin sat looking at the floor.

Ruth waited as he paused. He looked more serene now, lost in the memory of a time in his youth. "What are you thinking, Franklin?" Ruth asked in a soft voice.

Franklin leaned back on the sofa. His restless fidgeting and manic behavior had dissolved into a look of introspective contemplation. His breathing became slow and regular. Ruth noticed a faint smile begin at the corners of his mouth and spread across his lips as he recalled the story.

"It was a beautiful summer day. We were both about nineteen at the time. The thing we most enjoyed doing together was fishing on the lake. I always talked about the fish I was going to catch and the best bait or lure to use, but I don't think any of that really mattered to Dennis. He seemed content just to be out together on the water. Most of the time I would talk and Dennis would listen. Nobody else ever really listened to me the way he did. When I would tell a story, and I often did, he would hang on every word. Most of the guys we knew would just tell me that I was full of crap, that I talked too much, but not Dennis—not Dennis."

Ruth sat quietly, observing the gentle tone that had overtaken Franklin's voice as he spoke of Dennis. It was a warm tone, rich with affection.

Franklin closed his eyes, and he was back in the boat on Lake Oneida. "I sat in the bow with my feet dangling over the side, staring at the red-and-white bobber tied to my fishing line, waiting for a fish to pull it under. Dennis stood in the stern next to the outboard motor, casting his line. He never was patient enough to sit and wait for the fish to bite."

"It sounds Rockwellian," Ruth said.

"The water was smooth as glass, yet the boat rocked as Dennis cast and then reeled in his line, trying to place his lure in one specific spot about fifty feet away." Franklin went through the motions of casting and reeling with an invisible fishing pole and line.

"'Hey, sit down,' I told him, 'you're going to tip us over, and I forgot to bring the life preservers.' I felt pretty guilty about that, but Dennis didn't care. He said we didn't need them. He could swim back to shore without even breathing heavy."

"Was he that good a swimmer?"

"Not really, but he could swim better than me. Dennis always joked that I looked like a chicken when I swam."

Ruth laughed, put down her notepad, and settled in her chair. "Sounds like you were both enjoying the day."

Franklin continued, "I looked down and noticed the reflection of a few small clouds in the water. I tried to sense their movement across the lake, but I couldn't tell because of the ripples generated by the rise and fall of the boat. Minutes later, when I looked up, they had increased in number. I asked Dennis if it was supposed to rain. I hadn't even checked the weather report that morning. He said he hoped it would. That fish loved to bite during a rain.

"Soon the clouds filled the sky, and only shafts of sunlight streamed through between them. I remember holding my palm out, waiting for the rain to start.

"'You think we should head in?' I asked. Dennis laughed. He said, 'Don't be such a wuss. Haven't you ever been caught in the rain before? It'll probably pass in a few minutes.'"

Ruth folded her hands in her lap and laughed at Dennis's remark. This was the most relaxed Franklin had been since she'd met him. Then he leaned forward and picked up the pace of his story.

"The attack of the storm was subtle," he said. "First those small lone clouds gathered and combined into bigger clouds in what just minutes before had been a clear afternoon sky."

Franklin closed his eyes and again saw the dark-gray clouds begin to arrive from the north, pushing their way into the gathering, their count increasing, until the dark clouds outnumbered the white. He remembered the tenor of the moment changing. The new gray clouds bumped and merged with the original white puffs agitating them, provoking them. Then he recalled the battle. The dark clouds ebbed and flowed. They began to look like hills and valleys and then massive mountain peaks, towering up for what seemed like miles into the sky.

"It was frightening," he said as he opened his eyes. "The surface of the clouds began to boil and churn until they transformed into a raging sea."

Ruth wrote on her notepad: *Franklin does have a way with words.*

"Then the rain began. A huge bolt of lightning leaped from one dark peak to another. It made a loud hissing and crackling noise. We ducked down in the boat, shielding our eyes and cringing at the explosive sound of the thunder. The trees on the shoreline seemed to be dancing to a flickering strobe light show, like in a disco club. They had those back then."

"Yes, unfortunately I'm old enough to remember them," Ruth said, nodding.

"A sharp crack of thunder shook the far bank; the echo seemed to roll on and on and on. The storm had arrived," Franklin said.

"I would imagine that was enough to get Dennis to pack up and leave," Ruth offered.

"Yeah, I think he was as scared as I was, although he would never let on. He struggled to the engine, fighting his way through gusts of wind. The boat kept turning. We were being pushed farther out into the choppy water. The shoreline had receded into a faint, misty band at the limit of our vision. The rain was now coming down in sheets, making a pool out of the bottom of the boat. I grabbed a bait can and started to bail water over the side. The water was up to our ankles and still rising. Dennis pulled on the starter cord, yanking again and again. The engine only coughed and popped. He adjusted the choke, and he advanced the throttle. He tried everything. Then he pulled again with all his might. I could see tension in the muscles of his arms. The engine sputtered and coughed, but started running. Dennis worked at the throttle and choke, desperate to keep the wheezing motor alive. Soon the rasping sound became smooth, and the engine roared.

"'That's it,' I said. 'Help me bail some of this water before we're swamped.' Dennis left the engine idling, grabbed another bait can, and moved to the bow. Both of us bailed as fast as we could, splashing as much water on each other as back into the lake. There was still about six inches of water in the boat, but we were going to make it."

Ruth blew a breath of relief. "You must have felt ecstatic when the engine started."

"At that moment we did, but an instant later the whole world turned white. A loud buzzing clogged my ears, and the smell of ozone filled my nostrils. I didn't even know what ozone was back then, but I learned later. Anyway, my muscles started to twitch uncontrollably, and I fell facedown in the bow of the boat."

"You were struck by lightning?"

"Practically cut the outboard motor in two. I pieced together what happened later. At the time, I must have been unconscious. The next thing I remember was Dennis lifting me by the collar and flipping me onto my back. I think there was smoke and steam rising from my clothes. I remember Dennis breathing life back into me and pressing on my chest until I choked the water from my lungs. He smoothed the wet hair from my forehead, pressed his cheek to my face, and told me that I was going to be all right."

Franklin placed a finger under his glasses to catch a tear before it fell, and so did Ruth.

He sniffed and went on, "The outboard motor and part of the stern had been demolished by a nearby lightning strike. Maybe it was the high rubber boots that Dennis was wearing that insulated him from the charge. Maybe it was an act of God, but Dennis was unscathed—dazed but unharmed. He propped me up against the bulkhead. I remember he looked right in my eyes. He held my face with both hands and shouted over the storm. He told me that the boat would stay afloat. That he was going to swim ashore and get help. Just stay put, he said, and he would be back in a few minutes.

"I shook my head. I didn't want him to go, but I couldn't speak. Then he slipped off his boots, dived over the side, and was gone.

"It seemed like I lay there for hours. The boat was rocking, and I was so sick I vomited onto my own shoulder. I didn't even have the strength or the coordination to roll onto my side.

"All I kept thinking was—he left me. I've been a terrible friend, and he left me. Why did he leave me? I wouldn't have left him, I told myself, but the truth of the matter was I had left him long ago.

"I thought about how close we had been for so many years. Dennis had always been my strongest ally and my most loyal supporter. I always thought of him as my avenging angel, quick to rebuke anyone who disrespected me. I should have been a better friend. I shouldn't have let Myra separate us. I let Dennis down, and now I was going to pay for it with my life. He was not coming back.

"I wiped my hand across my eyes to clear my vision. Some of it was rain, but most of it was tears. I felt weak and nauseated. It was time to sleep. I was so tired. Then something bumped against the crippled boat. A hand grasped my collar and lifted me to a sitting position. My eyes began to clear, and the face of the man holding me came into focus. I never felt so relieved or joyful to see anyone. Dennis had come back with a fisherman who lived near the lakeshore. He pressed his forehead against mine and said, 'Franklin, are you all right?'" He paused.

"Franklin, *are* you all right?" Ruth Klein asked.

"Fine, I'm fine," Franklin said, blinking and shaking his head to focus his attention back to the present day.

Ruth poured a glass of water and handed it to him. "It was a marvelous story. You must have been traumatized. Was there any permanent damage from the lightning strike?"

Franklin looked at his cane leaning against the couch as he wiped the sweat from his forehead and dried his eyes with a tissue.

"I'm sorry," Ruth said, chastising herself for the thoughtless comment. "I think I understand a little about the bond that you and Dennis shared. If he's here, why hasn't he spoken to you?"

"Well, when we finally parted company, we were not on the best terms. I wasn't a good friend."

"But it sounds like he loved you."

"Maybe once, but if you're rejected enough, love can turn to hate."

"Do you think he hates you now?"

"I don't know. I don't even know if the man I saw was really Dennis." Franklin got up and walked back to the window. "It's been more than twenty-five years. It was probably somebody else. I think that's enough for today. I need to go."

Ruth stood and watched Franklin as he walked directly to the door and left without another word.

***

Ruth sat reflecting on the session for quite a while before beginning to edit her notes. She had been so enraptured by the story that her note-taking was sparse at best. However, her recollection of the story Franklin had told was clear and vivid. She shuddered as she relived the lightning strike, and her eyes again became moist as she noted the tearful reunion of two friends.

Ruth had never had a really close friend. There were girls in college that she'd hung out with, but never anyone close enough to share her problems or help her with difficult decisions. Her father was always there for her and willing to listen, but there were things a young woman just couldn't share with a father. *Maybe when Emma grows a little older we could...*

"Session notes, session notes, you're writing session notes," she scolded and directed her focus back to her notebook. She wrote:

> Franklin is exhibiting feelings of guilt relative to the demise of his friendship with Dennis. Whether or not the person he observed outside the office window was really his old friend is moot. It is possible that these feelings of guilt are the cause of the insomnia he is experiencing and the nightmares that plague what little sleep he achieves. He may even have found some other, as yet unknown, way of punishing himself.

Ruth began to plan her approach to resolve Franklin's guilt. If Dennis had returned, the best course of action would be for Franklin to make amends and mitigate his guilt. At least it would be a start.

Satisfied, Ruth closed Franklin's file and stuffed it into her file drawer.

8

Franklin kicked off his covers and staggered barefoot to the bathroom. He rubbed his hand across his face and scratched the three-day growth of stubble on his chin. Squinting into the mirror over the sink, he opened his mouth and looked at the fuzzy tan coating on his tongue. He massaged the dark circles under his eyes and tried to smooth down the hair on the left side of his head. It was the side on which he had been lying, off and on, as he tossed and turned for the last four hours, trying to fall asleep.

Franklin didn't want his nightmares to get the better of him, but he kept finding it harder and harder to sleep for fear of having another frightening dream. He opened the medicine cabinet, grabbed the three bottles of pills from the bottom shelf, and placed them in a row on the sink. One by one he held them up to the light to read the label. It would have been easier had he taken his glasses from the nightstand, but Franklin wasn't thinking at his best. He yawned deeply and opened the bottle he assumed was Ambien and took out two pills. They were pink and oblong. He felt sure that Ambien was the only pill in his medicine cabinet shaped like that; besides, if he was wrong and it was something that would kill him, he would welcome it. At least he wouldn't be awake. He tossed the pills into his mouth and bent over the sink to drink directly from the faucet.

He sat on the side of the tub, closed the drain lever, and adjusted the water to run a hot bath. While the tub was filling, Franklin shuffled in his bare feet to the kitchen and warmed a cup of milk. By the time he returned to his big soaking tub with its rows of bubble jets, the tub was three-quarters full. It was time to pull out all the stops. He opened a box of bubble bath and shook in half the box. The mounds of suds nourished by the churning hot water formed peaks rising high above the rim of the tub.

A nice soft bath towel was next on the list. Franklin chose a large blue bath sheet and pulled it from the stack in the linen closet. Threads were hanging from its frayed edges. He wound them around his fingers and tore them off with his teeth. It looked like time to buy some new towels. Being a bachelor again had its benefits, but it had its drawbacks too. Franklin had always depended on Myra for domestic chores like buying linens and household items. Things were starting to wear out. *She could have stocked the house before she divorced me*, he thought. *That would have been the right thing to do.*

Franklin hung his bathrobe on a hook next to the tub, stepped out of his pajamas, and tossed them into the hamper. He shook his head to chase away the thoughts of Myra. He had taken the divorce hard. It wasn't that he thought he still loved her. It was more because he never understood why she left him. He glanced in the mirror and noticed how the last two years of sitting around and eating lots of any kind of food he wanted had changed him from a hard-bodied young man to the softer, overnourished fellow in his reflection. He raised his arms and flexed his biceps at the mirror. "You look ridiculous," he said. "Knock off the muffins and ice cream before you give yourself a heart attack, you jerk."

One more big yawn and he stepped into the tub. Steam was rising through the patches of bubbles, and he had to lower himself very slowly into the water. He grunted and groaned several times, and after a final long sigh, he was settled in. He leaned back, rested his head against the rim of the tub, and stretched out to his full length. Within minutes the tension in his body that had accumulated over days of limited sleep began to dissolve away into the warm water. With a long exhale, he closed his eyes and began to relax.

Just as his mind cleared and he began to slip into a light sleep, he heard a noise. *Damn it*, he thought, *I can't catch a break.*

He opened his eyes. "What the...?"

A woman wearing a nightgown had run into his bathroom. She ran barefoot across the tile floor, slightly out of breath, her breasts heaving under her sheer lingerie. Although he couldn't see her face, he could sense panic in her rapid movements. She looked over her shoulder back at the bathroom doorway and hurriedly began to open the vanity drawers, throwing things out onto the floor as she searched. The long black hair that flew behind her as she ran into the room now covered most of her face as she bent over the drawers. Franklin stared, mesmerized. Her figure was stunning. The muscles of her naked torso tensed under the sheer fabric of the nightgown as she moved from drawer to drawer until her hand closed around the object of her search.

Franklin grasped the sides of the tub to lift himself out of the water, and then he quickly dropped back in as a second person ran into the room. He pulled the towel in over his body. The towel would afford no protection from the intruder, but he covered himself almost as a reflex, a reaction to his vulnerability, like a drowning man grabbing at twigs that couldn't possibly keep him afloat.

The woman wheeled around to face her attacker, a long pair of stainless steel scissors held like a dagger in her hand. The man had a nylon stocking pulled over his head. He stood in a crouch with his arms spread wide at his sides, his hands flexing, anticipating the feel of his prey. They slowly circled the room in a standoff between a powerful aggressor and a would-be victim who was now armed.

Long black streaks of eye makeup mixed with tears ran down her face. Drops of blood from her nose covered her upper lip. She sniffed and wiped the droplets of blood with the back of her free hand, forming a smear that covered her right cheek. Through the fog of steam rising from the tub, Franklin could see the determination in her eyes, a determination that was only slightly betrayed by a soft whimper as she wielded the scissors.

They continued to move in a slow circle around the bathroom. Each breathed heavily, trying to anticipate the other's next move. A quick feint to the left by the man caused the woman to strike out with the scissors, but the man dodged the blow and grabbed her shoulder with his right hand and her throat with his left. She raised the scissors again, and this time she thrust them squarely at his chest.

Her worries would have been over had he not turned quickly to the left, causing the blades to miss their mark and to catch in his shirt pocket. With a grunt he ripped his shirt free, released her shoulder, and grabbed the scissors out of her hand. She twisted left, breaking his grip on her neck, and began to run from the room. As his fingers slipped from her neck, they closed around the top of her nightgown, ripping it to her waist. The woman ran screaming with her arms folded in front of her, protecting her breasts.

The man stood in the center of the bathroom with the scissors in one hand and the torn top of her nightgown in the other. Franklin looked up from the tub into the man's face. The nose was bent to one side and the lips were pressed into a wide sneer by the stocking mask, but the face was not so obscured that Franklin couldn't recognize the evil in its stare. Franklin lay motionless, trembling. He took little note of the sudden warmth spreading across his legs as his bladder emptied.

The man took one step toward the tub. Franklin flailed his feet, thrashing wildly, trying to get up, his hands and feet losing what little grip they had on the tub's bottom and his body sliding down until his head slipped under the water. He could hear his heart beating wildly, trying to break free of his chest. It pounded among the bubbles and echoed off the sides of the tub into his water-filled ears.

Through the soap film he could see the man looking down at him. Franklin was alone, naked, and more vulnerable than he had ever been, but he was determined not to be drowned in his own tub. Not without at least putting up a good fight. His eyes burned in the soapy water and his lungs ached for a breath of air, but he wasn't beaten yet. He forced both hands to the bottom of the tub and pushed down as hard as he could to raise his head out of the water. He broke the surface, coughing and gasping for air. He grabbed the side of the tub for support, waiting to feel the force of being pushed back down under the water. A moment passed. Nothing happened. Franklin opened his eyes, but his vision was still blurred from the soapy water. He waved his arms furiously in the direction of his assailant, and then slowly, as his eyes cleared, he realized that he was alone in the room.

Slipping and sliding on the wet tile floor, Franklin reached for his robe and pulled it from its hook with a rip. He grabbed at the bathroom hamper and leaned on it for support until he regained his balance. His hands fumbled through the pockets of his robe to retrieve his glasses until he remembered that he had left them on the nightstand. He stood, one hand on each side of the doorway, breathing heavily and squinting as he scanned the bedroom. The room seemed different somehow.

Movement at the bed caught his attention. Covers flew into the air as the woman clawed and punched at the man leaning over, pressing her to the bed. His hands were wrapped tightly around her neck, his fingers and knuckles white from the pressure of squeezing her throat. Blue veins pulsed at her temples and her eyes bulged as she kicked and pushed against the footboard of the bed. Her fists bounced off his body. The man was oblivious to all but the act he was intent on completing.

Franklin stood immobilized by the horror all around him. He should be doing something to stop this. He should pull the man off her, or at least hit him with something, but he couldn't move. He looked at his feet. "Take a step, you coward," he said, but he didn't move. He was frozen in time, frozen in space. He couldn't do anything.

"Stop," Franklin shouted, hoping to distract him long enough for the woman to take a breath. To divert the man's attention even for a second could prolong her life. Her attacker didn't turn; he didn't pause. It was as though he hadn't heard Franklin's voice. Franklin shouted again, "Leave her alone, you…" He stopped midsentence. Not only had the man not heard his plea, but Franklin hadn't heard his own words either.

Suddenly Franklin realized that he didn't hear anything, nor had he heard anything since he entered the bedroom. Not the man grunting as he strained to hold the woman to the bed while she struggled to breathe. Not the sound of her feet kicking at the footboard. He didn't hear the thud of the man's hand as he released her neck and struck her face with his fist or the slash of the scissors, ripping through her flesh again and again.

It was about this time that Franklin began to realize that the events he was watching unfold could not be real. A half-naked woman running into his bathroom? A murder taking place in his bedroom? These were the things of science fiction novels—or nightmares.

He slapped his own face as hard as he could. He didn't feel it. He looked around the room carefully for the first time. There was a fireplace on the far wall that didn't belong there. The dresser was similar to his, but on the wrong side of the room. Even the bed was wrong; it had posts and a canopy. Nothing in this room was familiar. It wasn't his room. He was in a strange house, and now he knew. He knew that none of this was real; it was all a dream, a nightmare. He was probably still asleep at home in his bathtub.

Franklin took a deep breath and slowly exhaled into the silence. He felt relieved knowing that he would awaken from this nightmare, but he still felt uncomfortable—and guilty. He hadn't done anything to help this woman, even if it was only a dream. He just stood by and watched a horrible beating inflicted on a defenseless woman by a maniac.

Drip! Drip! He cocked his head to one side and listened to the new sound. Franklin looked down. Water was dripping from his wet bathrobe onto the floor. The dripping sound became louder and louder until the room shook as each exploding drop hit the hardwood floor. Franklin covered his ears with both hands. Suddenly the room erupted into an ear-shattering cacophony of sound, as though a switch had been thrown and the volume turned to its maximum level. The woman was screaming a blood-curdling scream. There was a crash as a lamp shattered on the floor. He heard the loud crack of breaking wood as the footboard of the bed gave way under the frantic kicks of the woman's feet.

All the sounds previously absent swelled into a deafening crescendo of ear-splitting noise. Franklin pressed his hands tighter to his ears, squeezed his eyes shut, and yelled, "This is my dream—you have to stop!" But the man didn't stop. He raised the bloody scissors high and thrust them again and again into her twitching body. Seconds later there was silence again. The woman lay still on the bed. She no longer struggled for breath, her arms limp at her sides and her legs now lying still, on top of the broken footboard.

Now that Franklin knew he was dreaming, and that these people were figments of his imagination, he could move among them without fear.

He walked to the side of the bed and looked down at the battered body. Her face looked somewhat familiar, but her features were distorted from the punishment of the attack. The remnants of her torn nightgown had been raised almost to her waist by her frantic kicking during her last moments alive. Franklin could see a pattern showing through the sheer fabric covering her right hip. He lifted the swatch of bloodied cloth and exposed a small tattoo: a tattoo in the shape of a yellow rose.

Franklin jumped back; the man bent over and seemed to pass right through him. He lifted the dead weight of the woman's body from the bed and carried her out of the room, down the stairs.

Franklin followed him as if in a trance. He felt detached. He was there, yet he knew this was a dream, and he was really safe at home asleep, and none of this was really happening. He followed the masked man out of the house, through the garage, and watched as he placed the body in the trunk of a car. Franklin touched the silver midsize late-model car, not much different in size and shape than his own car. Since he was sure this was a dream, Franklin tried to pass through the closed door of the car and sit in the backseat. He was astonished to find that he could. It was like being a ghost. Moments later the killer started the car and drove out of the neighborhood. Franklin looked out the window and saw a woman walking a large gray dog. The dog pulled at the leash and barked at the passing car. She was almost jerked off her feet but steadied herself by clinging with one hand to a sign that read *Golf Cart Crossing*. The old woman stared at them as they sped away.

Soon the driver came to a stop on a small bridge over a rain-swollen stream. He took the body from the trunk of the car and dropped it over the side of the bridge into the fast-moving water. Franklin watched the body, carried by the swift current, disappear into the darkness. He closed his eyes and wished that this dream was over. He waited for the car to start moving again, but it did not. As he reopened his eyes, he saw that he was no longer in the backseat of the murderer's car. He was now alone and in the driver's seat of another car, his car, and it was parked in his driveway just where he always parked. Franklin looked down at the wet bathrobe he was still wearing and began to shake and rock back and forth in his seat. What insanity had entered his dream? What had happened to him, or more importantly, what had he done?

9

Franklin pulled into the circular driveway and parked in one of the spaces to the right of the large colonial house. He raised his collar and held it close against his neck as he walked down the flagstone path leading toward the front entryway.

"Good to see you," shouted Elaine Green as she walked down the white marble steps from the large mahogany double-front doors. "It's been quite some time since you've paid us a visit."

Elaine was bundled against the cold in a leather coat topped with a collar Franklin recognized only as some kind of exotic fur—maybe bobcat. He remembered stories Hyrum had told him about Elaine's college days. She was a fighter for causes back then. The environment and animal rights were the vanguard of her crusade. Franklin wondered whether age or affluence had had a greater numbing effect on her principles. He decided that it was probably money that had changed her view of the world.

He remembered the changes that had taken place in Myra as their wealth grew. When they first met, she was a vegetarian and wouldn't even sit at the same table where animal products were being served. After Franklin earned his first few million, crown roast of beef and lobster became staples on her dining table. She'd never succumbed to a desire for fur, but leather coats and alligator boots were rationalized purchases that found their way into her closet. Franklin really had no right to cast aspersions. He had wholeheartedly embraced Myra's proenvironment convictions when she professed them, then just as quickly he gobbled the roast beef to the last morsel when her views became, shall we say, less puritanical.

"Have you been waiting outside in the cold for me?" Franklin asked with a smile.

"I'm sorry, but I'm on my way out. Hyrum is in his study; go right in."

She watched as Franklin negotiated the stairs using his cane and offered him her arm for support since there was no railing. He leaned forward and kissed her on the cheek as he reached the top step. Elaine smiled and walked toward her car.

Franklin stepped through the front door into the spacious foyer and started down the long tile hallway to Hyrum's study. Along the walls of the hall were photographs of Hyrum and Elaine taken over the years. There were pictures in ski outfits, on horseback, and even a picture of Hyrum in scuba gear. Franklin hadn't realized that Hyrum was so athletic, or that his own dental work had paid for such lavish vacations.

"Are you busy?" Franklin asked as he peeked into the study.

"Franklin, I'm glad you came. Sit and talk for a while."

"I was just looking at how much vacation a root canal can buy. Where are you off to this year?"

"There'll be no vacation this year, at least not for both Elaine *and* me. She'll go on a trip, and I'll stay here and work. Insurance companies have cut back so far on their payments that I have to see three times the number of patients I treated two years ago just to make enough money to keep my head above water. It's criminal, but you didn't come here to hear my tale of woe. How are things with you?"

Franklin sat in a Chippendale chair and leaned forward with his elbows on his knees and his head down. "Hyrum, something strange is happening to me. I'm having horrible dreams, and I'm afraid the nightmares are affecting my mind."

Hyrum opened his mouth to reply in his normal wisecracking style, but stopped short. He saw the fear in Franklin's eyes. He looked vulnerable and confused. Hyrum decided to listen instead.

Franklin began to chronicle each of his dreams in detail. Hyrum listened, totally engrossed in Franklin's story. He was particularly interested in the murder dream and moved to the edge of his seat as Franklin described his feelings of helplessness when he could not alter the woman's fate. Hyrum rubbed his chin with his hand and scratched his head, trying to think of something to say that might ease Franklin's pain.

"Have you been reading murder mysteries before going to bed, or maybe watching the news on television?" Hyrum asked.

"Not more than usual, but that's not the worst part. I think I've been walking in my sleep. Two nights ago I woke up in my car, and now I'm afraid to go to sleep."

"That's it?" Hyrum said. "Lots of people walk in their sleep. It doesn't mean you're losing your mind. Aside from the sleepwalking, is there anything else unusual that's happened recently?"

"Well, I'm embarrassed to say this…"

"Please, we're friends; you can tell me anything." Hyrum leaned still closer.

"I was talking to myself the other day."

"Franklin, everybody talks to themselves now and then. It's normal."

"But I was answering myself, Hyrum. I don't feel normal."

"Have you thought about professional help? If this were a gum infection, I could tell you what to do, but this is out of my league."

Franklin thought of telling Hyrum about his session with Dr. Klein. There was no shame in receiving professional help, but since Hyrum's office was in the same building and just down the hall from Dr. Klein's office, he was afraid his friend and his psychologist might compare notes about him. Intellectually he knew that would never happen, but if he had any trust left for his intellect, he wouldn't be having this conversation at all.

"No, I think I just need to get some rest. Everyone has nightmares now and then, right?" Franklin said, trying to lighten the mood.

"Maybe you're psychic," Hyrum said. He didn't know why, but somehow he thought it would be helpful if he could offer a reason for Franklin's dreams.

"What?"

"Maybe you're psychic. One of your dreams was about a burglary, and there have been many in the area lately. Maybe the burglary you dreamed of really happened," Hyrum said, hoping this suggestion might quell Franklin's appetite for a diagnosis of his fears.

"You know, that could be. Maybe the burglary happened just as I dreamed it did, but it happened to someone else. Or maybe it didn't happen yet. Maybe it was a premonition." Now Franklin became excited. "You know, I dreamed of a wolf, and then two days later I read that one had escaped from a preserve in New Jersey. I'll have to think about that." Franklin paused and stared at the floor.

"What's wrong now?" Hyrum asked. "I thought the possibility that you had a talent, an ability to see the future, would make you feel better."

Franklin hadn't thought about his dreams being premonitions. If it were true, it would explain the detail and intensity of the dreams. It would mean that he was not going insane; on the contrary, he was gifted. But there was a downside to that scenario. If he was psychic and the dreams were harbingers of the future, then a woman was about to be brutally murdered. Franklin didn't want that to be true. He wanted his dreams to be just dreams with no real meaning. They had to be.

"It should make me feel better, but if it's true that my dream was a premonition, then that means that a woman will be murdered in her bedroom," Franklin said, his voice beginning to crack.

Hyrum thought for a moment. "It means no such thing," Hyrum said. "I'm sure I'm wrong. I'm sure they're not premonitions, only dreams. Tonight you'll dream that the same woman is alive and well. It's all fantasy."

Franklin decided that this conversation was not helping and decided to end it.

"Well, thank you for the input," Franklin said. "I'm sure you're right. I'm just overtired. I'm sure I'll feel better in the morning."

"Franklin, Elaine won't be back until late. Why don't we grab a couple of beers and go into the living room? You need a distraction. Let's try to forget about your dreams for a while and watch some television, preferably a comedy."

Neither Franklin nor Hyrum heard the soft patter of footsteps as Elaine Green hurried from just outside the study door. She stopped at the small telephone table near the stairway.

"Elaine, I thought you were gone," said Hyrum as they emerged from the study. Elaine held up her keychain and rattled the keys.

"I couldn't get very far without these," she said, and she turned to rush out of the house.

10

Franklin paced back and forth across his kitchen floor. It was six o'clock, barely half an hour before he had to leave for his therapy appointment with Dr. Klein, and he still hadn't decided just how much of his dream he was willing to share with her.

"She'll probably have me committed before I get half the story out," he said out loud. "Shit, I'm talking to myself again." He picked up the cup of tea on the counter and took a long pull.

"Damn," he shouted, pressing a dish towel to his scalded lips. "And I'm still talking to myself." He dumped the tea in the sink and watched it circle down the drain.

His computer was booted up and waiting in his home office. He walked to the desk and sat at the keyboard. He decided that an entry describing the events of his dream written in the order they happened would make it easier to relate the story—keep him on the right path.

He typed, "My Murder Dream, by Franklin Jameson." For some reason typing the title made him chuckle. It reminded him of a grade-school essay, like "My Summer Vacation," or "My Favorite Things." Only this essay could have been titled, "How I Watched Someone Die at the Hands of a Maniac." He took a deep breath and exhaled slowly. He knew it was just nervous laughter, but he still felt guilty. Franklin shook his head to clear it and sat staring at the blank page while he formulated his thoughts. As he sat staring at the title, a small snicker again rose up in his throat, then a slight giggle leaked from his lips, and eventually a full-blown belly laugh as he convulsed into hysterics. He lost all control and rocked in his chair. It wasn't funny, but each time he strained to stifle his laugh and force his face into a scowl, he would think of the title and snort and again break up in a burst of renewed laughter. He pounded the desk and held his ribs as his sides began to ache. "This has to stop," he said through tears. Eventually the laughter subsided, and the mirth decayed into a quiet sob. He pinched his thigh as hard as he could. The pain shocked him back to the horror of the dream. Slightly out of breath but finally in control of his emotions, he dried the tears from his eyes with his handkerchief and focused back on the computer screen, now feeling even more guilty than before. "Let's do this," he said.

He closed his eyes and tried to relive the experience of the dream. He took several deep breaths and began to reconstruct the scene in his memory. Once he had a clear picture of the bedroom, he began to mentally walk through the murder room, trying to remember every detail. He looked in his mind's eye at the broken footboard and the bloody sheets pulled from the bed and scattered about on the floor. He conjured up the smashed lamp lying near the nightstand, and he tried to examine the contents of the dresser drawers carelessly dumped on the area rug.

Franklin remembered the dream as being vivid, but now many of the images were distorted. He wasn't sure if he was reviewing the dream or if his imagination was filling the gaps, amending the areas that were unclear.

He shuddered when he approached the body lying on the bed. He tried to recognize the victim, but her face was out of focus. He wanted his description of the dream to be accurate in every detail as he remembered it. He drew a diagram of the room layout, the location of the furniture, and all the bloody stains on the sheets and carpet. He described the victim, her wounds, and her struggle. He wrote about the bridge where the body was thrown and the dog walker who witnessed the murderer's getaway. Franklin read his notes. The account of the events wasn't complete, but he was satisfied that it would jog his memory adequately to explain the dream to Dr. Klein. He printed the document and folded the paper lengthwise to slip into his back pocket.

***

Franklin arrived early for his appointment with Dr. Klein, just in time to meet Hyrum Green as he was locking his office for the night.

"You haven't broken a tooth, have you?" Hyrum asked to cover his surprise at seeing Franklin at this late hour.

"No, I'm fine," he said, trying to cover his own surprise and embarrassment at meeting Hyrum while on his way to a psychoanalysis session. "I'm, uh…meeting a friend for drinks later at the pub across the street. I'm early, and since I saw your car still in the parking lot"—Franklin pointed over his shoulder in the direction of the lot—"I thought I would stop in and say hello." He stammered, red-faced. *This excuse is so lame he can't possibly buy it.*

"Don't be embarrassed, Franklin. I'm glad to see you found someone to talk to," Hyrum said with a wink. Franklin now felt extremely distressed, believing he had been caught in a lie. He reached into his back pocket for his handkerchief to mop his brow. "You think you might get a little tonight?" he said with another wink.

"What?" said Franklin, wondering what Hyrum knew about Ruth Klein's therapy that he didn't.

"Your new friend, the one you're meeting for drinks; Elaine and I have been hoping you would find someone soon. We miss seeing you, plus a little 'exercise' would be good for your nerves."

"Oh no, it's just a first date," Franklin replied, trying to regain his composure. "I had better get back there before I'm late." He shook Hyrum's hand and started toward the door.

"Good luck," Hyrum shouted as he continued to lock his door, a wide, adolescent grin on his face.

Franklin dodged heavy traffic on the busy street to reach the small local pub situated on the other side. He stood inside the pub and bent over to affect a line of sight between the fluorescent Miller Beer sign and the blinking "This Bud's for You" beacon that gave him a clear view of Hyrum's car.

The tavern was almost empty. Franklin scanned the room and noticed a woman sitting in the shadows at a small table in the corner. She was wearing business clothes: a dark skirt and a jacket. Probably navy blue or black, but the color was almost indistinguishable in the subdued light.

Her legs were crossed, and his eye traveled from the hint of thigh peeking out from under her skirt past a well-defined and nicely muscled calf to a pair of black leather, extremely high stiletto heels. The shoes were elegant but looked almost impossible to walk in.

The bartender, noticing Franklin's stare, leaned toward Franklin, holding his hand next to his mouth and speaking in a low voice. "They're CFM shoes."

Franklin cocked his head and shook it slightly. "CFM?"

"Yeah, they're called 'come fuck me' shoes."

Franklin again shook his head.

"They wear them when…ahh, never mind. What can I get you to drink?" the bartender asked as he placed a coaster and a napkin on the bar.

"I'll be just a minute," Franklin said. "I just want to make sure that my dentist has left for the night."

"Yeah, I feel the same way about my proctologist." The bartender laughed. "Can I pour you a drink?"

"OK, I'll have a draft beer." Franklin continued looking over his shoulder at the woman at the corner table.

"She comes in about twice a week," the bartender said, pouring a draft Michelob. "Don't waste your time. In about ten minutes, her boyfriend will come in for a drink. Then they'll both leave."

Even in the dim light, Franklin could tell that she was a looker. She never looked up from her magazine, just took a sip of her drink and reached into her purse, a large leather carryall, and plucked out her cell phone. She tapped the screen several times and waited for someone to pick up.

"Hi, it's me," she whispered. "Don't come to meet me right now. A guy who saw me leaving the building last week just walked in. I think he might be a patient of yours or of Dr. Klein's. Either way, it probably isn't a good idea if he sees us together. You go straight to the hotel, and I'll meet you there in a little while…Yes, he's tall and he has a cane. Do you know him?" Long pause. "OK, I'll see you soon." She tapped the phone, dropped it back into her bag, and turned the page of her magazine.

"Who's the guy?" Franklin asked.

"Hang around; you'll see."

"Why, do you think I'll know him?"

"You never know." The bartender busied himself wiping the bar, grinning from ear to ear. "I go to a dentist across the street too. He usually finishes up about now." The bartender's grin got even wider.

"It looks like I'm in luck; my dentist's car just pulled out of the lot," Franklin said.

"Well, I'll be damned," the bartender said, first looking at Dr. Green's car leaving the lot and then at the woman sitting at the corner table.

"You wouldn't happen to know her name, would you? She looks so familiar."

"I think it's Sally, or Sarah—no, Sylvia. That's it, Sylvia. I looked at her credit card receipt the last time she was here."

Franklin noticed that Sylvia was also watching Dr. Green's car leaving the lot.

Franklin was generally shy and rarely spoke to anyone he didn't know, but there was something very familiar about this woman. She had long black hair, was attractive, seemed to have a fine-looking body—just his type. But there was something else about her. He felt some sort of emotional attachment. It was like they shared a bond or an experience of some sort. He picked up his beer and walked to her table.

"Didn't I see you coming out of the building across the street last week?" he asked.

"Is that the best line you've got?" she asked with a smile.

He looked down and noticed that the label on the magazine she had just closed read Hyrum Green, DDS.

"Have you been seeing Dr. Green?" Franklin asked.

Sylvia locked eyes with Franklin. "Excuse me?"

"Is Dr. Hyrum Green your dentist? You were coming from his office last week, weren't you?"

"No one can pull the wool over your eyes," she said, lifting her purse and stuffing the magazine inside. "It was nice talking to you." She headed toward the door.

Franklin felt like a bashful schoolboy after talking to his first cheer-leader. He watched the rhythmic motion of those glorious hips sway out the door in spite of the height of her shoes.

Franklin looked at his watch. "Shit!" he exclaimed. He gulped down the beer, dropped a five-dollar bill on the bar, and rushed to the door.

"He's going to get you anyway; he uses a collection agency," said the bartender with a nod and a look of resignation on his face.

"Thanks for the advice," Franklin said, his cane clicking on the floor as he ran out the door and across the street.

Sylvia smiled, waved, and blew a kiss through her open car window as she turned onto the street in the same direction that Hyrum had taken moments ago.

Franklin again crossed the busy street and started up the steps to the building. A car horn and a screech of brakes caused him to turn back toward the boulevard. A driver was shaking his fist out of his window at a man in a hooded sweatshirt and a yellow plaid jacket as he dashed across the street and toward the pub. Franklin thought about going back to the pub to confront this man. Was this who he thought it could be, and if so, why was he stalking Franklin rather than talking to him? He looked at his watch. There was no time to spare, and the man was no longer in sight.

***

Franklin rushed through the door of Ruth Klein's office at ten minutes after seven. "Sorry I'm a few minutes late. I had to stop for gas, or I might not have made it here at all." He avoided her eyes as he walked to the couch.

Ruth caught a whiff of his breath as he walked past her. *He smells like he filled his tank with beer,* she thought, but said, "No problem, you're the last appointment of the day. We can run a little over if we need to. Have you had any more disturbing dreams since our last session?"

Franklin bit his lip and nodded a few times. "The night before last, I dreamed of a murder. It was frightening and horribly violent. A woman was stabbed with a pair of scissors in her bedroom. Every time I close my eyes, I see the carnage all over again."

"Did you recognize any of the characters in the dream?"

Franklin shifted his weight to his right side and reached into his back pocket for the folded paper. He didn't find it.

"I wrote some notes to help remember the details of my dream, but I seem to have lost them on the way over. Either they fell out of my pocket when I pulled out my handkerchief earlier in the hall, or I lost them crossing the street from the—ah, gas station. Hell, maybe I left the paper at home. I'm not sure of anything lately."

"Don't chastise yourself for losing a piece of paper. Just tell me what you remember."

"The victim looked slightly familiar. I didn't see her face clearly, but she had a yellow rose tattooed here." He touched his right hip with his hand.

Ruth Klein began to feel increasingly sympathetic toward this man who appeared to be having a breakdown in her office.

He continued, "It's like I was right in the room, but there was nothing I could do to stop it from happening. I knew I was dreaming, but I had no control. And the next thing I knew..."

Franklin stopped as he was about to describe the part of the dream where he followed the murderer out of the house and hid in the silver car.

"The next thing you knew—what?" asked Dr. Klein.

"I woke up," said Franklin. He dared not go any further.

Ruth summoned her most soothing tone. "Dreams can seem very real, but we have to realize that they're just dreams. The images they evoke can be frightening, but they are still just an illusion. There may be some fears or memories in your past that manifest themselves as nightmares, but usually bringing those fears or memories to the forefront of your mind will allow you to deal with them and end the nightmares. We can work on this together."

"What about not realizing if I'm awake or asleep?" Franklin blew his nose in a tissue.

"I've been thinking about that, and I can see several different sleep disturbances you're experiencing. None is necessarily serious." Ruth moved to the edge of her chair and leaned forward as she spoke. "First, let's talk about false awakenings. In a false awakening dream, the subject believes he is awake but remains asleep, still dreaming, until he truly awakens. We spoke of this in our last session. It's common and occasionally happens to everyone. You can minimize this problem by establishing a reality check upon waking. When you feel that you have awakened from a dream, test yourself by pressing your thumb into the palm of your other hand." She demonstrated while speaking. "If you are truly awake, all will be normal. If it's a false awakening and you're still dreaming, your thumb will pass right through your palm." She smiled. "I know it sounds ridiculous but it's an established test used by dream therapists. They say it works well to discover a false awakening." Franklin mimicked her actions with his own thumb and palm.

"As far as seeing people, such as the burglar, as you were falling asleep, it's called *hypnagogia*. It's a Greek word meaning the transitional state between wakefulness and sleep."

"Is it curable?" Franklin interjected.

"It's not a disease," she said, smiling. "It's a perfectly normal state of consciousness everyone experiences as they begin to dream, although not too many people experience both hypnagogia and false awakenings in the same dream."

"I always thought I was special," Franklin said, finally daring to smile.

Dr. Klein chuckled. "I think we have done as much as we should for one session. Try to ensure that you get enough sleep and call me during the week if you have any concerns or incidents before our next session. I'll see you on Tuesday at seven." They shook hands, and Franklin walked out the door.

Ruth Klein stood with her notebook in her hand, staring at the door for a full minute after Franklin left. She then settled in her chair and began to edit and transcribe her notes from the session.

11

Lt. Sam Peirce parked his dark-blue unmarked police car in the driveway of the two-story brick townhouse at the Silicon Springs Golf Links. He ran his fingers through his hair, then flipped down the visor and looked in the mirror. He carefully smoothed his hair to make the slight thinning on top a little less obvious. Sam wasn't a vain man, but he had some concern about the image he presented. A police officer should look fit and in control of every situation. He took the lit cigarette from the ashtray, placed it between his lips, stepped out of the car, and buttoned his suit jacket. The button pulled at the buttonhole, reminding him of the ten pounds he had promised to lose before the holidays. At just under six feet tall, Sam carried his weight well. But he had slowed a step or two in the last few years.

Sam Peirce rose from the rank of patrolman to sergeant during the fifteen years he had cruised the streets of Philadelphia. He was offered the position of lieutenant when the Luzerne County Police Department was regionalized in 1999.

Sam's record of solving crimes and making arrests was exemplary. He probably could have been promoted much earlier in Philadelphia, but that would have meant working from a desk. Lieutenants didn't work the streets in Philadelphia. But Sam was a street cop. He took the county promotion to homicide lieutenant only with the agreement that he could work some crimes from the field as well as manage his troops. Although the last few years of eighteen-hour days, solo restaurant meals, and a limited social life had seen his waist grow larger and his time at the gym cut shorter, he still enjoyed the thrill of the hunt and was happy only when he was working a difficult case.

It was dawn, and in the dim light of early morning, he could see rows of elegant brick-and-stone homes bordering the frost-covered fairways and glazed-over emerald greens of the well-manicured golf course.

Sam closed his eyes and took a deep breath of the chilly air. It was the first frost of the season, and he could still smell the clusters of roses, now brown, wilted, and bent, on the large rosebushes at each side of the front walk. It was a shame that no one had cut them and taken them in before the frost hit.

Lieutenant Peirce ran his hand along the two rows of neatly trimmed hedges on either side of the paving-stone walkway that led him to the large wooden front door with stained-glass windows. This was the kind of place he always dreamed about buying when he finally decided to pack it in. He had thought about putting in his papers several times in the last year, but he hadn't. Maybe it was the excitement he felt when he worked a difficult case that kept him going, or the satisfaction he enjoyed when he put the bad guys away. Either way, he wasn't quite ready to retire. Of course, the fact that he had less than a thousand dollars in the bank and still had a mortgage on his current home could have been factors in his decision as well.

"What the hell happened here?" he asked as he crushed out his cigarette on the top step with his left foot and reached into his jacket pocket for a pair of white latex rubber gloves. He held the gloves up to the porch lamp, blew into each glove in turn, and then stretched them onto his large hands in preparation for entering the first floor of the well-appointed home.

"I don't know," answered Sergeant Holloway, standing just inside the foyer and holding a paper cup of coffee. "I just got here a few minutes ago myself."

"That was a rhetorical question, Holloway."

"What?"

Lieutenant Peirce paused and looked at Holloway out of the corner of his eye. "Never mind. Who was first on the scene?"

Sergeant Holloway sipped his coffee and pointed to a uniformed private security guard leaning against the wall.

"I was," said the guard. He stepped forward as he tucked a shirttail into his trousers and straightened his tie.

"And who are you?" asked Lieutenant Peirce.

"James Chrystal, Silicon Springs Security. I was making my rounds at one a.m. when I saw the broken garage side door."

"You called me down here at five a.m. for a burglary?" Lieutenant Peirce asked Holloway.

"No, wait, he's got more," Holloway said, nodding at the rent-a-cop to continue.

James Chrystal walked to the side door. "I went to take a closer look, and I saw that the doorframe had something on it that kind of looked like it could be blood," he said, pointing at the red smudge on the frame. "I shouted into the open door—'Hey, is anybody home?' When no one answered, I went back to my car and looked up the telephone number for this house on my list of residents. It belongs to one Sylvia Radcliffe. I dialed the number, but when no one answered the phone, I called the police, just like I'm supposed to."

Sam bent and inspected the bloodstain. "You did the right thing." Then Peirce turned toward a sound coming from the next room.

A voice echoed from the top of the stairs. "My partner and I responded to the break-in call," said Sergeant Reagan as he came down the stairs. "We identified ourselves as police officers and entered the building. Officer Donavan and I cleared the first floor, and then I went to check the second floor."

Lieutenant Peirce walked past the sergeant to the staircase, grabbed the wrought-iron banister with his left hand, and began to pull himself up the stairs. After noticing that all eyes were on him, he released the banister and began to jog up the rest of the way.

"It's a mess up there, Lieutenant," said the sergeant. "Lots of blood everywhere."

When Lieutenant Peirce reached the top of the stairs, he could see light coming from an open door at the end of the hall. Looking down, he saw small drops of dried blood that almost blended into the pattern of the tweed carpet. He carefully stepped around the spots and shouted, "No one else comes up here. This is now officially a crime scene. Let's not contaminate it. Holloway, put a call in to forensics and get everyone else out of the building until they arrive. No one touches anything."

"You got it, Lieutenant," replied Holloway.

Lieutenant Peirce slowly walked to the open door, carefully avoiding the bloodstains on the rug, and scrutinized the hall for additional evidence or anything of interest. The door led to a grand bedroom suite. Peirce was impressed by the elegance of the four-poster bed and the large stone fireplace at the other end of the room. He looked at the scattered pillows and twisted bed clothes lying on the floor. Streams of dried blood had recently flowed over and around their folds. *There's enough blood here for a murder*, he proffered. Several of the dresser drawers were either partially open or pulled out of the chest completely and the contents dumped on an area rug. The footboard of the bed was cracked and pushed out from the bed frame. "Somebody put up one hell of a fight," he said out loud. Lieutenant Peirce studied the hardwood floor and noticed watermarks dried onto the wood just outside the open bathroom doorway. He took note of a bath towel soaking in a full bathtub of water with a film of soap floating on its surface.

He could smell the scent of lavender and assumed that the film was the residue of bubble bath or bath oil on the water. Lavender wasn't a scent he particularly liked, but it was a welcome relief from the metallic smell of blood that permeated the bedroom. Her bath appeared to have been interrupted. The vanity drawers were open, and on the sink and countertop were small droplets of blood, but not enough blood to have come from the same wound that caused all the stains in the other room. He stood very still, closed his eyes, and waited for some insight into what may have happened here.

As he stood waiting for the fruits of his intuition to gel into a plausible theory of the crime, he sensed his knees beginning to weaken. He held his right hand up in front of his face. It was shaking almost uncontrollably. A sour taste rose from his throat, and he felt a mild discomfort emanating from the center of his chest. It grew in size and weight until it became a pain so intense that it pushed the breath from his body. He groaned. "Not now," he said in a hoarse voice and reached into his jacket pocket for a small oblong metal box. Sam Peirce removed a pale yellow pill from the box and placed it under his tongue. After a minute, the pain began to subside.

"Lieutenant, are you still up there?" shouted Holloway from the bottom of the stairs.

Lieutenant Peirce took a moment to compose himself, then answered in as strong a voice as he could muster, "What is it?"

"The forensic team will be here in ten minutes. Everyone else is outside, and I posted a guard at the door. Shall I come up?"

"Not necessary," replied Lieutenant Peirce. "Wait until the team arrives, then bring them up."

Sam Peirce sat on the closed toilet lid in the spacious, elegant bathroom, pulled his handkerchief from his pocket, and mopped the beads of perspiration from his brow.

After a few minutes, he walked cautiously back into the bedroom. The sunlight was now beginning to penetrate the curtains with a brightness that disaffirmed the events of the previous night. *A good cleaning and the next owner of this house would never know the violent atrocities that happened here, or, if it was publicized, the house would probably go for a song. I wonder how much...*

He shook his head as he thought of how callous he had become in the last twenty years. Bloodstains and the destruction of property had become no more than clues. Victims and murderers had become case numbers to be closed or to grow cold and remain forever in an open file. At what point, he wondered, had he lost his sense of humanity?

A minor commotion on the first floor signaled the arrival of the forensic team. Startled back to full awareness, he straightened his tie, buttoned his jacket, and walked to the hall to meet the arriving officers.

The forensic team began to collect evidence at the scene. They placed small yellow placards with numbers next to anything they believed to be of value and photographed its location before sealing any evidence in plastic bags, labeling them, and filing them away. Small fiberglass brushes were twirled about on any surface that might hold a latent fingerprint. Each time a print was found, it was transferred by clear tape to a card and again labeled and filed.

"Holloway," said Lieutenant Peirce, "everything seems to be covered here. I'm going back to the office. Bring a prelim of anything they find as soon as you can."

***

8:30 a.m. Thursday

Lieutenant Peirce sat in his office sipping a steaming cup of coffee—cream, two sugars—and perusing the morning paper. At 8:32 Sergeant Holloway walked into Lieutenant Peirce's office, carrying the forensic report.

"Anything important?" asked Lieutenant Peirce.

Holloway stared at Peirce for a second. "Nothing earth-shattering. The home belongs to one Sylvia Radcliffe. We tried locating her, but no luck."

"Could she be away on business or a vacation?"

"Her clothes and suitcases are still in the closet, so we don't think she went on a trip. We're trying to reach her next of kin; she has a mother, Henrietta Radcliffe, and a younger sister, Emily. They both live in Allentown." Holloway searched through the jar of jelly beans on Lieutenant Peirce's desk, picking out as many orange candies as he could find.

Lieutenant Peirce looked up from his newspaper, locked his eyes on Holloway, and placed the lid sharply on his candy jar, almost trapping Holloway's fingers. "She married or single?"

"Divorced. A neighbor told the officer doing the canvass that the ex moved to Utah a year ago." Holloway carefully looked at his fingers, then slipped the five orange jelly beans into his shirt pocket.

Lieutenant Peirce stretched out his open hand toward Sergeant Holloway and waited in silence. As Holloway reached back into his shirt pocket to retrieve the candies, the lieutenant looked at the ceiling. Then he squeezed his eyes shut and said, "The forensic report?"

After Holloway handed it to him, Lieutenant Peirce leaned back in his chair and began to read the document.

"Did the canvass of the neighborhood turn up anything else?" Lieutenant Peirce asked, looking up from the report in his hand.

Holloway flipped a few pages in his notepad and replied, "A Mrs. Maxwell was walking her dog about eleven thirty last night. She said she saw a silver sedan, she didn't know the make, speed out of the development coming from the direction of the Radcliffe house. She said he almost hit her dog. And I quote, 'I didn't see the face of the bastard who scared my Rodney, but he was in a silver car. If you catch him, I'm going to sue him for all he's worth. My Rodney's had diarrhea all night.'"

Lieutenant Peirce shook his head, chuckled, and returned his eyes to the report while Holloway quietly extracted orange jelly beans from his shirt pocket and one by one covertly placed them in his mouth.

The report indicated that there was indeed enough blood in the bedroom to support a homicide investigation. All the blood in both the bathroom and the bedroom was of the same type, type A. Future DNA data should indicate if all the blood samples were from the same individual. A clear trail of blood droplets was apparent and could be followed from the bedroom through the hall, down the stairs, and out the garage side door, eventually ending on the driveway. A pair of long stainless steel scissors was found among the bloody sheets. They would be evaluated as a possible murder weapon once a body was found. A small piece of blue fabric was caught in the joint of the scissors. It didn't match any fabric at the scene. Fingerprints from at least four different individuals were present in the bedroom, and prints from an additional three people were found throughout the rest of the house. The lieutenant looked up from the report.

"Holloway, see if any of the prints they picked up in the house are in the system. The blood trail would indicate that the victim, assumed dead from the amount of blood loss, was carried out of the building through the garage. The trail ended on the driveway. I would assume that the body was placed in a vehicle of some sort and removed from the property. Check to see if any neighbors can remember a silver sedan parked at the Radcliffe house last night. And get me the address of the mother and sister; I'll want to interview them."

"You got it, boss," said Holloway as he hurried out the door.

12

Red lights flashed, a whistle sounded, and clouds of dust and soot rose into the air, blown by the wind emanating from the train roaring through the crossing. Lieutenant Peirce waited, drumming his fingers on the steering wheel of his car as an untold number of freight cars passed before he could drive to the other side of the tracks where Henrietta and Emily Radcliffe made their home.

As he stepped up onto the wooden porch of the two-story house, he ran his finger along the peeling gray paint of the railing and walked to the front door. He could hear music and voices within, which he assumed were from a television game show. Someone was being asked to "Come on down." Lieutenant Peirce summoned his official-duty face and poked the small, round, worn button on the doorframe. At the sound of the doorbell, the game show host was suddenly silenced. Lieutenant Peirce heard muffled voices inside; there was a momentary pause, and then the door opened, but only a crack.

"I'm Lieutenant Sam Peirce of the Luzerne County Police Department. I'm looking for Henrietta Radcliffe," he said as he held his shield and ID in full view of the opening. The door opened wider, and a large woman in a yellow flowered housecoat leaned forward to inspect his credentials.

"I'm Henrietta Radcliffe. Is something wrong, Officer?" she asked.

"It's Lieutenant, ma'am. We are trying to locate your daughter, Sylvia. Would you know where she might be?"

"I haven't seen her for about two weeks. She do something wrong?" She opened the door the rest of the way and motioned for the lieutenant to follow her in.

Lieutenant Peirce stepped into the cramped living room and automatically began to survey the area. No one else was in the room. The sofa and side chair seemed to be showing some signs of age and wear in contrast to the apparently new fifty-inch flat-screen television that sat on a chipped and scratched television stand. The television dominated the better part of one wall of the small room. A bowl of chips of some sort, a glass, and two beer bottles sat on a portable snack table positioned in front of the sofa. The glass was about one-third full, yet both bottles were half-empty. *Either Henrietta Radcliffe pours drinks with both hands, or that second bottle was being drunk by someone else who didn't want his or her identity known.*

"Would you please have a seat, Mrs. Radcliffe," Lieutenant Peirce said in his most compassionate tone. Henrietta remained standing.

"There was a break-in last night at your daughter's home. I don't want to frighten you, but we think someone may have been home when the break-in occurred and may have been injured. Is anyone else here with you?" he asked, hoping that the shy guest would come forward and give support to this woman in her time of crisis.

"No, I'm alone," she said in a firm voice. "My daughter Emily won't be home until later this evening."

Peirce was momentarily confused by her answer, but he quickly regrouped. "Does anyone besides Emily live here with you, Mrs. Radcliffe?"

"Lieutenant, has something happened to Sylvia?"

"We don't know. There were signs of violence, and we haven't been able to locate her."

"Was anything taken from the house?" she asked.

Sam Peirce paused. This did not seem like the most natural follow-up question to ask. "We don't know. Until we find Sylvia, we have no way of knowing what was in the house."

"Maybe I could come by and see if I can tell what's missing," she said. "That might help with insurance claims." Sam Peirce felt his stomach turn as he observed all the concern for her daughter suddenly melting into distress over the potential loss of property.

"The crime scene is sealed, Mrs. Radcliffe." There was a sharp tone to his voice. "Please let us know if your daughter contacts you. Someone was hurt in that break-in. I'm sure you're hoping it was someone other than your daughter." He reached into his inside jacket pocket. "Here's my card; call if you hear anything."

Sam Peirce turned and walked to the door. As he slid into his car, he heard Mrs. Radcliffe call, "And please let me know as soon as I can get into my daughter's house, Lieutenant."

***

Ruth Klein sat at her desk, watching the second hand on her desk clock steadily sweep toward the twelve. She counted down the last few seconds as it progressed: "Five, four, three, two, one," and pointed at the door, but there was no knock. She checked her desk clock against her wrist-watch and looked at the door again. This was the first time in almost four years that Sylvia Radcliffe had not arrived exactly five minutes early. Ruth smiled. *Maybe we've made more progress with her compulsive behavior disorder than I thought. Now all we have left to deal with is her narcissistic personality disorder and her relationship problems. That should keep us busy for at least a few more years.* At two minutes after six, there was a knock on Ruth's office door.

"It's about time," she shouted in a jovial voice. "I was just about to send out a search party for you. Come in, come in!"

The doorknob turned, and as the door slowly began to open, Ruth observed that this was not Sylvia's usual high-speed entrance. Instead, when the door fully opened, it exposed a man with a slightly receding hairline wearing a rumpled gray suit, a white shirt with an unbuttoned collar, and a loosened blue tie. He was about six feet tall. His strong chin was one of his most prominent features, and in spite of his slightly over-nourished appearance, he seemed quite well built. Ruth's smile dissolved as her impish demeanor changed to one of slight humiliation.

"I'm sorry," she said penitently. "I was expecting someone else. May I help you?"

"I was hoping to find Sylvia Radcliffe here, but as I feared, she has missed her appointment."

"I'm afraid I can't comment on who does or does not have an appointment, sir. If you would—"

"My name is Lieutenant Sam Peirce. I'm with the Luzerne County Police Department," he said as he held up his credentials. "I'm trying to find Sylvia Radcliffe. We found her appointment book, and I was hoping—"

"Where did you find her book?" Dr. Klein rose from her chair and started across the office toward the lieutenant.

"It appears that Ms. Radcliffe is missing," he said, his eyes scanning her full height. "May we sit down?"

Ruth guided him to the sofa and sat on a chair facing him. "Has something happened to Sylvia?" she asked, leaning forward on the edge of her seat.

"We're investigating an apparent burglary at her home. We believe some sort of violence did take place, but until we have more facts, we can't draw any conclusions as to who may have been injured." As he spoke, he automatically reached for the pack of cigarettes in his shirt pocket. He looked up at the frown forming on Dr. Klein's face, paused for a moment, and then put the pack back in his pocket.

"I was hoping that you could help with some information as to where she might have gone."

"Actually, I have no idea where she might be, and of course you know that I can't tell you anything she may have said here. I could, however, give you her address and that of her next of kin, but since you have her appointment book, I'm sure you already have that information."

"Dr. Klein, would you know of anyone she may have had difficulty—"

"Lieutenant, as I said, anything said here falls under doctor-patient privilege. I'm afraid I can't—"

"I understand." Lieutenant Peirce removed his business card from a small leather card case and offered it to Dr. Klein. "If you should hear from her, please ask her to call."

"I will," said Dr. Klein as she accepted the card. "And could you also keep me informed if there are any new developments, Lieutenant?"

"We've kept it out of the press so far, but I'm sure that won't last. We would appreciate your discretion. Thank you for your time, Dr. Klein."

Lieutenant Peirce rose from the sofa, smiled, and walked out of the office, reaching into his jacket pocket for his cigarettes as he left.

***

Ruth Klein was an educated woman, worldly to an extent, or so she believed. She was not the type to become unduly alarmed before all the facts were in. Yet an uneasy feeling had begun in the pit of her stomach and welled up within her throat. She opened a bottle of antacid tablets and quickly tossed three into her mouth with no regard for their flavor. Normally she matched the colors. Purple—grape—was her favorite, but there just wasn't enough time. *Bile is not a gourmand*, she thought as she chewed and swallowed the medicine.

A few minutes later, her indigestion had passed in spite of the mismatched flavors, and she began to settle down in her desk chair to write notes from her sessions earlier that day.

Suddenly the lights went out. She waited at her desk for the twenty-three-second delay to pass before the emergency power would come on. Power failures were not that common, but she remembered a time last year when a drunk driver hit a utility pole, causing a chain reaction that plunged the town into darkness for twelve hours.

Ruth usually felt safe in her office, but that visit from Lieutenant Peirce, and the thought of a break-in at Sylvia Radcliffe's home, made her feel nervous. And now this damn darkness had her ready to jump out of her skin.

As she sat waiting for the lights to come back on, Ruth's attention was drawn to a low but rather consistent tapping. She tried to look around to locate the source of the annoying sound, but she was completely confounded by the darkness. Ruth sat still, waiting.

Ruth claimed that she had never been afraid of the dark. Not even when she was eight years old and accidentally locked herself in the trunk of her father's car. Her father didn't find her for hours. He and her mother searched every inch of the house and the yard. They called most of the parents of her friends, and finally, when her dad got in his car to drive around the neighborhood to look for her, he heard the muffled sound of her kicks and screams coming from the trunk. Ruth hadn't admitted, even then, that she had been afraid of the dark, but she slept with her Sleeping Beauty night-light on for at least a week.

What is that noise? she thought. Twenty-three seconds must have passed by now, but the emergency power still had not come on. As her eyes became accustomed to the dark, Ruth noticed that some faint light was coming into her office through the open waiting room door. Yes, she remembered, the corridor outside the frosted-glass door of her waiting room had small battery-operated emergency lights. At least she'd be able to see well enough to pack up her things and leave for the night. *And what is that awful tapping noise?* With her eyes somewhat adjusted to the darkness, she focused on her desktop. Then she placed her right hand over her left to stop it from shaking and beating her pen against her clock. "Oh," she said, and with a smile touched with embarrassment, she placed her pen in her purse.

The battery-powered light from the hall was dim, but after opening the vertical blinds to let in light from the distant streetlamp, there was an adequate amount to help find her way around the office. *No use staying any later*, she told herself. She had no other scheduled patients tonight, and this would be a wonderful opportunity to spend some extra time with her daughter, Emma. Going home early was the silver lining behind a power failure.

First, she picked up the three file folders and her digital tape recorder from her desk and haphazardly dumped them into her Tratavere briefcase, handmade in Tuscany. Next she slid her laptop into the case, bending and creasing at least one of the folders. Lastly she tossed in her bottle of spring water, then quickly retrieved it and checked the cap for tightness. Having dodged that messy bullet, she gave a sigh of relief, dropped the bottle back in the case, and closed the gold-plated clasp.

Ruth waited impatiently for someone to answer the telephone as she called home to let her daughter know she would be home in half an hour. "Emma, pick up, pick up, pick up," she said into the ringing phone. "You're supposed to be there, and where is Sophia? She doesn't leave for at least two more hours. What am I paying her for?" Frustrated, she hung up the phone just as her voice mail message began.

Ruth stepped into the hall, closed her office door, and searched through her handbag for the key to her deadbolt lock. She heard the sound of soft footsteps coming from somewhere down the hall, but she couldn't see anyone in the dim glow of the battery-powered emergency lights. Her hands were beginning to shake as she stood in the dark corridor, and after several unsuccessful tries, she used both hands to steady the key and guide it into the lock. As Ruth squinted at the glowing red exit signs at the middle and end of the long corridor leading to the front and side doors, she perceived a shadow slightly protruding from the wall about halfway down the corridor. "Is someone there?" she called out. No answer.

She looked down the hall and called out again, but this time in a shakier voice, "Is someone in the hall?" Still no answer, but the shadow now appeared to be closer than it was just a minute ago. She reached into her bag to retrieve her keys so that she could get back into her office. "Where are they?" she mumbled. Desperately rummaging through the inside of her bag, she clutched at tubes of lipstick, a pen, a wallet, coins, something square that she didn't recognize but knew was not her key chain, and then, the key chain. "Thank God," she cried, but as she pulled the keys from her bag, the key chain opened and she heard the keys bounce and scatter on the corridor's tile floor. Ruth knew that there would not be enough time to pick up her keys from the darkened corridor floor, find the right key, unlock her office, and get safely inside before whoever was generating that shadow reached her. Each time she looked up, it had moved closer.

Her only chance was to escape. With no power in the building, the elevator was not an option, so she hurried to the exit door leading to the rear stairwell. *Up or down, up or down.* She paused and then decided. If she descended to the basement, she could run across the boiler room and then up the front stairs. She would emerge within twenty feet of the front door, probably well past her assailant. She decided to do it.

Ruth slipped as quietly as possible into the stairwell and gently closed the door behind her. The emergency lighting in the stairwell was brighter than the corridor, but not much. She took off her shoes and put them in her briefcase, then walked down the stairs and through the basement door. This was going to work out just fine, she thought. *I'm probably just imagining the whole thing anyway.* Then a sound reached her ears. The door—it sounded like the door at the top of the stairwell closing. *He's coming,* she thought, and began to run barefoot through the basement to the boiler room. The emergency lighting in the basement was even more limited than up in the first-floor corridor. She saw a faint glow from only one small bulb at the far end of the boiler room. Suddenly the basement door opened. Ruth sank into a shadow behind a series of large pipes and held her breath. A beam of light shone from the basement door as it opened, and the shadow of a man was cast onto the floor. Ruth crouched down in the darkness behind the pipes. Her body was shaking so much that she was sure he would hear her knees knock or her teeth chatter. She began to recite a meditation mantra in her mind to calm herself: *Om, I am; om, I am.* She concentrated on her breathing. *In, out; in, out.* Ruth sensed a figure pass her hiding place. She wanted to scream and run but did not. She had to keep her composure. Her life may be at stake. Who would raise her daughter if she were to be killed or severely injured? How would she live? She cursed herself for not buying a larger life insurance policy or establishing an investment trust to provide for Emma's education and future. The man's footsteps were receding. She listened and waited until they sounded as though he was almost back at the basement door, and then she grabbed her bags and ran for the light at the end of the room. She didn't hesitate; she didn't look back. Ruth reached the front stairwell door, threw it open, and ran as fast as she could up to the first floor. As she exited the stairwell, she looked to the right. The front door and safety were less than twenty feet away. Ruth dared to relax and started to walk to the door when a hand grabbed at her shoulder. At the same moment, the front door opened, and two figures peeked inside. Ruth screamed and yanked her shoulder free.

"Mom, what happened? Are you all right?" Emma cried.

"Dr. Klein," said Sophia, "what happened to you?"

Ruth took two steps toward the door and turned back to look at her assailant. Dr. Hyrum Green stood in the corridor with a flashlight in his hand.

"Dr. Klein," he said. "I'm sorry if I frightened you. I just came out of my office into the hall with a flashlight to see if anyone was here, and I saw these keys on the floor. Are they yours?"

Ruth took the keys from his hand. In a hoarse voice, she said, "I guess I'm a little jumpy."

"Your scream scared me half to death," Hyrum said. "I was just thinking of going to the basement to see if a circuit breaker failed or a fuse burned out. It looks like this is the only building without power. But now I think I'll call the building manager and let him do it. I don't think I want to go down there in the dark."

"Th...thank you for the keys, Dr. Green." Ruth didn't look him in the eye. She turned to her daughter and her nanny standing in the doorway. "Come on, Emma, Sophia, let's go outside. What are you both doing here anyway?" she asked as she stood on one foot while placing a shoe on the other.

13

ey, don't walk near him; he don't like people," the small, elderly man groused as he tried to tie his dog to the bike rack outside McDonald's. Franklin staggered backward to put distance between him and the ninety-pound German shepherd, growling and straining at his leash.

"Yeah, I can tell." Franklin barely avoided the dog's reach and flattened himself against a parked car. "Can't you calm him down? Buy him a Happy Meal or something."

"I told you he don't like people," the man repeated, more forcefully this time, as he grabbed the dog's collar and pulled him away from Franklin.

Franklin clapped the dust from the parked car off his trousers. He looked back at the little man, whose feet were now dug into the gravel, one sinewy hand straining to hold on to his pet, the other locked on to the bike rack to keep him from being dragged into the parking lot.

Suddenly Franklin's mind flashed back to a scene from his dream of the murder. He saw the image of the old woman restraining her barking dog as he and the murderer sped out of the development. The frail, stooped-over woman was clinging to a signpost with one hand to keep from being dragged into the street. The words on the sign flashed before his mind's eye, *Golf Cart Crossing.*

"Hey, are you drunk or something?" the old man asked, observing the blank expression on Franklin's face.

"No, no, I'm fine," Franklin said, and he rushed back to his car.

Once in the car, he sat with his face cupped in both hands. "This can't be happening," he mumbled. "Could it be true? Could I actually have been there? Was it not just a dream?" Franklin put his key in the ignition and started his car. "Well, it's time to find out." Franklin knew of three local golf courses, two of which had housing developments surrounding them. He drove out of the lot toward the nearest of the two.

The houses at Silicon Springs varied in size and value from rows of attached townhouses with single-car garages and cement walks to large, rambling estates sporting circular cobblestone driveways, stone facades, and acres of glass windows. Franklin drove down several darkened streets looking for anything he could remember from his dream. He turned corners at random, hoping to see something he recognized. The area *seemed* familiar, but he could chalk that up to coincidence; all these developments looked the same. It looked similar to the one in his dream, but nothing stood out to confirm this was the same place.

***

"Car three, this is base. You awake out there, Jim, over?"

"This is car three. Don't be such a putz, Frank; go ahead," said Jim Chrystal.

"Jim, a resident just called and reported a silver car circling their street three times. They said he just turned onto Hemlock from Pine, over."

"I'm sitting on Hemlock, Frank…Wait a minute. I see him. I'll follow and check him out, over."

Franklin glanced in his rearview mirror and saw the headlights of the security car turn on and the car pull away from the curb. Franklin turned left at the next corner and then right a block later in an attempt to distance himself from the security guard, but the car followed each of his turns and was now closing the gap between them.

"Looks like he's trying to shake me. I'm going to pick him up, over."

"Oh shit!" Franklin cried. He increased his speed and turned the next corner. As he did, he bolted past a golf cart crossing sign. The image of the woman stretched between the sign and her straining dog again flashed in his memory. The sign could be the one he saw in his dream. His heart started pounding, and his breath came in gulps. If the murder was real instead of a dream and he was caught driving through this neighborhood, he would have a lot of explaining to do. And right now, he didn't have any answers. Franklin glanced in his rearview mirror and saw that the security car was just a block away. Tires squealing, Franklin turned the next corner, spotted an exit from the development, and made for it. He turned onto County Road 6, and this time he pushed his foot to the floor.

"He's heading out of the development onto the county road. I'm going to have to break off, over."

Franklin kept monitoring his rearview mirror. The guard had stopped at the end of the development and was no longer pursuing him. Franklin eased back on the gas and drove along, feeling relieved and a little proud of his escape.

"Car three, did you get his plate, over?"

"No, I missed it, but call in a suspicious silver late-model Toyota to the county police. It might be that burglar from the other night back for another try, over."

"You got it, Jim; base over and out."

***

Franklin continued to drive down the county road after his narrow escape. There were no streetlights, and he turned his headlights to bright. The road ahead was bordered by small mountain laurel shrubs and sparsely foliated oak trees. The wind gusts whipped dried leaves and scattered paper debris alongside his car, twirling them into miniature twisters that formed and died within seconds.

He pondered the consequences of being caught. What would he have said to the police? Did his recollection of the golf cart crossing sign mean that he had really been there on that night, and that it wasn't just a dream? That somehow, while sleepwalking, he actually witnessed a murder, or worse, participated in one? It made no sense. Golf cart crossing signs were common to most golf courses. He could have seen a similar sign in the past and now his imagination was using it as a prop, a manufactured proof to lend false legitimacy to his dream. He smiled and shook his head. Speculation wasn't getting him anywhere.

A moment later, Franklin noticed something on the road ahead and came to a sudden stop. His hands started sweating and his knuckles turned white as he squeezed the steering wheel. *That bridge*, he thought as he looked ahead on the road. *That's the bridge, the one the murderer stopped at to dispose of the body.* Franklin pulled to the side of the road, got out of his car, and walked to the center of the stone bridge. He looked at the fast-moving creek passing under it. It looked the same, but all these bridges looked alike. *I must have driven over hundreds of them in the past; I may have even driven on this very road before.*

Then, as he looked into the stream, he noticed something stuck on a branch rising up out of the water. It looked like a piece of fabric of some sort. *Her nightgown*, he thought. He stumbled, then regained his footing as he ran back to his car, grabbed his flashlight from the glove compartment, and shone the light on the object clinging to the branch. "A plastic bag," he said out loud. Relieved, he began to turn to leave. *Paranoia, thou art my master.* As the light beam moved from the plastic bag, he caught sight of another foreign object in the stream; this one looked like a hand. Franklin stared at what he believed to be the latest product of his disturbed mind. *It's probably an old glove*, he thought. Was his imagination beginning to run away with him? He needed to know.

Franklin walked to the edge of the bridge and eased himself over the embankment. The roar of rushing water filled his ears and drowned out all other sounds. The bank was slippery, covered with leaves wet from the spray. Franklin worked his way down to the stream, holding on to low tree limbs for support; it was slow going. At the water's edge, he focused his light on the object. Tears began to form in his eyes. He looked away and blew his nose into his handkerchief, hoping that when he looked back at the stream the object would be gone, or changed into an old tire, or a pile of garbage bags entangled in the rocks. He knew it wouldn't.

The flashlight beam trembled as it exposed the naked body of a woman just below the surface of the water. Sobbing, Franklin trudged back up the bank and climbed into his car. He drove away, knowing that he had no choice but to call the police and tell them everything that had happened, no matter the consequences.

***

"This is 911. What is the emergency?" said a nasally sounding female operator.

"I...uh...want to report a dead body," the muffled voice said.

"Who am I speaking to?" asked the operator.

"It doesn't matter," said the voice. "She's in a creek under a stone bridge on County Road 6, about five miles south of Silicon Springs."

"Would you repeat that for me, sir, I'm not sure I got it all. Sir, are you reporting an accident? Can you give me more details? Is there—"

Franklin slowly pressed down the switch hook of the pay phone, removed his handkerchief from the mouthpiece of the receiver, wiped down the telephone, and started walking back to his car. His view of the road in front of the deserted gas station was limited by darkness. Franklin looked left and right. A dim light, barely a soft glow, began to illuminate the farthest point of the road in the direction from which he had come, and the sound of a car engine slowly began to build. Franklin ducked behind one of the rusted-over gasoline pumps and held his breath. If the oncoming car was that of the security guard from Silicon Springs, he was as good as caught. Franklin's silver Toyota was sitting just off the road in front of the abandoned minimart. The gas station was in almost total darkness, and Franklin hoped that his car, parked not far from a blue stripped-down derelict vehicle, would pass for just another hulk in this testament to business failure. Franklin exhaled and watched a red pickup truck speed by, its radio blasting a country tune. He watched until it was out of sight, then got into his car. No more headlights could be seen in either direction. He loudly blew his nose one more time, stuffed his handkerchief into his back pocket, and drove toward home.

Although he had intended to call the police and tell them all the details of his dream and how it had led him to the discovery of the body, he realized how preposterous it sounded. And the farther he drove from the scene, the less willing he was to face the inevitable repercussions of the call. He could barely believe it had really happened. Why would anyone believe him? Why wouldn't the police think he killed her? At this point even he wasn't sure what he had done or not done. Then he had another thought. Maybe *this* was a dream, just another lucid dream. What was it Dr. Klein had said to do? Oh yes. He took his hands off the wheel to press his right thumb into the palm of his left hand. The car drifted toward the side of the road. His first impulse was to grab the wheel, but if he was dreaming...If this wasn't real, and he was at home in bed...He pushed his thumb into his palm—his palm was solid. His thumb didn't pass through.

"Oh shit," he cried, grabbing the wheel and jerking the car off the shoulder and back onto the road. He knew now that this entire evening was real. That the woman was actually dead, and there was nothing he could do to change it.

14

4:30 a.m.

Lieutenant Peirce drove south at high speed along the dark tree-lined county road. His broad face flashed alternately blue and red as it reflected the revolving colors of the portable police dome light magnetically attached to his dashboard. Up ahead he could see a tiny oasis of daylight in the surrounding darkness. An image of an alien spacecraft emitting brilliant light as it hovered just over the road formed in his imagination. The image of the UFO was complete with minions scouring the lighted ground, collecting samples of flora and fauna to bring back to their far-off galaxy.

As he got closer, he could see the massive glow of bright light transform into two rows of spotlights standing on tall tripods lining both sides of the stone bridge. On the roadway, the tiny alien minions, now full-size forensic investigators, methodically roamed up and down the road, searching for any evidence that might lend clarity to the crime scene.

He pulled onto the side of the road, stopping just short of the police barricade blocking access to the stone bridge, and surveyed the scene. Two state police cars parked diagonally across the road highlighted the barrier with their headlights. The county medical examiner's ambulance waited on the side of the road with its back doors open, ready to accept its morbid charge. Several other vehicles sat outside the barrier on the far side of the bridge. *They probably belong to the forensic team*, he assumed. All was going as it should. Lieutenant Peirce removed his shield from his jacket pocket, clipped it to a black lanyard, and hung it around his neck. He rolled down his window and threw his cigarette out onto the road, then took his notepad and pen from the unmarked car's console and placed them in his outside jacket pocket. He exited his car.

Lieutenant Peirce acknowledged the state troopers with a wave of his hand, squeezed between the two wooden barriers, and called out to the forensic investigator taking photographs of tire prints on the side of the road.

"Did you get this yet?" he asked in a loud voice while pointing at the bridge.

"You can go through, Lieutenant. We got everything we need from that area."

Peirce walked onto the bridge and rested his elbows on the stone wall. Below, two men wearing hip boots were standing in the shallows of the stream watching a third, the medical examiner, knee-deep in the icy water, studying the position of the body. She lay faceup just under the surface, held in place in the fast-moving current by a tree branch wedged against a large stone.

"Do you want to come down and see the body before we move it?" called Holloway from the shallows, beckoning to the lieutenant to join him.

"No need, the perp threw the body from here," shouted Lieutenant Peirce. "You'd like to see me slide down that embankment, wouldn't you?" he whispered. Disappointed, Holloway joined the other officer and the ME to help pull the body from the water.

"Did you find anything near the body?" Peirce asked the forensic investigator.

"We took a cast of a footprint on the shore opposite the body, but the ground was so spongy that I don't think we got much definition. I'm not sure we'll be able to identify anything but the size of the shoe—eleven, I would guess. We've got lots of tire tracks on the shoulder, maybe four different cars." The officer pointed at the tire marks leading on and off the shoulder. "No way to tell when they were made, so we can't tell who wins the prize."

"Get me a sample of the mud from the stream bank and some soil from this shoulder," Lieutenant Peirce said, pointing at the dirt at their feet. "Log it into evidence for me."

After a few minutes, the corpse was brought up in a body bag and placed on a gurney behind the ambulance.

"What have we got, Doc?" asked Peirce as he began to unzip the bag.

"Multiple stab wounds, probably the cause of death, but I'll know more later," said the ME.

"I'll assume she doesn't have any ID on her." Peirce looked at the naked corpse.

"Well, actually she does," said the ME. "A yellow rose tattoo, still visible on her right hip in spite of some slight decomposition."

***

Sam Peirce removed his suit jacket and tossed it onto the uncomfortable-looking chrome-and-white plastic chair sitting against the wall. A sheet of white paper pulled from a roll at its head covered the examining table. Peirce studied it for telltale wrinkles; it looked unused.

He slipped his suspenders off each shoulder and let them hang at the sides of his trousers. His shirt came off next. A button popped from his cuff as he fumbled with it. It fell to the floor and rolled to a stop under the chair. It was the third time that same button had come off. *Maybe I should find some stronger thread.* He laughed. *Or better still, get someone else to sew it on.* After laying his shirt on top of his jacket, he sat down on the paper-covered table, making a crinkling noise. Sam grabbed the sleeve of his undershirt, pulled it toward his face, and sniffed. A satisfied nod gave outward expression to his feeling that, in spite of a long night, his careful morning attention to daily hygiene would keep him from being embarrassed.

Sam heard the click of the doorknob turning and immediately flexed his abdominal muscles to pull in his stomach. Sam had been quite athletic in his youth, but the long, irregular hours of police work, catching meals on the run, and long stakeouts in his car had taken a toll on his once rock-hard abs.

"Good to see you, Sam," said Dr. Alicia Goodman as she walked in and closed the door.

Alicia Goodman had been Sam's cardiologist since she joined her father's practice five years ago. She had been working for a large managed health-care organization after her residency, but had left the security of that steady salary and bright future to help her ailing father. As his health deteriorated, many of his patients started looking for alternative care, and his practice developed financial difficulties. She took a leave of absence from her job and placed her dreams on hold until she could bring his practice back to solvency. Inheriting her father's practice was not one of Alicia's career goals. She had always believed that her medical future would eventually consist of research and the development of new procedures or techniques to reduce or even cure some form of heart disease.

He died a year later. Since then, through her hard work and a good number of referrals from other medical associates, her number of patients had steadily increased as well as her financial stability. Her old job and her dreams of glory were gone, but she believed that she was making a difference for some patients. She felt satisfied that she had improved and even saved a few people's lives in the last few years.

"I had another episode," Sam said as he unconsciously rubbed his chest with his right hand.

"Tell me what happened," she said as she placed a blood pressure cuff on his upper arm and pumped it full of air.

"Nothing important—I was working, and I felt some pain in my chest. I took one of those little pills you prescribed, and it went away. Probably just something I ate."

"Probably angina," she said sharply as she pressed her stethoscope to his arm and listened to read his blood pressure. "You're forty-five years old, Sam, and you look like sixty." She wrote his results on his chart. "You're thirty pounds overweight, you don't exercise, your BP is high, and I'm almost afraid to open the results of your cholesterol test. At least you've stopped smoking. Have you cut out the fatty foods at lunch as we discussed?"

Sam Peirce glanced at his jacket lying on the chair, hoping his pack of cigarettes had not fallen out.

Dr. Goodman followed his eyes to his jacket. "You *have* stopped smoking, haven't you?"

"You know, your father never treated me with this little respect. He didn't tell me I should quit being a cop, or try to control everything I ate." Sam began to tear little pieces of the crinkly paper from the edge of the examining table.

"My father didn't control his own life. Maybe if he had, he would be watching you kill yourself instead of me." She placed her stethoscope on his back and said in a loud, demanding tone: "Deep breath!" After brusquely checking his heart and lungs, she said in an even angrier tone, "If you continue your current lifestyle, the next 'episode' you have is going to be a cardiac arrest."

"Well, that's just fine," he snapped. "Arrests are something I'm good at!"

"Well, you might as well put your shirt back on," she said, almost shouting. "You're just too pigheaded to take good advice."

"When I hear good advice, I'll consider taking it," he bellowed. "Pick you up for dinner at seven as usual?"

"I'm working tonight until eight—be on time," she screeched and stormed out of the examining room.

"That's the last button she sews on for me," he said with resolve. Then he laughed and continued dressing.

∗∗∗

"The subject is a Caucasian female, approximately forty years of age," said Tom Craig, the county medical examiner, into a microphone hanging above the autopsy table. He released the button on the microphone and turned to Lieutenant Peirce and Sergeant Holloway as they entered the lab.

"I was just about to record my findings," Tom said. "You're right on time."

"Could we possibly get the abbreviated version? We need to get right back out on the street."

"OK, here's what I've got. The pair of scissors found at the crime scene is definitely the murder weapon; it matches the wounds perfectly.

The time of death is a little harder to determine because of the immersion of the body in the stream, but from the wounds and the amount of blood at the house, I would put the death at the same time as the burglary, sometime on Wednesday."

"Well, we know she left work at Stanton's at five o'clock on Wednesday evening, and a neighbor walking her dog reported a car speeding away from the house at eleven thirty, so I would say that's our window, minus the twenty minutes or so it took her to get home," said Lieutenant Peirce.

He stood and stared at the body for a full minute. He looked closely at the deep punctures in the abdomen and the slashes to the chest. "Somebody really didn't like her," he said. He looked closely at the purple ligature marks on her throat and the cuts on her hands she'd received while trying to block the violent thrusts with the scissors.

"Any sign of a sexual attack?"

"No evidence of rape or any sexual abuse at all," said Tom Craig.

"Could be just a burglar caught in the act. Maybe she was just in the wrong place at the wrong time," said Holloway, standing back from the corpse at least five feet.

"No, this was a crime of passion," said Lieutenant Peirce. "I'll bet he knew her; it looks too personal."

"Do you have any leads to go on?" asked Tom Craig.

"We received a call about a half hour before the 911 call from Silicon Springs Security, reporting a silver Toyota driving near the victim's house and then leaving by the same road where the body was found. It's thin, but the woman with the dog said the car she saw leaving the development was silver. Could be the killer returning to the scene of the crime, but that usually only happens in crime novels," said Peirce. "It looks like we're nowhere. Holloway, let's look at the crime scene again and then take another run at the victim's mother and sister."

15

Ruth Klein was having a pretty good day. All her patients were on time, she stayed focused on each session no matter what distraction competed for her attention, and the blueberry muffin she had with her lunch was the best ever.

"This is Dr. Ruth Klein, may I help you?" she said with much enthusiasm, answering her telephone on the first ring.

"Good evening, Dr. Klein, this is Lieutenant Sam Peirce. Do you have a minute to talk?" Sam asked as he sat up straight in his chair, caught slightly off guard by her quick and jovial response. Peirce had made hundreds of calls to tell people bad news, but he still had trouble beginning the conversation. He used to rehearse his opening line: "I'm very sorry to have to tell you that your husband has been injured in a car accident," or, "It's with great sorrow that I must inform you of the death of your loved one." He got most of that last one from a sympathy card sent to him when his father passed away. Over time he learned that the best thing to do was to just say it and get it over with; no one remembered the exact words you used anyway.

"Dr. Klein, I'm calling to tell you that Sylvia Radcliffe is no longer missing. We—"

"How wonderful, Lieutenant. When and where did she show up? I was beginning to think she was avoiding my treatment." She laughed. "Is she back at home?"

Lieutenant Peirce closed his eyes and tapped his forehead with the telephone receiver. That didn't work. He would try it again.

"No, Dr. Klein, she is not back at home. I just spoke to her mother a few min—"

"Well, I'm surprised that she was at her mother's house. She—"

"Dr. Klein, she isn't at her mother's house. We took her to the city last night. She—"

"She isn't in trouble with the police, is she? I'll be glad to help her find a lawyer if she needs one. I can come there myself…"

Lieutenant Peirce placed the telephone receiver on his desk, sat back in his chair, and stared at it, trying to figure out how this call could have gone so wrong. Maybe if he approached from a different angle. He picked up the receiver and held it to his ear.

"Lieutenant, are you there? Lieutenant Peirce?"

"She's dead, Dr. Klein," he said, a little too loudly.

"Oh, that's horrible," Ruth said, her voice slightly cracking. "How did it happen? Was it an accident?"

"It's an ongoing investigation, but considering the burglary at her home and the location of the body, we've classified the death as a homicide."

"You know, you could have broken the news more gently."

"I'm so sorry. I don't know what I was thinking," Lieutenant Peirce said as he slowly strangled the telephone receiver with both hands.

"Are you sure that it's her—I mean, has someone identified the body?"

"Yes, we just got a positive ID from her mother. We had a preliminary from her ex-boyfriend, but that was mostly based on her tattoo. It was hard to identify her with the amount of de…, ah, confusion around the discovery of the body." He had almost said *decomposition*. That would have been indicative of his usual lack of sensitivity, which he had been trying to avoid, but she wasn't making it easy.

"Tattoo? I seem to remember something about Sylvia getting a tattoo, but I don't think she described it to me. What did it look like?"

"It was a yellow rose on her right hip, but that's not for public knowledge. Please consider it privileged information."

Ruth Klein quickly opened Sylvia Radcliffe's file and began to run her finger along each line of the notes from her last session looking for the description of the tattoo, but it wasn't there. She saw the note telling her that Sylvia had gotten a tattoo, but not that it was a yellow rose. Yet

Ruth distinctly remembered hearing the description of a tattoo as a yellow rose and even the location, on the right hip. Confused, Ruth reread her notes. She still found nothing describing the tattoo. Maybe Sylvia had described the tattoo to her while she wasn't paying attention, and maybe she remembered it subliminally. That was possible. She recalled being distracted by Sylvia's rant about her mother and the subsequent daydream about her own mother. That little head trip had caused her to miss half of Sylvia's session. That was unacceptable, and she vowed never to let that happen again.

I need to stay more focused on what I'm doing and not get so lost in my own thoughts...

"Hello, Dr. Klein, are you still there?"

"Yes, yes, I'm here, Lieutenant. I was, ahh, just picking up something I dropped." *I will never learn.*

Then she recalled that she had a recording of a session that she had not yet played. Problem solved—if Sylvia described the tattoo during the session, it would be on the memory card. With the distraction of trying to remember how she'd heard about the tattoo now past, Ruth began to face the realization that Sylvia was gone. Her eyes began to well up with tears.

"Lieutenant, I'm afraid I have to hang up now; I have a patient coming in." She hung up the phone without waiting for Lieutenant Peirce to answer. There were no patients scheduled for over an hour, and she thought that might be just enough time for a good cry.

She decided that it was not necessary to hear Sylvia's recording since that was the only place she believed she could have heard about the tattoo, and besides, she felt too sad to hear Sylvia's voice right now. Maybe she would listen to it at a later date. Ruth stuffed Sylvia Radcliffe's file, notes, and the recording into an envelope and placed it in her briefcase.

***

The picture on the front page of the morning newspaper looked like a high school graduation photo. It was the only photograph of her daughter that Henrietta Radcliffe could supply. The attractive young woman in the picture was smiling, her eyes bright and her hair pleasantly arranged, albeit not in a style still popular today. One could view this photo, and from its blissful visage, suppose that as she posed in the photographer's studio, her mind had wandered to the achievement she had just attained. There was a look of pride, satisfaction, and contentment on her face. One might be compelled to believe she was visualizing a long life, a successful career with new relationships, and travel to exotic places in the world. She looked like a young woman who believed her future would soon abound with wealth, excitement, and romance. Franklin imagined that he saw all these things in her graduation photograph, but then felt sorrow, knowing full well that none of them were possible any longer.

The promise of the future that Franklin could see in the face smiling back at him from the newspaper was now replaced by his memory of a body lying naked, half-submerged in an icy stream. Her eyes cold and sightless, her mind stilled by the violence perpetrated against her.

Franklin pondered the details of the murder in the newspaper article. He read and reread the account of the burglary and the subsequent 911 call leading to the discovery of the body. He looked for any facts that might contradict the details in his dream. He searched his mind for any evidence or even a rationalization to explain his knowledge of this crime, a knowledge that seemed far more detailed than the account in the paper.

Could his dream of the murder have been coincidental? Had it simply been concocted by his imagination from bits and pieces he may have heard or read or seen—a dream that was just a dream and no more? If so, where did he read or hear or see these details? He couldn't remember. Was the dream somehow a clairvoyant emissary reporting a future horror that only his mind's eye witnessed and not his physical being? He had never experienced any sort of premonition or psychic event before. Or, he thought with much trepidation, was it possible that the dream was part of an insidious plot hatched by his subconscious mind to secretly make him aware of something he had really done while sleepwalking and subsequently forgotten? That the dream was simply a mental cover-up to hide actions that his conscious mind could not endure? No, that was unthinkable. He dismissed that possibility with a wave of his hand and a shake of his head.

He returned again to the article. There must be something there that would prove he could not have been involved. He found few facts in the newspaper about the murder that contradicted his dream, but not many that supported it either. The newspaper didn't mention scissors as the murder weapon or the tattoo on the woman's hip. There was nothing to conclusively prove that it really happened the way he saw it in his dream. How did he know that the body he found under the bridge and reported in the 911 call was even the same woman that was murdered in his dream?

Franklin stood and turned to the large mirror on the wall behind his sofa. He studied his reflection for at least a full minute. He didn't look like a killer.

"Did you do it?" he said to his reflection, half in jest. "Did you kill that woman and think it was a dream? You don't even know who she was; why would you hurt her?"

"You know who she was," the reflection said.

Franklin looked around the room, trying to determine if he had just heard a voice or if his mind was playing tricks on him.

"You know who she was," the reflection repeated.

"What—no, I never saw her before," Franklin whispered to the mirror, cocking his head to see if the reflection's lips moved.

"Think about it," the reflection said. "Earlier that week, outside Dr. Klein's building?"

Franklin backed up a step, still doubting his eyes and ears. Although he moved back, the reflection remained where it was.

"On the front steps?" the reflection said.

"Was that the woman who was murdered, the woman that had been crying in Dr. Klein's office, the one I spoke with in the tavern last week?" Franklin asked. He was no longer challenging his senses.

His reflection smiled.

"But I couldn't have hurt her; I was home in bed," Franklin said unconvincingly. "I never left my house."

"You woke up in your car in your driveway."

"But that was almost a week before the murder. It was a dream. She was alive the next day."

"What makes you think you didn't drive back to her house a week later, kill her, and dispose of the body in the stream?"

"But I was in Dr. Klein's office for more than an hour after she left; I couldn't have followed her home. How would I know where she lived?" Franklin said in a last attempt to counter his fears with reason.

"You don't know what you did," said the reflection. "You can't even tell when you're awake or asleep. You went back to her neighborhood just last night and then found the body in the stream where it had been dumped. Where *you* dumped it. How could you find the house, the bridge, and the stream if you hadn't been there before?"

"It was a dream, just a nightmare. I never touched her." Franklin pressed both hands over his ears to block out any response from the reflection that contradicted what he needed to believe.

"If it was only a dream, why do you feel so guilty?" the voice said in a calm yet forceful tone.

"No, you're wrong. I had no reason to hurt her," said Franklin as he ran from the living room to his bedroom and slammed the door. He sat panting on his bed, searching his pockets for his handkerchief to dry his eyes.

He jumped to his feet and dropped his handkerchief when he heard, "She looked a lot like Myra." The reflection was now in the wall mirror over his dresser. "No one would blame you after what that bitch did to you. She took half of everything you owned, and now that she spent it all, she wants more."

"But I'm not a violent man," he shouted. "I would never hurt anyone." Franklin stood, facing his accuser with new resolve.

"You hate her; you wished she was dead," the reflection chided. "You said so."

"I don't hate Myra," he yelled. "I didn't mean what I said. She had good reason to leave me. It was my own fault. You're wrong, I don't hate her; I hate you!" He ripped the clock radio from his nightstand and threw it at his reflection in the wall mirror. The mirror cracked, and large pieces of glass fell from the wall with a crash. In the pieces left standing, Franklin could see a partial figure looking back at him. It looked like a man who was losing his mind.

Franklin looked at his wristwatch—7:00 p.m. The time didn't really matter since he couldn't go another minute without talking to someone. He would call his friend Hyrum. Any voice other than the one in the mirror would calm him, and maybe Hyrum had information that would help. He dialed the phone.

"Hello?"

"Hyrum, this is Franklin. Did I catch you at a bad time?"

"No, no, we just finished dinner. You're saving me from helping with the dishes. By the way, how did your date go the other night?"

Hyrum's familiar wink was implied in his voice.

"Fine, fine. The reason I called was to ask if you read the article in today's paper about the murder in Silicon Springs."

"Yes, I did," Hyrum said in a slow, drawn-out manner. "This area used to be a safe place to—"

"Hyrum, you mentioned last week that Dr. Klein had some attractive patients. Do you remember if the woman in the newspaper, the one that was murdered, was one of them?"

Franklin knew that Hyrum always spoke slowly and deliberately; he chose his words well and pronounced every syllable carefully. However, this pause before answering was uncharacteristically long. "No," he said. "I can't say that I ever saw her before. Why do you ask?"

"No real reason," Franklin said. "I just thought she might have looked familiar. I thought I might have seen her in your building, and since you work there—"

"Would you like to meet somewhere for a drink?" Hyrum asked. "I wouldn't mind getting out of the house for a while."

"Maybe another time, Hyrum. There are a few things I have to do."

"Suit yourself. I'm here if you want to talk."

Franklin opened his wallet and dumped all the cards, pieces of paper, and money out onto the bed. He rummaged through them until he found Dr. Klein's business card and dialed the number.

***

Ruth Klein rarely enjoyed the benefits of modern technology. There was something about computers, cell phones, and other electronic devices that just seemed to conspire against her, and this new software she was trying to install on her laptop was no exception. It was designed to take the recordings of her patient sessions and automatically transcribe them into files and download them to her computer. There would be no need for her to type.

"What a great idea," she had said to the salesperson at Software City.

With this electronic wizardry, she could eliminate all the tedious, time-consuming corrections to her typing and spelling. It would make her life easier. At least that's what the salesperson had told her. Right now, it wasn't going well.

"What do you mean that operation cannot be completed at this time?" she hissed at her computer. "That's what you're supposed to do."

Ruth shut down and then restarted her computer, hoping that a brand-new beginning might make a difference. When the computer rebooted, she tried to open the new software again. "Shit," she cried as she received the same error message: *The operation you requested cannot be completed at this time.* She pounded the desk with her fist and then picked up her laptop. Ruth held it high over the desk, paused, composed herself, and then gently placed it back down. She was getting nowhere. She usually pulled the plug on her copier at the office and then plugged it back in when that mechanical prima donna refused to cooperate. She began to try the same cure for this obstinate contraption.

"Even if it doesn't solve the problem, I'll at least get some satisfaction from yanking your cord," she said. As she reached down to pull the plug from the wall, she heard, "That's not going to work, Mom."

Emma stood in the doorway of Ruth's home office wearing a pink robe with Hello Kitty on the front. Her strawberry-blond hair, still wet from her evening shower, was wrapped in a towel resembling a turban.

"Emma, how long have you been standing there?" Ruth asked, trying to remember if she had used any language she wouldn't want her eleven-year-old daughter to have heard.

"Not long, I just thought I would try to save your computer from the same fate as the telephone you couldn't figure out."

"That was an accident. It fell from my hand while I was looking out the window," said Ruth, blushing.

"It's more likely it committed suicide after the way you yelled at it." Emma chuckled. "Pulling the plug won't help; it has a battery. May I see what you're doing?"

Emma sat down next to Ruth at her desk and pulled the computer to a comfortable position in front of her.

"It's no use," Ruth said. "This software is defective. I'm going to take it back."

She paused, amazed as Emma's tiny fingers flew over the keyboard, opening and closing applications and adding lines of text as she referenced the installation instructions in the user manual.

Ruth leaned over her daughter and smiled. She could smell the scent of fresh peaches from Emma's shampoo. She moved close to the back of her neck, brushing it with her lips as she inhaled deeply. *Moments like this will be gone all too soon. They need to be savored, and then indelibly written in memory for a time later in life when memories are far more abundant than experiences.*

"That tickles." Emma giggled as she raised her shoulders and wrinkled her nose, never missing a keystroke as she squirmed in her chair.

"OK, it should work now," Emma said as she turned and ran from the room, dragging her feet in slippers—Ruth's slippers—much too big for a child's feet.

"The salesperson said even a child could install it," she yelled after Emma. "He should have said *only* a child could install it."

"I'll expect something extra in my allowance envelope this week," Emma said as she disappeared into her room.

Ruth sat staring at the door through which her young daughter had just disappeared. Emma not only demonstrated skill with a computer but exhibited poise and maturity far beyond her eleven years. "Well, at least she gets her good looks from me," she said under her breath.

The sound of her cell phone interrupted her thought. Ruth could tell by the ring tone that it was a business call rather than personal. "I'm getting good at this technology stuff," she gushed.

Ruth did not usually take business calls at home after business hours. It wasn't fair to Emma. This was her home too. Of course, Ruth's business did involve human suffering, and if someone was in dire need of psychiatric help, it would be unprofessional to refuse them.

Ruth then thought it might be about Sylvia Radcliffe. She had told Lieutenant Peirce to call her if he received any new information about the murder. She could let it go to voice mail; it was probably just a robo-call anyway. A digital panderer looking for a donation to the campaign of whatever political flavor of the month was running for office. *They're as bad as those telemarketers who dial every number exactly at dinnertime just looking for some unsuspecting kindhearted person to swallow their mouthful of mashed potatoes and jump at the chance to buy a magazine subscription to* Guns & Ammo. *They have a lot of nerve disturbing people at home. Isn't there a law to prevent this invasion of privacy?*

"Mom, are you going to answer that?" asked Emma, peeking back into Ruth's office from the doorway.

Ruth looked up, her mind slowly returning to the present, and said, "Sure, honey." *Maybe I'm the one in dire need of psychiatric help.*

Ruth smiled, waved at her daughter, and pushed the button on her phone. "Dr. Ruth Klein, may I help you?"

There was a long pause, and then she could hear someone breathing into the other end of the phone. Just as she decided that this must be the beginning of an obscene call and was about to hang up, a voice said, "Dr. Klein, this is Franklin Jameson. I'm sure I'll be dead before our next appointment on Tuesday."

16

The headline of the morning newspaper read, "LOCAL WOMAN MURDERED DURING BURGLARY." Lieutenant Peirce read the entire article to ensure that it did not contain any mention of the yellow rose tattoo on the victim's hip or the scissors, which had now been confirmed as the murder weapon. The newspaper story purported that the victim had returned home, interrupted a burglar, and a struggle ensued, resulting in her death, but Sam was skeptical. There had been many unsolved burglaries in the area. Most had the same MO and were probably the same burglar, but the thief had never been violent. The cruelty with which the woman was attacked seemed personal. Sam wasn't buying the "victim of circumstances" theory.

He leaned back in his chair and tossed the paper with its carefully edited details of the crime onto his desk. It was a common police practice to hold back certain critical facts of the case from the public. There was always the possibility that a suspect might divulge information during an interrogation that was not commonly known. Of course, this ploy was only useful assuming that he could find and arrest a suspect to interrogate. Peirce hoped restricting the facts of the case would at least help weed out the usual wackos who showed up at the police station to confess to every crime published in the newspaper.

The case was getting colder by the minute. Sam reached down and picked up the brown cardboard evidence box sitting on the floor. He placed it in the middle of his desk and lifted the lid. Sam rubbed his hands together, and then he stood and began to remove the sealed plastic bags of evidence from the box. Each clear bag was labeled with the case number, date, time, location found, and a description of the item it contained. Below the evidence label was a chart documenting the chain of custody.

The first bag Sam removed from the box contained an audio tape of the 911 call identifying the location of the body. The label read: *Quality of recording, level two.* The anonymous caller had obviously tried to disguise his voice and succeeded. There would probably be no voiceprint match from this fuzzy recording, even if the suspected caller was found. Sam placed the plastic bag on the left side of his desk. He handled the bags very carefully. They were tamper-indicating bags, which had intricate, weblike patterns in the clear plastic that would show stretch marks if an attempt were made to open them. Rough handling could be mistaken for an attempt to penetrate the bag. Even an extreme temperature change, suggesting that someone may have tried to open a bag's seal by heating or freezing, would call into question the integrity of the evidence.

Next he removed the bag containing the murder weapon. The label stated that there were no fingerprints on the scissors and that the blood was type AB, the same type as the victim. Nothing new there. The small piece of blue fabric caught in the joint of the scissors didn't match any other fabric in the victim's house and was a common blue cotton cloth with no identifying marks. It could have been from the killer's shirt, but if true, the killer would have burned the shirt by now. It looked like another dead end.

Sam lifted out an evidence bag containing a plaster cast of a shoe print taken from the muddy bank of the stream where the body had been found. The mud had been so soft and the detail of the casting so poor that the make and even the size of the shoe were indeterminable. At the bottom of the box were bags containing soil samples from the bank of the stream and photographs of tire prints from the road near the stone bridge. The soil was common to most of the state, and the tire tracks were of a very popular brand and size of tire. He signed and dated the chain of custody label on each bag and placed them back in the box. There was nothing here that he could consider hard evidence, nothing that would move this case forward.

"I'm going for coffee, Lieutenant. Can I get you one?" asked Holloway as he poked his head into Sam's office.

"I'm all set," Lieutenant Peirce said with a sigh. "You find out anything from the victim's ex?"

"From the ex-boyfriend or the ex-husband?" asked Holloway.

"Which do you think?" asked Lieutenant Peirce in an aggravated tone.

"Something bothering you, Lieutenant?" Holloway stepped into the office and observed that the lieutenant's usual cup of coffee had been replaced by a juice box. A slice of whole-wheat toast occupied the spot on his desk usually reserved for two cream-filled donuts. He chuckled, slightly shook his head, and then replied, "Both exes have solid alibis, and neither had anything helpful to say."

"Write up the interviews and put them on my desk before the end of the day."

"Yes, sir," said Holloway as he exaggerated a salute.

"I'm sorry, Holloway. I'm having an off day," said Peirce as he waved a dismissive gesture with his hand.

At the coffeemaker, Holloway overheard two officers commiserating about the lieutenant's foul mood.

"It's not you," Holloway said. "I think he's angry because his girlfriend won't let him have any more coffee."

"You mean she cut him off," said the first officer.

"Yeah, maybe that too," said the second officer, and all three laughed.

***

By noon, Lieutenant Peirce and Sergeant Holloway were on their way to revisit what now was believed to be the murder scene of Sylvia Radcliffe.

Holloway drove through the gated entrance to the Silicon Springs Golf Course and pulled the car to the curb of the house. A large yellow X of official police crime-scene tape crisscrossed the front door and the garage side door.

Lieutenant Peirce ran his hand along the yellow tape to see if it was loose. It did not appear to have been removed or replaced since its installation. He then inspected the repair made on the door lock that had been damaged in the burglary. Sam twisted the doorknob and gave the door a gentle pull to test its strength. Everything seemed in order, but he had this feeling—call it intuition, call it a hunch—that something wasn't right. He turned and started walking toward the back of the house.

"Hey, Lieutenant, aren't we going in?" asked Holloway.

Lieutenant Peirce placed his finger in front of his lips and whispered, "Watch the front. I'm going to check the back."

As Lieutenant Peirce walked to the back of the house, he noticed footprints from a man's gym shoes in the soft earth of the flowerbeds near a first-floor window. There had been no information about footprints near the windows in the forensic report. Peirce tried to push up on the window; it was closed and locked. He continued around to the back of the house. Soon he found what he was looking for: a basement window had been pried open. He thought about squeezing into the basement through the window but decided against it. The element of surprise was probably gone because of their noisy arrival; getting stuck halfway through a basement window at the mercy of the burglar—or murderer—would be a dumb move. He would call for backup and watch the house until a patrol car arrived.

There was a loud crash, and splinters of glass rained down on him from a dormer window set back along the roofline as a chair smashed its way through. Lieutenant Peirce covered his head with his arms to deflect some of the falling glass and sidestepped just in time to avoid being struck by the heavy chair. By the time he'd brushed off most of the glass shards and was able to look up, a man had emerged from the window and was running along the garage roof. When he reached the end of the building, he leaped from the roof over a stockade fence at the perimeter of the property and into the yard of the neighboring house. He was agile and quick, tucking and rolling as he hit the ground and immediately springing to his feet. Peirce called out to Holloway, who had heard the crash and was already running toward him.

"Next door," Peirce shouted, pointing in the direction that the man had run. Holloway turned without saying a word and ran back to the front of the house. Peirce climbed on top of a garbage can enclosure that afforded a view of the neighboring yard. From this vantage point, he could see a tall man in a blue shirt with a nylon stocking pulled over his head. The man leaped over hedges and other obstacles in the yard and then bounded over the far fence onto the next property. Peirce jumped from his perch and fell to his knees as he hit the ground hard. He struggled to his feet, his trousers covered with grass stains, and ran in the direction that Holloway had gone. When he traversed the corner of the house, he was steamrolled, knocked off his feet, the breath forced from his lungs, in a collision with the suspect. Peirce lay on the ground, dazed. As his eyes began to focus, he could see the man in the stocking mask standing over him. He turned and ran down the street. Peirce lay stunned for a moment, then collected himself and climbed to his feet. He drew his gun and yelled for the man to stop, but it was too late. Peirce couldn't risk firing his weapon in a residential neighborhood, and within seconds the intruder had turned the corner and was gone.

Peirce walked back toward the home. "Holloway, where the hell are you? You're supposed to stop the criminal, not let him pass. Holloway?"

Peirce ran to the front of the house and stopped. Holloway was lying on the ground. His head was bleeding just above his right eye. Peirce cradled his head in his arms. "What did the bastard hit you with?" he asked. "I'll call for a bus."

"No, I'm OK, Lieutenant, no ambulance. Actually, I ran into that lamppost chasing the guy. Everybody at the precinct will have a field day with this one when I turn in the report."

"Maybe you don't have to write it exactly that way," Lieutenant Peirce said.

***

"He's coming any minute, Mort. You better get out of here," said Emily Radcliffe. "He almost caught you the last time he was here."

"Don't worry, Em; I can stay upstairs. He can't go up there without a search warrant, and he has no reason to bring one." Mortimer Banks stood at the kitchen table, wiping chicken gravy from his chin with a white paper napkin.

"He's here! Go before he sees you," Emily said in a harsh whisper.

"Go ahead, Mort, I'll handle this," Henrietta Radcliffe said, peeking at the dark-blue unmarked car through the pinstriped kitchen curtains. "It's the same cop who was here the other day."

Mort dropped his napkin into the plate of chicken bones in front of him, took a long pull from his bottle of beer, belched, and walked across the checkerboard-pattern linoleum to the hall stairs.

"Emily," said Henrietta, "go upstairs and change out of that yellow blouse. We're supposed to be in mourning, for Christ's sake."

"You think he's going to notice?" Emily asked.

"Go!" said her mother, and Emily ran off, following Mort.

After looking to see that her boyfriend and daughter were safely out of sight, Henrietta took Mort's plate and beer bottle from the table. She dumped the chicken bones and the bottle in the small garbage pail next to the side door and placed the dish in the sink. Henrietta then went to the door, removed the chain lock, and opened the door before Lieutenant Peirce was halfway up the walk.

"Nice to see you again, Officer," she said, standing in the open doorway.

"Nice to see you again too," said Peirce. "And it's Lieutenant."

"Yes, Lieutenant. You said on the telephone that you wanted to talk to my daughter Emily. She's upstairs. Have a seat, and she'll be down in a minute."

"That's OK. I'll stand, if you don't mind." As he spoke, Lieutenant Peirce walked toward the kitchen doorway. "I didn't interrupt your dinner, did I?"

"No. Emily and I finished eating a while ago. You know, we still don't have much of an appetite with Sylvia being, you know, gone." She took a tissue from her housecoat pocket and made a show of dabbing at her eyes.

"Again, I'm sorry for your loss," Peirce said, surprised by her emotional display. On his last visit she only seemed interested in getting into Sylvia's house.

"Do you think I could get into my daughter's house soon? I'm sure there's a lot to be done, with the furniture and the property and all."

Now that's the Henrietta Radcliffe I know, he thought. "It's still an ongoing investigation, Mrs. Radcliffe. The house will be sealed off until further notice."

A noise at the top of the hall stairs attracted Lieutenant Peirce's attention. Emily Radcliffe was bounding down the steps wearing a black skirt and a black top with a black ribbon in her hair.

She must have been out of sackcloth and ashes, he surmised. As he watched her descend, he thought he caught a fleeting glimpse of a shadow at the top of the stairs, but he couldn't be sure.

"I just stopped by," he said, "to pay my respects and to ask if either of you remembered anything that might help us catch Sylvia's killer. Anyone she may have had trouble with, maybe had money problems?"

"No, like I told you last time, we didn't see Sylvia that often. We don't know much about her life," said Henrietta, placing her arm around her daughter.

"Emily, do you have anything to add?" asked Peirce.

"Sylvia didn't want to have much to do with us," she said. "She was rich, and she kept—ow!"

"Now, Emily, let's speak kindly of the dead," said Henrietta, squeezing Emily's shoulder somewhat harder than an affectionate caress.

Lieutenant Peirce offered another business card and, after saying his farewells, walked down the peeling gray painted porch steps, past the weed-infested dirt plot that served as a front lawn, and returned to his car. He thought about the contrast between the elegant home and manicured property that had belonged to Sylvia in comparison to the impoverished haunt of her family. That could be the reason for the animosity, and maybe a motive for murder.

Mort returned to the kitchen, walking to the window where Henrietta bent to look through the curtains at Lieutenant Peirce's retreat. He patted her on the hip and said, "That's the cop I knocked on his ass this afternoon."

"He didn't see you, did he?" she asked, turning quickly.

"No, I had a stocking on my head. I knocked him down and ran. He could never catch me, and he has no idea I have anything to do with you."

They both watched the unmarked police car drive off.

Sam Peirce continued to drive a few blocks away, then turned, drove back, and positioned his car so that he was out of view of the windows of the house but could still see if anyone entered or left.

He called into the station using his cell phone. Sam hated using the police radio and avoided it as much as possible.

"Homicide, Sergeant Holloway."

"Holloway, what are you doing there? You're supposed to be in the hospital."

"They checked me out, Lieutenant. It's just a bump on the head; I've had worse. How are your knees doing?"

"Now that the pleasantries are over," Peirce said, "I could use some help. I'm a block from Henrietta Radcliffe's house. She swears no one other than her daughter Emily lives with her, but I suspect that she's not telling the truth. The last time I was there I heard voices in the living room before I entered, and this time I saw a shadow at the top of the stairs. In the kitchen there were only two place settings at the table, but there were gravy stains and some food scraps on the floor where a third person would sit. I think someone else is in the house now, and I need to know who it is."

"OK, Lieutenant," said Holloway. "I'll have two teams of detectives there in twenty minutes to stake out the house. Whoever is in there will have to come out sometime."

***

The sun was just beginning to set. Sam Peirce adjusted the visor above his windshield to block the glare from interfering with his view of the house. *Where are those detectives?* He reached around into the backseat of his car and retrieved the brown paper bag that Alicia Goodman had packed for him that morning. Inside he found a plastic bag filled with strips of assorted vegetables. There were carrots, peppers, celery, and very small round tomatoes. He smiled, tossed the bag back over the seat, and reached into his jacket pocket for his cigarettes. He fished around in his pocket and found instead a note from Alicia that simply said, "Liar." He would have some explaining to do later when he met her for dinner.

Where are those guys? Sam picked up his cell phone from the passenger seat and was about to call Holloway for an update when he saw a tall man wearing a blue shirt, baggy pants, and gym shoes step out of the front door of Henrietta Radcliffe's house. The man had broad shoulders and walked with a quickness in his step that denoted good physical conditioning. Peirce watched, slumped down in his seat, while the man opened the door of a yellow two-door coupe with flashy mag wheels and a black racing stripe down the center of its hood. It was parked just a short way from the Radcliffe house. Sam started his car and waited for the man to pull out before following at a discreet distance.

"I need info on a yellow Ford coupe, license plate LP-752-Q." Sam waited to hear the owner's name as he followed along local streets. Within seconds the police dispatcher returned to the phone. The car was registered to Emily Radcliffe.

"Well, that didn't help," he said out loud, "but you do have a nice ride, Emily." Peirce knew that he had no legitimate reason to detain or even stop the man, but he needed to know who he was and how he might be involved in this case. Peirce felt that this certainly could be the man who had run into him while fleeing the crime scene at Silicon Springs this morning, but the man had worn a mask, and there was no evidence to prove this was the same person. Up ahead, the sporty yellow coupe almost, but not quite, made a full stop at a stop sign. "I've got you now," Sam said. He pulled his portable police dome light from the floor, turned it on, and stretched his arm out the window to stick the magnetic light onto the roof of his car. Then Lieutenant Peirce increased his speed to catch up with the coupe. With his dome light flashing, Sam followed close behind the yellow car until the man saw the police beacon, pulled to the curb, and stopped.

Sam Peirce quickly walked to the open window of the coupe. He held up his badge for the man to see and said, "License and registration, please." The man looked at Peirce, first with a questioning expression on his face and then with a look of alarm as he recognized him.

Without turning his head, his eyes still locked on Sam's face, Mortimer Banks made a costly mistake. He slipped the gear shift lever of the coupe into first gear, pressed the gas pedal to the floor, and released the clutch. The little yellow coupe bolted forward, engine screaming and smoke and dust rising from its tires. Sam jumped back to ensure that his feet weren't under the car and shielded his eyes from the gray cloud of burning rubber and debris.

Mortimer Banks accelerated to high speed as he roared down the narrow street. Sam Peirce ran back to his car, and as he fitted his key into the ignition, he could hear the sound of the coupe's engine growing faint in the distance. He had to hurry, or all was lost. Sam raced forward, determined not to let this man escape. He may no longer be in shape for a protracted chase on foot, but he could drive. When Sam attended the police academy, admittedly a long time ago, he was the best in his class in pursuit driving. He always felt that much of his driving skill had been developed during his reckless youth. As a teenager, he earned extra money modifying and drag racing cars on the boulevard in a town just like this one. He recalled many nights when he'd had to outrun the police to keep from losing his driver's license. He always believed that the experience he'd gained in those not-so-legal pursuits helped prepare him for days just like today.

Up ahead he could see his quarry slide into a right turn and sideswipe a car parked near the corner. There was the screech of metal scraping against metal and shards of glass from the side windows exploding into the air. Droplets of perspiration formed on Sam's upper lip, but there was no time to wipe it. He knew his car wasn't as fast as the yellow sports car and the only way he could possibly catch him was to outdrive him. Sam Peirce was focused and determined. He reached the corner and put his car into a controlled skid to negotiate the turn without further redecorating any of the parked vehicles. His tires squealed, and a wheel cover flew off his front wheel and flashed across the pavement like a buzz-saw blade. He accelerated out of the turn, sure that he had made up some time, when suddenly, half a block ahead, he saw a car blocking his path. The car was a blue sedan, and it was sitting diagonally across the road, obstructing both lanes. Its front right fender and wheel were badly crushed, and steam was rising from the hood. Sam had no choice but to slam on his brakes and skid to a stop within feet of the stalled car.

"No, no," he shouted. "Get that car out of my way!" The driver of the blue sedan appeared dazed, blood running from his forehead. He looked to be seriously hurt. Lieutenant Peirce knew no matter how much he wanted to catch this man, he would have to break off his pursuit and offer assistance. He pounded his steering wheel with his fists several times before accepting defeat. He called police dispatch on the car's police radio and asked for an ambulance, his cell phone now lost somewhere under the front seat.

He stepped from his car to walk across the street to the injured man. As he did, he heard a commotion and saw a crowd gathering at the other end of the block. Not one hundred feet away, the yellow coupe, after ricocheting off the blue sedan, had mounted the curb and come to a very sudden stop against a telephone pole. The coupe had struck the pole with such a strong impact that it had driven the pole almost to the center of the car, crushing Mort Banks where he sat.

17

D r. Klein, it's eight o'clock in the morning. I've never seen you here this early," said Hyrum Green as he unlocked the door to his dental office. "Would you like to join me for coffee? I'm buying."

Ruth held up her large caramel cream double espresso macchiato light as she rushed by. "Some other time, Dr. Green, I have a busy day ahead."

Hyrum frowned and stood watching her walk down the hall, her open coat flowing like a cape behind her, rhythmically hinting at the movement of her hips with each step. He closed his eyes. The corridor resonated with the click of her heels on the hard tile floor. He stayed until she disappeared into her office and the early morning corridor was again silent.

Ruth still had not fully recovered from her narrow escape in the pitch-black basement the other night, and although she had no real reason to suspect Dr. Green of any wrongdoing, she would feel uncomfortable being alone with him, even if she did have enough time.

The telephone call she'd received from Franklin Jameson last night sounded desperate. There was talk of sleepless nights, hearing voices, doing something he was sorry for, and even a threat of suicide. After an hour-long conversation, during which Ruth listened and comforted him, he seemed stable enough to get through the night on his own. Ruth tried to discover if he had a family member or a close friend with whom he could share his concerns, but he denied having anyone in his life that he trusted with his innermost fears—no one other than her. Although Ruth was pleased that he had begun to trust her and that he seemed to have faith in their therapy sessions, she still wished he had someone who could provide support outside her office, a social support group, or even one friend to help him through a crisis. After Franklin reassured her several times that he would not do anything rash before morning, she offered to open her office early and see him at 9:00 a.m.

Ruth dropped her coat onto an office chair and hurried to her desk to review Franklin's file. She recalled observing stress in his voice at their last session, but nothing that indicated such aberrant behavior. She would need to find out what had caused this episode if she was going to help him through it.

Ruth Klein quickly retrieved Franklin's folder from her file cabinet drawer. She was pleased with herself for having labeled and filed it properly immediately after his last session. She normally procrastinated, which usually necessitated a mad scramble through piles of seemingly camouflaged documents to seek out the unidentified culprit she sorely needed. She laid the file open on her desk, took a long sip of her coffee, adjusted her glasses, and began to read.

Ah, now she remembered, nightmares precipitating feelings of guilt, minor acting out of his dreams, but nothing as debilitating as the symptoms he's now presenting. Something new must have happened.

Ruth scanned her notes, running her finger down the page, then stopped at three words: yellow rose tattoo. Suddenly the full session with Franklin from Tuesday replayed in her mind. He described a burglary taking place in a large house and a woman stabbed to death with a pair of scissors, a woman with a yellow rose tattoo on her right hip. He was describing Sylvia Radcliffe's murder. *How could he know that? Unless...*

Ruth looked at her desk clock: 8:45. *He'll be here any minute.* She sprang from her chair, ran to the front door of her waiting room, and closed the deadbolt lock, making a loud *click*. She stood motionless with her hand on the lock, breathing deeply to regain control of her racing heart. After a calming moment, she decided that she may be overreacting. There was probably a logical explanation. *This could simply be a coincidence, or something he read in the newspaper.* She slowly unlocked the door. It made a "clunk" sound this time, and she backed away about a foot. *But the yellow rose tattoo—that's a bit much for a coincidence, and it wasn't in the newspaper.* She stepped forward again; *click* went the lock. Then she stepped back, thinking, *Tattoos are very popular right now. I would imagine a yellow rose is a very common design in tattoo parlors, particularly with young women. Clunk* went the lock as she opened it. *But on the right hip? Click.*

Being no stranger to paranoia, Ruth weighed her fear against her professional training and her obligation to her patient under the Psychologist's Code of Conduct and made her decision. *Clunk.* She commended herself for making the right decision, one favoring the welfare of the patient over her personal concerns, and then she ran to her desk and rummaged through her top drawer until she found her tube of pepper spray and slipped it into her pocket.

***

Franklin stepped quietly through the front door of 29 Office Park Place. When he passed Hyrum Green's office, he walked on his tiptoes. Only his cane clicked on the noisy tile floor. As he went by, Hyrum opened the door and stepped into the hall.

"Early for another date, Franklin?" He smiled broadly. "I knew you didn't stop by the other night just to see my handsome face. So what is it? You're dating Dr. Klein. It's all right; you can tell me," he said with his usual wink. "I wondered why she was here so early today. Now I know."

"No, I just stopped by to—"

"Enough—she's an attractive woman. You're a good-looking man. Go. You can tell me all about it later," he said and disappeared back into his waiting room.

"I'm going to have to see if this building has a back entrance," Franklin mumbled as he made his way down the hall.

He entered Dr. Klein's waiting room and took a seat. Within a few seconds, he got up from his seat and walked to her office door. Just as he raised his fist to knock, Dr. Klein pulled the door open. Startled by the sight of Franklin standing less than a foot away with his fist clenched and raised, she uttered a short, high-pitched shriek.

"I'm sorry," Franklin said, backing away from her. "I didn't mean to frighten you. I was going to knock."

"You didn't frighten me," Ruth said in defense of her pride. "I was just a little surprised to see you. I didn't hear you come in."

Any more "surprised," and I'd have to change my pants, she thought as she secretly slipped the pepper spray back into her pocket.

"Come sit down and tell me what happened," she said, intentionally leaving the door to the waiting room open as she walked to her chair.

Ruth watched Franklin rub his hand over the two-day growth of beard on his cheek. His hair was matted; it looked as though it hadn't been combed for days—he looked pretty scary.

"Do you mind if I record our session along with taking notes?" she asked. "Sometimes a recording helps when reviewing a session." *And it can also serve as evidence if you threaten me*, she thought.

"I'd feel better if you didn't," he said.

"You seemed extremely upset last night when you telephoned. Could you tell me what happened?"

"I'm still frightened by the dreams we discussed last time I was here," he said. "I don't know what they mean."

"What do you think they mean?" Dr. Klein asked. *That is the most overused response in psychology ever. We should give it a number. Then we could just say 'twelve' when that response is required, and everyone will know what we mean.*

"Is it possible to do something while sleepwalking and not remember doing it?" Franklin asked.

"It certainly is possible to not recall an activity while sleepwalking. Do you think you did something in your sleep?" Dr. Klein said. *Like kill somebody?*

Franklin sat on the couch with his hands clenched in his lap, looking at the floor. He tilted his head as though he were sorting out his thoughts. Then, he raised his head and began to explain.

"I think I'm psychic," he said.

Psychotic is more like it, Ruth thought.

"What led you to that conclusion?" she said instead.

"I know things I could not know any other way," he said with a new-found look of confidence on his face.

Unless you did them, she thought. "Can you give me an example?"

Franklin cleared his throat, stood, and began to pace as he spoke.

As he approached her chair, she instinctively placed her hand in her pocket and gripped the pepper spray. She relaxed her grip when he turned away.

"I know this will sound strange to you," Franklin said, shaking his index finger in the air as he spoke, "but I think the dream I described to you in our last session was a premonition of a real murder."

And there it is, Ruth thought.

He went on. "Have you read yesterday's newspaper about the murder of a young woman in Silicon Springs?"

"She was my patient," Ruth volunteered, then regretted saying it.

Franklin sat back down on the sofa and lowered his head into both of his hands.

"I'm sorry," he said, his voice now weak and slightly muffled. "I thought it was only a dream, but I guess I was seeing what was going to happen."

Or you were planning what you were going to do, she thought, her anger beginning to well up inside her.

"In our last session, you said that the murder weapon was a pair of scissors and the victim had a yellow rose tattoo on her right hip. Were those facts in the real murder?" Ruth asked, already knowing that at least the tattoo was real.

"I don't know. But if they are real, it would prove I am psychic, since I saw them in my dream. Don't you see?" he said, leaning forward at the edge of his seat.

It would prove something, she thought. "I've never seen any proof of psychic phenomena before. Have you?"

"I'll bet many of the dreams I dreamed recently have been premonitions of things to come. I never thought of it before. Even dreams I had as a kid probably came true, but I didn't know." Franklin began pacing again, this time with his hand on his chin as he walked faster and in a tighter oval pattern.

He's delusional, Ruth thought. *This fantasy of being a psychic is his escape. It's an opportunity for his mind to rationalize the memory of the violent events in his past as premonitions. It's a defense mechanism to hide his actions from his conscious mind and thus avoid the consequences of those actions. He doesn't know he did it.*

This man needs help, but the only way to institutionalize him would be if he committed himself voluntarily, since he has no family in the area that would have that authority. Of course I could contact the police and tell them what I know and let them take it from there, but I have no knowledge of a crime he is going to commit or proof he committed one in the past. The Psychologist's Code of Conduct forbids me to divulge any of his personal data to the police or anyone unless it's to protect someone from imminent danger.

"Dr. Klein—Dr. Klein!"

Oops, I did it again, she thought.

"How shall we prove you're right?" she said. "Should we call the police and tell them what you know? Maybe you could help them."

"No, no, no. We can't tell anyone until I can prove I'm right. They might get the wrong idea."

Might? Ruth thought.

Then suddenly Franklin walked through the open door into the waiting room. "Thank you so much, Doctor. You really helped me," he said. He continued walking to the exit.

"Mr. Jameson—Franklin—where are you going? What are you going to do?" she cried.

"I'm going to go home and write down everything about my dreams, all of them. Then I'm going to check each one out. I'll prove I'm a psychic, and the next time I dream of a crime, I'll be there to prevent it. Thank you again; I feel so much better." Then Franklin disappeared down the hall.

Ruth Klein stood stunned in the middle of her office. She thought of the seriousness of his illness and the need to take action, but then there was the conflict she felt with doctor-patient privilege and the Psychologist's Code of Conduct.

"Fuck the code. I'm turning him in," she said, speaking from pure impulse.

After a few minutes of calming meditation and rethinking the problem, Ruth came to a different conclusion.

She was still committed to her career and to her code of conduct, but she felt an overpowering urgency to act. She would never intentionally violate doctor-patient privilege, but this was an extreme

situation. Although she had no proof that Franklin would hurt someone in the future, she felt she could not allow him to roam the streets
at will in his current psychological state. What to do? That was the
question. She could call the police and give an anonymous tip that
he was the murderer. She didn't actually know that as a fact. She
could talk to Lieutenant Peirce and tell him she was concerned that
Franklin might hurt himself. That might get the lieutenant involved,
but she couldn't support her concern without telling him why, and
that would violate Franklin's privacy. How could she stop him? She
could wait for him to cross the street and then run him over with her
car. That would stop him. *OK, you're losing it now*, she thought. What if
she met with him again and tried to convince him to commit himself?
It was a long shot, but it might work. And if it didn't, she thought,
she could always revert to Plan B—the anonymous phone call, not
running him over.

***

"Here you go, Cochise," said the uniformed police messenger as he
handed a large manila envelope to Sergeant Holloway.

Holloway raised his hand and touched the bandage on his head. He
turned and looked at his reflection in the glass-topped partition dividing
his cubicle from the other precinct office spaces. He stared at the single
white band of gauze wrapped around his forehead and understood.
"How would you like an arrow in your ass?" he asked as he sat in his
chair to open his mail. The messenger did not reply, but as he walked
away, he flashed half of a peace sign over his shoulder.

"Whatever happened to respect for your fellow workers!" Holloway
shouted at the receding figure. An hour later he stood in Lieutenant
Peirce's office paraphrasing the arrest record of the recently deceased
Mortimer Schmidt, aka Mortimer Banks.

"This guy had a conviction for grand theft burglary and manslaughter. He served twelve years in a New York state prison," Holloway said
as he looked for the familiar jar of jelly beans on the lieutenant's desk.
"Banks has been out for about a year. He fell off the radar a month after

he was paroled. His parole officer in Albany issued a warrant for his arrest, but he was never found."

"I guess he figured he would be sent up for life if he was caught. That's probably why he ran." Peirce opened his top desk drawer, removed a bag of wilted vegetable strips, and tossed them onto the desk in Holloway's direction.

"Here's the good part, Lieutenant—he had a computer flash drive in his pocket. It contained a list of customer sales from the jewelry store where Sylvia Radcliffe worked. I checked with robbery division, and four of the addresses on this list have been broken into in the last month. I think we have our cat burglar."

Holloway opened the bag, took all the carrot sticks, and tossed the bag with the remaining vegetables back on the lieutenant's desk.

"I guess Sylvia could have been feeding information to her mother about who recently bought jewelry, and Mort did the smash and grab. Maybe Sylvia decided she wanted out, and the family needed to keep her quiet. Was anything other than jewelry stolen from those houses?" Peirce asked as he wondered about Holloway's fascination with the color orange.

"The usual stuff," said Holloway, "some cash, a big-screen TV."

"Good work," interrupted Peirce. "Get a detailed list of the stolen items from robbery, including the serial number of the stolen TV. Then get a search warrant for Henrietta Radcliffe's house. It's time to pay another visit to the grieving mother."

18

P olice sirens wailed and black-and-white police cars skidded to a stop, blocking off both ends of the street. Four uniformed police officers and two in plain clothes exited their cars and rushed to the front door of Henrietta and Emily Radcliffe's home.

"What do you want now?" Henrietta shouted at Lieutenant Peirce as she stood in the open doorway. Henrietta was dressed in a dark-blue pantsuit and black leather shoes instead of her customary flowered housedress and flip-flops. Through the open doorway, Sam Peirce could see Emily carrying two suitcases down the stairs. When she saw the lieutenant, she stopped midflight and ran back up the stairs to her bedroom, bumping her bags along the wall and stairs as she went.

"Henrietta Radcliffe," Peirce said as he held up a folded sheet of white paper. "We have a warrant to search these premises."

The four uniformed police officers immediately began to rummage through the house, lifting sofa cushions and opening drawers over the protests of Henrietta. She waved her arms and shouted profanities as she attempted to reset the sofa cushions and slam the drawers before a thorough search could be executed. Sergeant Holloway intervened, backed Henrietta to a chair, and cautioned her not to interfere under penalty of arrest. Lieutenant Peirce smiled as he observed the tenacity with which Holloway confronted the woman in spite of the fact that she was two inches taller and outweighed him by at least fifty pounds.

Peirce turned the big-screen television and checked the serial number on its side against the list of stolen items and found a match. From the top of the stairs, Officer Thompson called down to the lieutenant.

"Sir, you might want to come up and see this. It seems Ms. Radcliffe's suitcase is filled with some pretty expensive jewelry."

Sam Peirce climbed the stairs. He lifted a blue velvet bag from the suitcase and dumped its contents onto the bed. He lifted a diamond tennis bracelet from the pile of rings and watches and matched it against the description of a bracelet stolen just three weeks ago. "Those aren't mine," Emily said. "I didn't put them in there."

Peirce lifted her wrist and studied the white-gold and diamond-encrusted Patek Philippe wristwatch she was attempting to hide behind her back. He checked his list. "I suppose someone put this watch on your wrist without your knowledge."

"It was a gift. I got it from—"

"Shut up," Henrietta shouted from her chair in the living room. "Don't say another word."

"Well, that's at least possession of stolen goods. I think we have enough to continue this conversation at the station. Officers, read them their rights and bring them in. We'll meet you there as soon as we finish the search."

* * *

"We've had them sitting there for over an hour. From the way they're both fidgeting, I'd say they're ready, boss," Holloway said as he looked through the glass window into interrogation room three.

A single desk lamp barely illuminated the small observation room where Peirce and Holloway stood.

"Let's give them ten more minutes to stew. Make sure we're recording them." Sam walked out of the observation room. Holloway put on a pair of headphones, checked the volume control on the recorder, and resumed watching the two women through the one-way mirror.

Henrietta and Emily Radcliffe sat on metal chairs, both on the same side of a large stainless steel table. They sat under harsh light cast down from four strong spotlights recessed into the ceiling. Emily reached down and grabbed the sides of her chair and tried to pull it closer to the table.

"We're screwed," Henrietta said.

"What?"

"Our chairs—the chairs are screwed to the floor. You can't move them. And you see those big metal rings stuck on the table? They're to attach handcuffs."

"They're not going to put handcuffs on us, are they, Momma?"

"Maybe—we're dangerous criminals."

"I'm not a criminal; all I did was—"

"Emily, we talked about this. All that jewelry, we never saw it before, and the TV was a gift from Sylvia. We don't know how she got it. You know what to say."

"Maybe we should ask for a lawyer; they said we could have a lawyer."

"Just tell them we didn't do anything wrong, and we won't need a lawyer. Tell them what we talked about. OK?"

Peirce returned to the observation room with a juice box in his hand. He took a pull on the straw, made an unpleasant face, and threw the half-full container into the trash.

"Alicia pack your lunch, Boss?"

Peirce's eyes drilled into Holloway for a long moment. Then he said, "They say anything we can use?"

"Not really, but aren't the detectives from robbery going to do the interview?"

"I don't think this is just about robbery," Peirce said. "I think it's about our murder case, and I want first crack at them."

"You're the boss," he said, looking at the juice box in the trash can and smiling as he watched Lieutenant Peirce walk into the interrogation room.

"Are you ladies comfortable?" he asked as he stepped into the room.

"I could use a Diet Coke," said Emily.

Henrietta shook her head. "No, nothing, we're fine, we're both fine."

Peirce smiled and tapped the file folder he held in his right hand several times. Then he slowly walked once around the room, causing both women to turn their heads first right, then left, to follow him as he circled behind them and then settled in a chair at the front of the table, back where he had started.

"Would you like to tell me where all the jewelry we found in your house came from?" Peirce asked.

"First," Henrietta said, "I never saw that jewelry before. I don't even think it's real."

"Oh, it's real all right, and each piece was stolen within the last year. Here's another piece of news that you might be interested in. Most of the jewelry was originally sold, before it was stolen, by the jewelry department your daughter Sylvia managed."

"Well, I guess you'd have to ask Sylvia about that, if she were alive. Maybe she stole the stuff back and planted it in my house."

"What about Mortimer Banks?" Peirce asked. "Did he have anything to do with the theft?"

"Mortimer who?" she said. "I don't know anyone named Mortimer."

"Well, let me tell you what I know. First, I saw Mortimer Banks leave your house yesterday and drive away in Emily's car. I know you know him. Now, let me tell you what I think. I think both you and Emily took information from Sylvia, with or without her knowledge, about the purchase of jewelry from her store. I think you gave that information to Mortimer Banks, and he burglarized the houses."

"I don't know what you're talking about."

"I also think that Sylvia either found out about the thefts or wanted out if she was part of it, and either Mort, one of you, or all three of you murdered her."

"That's crazy," Henrietta said, her lip beginning to quiver. "I loved my daughter. I would never hurt my baby, and Mort was with me the night she died. We were all together at my house. Ask Mort, if you can find him. I haven't seen him since he left in Emily's car."

"We know where Mort is. He's here in this building."

"Then ask him. He'll tell you we were all together at my house when she was killed. You should be out finding the bastard who killed my baby; not accusing us. I loved her. She was my baby."

Sam Peirce sat in silence as Emily rubbed her mother's shoulder and offered her handkerchief to dry her mother's eyes. "None of us killed Sylvia," she said.

Sam turned to face the mirror on the wall behind him. He placed his thumb under his chin and motioned a cut sign to Holloway so that he would turn off the recorder. Although they may have been involved in the burglaries, he was satisfied that the two women were not implicated in the murder of Sylvia Radcliffe. Now he began to feel extremely uncomfortable. He knew the time had come to deliver more bad news to this woman. Sam raised his hand to his chin and felt the stubble already growing back on his face.

"Henrietta, there is something I have to tell you."

19

Three days had passed since Franklin, in a manic state, had run from Ruth Klein's office shouting that he would prove that his dreams were premonitions of the future and that his psychic abilities would lead him to find the real killer of Sylvia Radcliffe. Ruth tried again—well, actually for the tenth time in the last two days—to reach him by telephone. Her concern for his safety, and the safety of everyone around him, was growing with each failed attempt. Now she found herself driving through his neighborhood, not really knowing why, but feeling compelled to do something—anything. Her conscience just wouldn't let her rest until he was either checked into a hospital or in jail. The man had become a menace to himself and anyone who might cross his path. She pulled her car to the curb, directly in front of Franklin's house. His silver Toyota was parked in the driveway, and she could see lights on in several of the rooms.

He could have hurt himself or possibly even committed suicide. He said he might be dead before next Tuesday. Had he been making a threat? Guilt now became Ruth Klein's dominant emotion. While she was busy chastising herself for waiting so long to take action, she dialed his number one last time from her cell phone. Six rings, seven, eight, nine…maybe he was hurt and couldn't answer, or worse.

Ruth marshaled her courage and walked to Franklin's front door. Once on his wooden porch, she leaned over the railing to see into the brightly lit living room. Her attention was immediately drawn to the amount of debris on the floor and the furniture. There were pizza boxes, beer and soda cans, empty paper coffee cups, and cake wrappers everywhere. *At least he's eating*, she remarked to herself to ease the tension.

Maybe it's the maid's day off. Then she realized that she could be blowing this whole thing out of proportion; there may be nothing wrong at all. Leaning farther over the railing, she noticed that the mirror on the living room wall was covered by a bedsheet that had been tacked to the wall and reinforced with duct tape. That didn't seem exactly normal, but he could have a logical explanation, like maybe he's given up being psychic to become a vampire. That thought amused her.

Back to business. In the far right corner of the room, she saw an open doorway that appeared to lead to the kitchen. If she could just lean a little farther over the railing, she could see. Suddenly her feet began to slip on the porch floor, and she stifled a scream as she fought to regain her balance. Then a hand grabbed her arm just below the shoulder, and the scream was let loose with all its pitch, power, and volume.

"Dr. Klein. Are you all right?"

Ruth Klein caught her balance, with Franklin's help, by leaning back against the wooden porch railing.

"Fine, I'm fine. I was just about to ring your bell when I slipped. New shoes—I'm going to have to scuff up the leather soles a little before I kill myself."

"I'm glad you're here," Franklin said, either ignoring or not realizing that she had not been invited. "Come in, come in. Wait until you see all the progress I've made."

Franklin led Ruth to the kitchen, pulling her along behind him. "I'm almost ready," he said, "I just need another minute."

Franklin sat at his kitchen table reading from a newspaper clipping and making notes on a ruled yellow pad. He folded the clipping several times and placed it in a paper bag on the floor at the right of his chair. Ruth stood in the kitchen, shifting her weight from foot to foot, uncertain as to how to proceed.

"Franklin, I'm worried about you. We need to have a quiet discussion."

"No, it's OK. I'm just about ready."

With a sweep of his arm, Franklin cleared the table of paper plates, cardboard boxes, napkins, and empty plastic bottles. Ruth stepped back just in time to avoid being spattered by the rubbish on its way to the floor.

Then he reached into the paper bag and began to pull out strips of newspaper one at a time. Some of the articles were wrinkled from being stuffed in the paper bag, and some had stains from pizza sauce, coffee, and other unidentifiable substances. They all had torn edges, but the edges were very neatly torn. The clippings were straight and square and complete, and he handled them with reverence, as if each one was a precious record of an important moment in his life, a part of a scrapbook of his major achievements and noteworthy memoirs recorded for posterity.

Ruth watched as he carefully unfolded each of the clippings and arranged them in precise rows on the kitchen table. He aligned the articles into columns from top to bottom and the columns into rows from left to right. Her eyes widened as she observed how he moved with deliberate confidence, focusing on every minute detail of his task. She made a mental note: *Add anal retentive to his list of idiosyncrasies.*

The articles he had chosen to save were reports of crimes, mostly burglaries and other odd events that had occurred during the last few months. Each one had a date written across its top in black marker. Next Franklin placed a piece of yellow notepaper containing a few paragraphs of handwritten notes under each column. Ruth leaned over to read one of the yellow pages and then jumped back as Franklin said in a loud voice, "They're my dreams. Each sheet of yellow paper is a different dream, a dream of a crime or some other event like this one."

He pointed to an article on the table and handed Ruth the yellow paper beneath it. Ruth read the newspaper headline aloud: "'Wolf Escapes from Game Preserve and Frightens Hiker in State Park.' What does this have to do with you?"

"I dreamed it," Franklin said. He snatched the yellow paper back from Ruth's hand and read the account of his dream of walking in the forest and being confronted by a wolf.

"Look at the dates. The dream happened three days before the hiker reported seeing a wolf on a trail in the state park."

"That's an interesting coincidence, but that doesn't prove anything. You might have heard or read that the wolf had escaped from the preserve days before and forgotten all about it. Later, the dream was simply manufactured from your subconscious mind to match the real event."

Ruth shook her head. This was going nowhere, and he was becoming more agitated by the minute. She checked her pocket for the pepper spray, just in case. She pulled her cell phone from her jacket and, while Franklin was distracted with his clippings, typed in 911 but did not press *call*.

"No, that's not true. Here, look at another one." He handed her another clipping.

The article was an account of a break-in at the crime scene of Sylvia Radcliffe's home several days after her murder. The article described an intruder, a man in a blue shirt with a stocking over his head, escaping from the house by throwing a chair through a window, climbing on the roof, and evading police.

"This is the dream I told you about in our first session, weeks before it happened."

Ruth offered a dubious smile as she calculated the date of their session and then looked at the date on the article.

"I see the similarity," she admitted, "but I'm still not a believer. You'll need some harder evidence if you're going to convince me that you had some sort of premonition. I don't recognize that such things even exist."

Franklin scratched his shoulder and rubbed his chin, trying to think of a way he might convince her that his logic was sound.

"I've got it." He picked up another article and handed it to Ruth.

This one described an automobile accident after a police chase that took the life of a man, Mortimer Banks. The article went on to say that the police believed that Mr. Banks was in fact the burglar who had broken into the Radcliffe home. The suspicion was based on police eyewitness reports, a stocking mask, and other evidence, not described, found in his pocket.

"The burglar in my dream took something from the dresser and put it in his pocket. It looked like a small black plastic case just a few inches long and maybe an inch wide. If we could find out what he had in his pocket besides the stocking mask, it would prove that I really saw him."

Ruth was confident that this was all Franklin's active imagination and stemmed from his need to gain absolution for his crimes—or at least ease his conscience—but he made an interesting point. If she could prove him wrong, or at least show that his proof did not exist, he may more readily accept her advice. She carefully read the article and noted that the police officer involved in the incident was none other than Lieutenant Peirce. Maybe a call to the good lieutenant would help end this dilemma.

***

The hot shower poured down on Sam Peirce's head. Steam rose around him, forming a heavy fog that settled on the clear glass doors. He took a deep breath. The water vapor cleared his head. The streams from the jets beat against his sore muscles. The large tile shower enclosure sported six water jets to knead and massage aching body parts, but Sam liked the rain shower head best. He closed his eyes and breathed through his nose. The water beat against his head and then cascaded in rivulets over his face and down his body. He'd had only four hours' sleep and wasn't sure if this morning's shower was a help or a hindrance to preparing him for a busy day. He thought about the murder of Sylvia Radcliffe and how he might never know for sure if Mortimer Banks was the killer. Sylvia's mother and sister swore, of course, that he didn't do it, but if he had lived and been convicted, they very well could have been arrested as accessories to murder. Their testimony was useless. Of course there was no explanation, so far, for the mysterious silver car seen by a neighborhood woman the night of the murder and by the security guard days later. Probably just kids joy riding, an unrelated coincidence.

Sam reached for the temperature control and turned it all the way to cold to shock his system awake. A shrill scream sliced through his throbbing head, and a fist punched him in the middle of his back.

"Why did you do that?" Alicia Goodman cried as she pulled a towel into the shower to protect her naked body from the freezing cold water. "You're going to give us both a heart attack." She grabbed at the controls.

Sam wrapped his arms around her and pulled her close. "I'll keep you warm," he said. Then he pulled the towel from between them and tossed it to the back of the shower enclosure.

An hour later, Sam Peirce was out of the house and heading down Route 415 at a brisk pace. The new gray running outfit and Rockport shoes that Alicia bought for him fit pretty well, but he felt a bit uncomfortable wandering around the streets without his usual business suit or at least a sport coat. The hooded sweatshirt jacket he wore barely offered enough room to fit his shoulder holster and off-duty gun underneath, and he felt that anyone who saw him would see the bulge in his shirt and wonder. *Maybe I should have put the gun in my underwear; let them wonder about that bulge.* The sun was just rising above the trees. Sam raised his hand to his forehead to shield his eyes from the glare and squinted, watching for oncoming traffic as he crossed the road. He looked over his shoulder back toward the house. Alicia Goodman stood on the top step, straining to see his progress before she drove to the hospital for a day of surgery. Sam patted his pockets, then held up his empty hands. He made an exaggerated gesture as though he were smoking a cigarette and smiled. Alicia shook her head, offered a dismissive wave, and got into her car.

A satisfied smile materialized on his face and his eyes grew bright as he watched her drive away. He reached the far curb, crossed the sidewalk, opened the door, and walked into Dunkin' Donuts.

Sam hurried across the tan-and-black checkerboard tile floor and leaned both hands on the counter. He pointed at the rack of freshly made doughnuts and ordered two chocolate-covered Bavarian cream-filled and a large coffee.

At a small maroon table in the corner of the restaurant behind a fake potted yucca plant, Lieutenant Sam Peirce sat with his purchases and poured two small containers of cream and two packets of sugar into his coffee.

He stirred the cup and stared at the doughnuts, sure that the dough-nuts he bought in the past were bigger. Sam was about to lift one of the oozing sweet pastries to his mouth when his cell phone rang. *How could she know?*

He checked the incoming number and was relieved to find that it was unfamiliar.

"Lieutenant Sam Peirce—may I help you?" He hoped his voice would not show his annoyance at being disturbed while indulging one of his few remaining vices.

"Lieutenant Peirce, it's Ruth Klein. I'm sorry to call so early, but I was wondering if you could answer a question for me pertaining to the Sylvia Radcliffe murder?"

That sounds like something I'm supposed to say, he thought. "How can I help you?"

"I read in the newspaper that a man killed in an automobile accident was suspected of breaking into Sylvia's house because of items found in his pockets. Would you be able to tell me what those items were?"

This woman knows something more about this case, Sam thought.

"Dr. Klein, since this is an active murder investigation, and since your patient was the victim and is now deceased, isn't it true that doctor-patient privilege no longer applies?"

"That would depend on the question. Anything personal that doesn't pertain to the crime would still be privileged." Ruth had not yet offered any new information, but Sam was hopeful.

"I'll tell you what was in his pocket if you tell me why you want to know." Sam realized that his case had hit a stone wall and that Dr. Klein may be one of the few opportunities left for a new lead.

Ruth decided that she could do this if she trod carefully without rais-ing his suspicions about Franklin or herself.

"I have information that might be pertinent to the case and might not violate privilege, but it all depends on what was found."

"It was a computer flash drive, but I can't tell you what was recorded on it. Now what can you tell me?"

Sam now believed that Sylvia must have told Dr. Klein about the flash drive and maybe even about the burglaries in one of her sessions.

A confirmation that Sylvia knew about the crimes would go a long way toward motive for her murder.

"No, that doesn't help at all. I'm afraid there isn't anything else I can tell you. I'm sorry. I just don't have anything else I can say." Ruth had accomplished her task. She had learned what was in the burglar's pocket without incriminating Franklin or impugning her own veracity.

She's lying, Peirce thought. *This isn't over.*

"Well, thank you for trying," Peirce said. "Let me know if you remember anything that might be helpful."

After closing the call with Ruth Klein, Sam Peirce formulated a plan. His thought process went something like this: *Dr. Klein knows more than she's saying. Since Sylvia Radcliffe is dead and doctor-patient privilege no longer applies, any information she's withholding must be coming from another patient, one she's not at liberty to identify.*

Sam decided to find out who else might be involved in his case.

"Holloway, this is Peirce. Set up a stakeout in the parking lot outside Dr. Ruth Klein's office," he said, juggling his cell phone as he pressed the lid down on his container of coffee and placed the two doughnuts back in the Dunkin' Donuts bag.

"Twenty-four–seven or just during office hours?" Holloway asked.

"Office hours should do it. Keep an eye peeled for a late-model silver Toyota driven by one of her patients. Don't approach, just run the plate and call me."

Sam Peirce collected his coffee and bag of doughnuts, and as he reached the exit door, he unceremoniously dropped them in the round black plastic trash can and walked back to his car parked in front of Alicia's house. Once there, he drove home to change into a suit and continued on to work.

20

Ruth Klein had a dilemma. She had studied psychology and psychotherapy for twelve years and had been in practice, private and other, for at least eight more. In all that time, she had never seen any conclusive proof of psychic phenomenon and wasn't about to accept Franklin's theory of "How else could I know this?" without more proof. There were probably many logical reasons why Franklin's dreams so closely resembled future events. She just couldn't think of any.

He did tell her about the burglar jumping through the window in his dream on a Tuesday, and the newspaper said it happened days later. That sounded fairly convincing, but it could still be just a coincidence. Jumping through a window may have been a logical way for his subconscious mind to allow the burglar to escape and thus end the dream without Franklin being harmed. It could simply have been an escape mechanism his mind used for self-protection while dreaming. It's logical that a burglar might jump out of a window to escape police in real life, so why not jump out of a window in a dream. Coincidence!

Franklin said the burglar had stolen a small plastic box. That could have been the flash drive Lieutenant Peirce said was found on Mortimer Banks's body, but then again, Franklin only described a small plastic box. The box could have been a ring box or some other small jewelry box rather than the flash drive; that would be logical. Again, it was just a coincidence.

That seemed to explain the dream of the burglar, but she had a more difficult problem to work on. Franklin's dream of the murder was just too detailed and too close to the actual facts reported in the newspaper to be mere coincidence. And even if she could explain away (or maybe rationalize was a better word) some of the facts, how could she explain his description of the yellow rose tattoo on Sylvia's hip? The fact that she even had a tattoo was kept secret by the police. To Ruth's knowledge no one outside the official investigation (and herself, of course) knew about it—except for Franklin. How could he have known unless he actually saw the tattoo? He said he didn't know the woman who was murdered, although he did say she looked vaguely familiar. Well, it takes more than a vague familiarity with a young woman to see a tattoo on her naked hip. If he had a relationship with Sylvia, he was lying to hide it. That alone would make him a suspect in the murder.

Using all the logic Ruth Klein could muster still could not resolve this dilemma. Either Franklin was a violent person and had some involvement in the murder, which she was beginning to strongly doubt, or he was psychic and had had a premonition of the murder. *How else could he know?* "Well, that was a well-spent half hour," she said out loud.

* * *

Franklin arrived at the parking lot of Dr. Klein's office and parked his car at the side of the building next to the tall cedar trees, far from the lampposts illuminating the front lot. He felt a little uncomfortable parking in the dark. Normally he would be afraid of muggers lurking among the trees, but tonight he felt it was worth the risk. He had a plan, and if he decided to act on it, stealth and caution would be of paramount importance. Some of his fears were allayed by the fact that the parking lot was not totally empty. In the far corner of the lot, a man sat in a dark-blue sedan reading a newspaper, apparently waiting for his wife or girlfriend to come out of the building after a dental appointment, or maybe a Botox treatment, Franklin mused. He walked close to the building to avoid being seen, ambled up the stairs, and slipped into the front door while the man's face was buried in his newspaper. Franklin removed a Band-Aid from his pocket, peeled off the wrapper, and stuck the pad of the bandage to the tip of his cane. He tapped it on the floor to ensure that it didn't click against the tile as he walked.

James Bond couldn't have done better, he thought as he slunk down the hall to Dr. Klein's office.

***

Ruth Klein was sitting at her desk. She watched Franklin through her open office door as he entered her waiting room. He was wearing a black T-shirt, tight black jeans, and rubber ripple-soled black shoes. *Where's your black watch cap and mask?* He looked like a cartoon cat burglar on his way to steal a pie that someone had left cooling on a windowsill.

"Dr. Klein, I believe I can solve the murder of Sylvia Radcliffe. I'm sure that if I can see the room where she died, I'll remember more about the killer. I'm sure I can find a clue or a lead at the murder scene that will solve the crime."

He's further gone than I thought. "That sounds like a great idea. Let's call the police and offer your assistance. I'm sure they'll appreciate the help." *Whether he's clairvoyant or just nuts, this will work for me.*

"I can't go to the police until I have more proof. They might not understand and think that I had something to do with the murder."

"Franklin, as your doctor, I'm bound not to divulge anything you say to me, but if you plan to commit a crime, like breaking into a house, I would be required to report it to the police. Privilege no longer would apply."

"No, I'm not ready to go to the police yet," he said. "I'll just stand in front of the house for a few minutes. I need to feel some vibrations from it."

Nuts, that didn't work. If it's vibrations he wants to feel, maybe he should get a vibrator. I'd give him mine if I thought it would get him to forget this delusion and commit himself.

"Franklin, I don't think going to Sylvia's house is the right thing to do. You won't be able to go inside to see the room where she was killed, and I'm not sure any *vibrations* will reach you from the front lawn." *Did I really say that?*

"It's worth a try," he said. "Come with me. I need a witness and some help interpreting the clues."

Ruth Klein suddenly had an idea. She could go with him, and once he received his "vibrations," or more likely, he didn't, she would convince him to go with her to share his clues and evidence with the police. If she couldn't control him and he broke the law by entering the house or in any other way, she could still call the police and have him arrested. She decided to go with him, knowing it was probably a big mistake, but alone he might do something really foolish and get himself hurt or worse. After all, he was her patient and she had some responsibility for his well-being. She realized that she was beginning to feel some kind of emotion for him. Pity, she hoped.

***

Franklin and Dr. Ruth Klein walked down the corridor from Ruth's office to the side door of the building. Franklin put his finger to his lips and pointed at Ruth's shoes. Her heels were clicking on the tile floor. Ruth heaved a heavy sigh and took off her shoes. She shivered as she remembered the last time she removed her shoes in this corridor and hoped this evening would be less eventful.

Ruth walked in the shadows to appease Franklin's paranoia and carefully closed the car door with as little sound as possible. Franklin started his car and said, "Now that's the way to keep a low profile and make a clean getaway. I'm really quite good at this spy stuff." Ruth rolled her eyes and felt around in her pocket for the object that had become a prerequisite for all meetings with Franklin, her pepper spray.

As Franklin pulled out of the parking lot and turned north toward Silicon Springs Golf Course, the man in the dark-blue sedan at the end of the lot sat upright in his seat and started his engine. He waited until Franklin had cleared the lot, then turned on his lights and followed at a safe distance.

Franklin drove to Silicon Springs Golf Course and located the Radcliffe home from the address in the newspaper obituary. He continued past and parked his car four blocks away. He suggested that they climb fences and travel through backyards until they reached the house so that they wouldn't be noticed. Ruth had a better idea. She took his arm and walked down the sidewalk as if they were a couple just out for an evening stroll. It seemed a lot less strenuous and easier on her clothes.

When they reached the house, Ruth noticed a dark-blue sedan parked across the street and a second car just fifteen or twenty feet farther down the road. There was no reason why she should be suspicious, and she decided that both she and Franklin were so on edge that even a barking dog would probably frighten them enough to necessitate a change of underwear.

Franklin walked up to the home and placed his hand against the siding. Ruth would have laughed if she could have stopped her upper lip from trembling. Franklin began to walk to the back of the house. Ruth hissed for him to come back, and when he didn't, she ran to the backyard to find him. As she turned the corner, she stopped abruptly, almost tripping over her own feet. She saw Franklin and two other men standing in the shadows. One man was holding Franklin with one arm around Franklin's neck, and the other was twisting his arm behind his back. The other man shone a flashlight in Ruth's eyes and said, "Good evening, Dr. Klein. This is Detective Samuelsson. You may have noticed him sitting in your parking lot; I suspect you didn't. You must be Franklin Jameson. Samuelsson ran the plates on your car and called me just after you arrived at Dr. Klein's office."

Samuelsson placed a pair of handcuffs on Franklin's wrists while Lieutenant Peirce held out another set toward Ruth and said, "May I do the honors, Dr. Klein?"

"There is a very logical explanation for us being here. Actually, you'll laugh when you hear it," Ruth said.

"I'm looking forward to it, Doctor," he said. "I think I'll hear it at the police station."

"Wait, Lieutenant. We're here because Franklin has evidence that he believes will help solve Sylvia's murder, and he needed to see the house before he called to tell you what he knows."

"Why didn't *you* just call me?" Peirce asked. "I would have been glad to listen."

"I couldn't call you because of the Psychologist's Code of Conduct, and Franklin was afraid you might misunderstand and suspect him of the murder."

"Well, this little field trip seems to have defeated both your purposes. I do suspect him, and I don't think much of your conduct, psychologist or not."

"Please, Lieutenant, just let him see the murder scene. You have nothing to lose, and he may be able to tell you something that might help."

Lieutenant Peirce reached in his pocket, took out a key, and opened the lockbox on the wall next to the side door. He unlocked the door and swung it wide open, then motioned for Samuelsson to take Franklin into the house.

"Will I be needing these, Doctor?" he asked, waving the handcuffs in front of him.

***

Samuelsson held Franklin's shoulder, Franklin's hands cuffed behind him, as he climbed the stairs to the long hall leading to the master bedroom. Ruth followed, closely observing Franklin's reaction to his surroundings. He stopped several times on the stairs, causing Samuelsson, and, in turn, Ruth Klein and Lieutenant Peirce, to falter and almost run into him. Franklin closed his eyes and took long, deep breaths each time he stopped, apparently waiting for a sign or whatever psychic information he believed was forthcoming. Lieutenant Peirce leaned toward Ruth and whispered, "Great act. When do the voices start?"

Ruth turned and glared at the lieutenant.

"Do you really believe this crap?" the lieutenant asked.

Ruth was two steps above Peirce, facing him on the stairway. She towered more than head and shoulders over him.

"This man is under my care, Lieutenant, and I would appreciate a little understanding and some respect for his condition," she said just above a whisper.

Peirce craned his neck to look up at her and said, "This man is…"

He stopped, walked up one step, and turned to her again. This time he found himself about to talk to her throat. He took another step up, and they were finally face to face. "This man is a suspect in a murder investigation, and that is the way he will be treated."

Ruth pursed her lips, stepped up one step, and again forced him to look up at her six-foot-one-inch prominence.

"Being in a position of power is no reason to be disrespectful," she said in a slightly louder voice. Peirce bit his lip, climbed two steps above Ruth, and said in a louder voice, "For Christ's sake, you're a woman of science; you can't believe this crap."

Ruth clenched her fists, her cheeks red and quivering with anger. She turned, stomped up three steps, and shouted, "I think he's as nuts as you do, but that's no reason to humiliate him." She turned, and in a calm voice said, "Sorry, Franklin."

She then straightened her posture, raised her head so that her nose was almost even with her eyes, and slowly walked up the remaining steps with as much dignity as she could salvage.

***

Two halogen lamps on tripods left by the forensic team were the only lights in the master bedroom. Both brass nightstand lamps had been knocked over in the violence of the murder. The bloody bed linens and the debris from the broken window were gone, removed by a professional crime-scene cleaning service. A piece of plywood blocked the opening where Mortimer Banks had catapulted himself onto the garage roof on his way to his first abrupt meeting with Peirce and Holloway and his final abrupt meeting with a telephone pole.

"Can you take off these handcuffs?" Franklin asked, looking at Dr. Klein for support. "I need to touch things."

"Cuff his hands in front of him," Peirce said to Samuelsson. He then looked at Ruth and said, "That's the best I can do."

Ruth nodded to Franklin, and he accepted his fate without complaining.

Franklin walked around the bedroom, touching objects as he passed, with Samuelsson close behind. He stood in front of the broken footboard from the bed for almost a full minute, and then walked with his entourage into the bathroom. Franklin looked at the mirror, then stepped into the bathtub.

"This isn't right," he said.

"This is ridiculous," said Peirce. "Let's get out of here."

"What's not right?" Ruth interrupted.

"The whole thing isn't right, none of it," Franklin said. He seemed terribly confused and was holding his cuffed hands against his forehead.

"That's it, Samuelsson, take him outside." Peirce motioned to the hall.

"No, wait. Please give me one more minute."

Without waiting for Peirce to reply, she said, "Franklin, what specifically isn't right about the rooms?"

Peirce nodded at Samuelsson, who stepped back to give Franklin some room.

"Well, first, the mirror is the wrong shape—the one in my dream was rectangular; this is oval. There's no towel hook next to the tub. I hung my robe on a hook, and the bathtub is the wrong shape."

"What is he talking about?" Peirce asked.

"I dreamed of this murder a week before the night it happened. I saw it all, but the rooms were different. There was a four-poster bed, and the footboard was broken, but it was a different bed, not this one. It had carvings on the posts. The dresser was where it is now, but the stone fireplace was on the opposite wall. It's a very similar room, but it's not right."

"So you caused all this fuss over a dream that was similar to a murder you read about in the newspaper?" Peirce said to Franklin. "And you encouraged this fruitcake to come here and waste everybody's time?" he said to Dr. Klein. "I should arrest both of you for hindering an investigation and wasting police time. Samuelsson, take off his cuffs and get him out of here. We have a murder to solve."

Franklin backed away from Samuelsson as he approached. "I know about the tattoo, the yellow rose tattoo on Sylvia Radcliffe's hip."

Peirce took a step toward him. "I told Dr. Klein about the tattoo; she probably told you."

"What about the 911 call, the anonymous call telling you where the body was hidden? That was me. I'm sure you could match my voice to the tape to prove it."

Ruth placed her hands on her head and shook it from side to side.

"Samuelsson," Peirce said, "I think it's time to read Mr. Jameson his rights. Dr. Klein, I'm considering whether or not to arrest you for obstruction of justice or aiding and abetting a criminal or hindering an investigation. I'm not sure what you did wrong, but I'm sure you did something."

"She didn't know," Franklin said. "I never told her that I called in the location of the body. All I told her about was a dream, and she had no right to tell anyone what I said."

Ruth Klein looked at Franklin and silently mouthed the words, *Thank you.*

"Dr. Klein, you can go for now, but I'll be asking for a statement in the near future. Don't leave town," Lieutenant Peirce said in a stern, businesslike tone.

As they walked outside, Ruth said, "You can reach me through my office, Lieutenant. Franklin, can I call someone for you? A lawyer perhaps." She looked at the lieutenant from the corner of her eye.

"Call my friend Hyrum Green; he'll want to help."

"The dentist in my building? I didn't know you were friends," she said, not knowing why it seemed odd to her.

"Just call him, he knows all about my dream," said Franklin. Samuelsson placed a hand on the top of Franklin's head, guided him into the backseat of Peirce's car, and slammed the door.

Ruth stood in the middle of the street as both unmarked police cars drove away.

"Hey, wait," she shouted. "I came here in Franklin's car."

She took her cell phone from her pocket to call a taxi. "Well, that's a perfect end to the evening."

Part 2

Thirty days before Sylvia's murder

The wildest colts make the best horses.
–Plutarch

21

Sylvia Radcliffe met Hyrum Green during a routine dental visit. He was gentle and kind and eased her pain. She was smart and sophisticated with a bit of a wild-child nature. She wore her skirts a few inches above the knee with thigh-high boots and fitted blouses that were just tight enough to slightly stretch across her breasts, giving any red-blooded man an opportunity to peek between the buttons at her expensive, lacy undergarment.

Maybe what attracted her most to Hyrum Green was the fact that she could never catch him looking. By her third dental appointment—an extraction, a cleaning, and a complaint of a slight toothache for which Hyrum could find no cause—she began to push the limits of modesty. She opened an additional button on her blouse, thus allowing a slightly better view of what she believed to be her best assets. She positioned herself in the chair so the view was available but not blatant enough to appear slutty. Dr. Green approached the dental chair and immediately placed a bib under her chin, totally obscuring the invitation.

Well, covering the patient with a bib was standard, but again she watched his eyes, and although they seemed to scan the vicinity, there was no recognition of the assets.

It's understandable; he's concentrating on finding this mystery toothache. She felt guilty about the ruse, but his indifference to her slightly erotic behavior was having a damaging effect on her self-esteem.

Her right hand was resting on the arm of the dental chair, and as he leaned over her to examine her teeth, his upper body lightly brushed her knuckles. Sylvia took this opportunity to ever-so-slightly raise her hand, exerting a small amount of pressure against his chest. Hyrum immediately shifted his position, creating several inches of space between them.

Well, he is married. He could be very dedicated to his wife.

Sylvia was now in a contest she did not want to lose. As he worked, she began to scoot down a little in the chair, which caused her skirt to rise just above her boots. No reaction. Now she shifted as though she were trying to get comfortable, and in the process she slid down so that her skirt was high enough on her thighs to almost show the bottom of her panties. Without looking down, Hyrum grabbed a second paper bib from his instrument tray, unfolded it, and placed it on her lap.

Oh, my God, he's gay. This had now become a considerable embarrassment. Sylvia enjoyed flirting and the occasional tryst with a married man; it boosted her ego. She thought of these dalliances as opportunities to hone her seduction skills, preparing for the day she would meet Mr. Right. On occasion her advances had been met with some indifference, but she had never struck out so completely before. She knew she should have switched to fat-free lattes and cut out that occasional pizza at the mall.

Hyrum said, "Excuse me," and walked from the examining room. Sylvia immediately reached under the bib and buttoned her blouse all the way to her chin and pulled her skirt to its original length. When he returned he said, "Well, Ms. Radcliffe, here is an appointment card for your next checkup. Let me know if you have any more trouble with that tooth." Sylvia jumped from the chair as soon as he removed the bibs and walked as quickly as possible to the outer waiting room. She looked at the card he had handed her and began to laugh.

"Is everything all right?" asked the receptionist behind the desk.

"I'm fine. I thought I had lost something, but I guess I didn't."

She read the card again: *I'll call you during the week. We could meet for coffee. You didn't have to try so hard. I was interested from the first button, Hyrum.*

***

Hyrum called Sylvia and asked her to meet him for a drink about a week after her dental appointment. She knew he was married and that this relationship couldn't develop into anything other than a short affair, but he had such wavy black hair and light eyes that always seemed to sparkle when he smiled, and he smiled most of the time. His hands were delicate but strong, and she liked the way they felt against her skin. They would meet at a local pub for a drink and inevitably end their evening either at a motel or sometimes make love in his car if they didn't have the patience or restraint needed to reach the motel. Hyrum was forceful, yet there was gentleness to his lovemaking, although you couldn't prove it by the damage he inflicted on Sylvia's wardrobe. She knew that this affair was wrong—it wasn't fair to his wife—but she just didn't care; it was an outlet, a release from her day-to-day cares.

The "business" Mort and Sylvia had started was stressful. She always worried that someone would connect the recent string of jewelry thefts to the jewelry store that she managed. Hyrum was a diversion from that constant worry. He was calm and self-assured. Sylvia was safe when she was with him. Not like the time she spent with Mort. Mort and Sylvia never had any romantic interest in each other. "He's my mother's boyfriend, for Christ's sake," she'd said when her sister, Emily, accused her of trying to seduce him. Yet she never thought of him as a surrogate father either. He was more like an arrogant older brother who always thought he knew what was best for her, but could be easily manipulated with a smile, or a pout, though on occasion she found a good old-fashioned "Are you fucking crazy?" worked just as well. Ultimately Mort did whatever she told him to do. He was very skilled at the execution of the "job," but not the planning. The last time he did his own planning he spent twelve years behind bars.

Hyrum and Sylvia continued seeing each other once or sometimes twice a week. Since she was one of his patients, she would find excuses to stop by his office before her weekly therapy session with Dr. Klein. After all, they were in the same building. She would stop by to ask a question like "What kind of electric toothbrush should I buy?" or "Did I leave my phone book here on my last visit?" Some of her makeshift justifications for visiting must have seemed pretty lame because his dental hygienist, Michelle Ackerman, became suspicious. Each time Sylvia stopped by to see Hyrum, Michelle would stare and then look away when Sylvia met her eyes. At first she thought Michelle was jealous and wanted Hyrum for herself, but he assured Sylvia that he and Michelle had no personal involvement, only business.

Still, this presented a problem on several levels. First, if Michelle told Hyrum's wife of their affair, his marriage would be in jeopardy, not to mention the negative effect on Sylvia's reputation. Second, Michelle could cause Hyrum's wife to hire a private investigator who might accidentally find evidence of Sylvia's side business with Mort, an even worse disaster. Third, his wife might not leave him, but force him to end their affair, a result Sylvia was not quite ready to accept. So something needed to be done about Michelle.

Hyrum didn't seem to appreciate the seriousness of the situation. Either that, or he was afraid to approach Michelle about the subject. Sylvia called Hyrum from her cell phone as she arrived for her weekly session with Dr. Klein.

"I think she knows something."

"Who?"

"Michelle, your dental hygienist."

"What does she know?"

"Us, she knows about us. She keeps looking at me, and I can tell she knows."

"It's your imagination, Sylvia; she knows nothing."

"Talk to her, Hyrum. Talk to her today. Find out what she knows."

"Don't panic, I'm sure she doesn't have a clue, but I'll check before the end of the day."

"Please, Hyrum; I'm not the only one who has something to lose."

"I don't understand."

"You have your marriage to protect, and I have my reputation. I wouldn't want anyone delving into my past, and I'm sure you wouldn't want someone examining yours."

Hyrum was silent for several seconds. "What do you mean by that? What do you know about my past?"

"Ah, nothing. I didn't mean anything. It's just that everyone has something from their early life that they don't want exposed." Hyrum paused again while Sylvia bit her lip. She had said too much.

She could hear Hyrum breathing into the phone. Finally he said, "I said I'll talk to her.

See you tomorrow at seven thirty at the tavern?"

***

The next night, as they were leaving the tavern, Hyrum said, "You will be happy to know that I spoke to Michelle, and she is not going to be a problem. You were right about her suspecting that we were seeing each other, but we had a good, long conversation, and her friendship for me, and her wish that I remain happy, outweighed her perceived moral obligation to tell Elaine. She won't say a word."

"How can you be sure? She could change her mind tomorrow."

"No, she won't, and besides, she's leaving town for a few weeks. I gave her some time off, and she's going back to Colorado for a while. We can trust her."

Hyrum was confident that Michelle would keep their secret, but Sylvia couldn't leave that to chance. She would feel much more comfortable if she heard it herself from Michelle's lips.

***

Each night at about five thirty, Michelle Ackerman pulled into her driveway. She pressed the button on the remote garage door opener, parked, and closed the overhead door behind her. Sergeant, her big orange cat, would return home for his dinner after a day of roaming the streets, rummaging through the occasional garbage can, and discouraging any interlopers from upsetting the feline pecking order of the neighborhood. He would walk, head held high, to the kitchen door, where Michelle would greet him with the respect he was due and invite him in for his dinner. That is, if she didn't forget. Sergeant ran to the back door, sat, and waited. His tail flipped from side to side. Then he stood up on his hind legs and scratched at the door. Patience has never been a feline virtue.

The door rattled in the soft evening breeze; the cat's pawing and scratching was moving it. He hooked one paw around the edge and pulled. The door moved, and he squeezed in through the narrow opening.

First stop was the countertop that always held his bowl. He paced back and forth, waiting for Michelle—it was that patience thing again.

Soon Michelle entered the kitchen through the garage door carrying three grocery bags. She struggled to the counter and propped the bags against the backsplash.

"What are you doing here, Sergeant?" she asked. "Have you been in the house all day?"

Michelle scratched Sergeant's head and looked at the slightly ajar side door. She thought back, examining her memory of the last few minutes before she'd left for work that morning. She had put Sergeant out, and she was *sure* she had closed the door. Now she turned the knob and closed the door several times to see if it latched properly. It seemed to be working fine. Maybe she hadn't been quite *that* conscientious. The unexpected phone call from her boss may have been more distracting than she thought.

"I'd like you to come in early—now, if you can. I have something important to discuss with you."

He hadn't said what he wanted, but she knew. Hyrum's new girl-friend, Sylvia, had been staring at her with a hostile look, intimating that she thought Michelle was either jealous of her affair with Hyrum or about to expose their "relationship" to Hyrum's wife.

Of course, Michelle would do neither. She would simply add this indiscretion to the other offenses for which she was already blackmailing him. She would simply continue to take Hyrum's money to maintain her silence.

"What happened between us happened long ago," Hyrum had said that morning. "There is no longer any evidence, and there were no witnesses." Michelle knew that Hyrum was right. There was little she could do other than start a scandal. But even unproven accusations have their consequences, and she reminded him of that fact in no uncertain terms.

"I am the witness," she told him. "I was the one who was wronged. You hurt me, and you hurt my family. If I tell my story, your career will be over. No parent will send a child to you again."

Michelle wouldn't tell Hyrum's wife about this adultery or the other incident from their past for which she hated him. Destroying his marriage served no purpose, not while he was still paying. And she assured him that she expected their financial arrangement to continue until *she* decided to end it.

Michelle began unloading the groceries and thought about the trip she was about to take. She hadn't been back to Colorado in years. Her father had moved there shortly after her mother died. He never remarried and lived a small life on limited funds. Michelle sent him a monthly check, part of the blackmail money from Hyrum, to supplement his social security check. Her father's loneliness was another reason to hate Hyrum and to ensure that he never stopped paying. Michelle shook her head to clear away the pain of the past. There was much to do before her trip.

Sergeant sat on the counter, looking at the cabinet that held his box of food. If cats could communicate using telepathy, an ability many people believe they possess, he would have been fed by now.

A sound emanating from the second floor caused both Sergeant and Michelle to turn their heads toward the staircase. A man's voice, barely audible, was coming from her bedroom. Michelle opened the pantry door and grabbed the Louisville Slugger leaning against the doorframe. She had found the baseball bat at the Goodwill store and bought it for three dollars. She didn't play ball. The bat was intended to keep a single woman living alone safe from prowlers.

"Who's there?" she called. "I have a gun, and I'll use it."

Sergeant, sensing the distress in Michelle's voice, leaped from the counter and retreated to safety under a kitchen chair. Michelle, however, advanced, bat at the ready, and began to climb the stairs. With each step the voice became louder. She couldn't tell what he was saying, but there was nothing he could say that would justify his presence in her house.

Michelle reached the open bedroom door. She held the bat shoulder high and leaned into the doorway. Now the man's words became clear: "And if you call in the next ten minutes, we will include a second jar of Miracle Jewelry Cleaner at no cost. Just pay separate shipping and handling..."

Michelle set the bat against her shoulder and shut off the television. Hyrum's call this morning must have upset her more than she had thought. First she had failed to close the kitchen door after letting Sergeant out, and now she discovered she'd left the television on.

"Oh, Hyrum, I'm going to make you pay for this," she said with a smile.

Five minutes later the bat rested against the side of the dresser while Michelle packed for her trip. She shuttled outfits from the closet to the bed, then carefully folded each in an attempt to minimize their need for ironing when she arrived in Colorado. On the next trip to the closet, a man's hand slowly reached out, grabbed the bat by its handle, and pulled it behind the drape.

Michelle returned from the closet to find a stowaway in her suitcase. Sergeant had found the courage to join her in the bedroom and had worked his way into the middle layer of slacks and tops, undoing Michelle's careful handicraft.

"Sergeant!" she scolded. "You're not coming with me. Annabelle promised to take care of you while I'm gone. You like Annabelle, and you'll be right next door. She'll take good care of you; don't make me feel guilty for leaving you behind."

Michelle studied the cat's intense stare. "If I didn't know better, I would think you understood every word I'm saying."

Sergeant's ears perked up, and he raised his head. He was actually looking past Michelle at the movement of the drape behind her.

"I'll be back in two weeks. It won't be so bad." Sergeant arched his back as he saw the tip of the bat move out from behind the drape and rise up.

"Well, you don't have to make me feel bad about it. It's not like I'm giving you away."

Sergeant hissed, leaped from the suitcase, flinging clothes out, and ran out of the room.

"Hey, come back here. I would take you with me if I could. I still lo—"

Her last word was interrupted by the cracking sound of the bat against the side of Michelle's neck, a moment of silence, and then the thud of Michelle's body collapsing to the floor.

Sergeant stood under a kitchen chair and watched the man with the baseball bat carry Michelle down to the living room and sit her on the sofa. He arranged her hands in her lap and leaned her head, now angled at thirty degrees to her body, against the sofa back. Next the man walked into the kitchen, tapping the bat on the counter as he walked.

Sergeant crouched down. He stayed very still and only snapped his head up when startled by the chimes of the front doorbell. The man was also startled. He walked to the kitchen door and opened it without making a sound. He was about to leave when he noticed that he still had the bat in his hand. As he turned to lay the bat on the counter, Sergeant ran through the open door and hid under a holly bush next to the house.

***

Sylvia looked at the address on the folded scrap of paper on the passenger seat. The streetlights barely illuminated the numbers on the mailboxes. She drove slowly, studying each house. Hyrum had said that the situation was under control and that Michelle wouldn't be a problem, but something in his voice was unconvincing. Hyrum was her lover all right, but that didn't mean she trusted him unconditionally. No one received that honor from Sylvia without first earning it, and so far no one had.

Men lied, particularly married men. They lied to both their wives and their lovers. Hyrum had been too quick to dismiss the problem, and Sylvia was sure that there was something Hyrum wasn't telling her. Something she would have to find out for herself.

Two forty-eight, that was the number she was looking for. Sylvia pulled her car to the curb. It wasn't an elegant home, but it looked to be much more house than a dental hygienist should be able to afford. She made a mental note to research Michelle Ackerman's past and current finances.

Well, no use putting it off. If Michelle was going to be a problem, Sylvia would meet it head on as she did with everything in life. She walked to the front door and rang the doorbell. A set of Westminster chimes echoed through the house. Sylvia waited. Silence. Then she heard the faint sound of footsteps. Just a few at first, but soon the footfalls increased in frequency until they evolved into the cadence of a runner. She leaned toward the door to listen, but the sound wasn't coming from inside. Sylvia crouched down behind a hedge and closed her eyes. The rhythmic beats rose in volume and pounded in her brain. She feared being seen here, although she didn't know why. It was like walking down a dark street and being sure that someone was following you, even though you couldn't see anyone. Something bad was going to happen. Soon the steady patter began to diminish, and she peeked over the hedge. The jogger moved down the street with a measured pace while Sylvia's heart ran a four-minute mile. She took in long, slow breaths to try to control her over-whelming desire to leave, to run away and pretend she had never come here. What did she hope to accomplish by talking to Michelle anyway? The hood on the runner's sweatshirt was pulled up over his head, and the words "Pittsburgh Steelers" rippled across his back. The footsteps faded, becoming ever softer until she couldn't distinguish them from the rushing of the blood in her ears, and then the night was quiet again.

It seemed unlikely that both the living room and bedroom lights would be on and no one home, so Sylvia decided to walk around to the back of the house to see if Michelle could possibly be in the backyard. She stayed behind the bushes as she worked her way toward the back, still not comfortable with the prospect of being seen, and still not knowing why.

Her feet found the paving stones that connected the front walk to the rear of the house. She inched her way along the path in the dark. A loud screech and a hiss startled her. She put both hands over her mouth to stifle a shriek. An animal ran from just under her foot to the back door. The narrow slit of light from the kitchen widened as the cat clawed at the slightly ajar door. Sylvia walked toward the crack of light and pulled on the doorknob. The orange cat squeezed through into the kitchen.

"I hope you're Michelle's cat," she whispered as it ran toward the living room. Sylvia wouldn't normally walk into someone's home uninvited—that was Mort's job—but that feeling of something being terribly wrong was back again. She stuck her head in the door and softly called out, "Michelle?" There was no answer. Through the archway leading from the kitchen to the living room, Sylvia could see the tail and hindquarters of the cat. He seemed to be rubbing against something just out of her line of sight. Sylvia stepped carefully into the kitchen and closed the door.

The cat ran back and jumped to the counter, causing the Louisville Slugger to roll toward the edge. Sylvia lunged forward and caught the bat by its handle. Sergeant walked up and down the counter, purring. He lay on his side, then rolled on his back, exposing his belly.

"I'll bet you're her cat, and you haven't had your dinner yet." She scratched the animal's belly. The cat kept rubbing his chin against Sylvia's arm, but now her attention was elsewhere. From this angle she could see a shadow on the wall, a shadow cast by someone sitting on the living room sofa. So Michelle *was* home.

"I'm sorry to barge in," she said, "but your door was open and..." She approached the couch, and that old feeling came back again for a third time, but this time she knew what was wrong. Michelle was slumped down on the sofa seat, her eyes closed, and her arms limp at her sides. The bat dropped from Sylvia's hand and rolled across the floor. She placed two fingers against the side of Michelle's neck and felt for a pulse. At first she thought there was none, but as she held her fingers against the carotid artery, she could feel a faint movement. Sylvia put her ear close to Michelle's mouth and heard an almost imperceptible wheeze. She was alive.

Sylvia pulled her cell phone from her pocket and poked 911 on the digital keypad, then stopped before pressing *call*.

Several thoughts flashed through her mind at once. The jogger who had run by could have come from the back of the house; he could have been Michelle's attacker. Her second thought was even more disturbing: Hyrum Green was a Steelers fan. She had seen him, on many occasions, wearing a hooded Pittsburgh sweatshirt, just like the one worn by the jogger.

Sylvia didn't want to believe that Hyrum would try to kill Michelle. What reason would he have? Surely exposing their affair could make Hyrum's life difficult, but not difficult enough to warrant murder. If Hyrum did this, he had to have a bigger reason than was apparent, and if he *did* do it, an investigation into the murder would probably expose their relationship. Normally that would be inconvenient for Sylvia, but not devastating, unless...

If the police looked at Hyrum's lover as a possible accomplice to the murder, and if they dug deep enough, they might even expose the burglaries she and Mort committed as well. Calling 911 and having her phone traced to the scene of the crime would not be helpful either. This was becoming a nightmare.

Sylvia paced back and forth across the living room, trying to think. She sat in an armchair and stared at Michelle for several minutes. She jumped up. She couldn't just sit there and let a woman die. She took out her phone again and began to dial. Suddenly Michelle gasped and tried to raise her hand to her neck. Then, just as suddenly, she exhaled. It was a long, hissing exhale. Her eyes opened, and her body went limp. It was over. Sylvia stuffed her phone back into her pocket. She was surprised at how calm she felt. She needed to stay calm until she was safely away with no trace that she had ever been here.

Sylvia thought about calling Mort to get his advice. Mort was very experienced at removing all traces of his presence at a crime scene. She speculated, if *he* had killed Michelle, which of course he hadn't, he would know how to dispose of the body and cover his tracks. But if she called him, he might think that *she* was responsible for Michelle's death, and he could use that knowledge as leverage against her in the future. No, she couldn't tell him she was here or that she suspected Hyrum.

Then she had an idea, a brainstorm that might cause Mort to unwittingly solve her problems for her. *What if Mort thought he killed Michelle? What would he do? He would probably clean up the murder scene and then get as far away as possible.* Of course there was always the chance that he might be caught, and the police might still find a path to her, but he was a professional. That was less of a risk than if they found clues and investigated Hyrum. Sylvia quickly formulated a plan. If it worked, Mort would believe that he killed Michelle, but it would only work if she could get him here tonight. She took out her cell phone and speed-dialed his number.

"Mort, I have a job for you. Meet me at the usual place at seven thirty. You need to do the job tonight." She hung up the phone before she gave him a chance to object. She would have to hurry. She looked at her watch: 5:35. She had less than two hours to prepare and much to do before she met Mort at the bar.

***

Mortimer Banks, alias Mortimer Schmidt, carried the small black burlap bag to the bed in his one-room apartment and dumped out its contents. He carefully checked to see if he had everything he needed: a blank plastic card the size and thickness of a credit card, a cordless screwdriver with assorted tips, a set of bent wire lock picks, a pry bar, a glass cutter, rubber gloves, about ten feet of copper wire, and a small pruning saw. He walked to the dresser and reached into the top drawer. Mort opened a package of nylon stockings, pulled one over his head, and faced the mirror. His low-pitched laugh sounded eerie as it passed through the fibers. Mort studied his masked face for a moment. The pressure of the nylon on his features distorted them beyond all recognition and made him look evil. It was good, and he snorted with pleasure. He repacked the bag with his tools and mask. He was ready.

Mort had been a cat burglar for a good part of his life. He was very skilled and extremely successful until one day when a man walked in on him before he could escape through an open window. In the struggle, Mort took quite a beating. His nose was broken as well as a few ribs. Unfortunately for both of them, the man who had just kicked his ass fell over and died of a heart attack. Mort lost the fight but won fifteen to twenty in a New York State prison for manslaughter.

He decided that one major mistake in his life was enough, and he worked hard to prove he was rehabilitated. He became a trustee of the prison and pushed the book and magazine cart through the cell blocks.

He volunteered for a road crew. The digging and raking was hard work, but it reminded him of his early years working as a gardener, and it helped the time pass. His new positive attitude and cooperative behavior won him parole after just twelve years. As a reward for his impressive rehabilitation, he was given a new suit of clothes, a room in a halfway house, and help finding a job bussing tables at a local Denny's Restaurant. Mortimer Schmidt had turned over a new leaf; he had a new beginning.

Now, three years later, his name was Mortimer Banks. The new leaf had lasted for just about two weeks. Mort violated parole by leaving the state. He changed his name from Schmidt to Banks and started over in Pennsylvania—but this time he would be a whole lot smarter.

Mort grabbed the black bag from the bed, took his car keys from the hook next to the door, lit a cigarette, and walked out of his apartment.

***

Sylvia sat at a small round table in the corner of the darkened bar nursing a scotch, neat. Headlights from passing cars on the boulevard shone through the large plate-glass window and migrated across the backs of the neighborhood patrons as they sat on their barstools. She pulled a gold case from her vintage Christian Dior handbag, took out a long filtered cigarette, tapped it on the table a few times to compact the tobacco, and placed it between her lips. A man's hand suddenly appeared, holding a silver-plated cigarette lighter. She didn't look up. She drew the flame into her cigarette and slowly exhaled a long stream of smoke.

"Can I buy you a drink?" the man asked.

"Thank you, but I'm waiting for someone," she said, barely glancing in the man's direction. He nodded and walked toward the bar.

A woman in her early thirties sat on her barstool sipping her beer from a longneck bottle. Sylvia watched the woman's reflection in the mirror behind the bar. Her hair was long, bleached, and slightly tangled as it hung over her open cloth coat. Sylvia supposed that Blondie was ready to leave with any man who would buy her dinner and drinks.

The woman looked at each man who passed her seat and smiled, then turned back to her beer as the men kept walking. She reminded

Sylvia of her mother and how she must have dealt with men at that age. She took pleasure as it came and never seemed to have a plan that carried her past tomorrow morning, wherever and with whomever she awoke. For all she knew, Sylvia's father may have been a man who just happened by when her mother was in need of a light for her cigarette and offered to buy her the next drink. She hated her mother for raising her in poverty, but she also pitied her, as she now pitied the feckless matron at the bar.

She wondered about this woman's life. She supposed that if her luck matched her appearance, she would return to her three-room apartment when she either became tired of waiting for Mr. Right or her money ran out. She would probably watch *The Price Is Right* on television and fall asleep in her clothes on the couch. Her kids, maybe two little girls, would have to fend for themselves, and in her absence, they would make their own meals and sometimes shoplift when they needed school supplies or just wanted something pretty to wear. She pictured them sitting in their room, ears pressed against the door, listening to their mom "entertaining" the latest man she brought home. They would pray that he wouldn't be mean to her and that she wouldn't be angry and yell at them because her night didn't turn out as expected. She probably never had dinner with her girls, asked them about school, or held them close when they were frightened or just lonely, but at least they'd grow up tough and resourceful. They'd learn to make their own way in the world. To take what they needed and have little concern for others. Yes, she both hated and pitied this woman.

Sylvia watched the bartender point to the woman's empty beer bottle. The woman frowned, opened her purse and rummaged through it for a moment, and then waved off the bartender with a shake of her head. Sylvia raised her hand to attract the bartender's attention, pointed to the woman on the stool, held up her own check, and nodded.

The bartender handed the woman another beer and pointed to Sylvia when she looked at him questioningly. The woman turned toward Sylvia and smiled. Sylvia barely acknowledged the smile with a nod and turned away as she sniffed and secretly wiped a small tear from her eye.

***

Mortimer Banks stood in the middle of the bar and carefully scanned the patrons. His eyes brightened when he found Sylvia at the corner table. He swaggered over to her. He turned a chair away from the table, straddled it, and sat down. Mort waved his arm at the bartender. "Club soda." Then he turned back to Sylvia. "I'm working tonight, right?"

"Two forty-eight Walden Avenue," Sylvia said.

"What am I after, and what time will the place be empty?"

"It won't be empty," she said, not making eye contact. "A woman will be home alone."

"You're nuts," Mort said, throwing down the paper on which he had written the address. His pretense of joy at seeing her had now dissolved. "I'm not doing it. It's always my neck on the line, and you always take half of the prize. I don't need to run into some housewife with her husband's shotgun just because you want her ring. What else have you got?"

Mort had been showing signs of dissatisfaction with their arrangement for some time now. He played along because the information Sylvia collected about each job was valuable, and because he was seeing her mother, but the information was not valuable enough, nor her mother good enough in bed, to take this unwarranted risk.

"I need this, Mort," she said, now looking directly in his eyes and holding his hand on the table. "You have to help me."

"What's the story?" Mortimer asked, still not convinced.

"This woman is ruining my life, and I need her gone. I want you to scare the piss out of her. Send her running back to Colorado."

"You want me to scare her? What do I get out of this?"

Mort stood, bending toward Sylvia, both his palms flat on the table, his face within inches of hers. "If you want her gone," he whispered, "you get rid of her. I've wasted enough time working with you. I'm going back out on my own." Mort straightened and turned to leave.

"I wouldn't do that if I were you, Mr. Schmidt."

Mort stopped and walked back to the table.

"Be very careful what you say next," he said through clenched teeth.

"I didn't mean anything by that," Sylvia said, again not meeting his eyes. "I really need the favor. I'll make it up to you on the next job. I'll raise your cut."

"What did she do to you—steal your guy or something?"

"Not exactly," Sylvia said. "She knows about me and a friend, and she threatened to tell his wife."

"Making threats can get you in a lot of trouble," Mort said, catching her eye and maintaining his stare.

"She pissed me off, Mort. I want her gone." Sylvia smiled and reached out for his hand again. If threats wouldn't work, maybe charm would. Mort pulled his hand away but decided this was not the time or place for this argument. He would humor her this one last time. Things would change when this job was over, but he didn't need to tell her that now. He sat back down at the table.

"What if she calls the cops as soon as I leave?"

"Scare her good and send her packing, and you won't have to worry about that. It's just another burglary, Mort," she said, whispering now. "The newspapers are full of home invasions. She'll just think she was unlucky enough to be home when her house was being robbed. Tell her if you see her again, you'll hurt her. You could be scary enough to send anyone packing. I've made a lot of money for you over the last year—give me this."

Mort resented Sylvia's attitude. He was the one who made money for *her*. It was his skill that made this partnership work. But, again, he would avoid this discussion and resolve the problem later in his own way.

"I don't like it, but I'll do it this one time."

"Thanks, Mort. Now do it tonight," she said, smiling at her victory.

Sylvia opened her handbag and removed a folded piece of paper containing the product of her prerobbery research and handed it to him.

"Who's this guy in the hooded Eagles sweatshirt you say to watch out for?"

"I don't know, just a jogger who passes her house between eight and eight thirty each night. He's pretty consistent. I saw him from my car as I checked out the neighborhood. Don't let him see you." She had seen a jogger, but the rest of the story was window dressing.

"I'm a ghost," said Mort. He refolded the paper, stuffed it into his pants pocket, and strolled out of the bar.

***

Mort sat in his car and took a slightly bent cigarette from the open pack on the passenger seat, straightened it with his fingers, and placed it in his mouth. He flipped up the top of his lighter and brushed the flint wheel with a snap of his fingers to light the flame. It was more dramatic than simply stroking the wheel with his thumb, and besides, he thought it looked cool.

When it didn't light, he closed the cover and shook the lighter several times, then attempted to light it again. No joy. He held the misbehaving lighter in his palm and stared at it for a moment. He took in a deep breath and with a guttural cry smashed the lighter into the dash. The lighter fell to the floor near his right foot, and he began to stomp the little metal object into the floorboard. He closed his fists and pounded the steering wheel with both hands and roared, "That bitch is going to get me killed."

A man who happened to be walking by the car tapped on the window and said, "Are you all right?"

Mort glared at the man and pushed his door open, knocking the man back a few steps. Mort stood behind the open door and said, "Walk away—walk away now!"

The man turned and quickly walked away, almost running, and never looked back.

***

Two hours later Mort drove through the streets of Michelle's housing development, looking for just the right place to park. The neighborhood was reasonably quiet and had tall oak and maple trees lining the streets. The light from the lampposts cast spots of daylight on each street corner, and Mort was uncomfortable leaving his car where it may stand out to residents as an unfamiliar vehicle. "There it is," he said in a low voice.

On the street in front of him were nine or ten cars all parked at the curb in close proximity to one house. All the lights in the house were on, and from the sounds emanating from the home, a party was in progress. Mort parked at the curb just past the row of cars and out of reach of the light cast by the nearest lamppost, his car now becoming that of just another partygoer.

Mort checked his wristwatch; it was 9:00 p.m. The jogger in the hooded Eagles sweatshirt that Sylvia had warned him about should be back at home by now, hopefully in for the rest of the night. Mort reached under his seat and pulled out a plastic bag. He unfolded a new Eagles hooded sweatshirt and slipped it over his head. He put several items from his black burglary bag into his pockets and waistband, checked to see that no one was on the street, and began to jog the five blocks to Michelle's house.

Mort kept his head down and his hood up as he traveled along the quiet street, the vapor from his breath visible in puffs that dissolved in the night air as he jogged. He would raise his hand to wave at passersby, and more often than not, they would wave back. He smiled at his own cleverness. *What rubes these people are,* he thought.

When he reached her house, he ducked into the shadow of a tall bush and worked his way into the backyard. There were lights on in the house, but the yard leading to the back door was dark, giving him plenty of cover. Peeking out from behind a tall evergreen tree next to the porch, he studied the lock on the back door. Even from this distance of fifteen feet, he could see that this would be an easy entry. He took the blank plastic credit card from his pocket and crept to the door.

The door opened into a small kitchen. It was dark except for the light from the digital clock on the range, and the room had a slight smell of disinfectant. All the counters were empty. There were no dishes in the sink or pots on the stove. He wiped his feet before entering, more to preserve the kitchen's neat, clean appearance than to eliminate any evidence of his presence. He moved silently through the kitchen toward the light from the open archway to the living room.

On the floor just a few feet from the opening to the living room were three tan suitcases. Two stood closed and one was open, partially filled with clothes. He bent down to feel the soft silk of a pink night-gown between his rough fingers. He lifted the nightgown to his face to drink in the scent of the woman he had come to see, but it smelled only of laundry detergent. Disappointed, Mort dropped the nightgown and listened for the homeowner. He assumed she had gone back to the bedroom for more items to pack.

He started up the stairs and froze as a step creaked under his foot. He heard no sound and saw no movement from above. As he approached the bedroom door, he still could not see his target, but a shadow dancing across the bed told him that she was in the room. He pulled his stocking mask down over his face and quickly stepped into the bedroom. He stood up tall, trying to look as big and as menacing as he could. To his surprise, the room was empty.

He looked around, trying to determine where she had gone. On the left side of the room, he saw an open door. At first he thought it must lead to a bathroom or a walk-in closet, but as he looked more carefully, a chill ran down his spine. Through the open door he could see what appeared to be a hallway, a hallway with the same rug and wallpaper as the hall he'd just left. He tensed and prepared to turn and move back to the door, but it was too late. Before he could complete his turn, the wind was knocked from his lungs by a blow to his side. He dropped to his knees. Next a sharp pain exploded in the left side of his head. Then everything was black.

Mort opened his eyes and tried to remember where he was. He was lying facedown on the bedroom carpet, his head pounding. He reached up and felt a lump the size of a baseball. When the spinning room slowed and his vision cleared, he saw a pair of eyes staring back at him from the floor, only inches from his face. They were wide-open eyes, but lifeless eyes. *She must be the woman I came to frighten into leaving. The woman Sylvia was afraid would cause trouble.* She would cause a different kind of trouble now. In her right hand was a baseball bat. The one Mort assumed hit him. His attention was now drawn to her neck. It was purple, and her head was resting at a grotesque angle to her body. He sat on the floor staring at his hands, trying to understand how he could have done this. He looked at his watch; it was eleven thirty. He must have been out for almost two hours. The more he looked at the body, the angrier he became.

Sylvia should never have sent him here. There was nothing to steal, nothing to gain. He shouldn't have listened to her. He needed to figure out what to do. This killing was Sylvia's fault. She was responsible.

***

Mort sat on the floor of Michelle's bedroom and cursed Sylvia for putting him in this situation. Michelle was dead. There was nothing he could do about that now. He rubbed the sore spot on his head and looked at his fingers for traces of blood. There was barely a drop, and none on the carpet. That was a good start. His head was still spinning, and he couldn't remember anything between being hit from behind and waking to find Michelle dead on the floor in front of him.

Mort's first impulse was to call Sylvia, but that might not be the smart play. If she were here, he would wring her neck, but calling and threatening her on the telephone would just give her a motive and the opportunity to turn him in to the police just to save her own skin. He was a wanted man in New York, and he was sure that Sylvia could arrange to have him arrested for parole violation, if not for this murder, without implicating herself. *She's a crafty bitch*, he thought.

Sylvia was his partner in the burglaries and he was sure that she wouldn't want to lose him as a source of income, but murder was a whole different story. Sylvia would avoid involvement in this business at all cost. He would be on his own if he got caught, and with his criminal record, he'd be lucky if they didn't give him life without parole. No, calling Sylvia would not be the smart play.

Instead, Mort decided to cover any traces of having been in the house and get far away as quickly as he could. He had to get rid of the body, of course, and remove any signs of a struggle. The woman was taking a trip, so she probably wouldn't be missed until he was well out of town.

He could tell Sylvia that he made Michelle believe she was in the wrong place at the wrong time as her house was being burglarized. He could tell her that Michelle was so frightened by him that she promised to leave the state and never come back. He could say how he threatened her, and how she pleaded for her life and swore she wouldn't call the police or tell anyone. He could even say she offered him her jewelry and cash if he would just let her leave unharmed. That sounded good to him.

Now that he had a plan, he began to inspect the bedroom for any evidence that might incriminate him. He moved her body into the hall and searched her closet and dresser for personal items. He found a cardboard box in the hall closet and filled it with all her possessions that had not already been packed in the suitcases on the living room floor.

As Mort walked down the stairs from Michelle's bedroom, a small panel in the ceiling of her closet silently began to rise, revealing an access passage through the closet ceiling to the attic. Next, two feet and then a pair of legs introduced a figure in dark clothing lowering carefully to arm's length and then dropping with catlike grace to the closet floor. Two eyes peering through holes in a black ski mask peeked through the louvered doors, found the way clear, and entered the room.

Mort was oblivious to the *clunk, clunk, clunk* sound made by Michelle's head hitting each step as he dragged the body feetfirst down the uncarpeted flight of stairs. He held both of her feet locked tightly under one of his arms and carried the cardboard box filled with her belongings on his opposite shoulder. *Clack, clack, clack* went the sound of her ring as her trailing hand struck each baluster on the way down to the living room.

Mort was now mumbling and making unintelligible sounds interspersed with fits of profanity and the occasional stomping of his feet. He dropped the cardboard box to the floor with a crash, sending hair brushes and jars of face cream bouncing and rolling across the living room and disappearing under the furniture. He groaned as he lifted the body and dumped her, facedown, on the sofa, leaving one shoeless foot hooked on the sofa back and one arm dangling down toward the carpet.

Mort lay on his back on the floor, stretching his arm under the sofa to retrieve the runaway beauty products. He then executed a verbal tirade, accusing them of intentionally trying to evade him, and threatened them with their eminent destruction if they didn't immediately submit to his attempts at their recapture. As he jostled the couch, stretching the full length of his arm, Michelle's hand fell that extra inch, causing it to brush across his cheek. Startled by the now cold touch, Mort jumped to his feet, almost tipping the sofa on its back. He caught it just in time and settled it back to the floor. He stood looking at the facedown body, not quite knowing what to do. First he took the dangling left hand and tucked it under her hip to keep it secure. After a moment's reflection, he felt guilt for placing her in what appeared to him to be a suggestive pose. He pulled out the hand and placed it under her chest, but felt no better about the mental image that conjured up either. Finally he bent the elbow and placed the hand under her cheek as if she were resting. This seemed acceptable, and he went on with his scavenger hunt.

The figure from the closet listened to Mort's antics and stifled a laugh. Then the intruder moved to the bed at the far end of the room without making a sound and carefully pulled down the covers. Next, the sheets and blankets were rumpled and twisted to look as though the bed had been recently used. With care, the intruder lay down to make a depression in the bedclothes. A slight squeak from a bedspring made the intruder freeze in place in the center of the bed. Without even risking a breath, the intruder listened for any activity from Mort on the first floor. Mort's footsteps moved closer to the stairs. The prowler sat up, ready to bolt back to the closet, but then Mort's footsteps receded back into the kitchen.

The masked intruder stood and admired the state of disarray of the bed. It looked as though someone may have struggled to fend off an attacker. All it needed now was the finishing touches. The agile prowler removed a folded piece of paper from a hip pocket and carefully opened it. It contained three black hairs that had been plucked from Mortimer Banks's head while he was unconscious. The stealthy interloper took a hair between two fingers and held it up to the light, smiling and nodding at the tiny root, still intact, on the end of the hair. The three hairs were then placed near the pillow where they might have fallen if they were pulled from an assailant's head during a struggle. The picture was almost complete.

Next, that same hip pocket produced a plastic bag containing the blank credit card that Mort used to slide between the lock and the frame of the kitchen door to gain entry. The intruder removed the card from the bag, holding it by its edges. Two full fingerprints and a partial print were clearly visible on the smooth face of the card. The rectangular piece of plastic was then placed on the floor just under the bed where it might have fallen without notice during a struggle.

Mort was still cursing and mumbling in the living room as he retraced his steps on the first floor to ensure that he'd left no sign of his presence. He finished Michelle's packing and closed the suitcases. He wiped down everything he remembered touching using a kitchen dish towel, which he then stuffed into his sweatshirt pocket.

The intruder stood in the bedroom peeking out of the doorway to watch Mort's progress with the cleanup. Mort was now rummaging through the kitchen counter drawers, looking for something. Suddenly he turned and started walking toward the stairs. The intruder quickly ducked back into the bedroom and looked at the closet with its access to the attic. There wouldn't be enough time to get through the door, open the ceiling hatch, and climb to safety.

Near panic, the intruder dashed to the bed and was about to roll under, but stopped. The room no longer looked as it did when Mort left it. Mort would know someone had been here, and under the bed would be the first place he'd look. Mort had been bested the first time by getting hit from behind, but this time the element of surprise would be forfeited the second Mort reached the doorway and saw the unmade bed. In a fair fight, Mort would be a formidable adversary—particularly for the slender prowler.

Just as Mort reached the center of the stairs, the intruder spied the baseball bat leaning against the wall where Mort had placed it when he moved the body. The intruder stood behind the door and held the bat ready to strike Mort a second time when he entered the bedroom. The plan was to hit him hard and run from the house before he came to his senses.

With a pounding heart, a heaving chest, and every muscle tensed, the prowler waited for Mort to enter the room. Several seconds passed, but Mort didn't appear.

The waiting was agonizing. The prowler raised the bat and stopped breathing, listening for the footsteps that would start the war. The bat was beginning to shake, and the intruder worried that it might knock against the wall and alert Mort.

Then the intruder exhaled and lowered the bat as Mort's footsteps were heard descending the stairs back down to the living room. The prowler lay on the floor and looked through the balusters of the railing just in time to see Mort take Michelle's car keys from an ashtray on the coffee table.

Mort entered the garage through the door in the hall and loaded the body, suitcases, and the refilled cardboard box into the trunk of Michelle's car. He had to slam the trunk several times, cursing and kicking it, to smash down its contents enough to make it latch. When he regained his composure, he took a last look at the kitchen and the living room and opened the garage door.

Mort drove the car out of the garage and used the remote control clipped to the visor to close the door behind him. At the sound of the door closing, the intruder ran gracefully down the stairs, stepped up to the living room window, and removed the black ski mask. With a shake of her head, long black hair cascaded to her shoulders.

"Perfect," said Sylvia.

***

Mort turned onto the two-lane road that led out of the development and toward the interstate. The streetlights along the road were far apart, which gave him the cover of darkness for most of the ride through the suburban streets. He was so angry that he feared losing control and flooring the gas pedal to speed away. To help suppress his rage, he punched the ceiling of the car as hard as he could. The pain helped him focus on his tasks—dispose of the body and then hide the car. He drove slowly and remained alert for police.

The kitchen door to Michelle's house slowly opened. Sylvia looked left, then right, and slipped into the backyard. She ran a few steps and vaulted over the short fence to the adjoining property and dashed to the gate at the far side of the house. Just outside the gate, sitting at the curb, was the Suzuki Hayabusa motorcycle she had parked there just three hours before. She unlocked the cable holding her helmet, strapped it in place, and mounted the bike. The engine sprang to life with a high-pitched whine, and within seconds she was slowly cruising two blocks behind Mort as he drove Michelle's little red car. She kept her distance and followed until he came to a stop near an abandoned strip-mine pit. Sylvia continued past the parked car for about a quarter of a mile and stopped behind a dune of coal. She then ran back to the pit, keeping out of sight among the small trees and bushes that lined the road.

Sylvia squatted behind a bush and watched Mort place Michelle's body at the foot of a pile of loose stones and then climb the pile and kick stones down until he started a mini avalanche that completely covered the body. Satisfied that his work was done, he returned to the car and drove off. Sylvia raced to her motorcycle and resumed her clandestine chase. Shortly after, Mort pulled into the local municipal airport parking lot, wiped down the car to remove any fingerprints, and walked to the terminal taxi stand. He took no notice of the black-clothed figure bending low to the motorcycle's handlebars and speeding past on her way back to the highway.

***

Sylvia rode back to the city, to the apartment she kept under her birth record name of Laura Carpenter. She parked her Suzuki in her garage and drove her car back to her house in Silicon Springs.

So far the plan was going well. She was still upset about the outcome for Michelle; she didn't deserve to die, or for her body to be so disrespected. To be dumped in a strip mine with no proper burial and no loved ones to grieve for her was despicable. That could all change by tomorrow. A phone call from Sylvia to the police would solve most of her remaining problems. Sylvia thought hard about exactly what she would say to the police. She could give them the location of the body, and that would start the ball rolling. Once they identified Michelle's body and investigated at her house, the evidence Sylvia had planted would make Mort the prime suspect. Mort was smart enough to know that no matter how careful he was, there was always some piece of evidence that could trip him up. Of course he didn't know that she had planted enough evidence to put him on death row. *He was probably two states away by now*, she thought, and would never be seen again.

Or, she could call the police and anonymously report Michelle missing. She would have to alter her voice somehow and call from a telephone that was untraceable, but that could be arranged.

The police would do nothing for at least seven days, and that would give Mort plenty of time to get out of town. She'd coax him to leave if he was foolish enough to think he wouldn't get caught. That might be a better plan.

22

Sylvia stepped out of the shower and began to dry her hair. The smell of coconut-scented conditioner and a brisk massage of her scalp helped calm her. She tilted her head from side to side to release tension from the muscles of her neck and shoulders, stopping abruptly when she noticed the reflection of her naked body in the mirror. She smiled, pleased with the trim, supple woman looking back at her. Sylvia dropped the bath towel to the floor, drew in a deep breath, expanding her chest, and ran her hands along the smooth skin on her flat belly and narrow waist. She turned slightly sideways to admire the shape of her buttocks in profile. *Forty is only a state of mind,* she thought. Sylvia wrapped her hair in a white towel, tucked in the ends to form a turban, and slipped into her terrycloth bathrobe, never taking her eyes off the woman in the mirror.

A sound from her bedroom interrupted her narcissism. At first she thought a gust of wind had closed the bedroom closet door, but it was a cold evening, and all the windows were closed.

"Is someone there?" she called. No response. Perhaps it had been a falling tree limb or a passing truck, she thought. She remembered not long ago being startled by the sound of a golf ball striking the side of the house, dimpling the siding. It was one of the hazards of living in a golfing community, but even the local zealots wouldn't be out playing this late in freezing weather.

Sylvia opened the bathroom door only a few inches and peeked out. The closet was still open; that wasn't it. Everything seemed to be as she'd left it. The noise must have come from outside the house. Nothing to cause concern.

There was a loud creak on the stairs, and her heartbeat quickened. She closed the bathroom door, pushed the button on the handle to lock it, and stepped back. Sylvia wrapped her robe tightly around her body and knotted the belt. She paced across the bathroom floor, not yet fully believing that someone was in her house, but sufficiently convinced to keep the door locked until she was positive. For more than a year, at her direction, Mort had been breaking into houses at least once a month, roaming through the homes at will, and taking anything he desired. She now began to feel the violation those homeowners must have experienced, knowing that the security of their belongings—or more importantly, their personal safety—could not be guaranteed by a locked door.

Sylvia leaned out the bathroom window and looked left and right. The streetlamp at the curb illuminated the sidewalk twenty feet below—there were no passersby. *Doesn't anyone walk their dog anymore?* She thought about jumping from the window, but at that height, she probably risked more injury from the fall to the concrete walkway than from confronting the prowler.

Sylvia pressed her ear to the door and listened for any sounds of movement in the bedroom. The silence was encouraging.

Maybe this was all just her imagination. Sylvia carefully turned the doorknob to unlock the door while holding the button in so that it wouldn't make a click as it popped out. She peeked around the partially open door into a dark bedroom. The room hadn't been dark when she had looked through the doorway just a few minutes ago. She guessed that a light bulb could have burned out, but it was too much of a coincidence to believe.

Sylvia opened the bathroom door just wide enough to slip through. The bedroom appeared empty.

She moved along the wall to the dresser and leaned against it while she studied the room, considering every corner as a potential hiding place. The room was quiet and still. Things seemed normal enough, other than the darkness, of course. Her courage began to return. Barefoot, she crept to the nightstand and picked up the telephone receiver. She waited for the dial tone that never sounded. Her hands explored the bed, groping through the rumpled covers for her handbag with her cell phone inside. The bag was gone.

Her breathing was now extremely rapid and shallow; she began to feel faint. Sylvia concentrated on breathing deeply to retake control of her racing heart.

Maybe he's gone, she thought. *He has my bag, and God knows what else. Maybe he's taken all he wants, and he's gone.* Sylvia reached for the thin brass lamp that sat on her nightstand next to the phone. She turned the switch on the lamp. Nothing. She gently pulled on the lamp cord and found it loose from the wall. Plugging it back into the outlet behind the bed would be difficult and would put her in a vulnerable position during the attempt. She could use more light, but right now she had a better use for the lamp. She unscrewed the cap to remove the lamp shade, unscrewed the bulb, and held the metal lamp in her fist. If she couldn't use it to light her way, she could use it as a club. Sylvia wrapped the lamp cord around her hand to secure her grip. She gave it a few shakes and swung it in the air a few times. The feel and the weight of the metal lamp swishing through the air gave her confidence. "Where are you, you bastard?" she whispered.

With a weapon now in her hand, she moved to the door leading to the hallway and reached for the wall switch. She paused. If she couldn't see him, he probably couldn't see her either. Since he was most likely stronger, she would have a better chance in the dark.

Sylvia crouched at the top of the stairs. She held the lamp over her head and listened for the slightest sound, ready to pummel whoever had been arrogant enough to break into her house. From the middle of the stairs, she could see into the living room and part of the kitchen. With her eyes now accustomed to the dark, and with the small amount of light from the lamppost on the street filtering in through the windows, she saw that the rooms were empty. However, a light *was* shining into the hallway just off the kitchen. The light was coming from the garage.

Sylvia entered the kitchen walking on the balls of her bare feet, ready to run at a moment's notice. With a shaking hand, she pulled an eight-inch chef's knife from the kitchen rack. Now armed with two weapons, Sylvia approached the door to the garage. The exterior door leading from the garage to the street was open as well. Sylvia let out a long sigh of relief. She laughed and mumbled, "Now I know how it feels to be robbed."

Sylvia was glad that her relationship with Mort had finally ended. They'd had a good run of luck. Getting out now was the right thing to do. The robberies she and Mort had committed had amassed a small fortune in jewelry and cash. Mort had sold most of the loot through contacts he had made while in prison or during his early years. She knew their luck couldn't last. Sooner or later Mort would slip up and get caught. Then, if the police offered him a deal, he might sell her out.

Sylvia smiled. Her plan that caused Mort to believe *he* had killed Michelle in a fit of blind rage was a stroke of genius. Mort knew that Sylvia could put him at the scene on the night of the murder. No, he wouldn't want her implicated at all. An arrest for burglary was bad enough, but a murder...As long as she could hold the murder over his head, he wouldn't dare implicate her in the burglaries.

Sylvia had already established a second identity using her birth name, Laura Carpenter, and most of her money was now stored in a safe place. All that was left to do was cover her departure so that no one would look for her. She chastised herself for having started the affair with Hyrum. Had they not gotten involved, she would have already planned her exit. Now there was an additional complication.

Sylvia closed and locked both doors, and placed the knife back in the rack. As she walked back up the stairs to her bedroom, she laughed out loud at the thought of being considered a criminal. It was Mort who robbed houses and stole jewelry. All she did was make information available to him, and split the profits, of course. The thought suddenly crossed her mind that Mort might not be satisfied with his share of the loot. After all, he did take most of the risk, and if he found out that she had fooled him into thinking that he killed Michelle...No, she dismissed the thought and continued up the stairs to her bedroom.

It had been a daunting evening. Sylvia collapsed on the bed, unwinding the tight lamp cord from her hand. She tossed the lamp off the other side of the bed and began to massage her aching palm. Seven thirty. She didn't plan to leave the house for at least another two hours; she had just enough time for a short nap.

The tune "You're So Vain," by Carly Simon, began to echo through Sylvia's bedroom. For a moment, half-awake, she was confused, wondering who could be playing the music. Then she realized that it must be coming from the cell phone in her purse. One evening last month, while consumed with boredom, Sylvia had assigned a different ringtone for each of the people on her cell phone contact list. This song "You're So Vain," she remembered, was selected for her sister, Emily. She had chosen "Honky Tonk Women," by the Rolling Stones, for her mother, and "Bad, Bad Leroy Brown," by Jim Croce, for Mort Banks.

Sylvia sat up so quickly that she became dizzy. Shocked out of a light sleep by the sound of the missing cell phone, she felt disoriented, and frightened. She heard a rattle of plastic against the bathroom tile floor, then a cracking sound and the splintering of plastic put an end to the ringing phone. *He's still here*, she thought. *He's in the bathroom.*

Suddenly a man appeared at the bathroom door. He was wearing a ski mask pulled down over his face under a hooded sweatshirt. He stood in the doorway for a moment, holding a large pair of stainless steel scissors.

Without saying a word he came toward her, the scissors held high. Sylvia rolled across the bed to the far side and scrambled to her feet. The man leaped across the bed and grabbed at her hair but only came away with the towel and a few strands.

Sylvia found her voice and screamed as she ran to the bedroom door. The man rolled off the bed and was on her in a second. He caught the belt from her robe at the middle of her back and tried to yank her back into the room. The belt cut into her stomach. Sylvia tried to untie it, but she had knotted it too tight, and her long fingernails bent as she picked at the knot. The man wrestled her to the ground, rolled her onto her back, and straddled her, his left hand on her throat and the scissors held high in his right.

She couldn't breathe. His fingers squeezed her windpipe and the weight of his body on her chest forced the breath from her lungs. Sylvia kicked her feet and tried to punch him. It was no use; he was too strong. As her arm fell helplessly back to the floor, her knuckles touched something. From the corner of her eye, she could see the brass lamp. She wrapped her fingers around its thin shaft and swung at his head as hard as she could.

There was a loud ringing sound in her ears from the lack of oxygen. Sylvia was afraid she might pass out. She gasped for breath and tried to get to her feet. The man lay on his back, his hands holding his head. Sylvia wanted to lift his mask, and kick him; she didn't know which to do first.

Just then he started to move, and she stepped over him in order to run down the stairs and out to the street. As she reached the top step, running as fast as she could, he stretched out his arm and grabbed at her ankle. His grip was not secure, and her leg slipped out of his hand, but he delayed her foot just long enough to throw her off balance. Her body was launched into a headfirst flight down the stairs, ending in a crash at the bottom step.

***

The man picked himself up from the floor, turned on the hall light, and walked unsteadily down the stairs. He clung to the banister, still dazed from the parting gift Sylvia had bestowed on the side of his head. Her body lay in an inelegant pose, limbs carelessly splayed. A quick check of her pulse satisfied him that her battle was over. He stood before her, removing his ski mask and stuffing it into his pocket. The lump on the side of his head was painful, but the hood from his sweatshirt had somewhat cushioned the blow. He took measure of the bump in the hall mirror. It was above the hairline. A cold compress later tonight and a comb-over tomorrow morning and no one would know the difference, he thought.

There was a lot of work to do and not much time to do it. First he hoisted the body over his shoulder, carried her back up to the bedroom, and plopped her down on the bed. He pulled out several of the dresser drawers and dumped the contents on an area rug in the middle of the room. The light cast from the hall and the bathroom was dim but adequate to find what he needed.

Sifting through the pile of clothes on the floor, he chose a nightgown, something light in color and fairly translucent. Next he attempted to remove Sylvia's robe, and he learned that dead bodies can be very uncooperative.

He struggled to pull the robe from her dead weight, but her arms were hopelessly stuck in the sleeves. He rolled her onto her back and pulled each arm free. As he did he cupped her breast with his hand. It was warm and firm, and he sighed. "What a waste."

He pulled a folded piece of paper from his pocket and stared at it, studying the writing. He needed to ensure that every detail was exact—nothing left out, nothing added.

He then attempted to slide the nightgown up onto her body from her feet. He wished she had been dressed for bed before he killed her. It would have saved so much energy. When he was finished, he tore the top off the nightgown, again exposing her breasts.

Now it was time for the difficult part. He picked up the steel scissors from the floor and held them over the body. He raised his arm but then stopped. She looked as if she were sleeping. Not comfortably—her face was contorted, and large purple patches were growing across her forehead. He knew he needed to finish this, but not while he could see her face.

He closed his eyes and raised the scissors high over his head. "Sorry, but I've come this far; I must make it look like his dream." He held his breath and drove the scissors down toward her abdomen with all his strength. Just before the scissors found their mark, his arm was struck from the side. It was a glancing blow that caused him to miss the body and stab the bed. A scream pierced his aching head, and fists began to pound his arms and shoulders. She was alive.

He straddled her body, pressing her shoulders down with his knees.

Her screams—would someone hear her screams? He left the scissors embedded in the mattress and wrapped both hands around her throat. He squeezed with all his strength. She kept trying to punch him but her arms were flailing wildly, having no effect, and her leg was kicking at the footboard of the bed. Suddenly he heard a loud crack, and the wooden footboard gave way. He turned his head just in time to see Sylvia's hand close around the handle of the scissors. She was trying to pull them from the mattress. They were coming loose. Her shoulder was pinned by his knee, but her hand holding the scissors was free. Free to stab him.

He released his right hand from her neck, still squeezing her throat with his left, and slid off her chest to avoid her thrust. She gasped as he changed his grip, finding part of a breath, and raised the scissors to follow his dodge. Leaning all his weight on his left arm and hand and pressing her neck to the bed, he reached out with his right hand, caught her wrist, and forced her arm down, thrusting the scissors deep into her rib cage. Her head tossed violently from side to side as he wrestled the scissors from her hand and stabbed her deep in her belly. Blood spurted from the wound hitting his face, filling his eyes, blinding him. Sightless and panic-stricken, he thrust the scissors again and again, harder and harder, until she finally stopped struggling and lay silent.

Out of breath, he fell onto his back on the bed next to her body and dropped the scissors to the floor. This time it *was* over. She lay still on the bed.

He stood and took several deep breaths to calm himself. He took the paper from his pocket and reread it. He looked at the scene on the bed and around the room and then at the paper again. Although he had planned to match the condition of the room and the body to the description of Franklin's dream, there was no need. The murder had played out in real life just as it had in the dream. The blood on the bedclothes, the wounds on the body, the broken footboard, even the position of the scissors on the floor—it all matched the paper.

He was unnerved, fearful that some unseen power was at work here. Was he the perpetrator of this crime or simply an instrument of fate? Was he copying Franklin's dream or was the dream controlling the events, guiding his moves to this very outcome, an outcome that had been determined in a dream weeks ago?

He couldn't think about that now. There was still work to be done. He wiped the blood from his face on a bedsheet and attended to the finishing touches. He filled the bathtub with water and bubble bath, pulled out the vanity drawers, and placed drops of blood on the vanity counter. Then he wrapped the body in the robe and scattered the bloody bedclothes around the room. Last, he took a small piece of blue fabric from his pocket, wedged it in the joint of the scissors, and placed them back on the floor.

The silver midsized sedan was in the driveway. He checked to see that no one was around and placed the body in the plastic-lined trunk. A small amount of blood from the body had rubbed off on the doorframe of the garage as he squeezed through. He was ready for the most dangerous part of his plan. He took a nylon stocking from his pocket and pulled it over his head. Then he drove around the late-night neighborhood, looking for a witness. Not just any witness—it had to be a person walking a dog.

He had to drive around several blocks several times, always on the lookout for a security patrol car, before he finally found a dog walker. To ensure that he was noticed, he swerved the car and almost ran over the dog.

With that piece of theater out of the way, all that was left to do was to drive to the county road, find a stone bridge, and throw the body into the water. The rest of the cleanup was easy. He disposed of the robe, rubber gloves, and plastic lining from the trunk, changed his bloody clothes, and returned the car. It had been a difficult task, but a job well done.

Part 3

Fate leads him who follows it, and drags him who resist.
—Plutarch

23

The yellow Piper Cub flew in a straight line across the strip-mining field. It began to circle the field, slowly gaining altitude, constantly moving higher and higher until it was almost out of sight in the clear blue sky. Then the engine slowed to what seemed like an idle, and the nose of the plane dipped toward the earth. The angle of attack increased until the nose of the single-engine plane was pointing almost straight down, falling through a silent sky. The engine sprang to life again, and the speed increased. It was in a power dive. It plummeted, gaining speed and spiraling down on the verge of being out of control. Just when it looked as though the pilot would never be able to avoid a crash, the nose began to come up. The plane leveled off and began to gain altitude again.

"Wow, that was too close. I was sure you were going to lose it," said Tom Haskins.

"That was nothing," said Hank, trying to hide his hands shaking on the controls. "I'm going to do a hammer stall next—hang on."

"I don't think that's a good idea; you haven't been flying that long."

"Don't be a pansy. I can fly this thing in my sleep."

The Piper Cub engine roared. The yellow plane gained speed and flashed across the sky. Suddenly the nose again pointed skyward and the plane began to rise, steeper and steeper until it was flying almost straight up. The engine strained, propelling the plane into a vertical trajectory high above the old strip mine. Gravity, being all that Newton said it was, began to take its toll on the plane's airspeed. There was a second where the world appeared to stop. The engine was still whining at full throttle, but the plane just stayed in one spot, at the point where the engine's upward power was matched by gravity's relentless downward pull. It hung there, still, for what seemed like minutes and then slowly began to fall to one side as Hank turned the rudder to the full right position. The plane's wing now became the head of the hammer, as its body—the hammer handle—tilted down with great force. No longer having any airspeed, the plane began to tumble out of control. It was a perfect hammer stall.

Hank Haskins pushed forward on the throttle, trimmed the rudder and ailerons, and tried to counter the tumbling motion of the plane. The object of the recovery from a hammer stall was to get the nose pointing down and the airspeed and power up sufficiently to pull out of the dive before you ran out of sky. Everything was going well. The plane was beginning to level off, and Tom was just about to start breathing again, when the strain on the plane's wings became more than it could bear. First the left wing tip tore off, and the plane began to spiral. Next the right wing folded in half and ripped from the body of the plane.

Tom yelled, "Pull up, pull up!" But there was nothing Hank could do. Then neither said a word as the yellow Piper Cub disintegrated on contact with the old coal field.

Tom and Hank stood in silence for a few seconds, and then Tom said, "I told you you weren't ready for a hammer stall. That's a hundred bucks down the drain."

Hank shut off the radio control transmitter and began to walk to the crash site. "Maybe if you built the wing a little stronger, we would still have a plane."

Tom began to pick up pieces of the little yellow Piper Cub from the hill of rocks. Hank sat on the ground and opened his backpack. "What kind of sandwiches did you make?"

"Cheese—it was all I could find in the refrigerator."

"It smells like rotten cheese," Hank said. "Why didn't you make peanut butter sandwiches?"

"Stop complaining," Tom said as he collected model airplane parts. "It's not the sandwich you smell; it's this place. The whole hill stinks. Hey, I think I see the engine under those rocks." He reached under an overhanging rock.

"Snake," yelled Tom as he touched something soft. Hank dropped the backpack and picked up a stick. He kicked the rocks away, ready to protect his brother. Both boys stood motionless, staring at the woman's arm Hank had just uncovered.

24

Franklin lay in the upper bunk of the bed in his jail cell. He stared at the cracks in the gray concrete ceiling while trying to understand how he'd ended up here. The steel springs creaked and moaned as he turned and fidgeted on the bare gray-striped mattress, trying to find a spot that wasn't lumpy. The odor of mildew caused him to sneeze. Until a few weeks ago, he was just another normal guy leading an uneventful life. Well, maybe not totally normal. He had a very vivid imagination, and he seemed to have unusual dreams, but hell, didn't everybody dream from time to time? Granted, most people didn't have vivid dreams of a murder and then find that a murder was committed almost exactly as they dreamed. That was a little odd, but he chalked it up to a clairvoyant moment. A glitch in time and space that revealed to him, and only him, a glimpse into the future. Actually, he was blessed. He should be honored for his gift, not punished as though he had done something wrong.

Franklin jumped down from the upper bunk, landing flat-footed on the painted cement floor. It stung his feet and sent a shock wave up his spine.

"They can't do this to you," a voice said from across the cell. "You didn't do anything wrong."

Franklin's head snapped around to see a man sitting in a chair facing the far wall. His voice sounded familiar, but Franklin couldn't quite place it. He knew, however, that this cell mate sounded belligerent, and even though his words seemed sympathetic to Franklin's plight, Franklin feared encouraging the man's combative attitude. He tried to change the subject.

"Did you come in while I was sleeping?" he asked. "I thought I was alone."

"Nope, I've been here all along," the man said without turning to look at Franklin.

"I didn't see you when I came in. Did they let you out for exercise? I could use some exercise," Franklin said as he pulled on his socks and banged his shoes against the frame of the bed. He held up each shoe to check inside for spiders or roaches, or whatever awful creatures might have crawled in while he was asleep. *Who knows what inhabits this place*, he thought.

"Nope, I've been here all along," the man repeated, this time with an exasperated tone.

Franklin thought it was rude of his cell mate not to turn around to face him as they spoke, but Franklin didn't want to add to the quarrelsome nature of the conversation. "So how long have you been stuck here?" Franklin asked.

"As long as you have," he answered and folded his arms across his chest.

There was a heavy clanking noise, and Franklin looked to the cell door; his cell mate did not. A guard holding a clipboard said, "Jameson, step outside the cell."

Franklin stood. "Maybe I'm being released. They probably realized that they made a mistake." He turned, feeling a bit uncomfortable talking to the back of the man's head, but if he didn't want to turn around, that was his business. "If I don't see you again, I wish you well," Franklin said, feeling a little confused by the man's indifferent tone, yet sensing familiarity and a feeling of kinship.

"You'll see me again," the man said in a dispassionate tone.

The cell door slid open with a loud rumble, and Franklin stepped into the corridor. His new orange jumpsuit fit so loosely that the cuffs of the trousers bunched up against his shoes and its sleeves fell over his hands. He would have been embarrassed by his appearance if fear hadn't already overwhelmed all his other emotions.

"Where are we going?" he asked the guard leading him through the cellblock.

"You have visitors," the guard said in a monotone. Franklin asked who his visitors were and how much time he would have with them. He asked the time of day and if the guard was married. He talked incessantly until the guard turned to face him and stared into his eyes with a totally blank expression. Franklin nodded, said "OK," and followed silently for the rest of the journey.

After a short walk, the guard opened a large steel door and motioned for Franklin to step inside. In the center of the room were four chairs and a small metal table. Three chairs were lined up on one side of the table, and the fourth chair was centered on the opposite side. Franklin was guided to the single chair. As he attempted to pull the chair back from the table, he observed that it was bolted to the floor. That seemed unnecessary. Next the guard placed a handcuff on Franklin's right wrist and secured the other end of the cuffs to a ring welded to the tabletop. *Equally unnecessary*, Franklin thought.

Up in the corner of the room near the ceiling was a small video camera. Franklin couldn't help waving at the camera with his free arm.

After about five minutes, the door opened and a tall man with a reddish beard and dark horn-rimmed glasses entered the room carrying a letter-size notebook. He wore a three-piece gray suit with a gold chain and a watch fob strung across the front pockets of his vest.

"I'm Dr. Fielding," he said. "I have been asked to speak with you."

"What kind of doctor are you?" Franklin asked. "I'm actually feeling quite good. I don't think I need a doctor."

"I'm a psychiatrist, Mr. Jameson. I'm here to help determine if you understand the severity of the charges against you. Do you understand the charges?"

"It's all a big misunderstanding. You see, I had a dream about a murder, and then it came true, and I thought I could help the police since I saw the murder happen—in my dream, that is—but these fools think I had something to do with it."

"And where were you when this murder dream occurred?"

"I was home, asleep. Well, I was asleep during the murder dream. When I woke up, I was in my car in the driveway."

"Where had you been?" asked Dr. Fielding.

"I don't think I was anywhere. I was dreaming that I was at the murder, and then I went with the murderer to dispose of the body, and when I woke up, I was in my car in my driveway. Besides, the murder didn't actually happen for another two weeks." Dr. Fielding opened his notebook and scribbled several lines of notes.

"I understand that you called 911 to report the location of the body. How did you know where it was?"

"I told you. In my dream I rode with the murderer to dispose of the body. He drove to a bridge on the county road and threw the body off the bridge. More than two weeks later, I drove to the same bridge and found the body. That's when I called 911."

Suddenly the door opened, and Lieutenant Peirce poked his head into the room. "I'm sorry to interrupt, but Mr. Jameson is a patient of Dr. Klein's." Ruth Klein leaned around Lieutenant Peirce and also poked her head into the room. "She was hoping that she could sit in on your evaluation."

"That would be all right, as long as you don't interfere, Dr. Klein."

"She has promised to sit quietly and observe, isn't that right, Doctor?"

"I'll be a fly on the wall," she said. "Are you all right, Franklin?"

"I'm fine. I was just telling Dr. Fielding, was it, how I came to know where—"

"Please talk to *me*," Mr. Jameson," said Dr. Fielding in a very authoritative tone.

"You don't have to be so harsh with him," said Dr. Klein.

Lieutenant Peirce held up his index finger and said, "That's one." Ruth sat down and did not reply.

Dr. Fielding straightened his tie and cleared his throat. As he began to ask his next question, he noticed that Ruth Klein was leaning toward him, trying to look at his notebook. He moved the notebook and looked questioningly at Lieutenant Peirce. The lieutenant closed his eyes and slowly shook his head from side to side. Ruth immediately sat back in her chair and returned her gaze to Franklin.

"Now," said Dr. Fielding, "have you had any other dreams that eventually became real events?"

"Yes," said Franklin. "I dreamed of a burglary, and then the house of the murder victim was burglarized, just as in my dream."

"That was just a coincidence," said Ruth. "His dream was so general almost any burglary in the last six months would have looked the same."

"*Please*, Doctor?" said Fielding. Ruth placed her hand over her mouth and nodded her understanding. Lieutenant Peirce looked her in the eye and held up two fingers.

Dr. Fielding looked at Ruth for a moment, gave a slight sigh, and turned back to Franklin.

"What do you think caused these strange dreams, Mr. Jameson?"

"Isn't it obvious I'm psychic? That's why I went to the murder scene the night they arrested me. I was waiting for a premonition, a sign to tell me who the murderer was."

"I know this looks bad for him," said Ruth, "but he's just overzealous about finding the murderer, he—"

Lieutenant Peirce stood, held up three fingers, and with the other hand pointed at the door. Ruth bowed her head and slowly began getting ready to leave the room.

"Franklin, you should ask for a lawyer before you say another word. And, Lieutenant, nothing he has said can be used against him; doctor-patient privilege applies. And turn off that camera," she said, pointing at the ceiling as she walked out of the room.

Franklin was led along a concrete walkway back to his cell. He tried looking into each cell he passed but was prodded to continue by the guard.

"Most inmates don't like to be stared at," the guard said. "It's not smart for a new guy to make enemies on his first day."

"I'm just looking for someone to talk to," Franklin said. "Well, I guess I can talk to my cell mate. He seemed like a nice guy. Do you know what his name is?"

"You don't have a cell mate," the guard said. "We don't put anyone in a cell with someone who's under a psych evaluation."

"Oh," said Franklin, now not sure if he hadn't been the victim of another dream.

25

Hyrum Green was walking from his car to his office building when he heard a woman calling his name. He turned and saw Ruth Klein running across the parking lot as best she could in uncomfortable business shoes. She waved, and once she saw that she'd attracted his attention, she slowed to a slightly limping walk and caught up with him.

"Dr. Green, I was hoping to catch you before you started your day. I was with a friend last night, and he asked me to contact you. He needs your help."

"Really, why doesn't your friend just call my office and make an appointment? I can treat him on an emergency basis if that's needed."

"No, it's not a professional matter, and he's not my friend, he's a friend of yours, Franklin Jameson." Ruth felt a little strange saying that Franklin was not her friend. He was a patient, but she was starting to think of him as a friend, albeit a troubled friend.

"He was arrested night before last, and he asked me to notify you. Your home number must be unlisted, so I came in early to catch you as you arrived."

"That was very good of you. What kind of trouble is Franklin in?"

"It's a bit of a long story—can we talk inside?" Ruth asked. She stopped walking, took off her shoes, and pulled a pair of old tattered clogs from a small canvas shopping bag. "I wear these in the office between patients," she said, averting her eyes.

"By all means. My first appointment isn't for two hours," he said, looking at his watch. "We can talk in my office."

As Ruth walked up the front stairs of the building, she noticed that Dr. Green had dropped slightly behind her, and although she didn't turn, she could feel his eyes on her body. *It must be the clogs*, she thought.

"What time does your staff come in?" she asked, feeling uncomfortable being alone with him. Ruth still had not completely recovered from the night someone chased her through the basement of the building. She had since concluded that someone was trying to frighten her; if the person had wanted to catch her, he (or she) probably would have. She had spent a considerable amount of time trying to decipher who the culprit might be. She didn't believe she had any enemies, and she knew of only two men who had recently been in the building. Lieutenant Peirce had just left her office before the lights went out, but he was a police officer. He had no reason to try to frighten her. Unless he thought it was the only way he could cause her to stop meddling in police business. Possible, but very unlikely. Dr. Green was in the hall when she emerged from the basement, so he couldn't have been behind her. Of course, he could have run up the back stairs and reached the corridor at the same time she did, but for what purpose? They'd never had any involvement with each other. He would have no reason to want to frighten her.

Then there was Franklin. She wasn't really afraid of him, yet she seemed to always carry her pepper spray whenever he was near. He had considerable psychological baggage that they hadn't yet explored, and in some way he could have been asserting his dominance over his doctor. He said he made the 911 call to the police, but she thought he said that just to support his theory of being psychic. *Well, he's in jail anyway and not a threat for now.*

Then she had an extremely uncomfortable thought. Sylvia's murderer may have discovered that Sylvia was in therapy. If he thought she might have confided some information that could lead to his identification, he would have a reason not only to frighten her, but to eliminate her. That was a seriously disturbing supposition.

She looked up and found that Dr. Green was staring at her.

"Nine," he said. "My staff starts at nine. I usually come in an hour early to prepare any bridges or crowns that will be installed that day."

"How interesting," Ruth said, not really hearing a word he said. "I believe Franklin is going to be charged with the murder of Sylvia Radcliffe. She was one of my patients. Did you know her?"

"Radcliffe, Radcliffe, I don't think so. Oh wait, I think I extracted a tooth from her several months ago, but I never associated the name with the article in the newspaper. What a shame…I guess I did know her."

Ruth thought that his speech seemed slightly affected and he was acting a bit strange, but she decided that he must be embarrassed not to have realized that a murder victim whose picture was in every newspaper had been his patient.

"But tell me, why do the police think Franklin is involved?"

"Franklin claims to have had a dream, a premonition of the murder. He described it in such detail that the police believe he must have been involved. But you know all about the dream—Franklin said he described it to you weeks ago."

"No, I'm afraid Franklin's memory must be failing him. He never told me about a dream. What did he tell you?"

"I'm sorry, I can't tell you anything other than the fact that while I was at the police station, Franklin asked me to contact you, and he told me you would know all about it." Ruth was suddenly aware that she might be giving away too much information. It wasn't her place to tell Dr. Green that Franklin was her patient. She needed a cover story.

"I've been working with the police," she said, "unofficially, helping to solve Sylvia's murder. I happened to be present when Franklin was questioned."

"I know Franklin has been having some problems lately and has been distraught, but he seems worse than I imagined," said Dr. Green. "I'll contact an attorney and have him call Franklin today. I'm sure this will all sort out."

***

The door opened just a crack, and two eyes gazed into the darkened room. At first, everything looked normal. A medium-size lump under the covers, about the length of a sleeping child, indicated that all was as it should be and the day had come to a peaceful end. Just as Ruth Klein was about to quietly close the door and back away, a strange light caught her eye. It was as though the child under the covers was glowing, radiating light that increased and decreased periodically with movement from under the covers. Ruth tiptoed to the side of the bed, leaned over her iridescent progeny, and said, "Emma, what are you reading under there?" The light was immediately extinguished. Not another movement or any sound came from the bed.

"What are you doing under there?" Ruth asked. While the words were still falling from her lips, Ruth wished she could take them back. She always thought of Emma as a small child, a baby, but time was passing, and Emma had now grown into adolescence. Ruth put her hand to her mouth to symbolically stifle any ill-considered words. Could she have just embarrassed her young daughter? She tried to think back to when she was first reaching puberty. A thoughtless remark by a parent could leave emotional scars that could last throughout adulthood. *You're a psychologist*, she told herself; *how could you be so crass?*

Ruth leaned over the bed and gently placed her hand on what she hoped was her daughter's shoulder. "I'm sorry, sweetheart. I didn't mean to embarrass you. You know you can talk to me about anything. If you have any questions about anything at all, you can ask me. Now don't be frightened; you haven't done anything wrong, and I promise, no matter what you ask, I won't be upset."

The covers slowly began to roll back, and Emma's face appeared. "I do have one question," she said in a low, halting voice. She reached under the covers and retrieved one of Ruth's manila folders. "Do all your patients tell you their deepest secrets?"

"What?" she said, confused by the playfulness of Emma's tone. Then she saw the patient record folder in Emma's hand. "Where did you get that?" she almost shouted. "You know you're never to read anything from my files. You're in a lot of trouble, missy. Give me that folder, and the flashlight, and go to sleep. Taking that folder was a very bad thing to do, and we're going to talk more about this in the morning." Ruth tossed the covers back over Emma's head and stormed out of the room.

After Ruth closed the door, she thought about what had just happened. She was angry about the stolen file folder but also relieved. She reviewed her compassionate response to her fear of having embarrassed Emma, and then her anger at the child's infraction. She settled into a living room chair and said aloud, "Well, that should screw her up for about a year."

Ruth looked at the tab on the folder. It said "Sylvia Radcliffe" in bold letters.

She hoped that Emma hadn't associated the name on the folder with the reports of Sylvia's murder on the TV news. Ruth reached out, lifted the wineglass she had filled before checking on Emma, and took a sip. She leaned back and felt a melancholy mood coming on as she opened the folder. Ruth hadn't reviewed any of her notes about Sylvia since her death. Now would be a good time to close out the file and store away the records.

A blank space in her notes from one of their last meetings reminded Ruth of her lapse of concentration during that session. She smiled as she recalled how relieved she was when she realized that she had recorded the discussion. *Discussion? It was more like a monologue,* she remembered.

Ruth reached down next to her chair and rummaged around in her briefcase until she found the recording. She placed the memory card into her handheld recorder and pushed play.

She felt disheartened at the sound of Sylvia's voice. It was hard for her to believe that she was gone. She sounded so animated, so opinionated, so alive. Ruth drank her wine, only half listening to the recording and picturing Sylvia rushing through her door at exactly five minutes before the hour every Tuesday. Every Tuesday except the last one, when Lieutenant Peirce showed up in her place to say she was missing.

Suddenly, something on the recording registered in Ruth's mind. She pressed stop and then rewound for several seconds. She wasn't sure what concerned her, but she had to hear it again.

"I knew he was married, but I think he was coming on to me. Or maybe I was coming on to him, I'm not sure. He gave me his card and said he would call me next week to meet for a drink, he…"

Ruth rewound more of the recording and played it again.

"I know it was a terrible thing to do, but I made up reasons to see him. I told him that I had this pain in my tooth…"

Ruth began to feel very uncomfortable. Something about these statements seemed wrong. She rewound further.

"Dr. Green had extracted a tooth just two weeks before…"

Ruth stopped the tape. *He knew her well*, she thought. *Why would he lie?*

If they had been having an affair, he might have lied because he was married and needed to keep the affair secret, she suspected. That made sense to her. But now that Sylvia was gone, he could have said it was nothing more than a doctor-patient relationship, and no one could have proven otherwise. Ruth felt that there was more to the story of Sylvia and Dr. Green and maybe more to the murder than a senseless killing during a burglary. She felt excited by the possibility of solving this case. Now she needed to know more. She needed to know it all. She needed to know who murdered Sylvia and why.

She wondered if Dr. Green's reluctance to state the extent of his relationship with Sylvia had a darker purpose. Now Ruth didn't usually jump to conclusions—well, actually she did—but she was trying to avoid doing so again. She walked to her desk and took a fresh manila file folder from her drawer. She wrote across the top of the folder: *Who killed Sylvia Radcliffe?* She then tore a page from her notepad and divided it into three columns, printing a title across the top of each column:

1. A murderous act by a serial killer.
2. Sylvia knew her murderer.
3. A random killing during a robbery.

She sat with her elbows resting on the desk and her head in her hands, wondering which of these possibilities she should pursue. She drew a circle around number two, Sylvia knew her murderer—that seemed to be the most logical place to start. Ruth downed the rest of her wine and thought about her next move. Solving this murder was important to her, but she had to ensure that it didn't interfere with the more important priorities in her life. Emma's welfare and happiness were her number-one priority. Her psychology practice, from both a professional and a financial standpoint, was second. Now there may have been other pressing priorities that she should have considered, but finding Sylvia's killer seemed to be right up there just below the other two.

***

"You're going to be late for class," Ruth shouted as she sat in her car with the motor running and the window rolled down.

The front door to the two-story colonial home opened, and Emma called out, "I can't find my karate uniform."

"It's in your gym bag on the chair in the foyer. You put it there your-self when it came back from the laundry so that you wouldn't forget it," Ruth answered. Then she smiled and thought, *I swear that girl gets more like me every day.*

On this Saturday morning after dropping Emma off at her karate class, Ruth decided to drive to her office and spend the morning orga-nizing her work for the coming week. Out of the corner of her eye, as she passed the art supply store on the boulevard, she saw something of interest in the window. She abruptly stopped her car. A screech of tires, honking horns, and a string of expletives from the drivers behind her indicated that she may have stopped a little too abruptly. "Sorry," she yelled and waved her hand as she pulled to the curb.

A half hour later, upon reaching her office building with her pur-chase, Ruth found a parking space just twenty feet from the front door. How lucky. She opened the trunk of her car and lifted out the three dry-erase whiteboards, each two feet by three feet, and the three alu-minum easels on which they would stand. *I can do this in one trip*, she thought. Ruth was proud of being self-reliant and clever enough to solve her own problems. She connected the shoulder strap to her briefcase and slung it over her head and left shoulder. The shoulder strap on her purse assumed the same position, but on the opposite shoulder. Next she tucked the three whiteboards, neatly tied together with string, under her left arm, placed the bag with the markers in her teeth, and leaned the easels against the car. Next she slammed the trunk, tucked the easels under her right arm, and finally started toward the building. *Not so difficult,* she thought. Unfortunately this left no body part available to turn the doorknob to the office building's front door. Ruth stood at the door, trying not to drool on the paper bag in her mouth while contemplating her next move. Just then a man opened the door from the inside and held it as she squeezed, decked out with all her visual-aid paraphernalia, through the narrow space.

"Can I help you with some of your packages?"

"No, I'm OK," Ruth mumbled through the bag in her teeth. "I do this all the time."

Just then the bag began to slip from her lips, and as she lugged the packages down the hall, the bag fell. Her attempt to break its fall with her foot altered her balance and allowed two of the easels to slip from under her arm and clatter onto the tile floor. "I'm OK," she announced to the man watching at the door. "I do this all the time." As she leaned forward to push the two easels with her foot, the string on the whiteboards snapped, sending the boards to the floor in front of her. Unperturbed by the noise or the debris on the floor, Ruth just continued to systematically kick each item to her office door. "I'm OK," she grumbled. "I do this all the fucking time."

Upon reaching her office, Ruth calmly fished her keys out of her purse and turned and smiled at the man still holding the front door open at the end of the hall while she unlocked her office door. She put a doorstop in place to hold it open and proceeded to kick each item through the doorway, some of the larger items requiring more than one kick to make it through. After all the items were safely strewn about her waiting room floor, she leaned back through the doorway into the hall and waved at the man standing with his mouth open, still holding the front door. "Thank you," she said as she disappeared into her office.

***

Ruth was inspired. Her hands trembled as she set up her three easels and whiteboards, placing a marker in each tray. She picked up one of the markers from the floor twice and finally threw it in the wastepaper basket after it kept slipping off its holder because of the angle of the easel's bent legs, a result of its trip through the doorway.

At the top of each of the boards she printed: *Who Murdered Sylvia Radcliffe?* On the first board she wrote, "Franklin Jameson." Under his name she listed all the evidence that led her to suspect him. For some reason—maybe it was the timidity she'd observed in his personality, maybe it was his disability—she didn't really believe that he was capable of murder. Of course it could also just be his good looks that persuaded her.

The evidence was damning. He claimed to have made the 911 call giving the location of the body. He described details of the murder not published by the police, and his knowledge of Sylvia's yellow rose tattoo was very disturbing. He claimed not to have known Sylvia, but since Sylvia's appointment time with Ruth was just before Franklin's, he could have seen or even met her on her way out of Ruth's office days prior to the murder. It was possible that he knew her.

Ruth tapped her marker against the second whiteboard before committing a name to it. She hesitated and then wrote, "Dr. Hyrum Green." She really had no strong evidence to support an accusation, but he did lie about the extent of his relationship with Sylvia. Ruth wrote, "Dr. Green had an affair with Sylvia."

Ruth began to realize that Dr. Hyrum Green made her more and more nervous each time she saw him. The evidence of his involvement in the murder was pretty thin, but she was still suspicious.

On the third board she wrote, "Killed by an unknown burglar during a robbery." This was the conjecture advanced by the newspaper. It was purely circumstantial, but if Sylvia had surprised someone during the robbery...

Ruth stared at the boards lined up against the wall. Two of the suspects were known to her, the other was not. Which should she pursue?

She decided to handle this as professionally as possible. She would focus her investigation on a suspect that she knew and didn't like—Dr. Hyrum Green.

26

Sam Peirce stepped out of his car in the parking lot of 29 Office Park Place. He placed his hand on his stomach and felt a slight rumbling as he looked longingly at the fast-food restaurant across the street. He had been up since 5:00 a.m., and breakfast had been almost five hours ago. As he looked toward the restaurant, his hand slipped from his stomach to his belt. Peirce grasped his belt buckle and the waistband of his trousers and pulled them away from his body. He chuckled. The gap between his stomach and his belt had grown to three inches during the last few weeks and was becoming wider by the day. His eyes turned back to the restaurant, and with a short sigh, he walked away, toward the office building.

"My name is Lieutenant Sam Peirce. Would you tell Dr. Green that I need to speak with him for a few minutes?" Peirce said to the receptionist when he arrived at Hyrum Green's office.

"Do you have an appointment, Mr. Peirce?"

"No, I don't, and it's Lieutenant Peirce, of the county police. Please tell the doctor that it's important that I speak with him now."

The receptionist huffed a little and looked at Peirce in a way that convinced him that she was hoping he needed a tooth drilled, preferably without Novocain, but she got up from her desk and disappeared into the inner office to deliver the message.

Minutes later she reappeared and guided Sam into a dental examining room. "The doctor will be in shortly," she said and walked back to her post.

Sam paced back and forth between the examining chair and the counter containing a tray of stainless steel instruments. He wasn't good at waiting, especially when he was the bearer of bad news. On a large-screen television at the head of the room, a man was preparing a chocolate cream pie, and the television morning news staff was anxiously waiting for him to finish while they held their plates and forks at the ready. Sam reached up and pressed the off button, and the screen faded to black. Satisfied that he had removed the temptation as well as the distraction, he finally sat in the large dental chair and began to examine his fingernails. A handheld mirror on the instrument tray attracted his attention. While he waited, he held the mirror up to his face and studied his front teeth.

"We could whiten those within a few weeks if you like," said Hyrum Green as he entered the room.

Peirce placed the mirror back on the instrument tray. "Sorry, I was just killing time until you came in. Don't they look white?"

"What can I do for you, Lieutenant…"

"Peirce," Sam said. "When was the last time you saw your dental hygienist, Michelle Ackerman?"

"She left about three weeks ago to visit her family in Colorado. I was expecting her back last week. It does seem strange that she hasn't called. Is she all right?"

Sam stood up. "I'm sorry to have to tell you that she was killed more than two weeks ago."

Hyrum picked up the tray of instruments from the counter and stared at them for a moment, then placed them back on the tray stand a little too forcefully. Peirce watched Dr. Green closely. The doctor's hand was scratching his chin, and his eyes were downcast. He turned away from Peirce, staring at a point in space somewhere between the floor and the wall. Suddenly, he seemed to compose himself. "Was it an accident of some sort?"

Sam had been a police officer for more than twenty years, and during that time he had developed a keen sense of observation. He had watched the reactions of hundreds of people as they received unhappy news. Hyrum Green certainly had a right to be upset, but Peirce's instincts told him that something else was afoot here. This didn't seem to be sadness that Hyrum Green was exhibiting; it looked more like relief.

"The investigation isn't complete, but we believe she was murdered. The evidence might support a homicide during a robbery. We'll know more in a few days."

"This is the second murder during a burglary this month," said Hyrum. "I understand you have someone in custody for the first murder. Do you think both women were murdered by the same man?"

"May I ask where you got that information?"

"Why, from Dr. Klein. She approached me and asked if I could help find a lawyer for her friend. She said she was helping with the investigation. Dr. Klein thinks your suspect is innocent. Do you think he did it?"

Peirce bit his lip and tried to ignore the question. He noted the reference to Dr. Klein's involvement in the investigation and returned to his original line of questioning.

"Were you aware of anyone with whom Ms. Ackerman may have had difficulty, anyone who may have wanted to harm her?"

Dr. Green was again staring at the floor, apparently disconnected from the conversation.

"Dr. Green?"

"Oh, ah, no, no, I don't know much about her private life, but she was well liked here. Lieutenant, this has been quite a shock, and I have a waiting room filled with patients to attend to. If you've finished asking questions, I'm going to need a few minutes to compose myself before I get back to work."

"I understand." Peirce placed his card on the instrument tray. "If you think of anything that could help the investigation, please call me. Thank you for your time, and I'm sorry for your loss."

Hyrum Green watched Lieutenant Peirce walk out of the examining room. He dropped into his dental chair and leaned to the side, his eyes following Sam Peirce until he disappeared into the waiting room. As he leaned back into the center of the chair, he caught a glimpse of his reflection in the stainless steel autoclave on the counter. He realized that he was smiling and quickly reorganized his features into a frown, but it didn't last. Within seconds he was smiling again.

Hyrum slapped the arm of his chair, then massaged his chin with his right hand while his mind wandered back to the day he first started his practice.

When Hyrum had awakened on that morning, he had thought that that day would rank among the top five days in his life: his marriage to

Elaine, the birth of each of their two children, graduation from dental school, and now the opening of his very own practice. He hung his diplomas on the wall and stepped back to admire them.

"They're crooked," Elaine said.

"They look fine to me," Hyrum replied as he slightly cocked his head to the right.

"You think everything is a joke." Elaine dismissed his remark with a shake of her head and straightened the diplomas.

"You think everything is so serious," Hyrum said. "Sometimes you need to laugh at your mistakes."

Hyrum had worked for the last five years in Dr. Sol Feldman's practice as a second chair. He had a few patients of his own, but Sol controlled the office and took a piece of all the revenue Hyrum generated. He wasn't sure he was ready to open his own office and build a new practice from nothing, but Elaine had pushed until he finally acquiesced. She really did more than push. She researched several cities and towns until she found just the right location. It wasn't a terribly affluent area, but a community with lots of kids and lots of factory workers with dental insurance.

"We received five résumés for the dental hygienist position," Elaine said. "I set up the interviews starting this afternoon." She stretched out her hand, offering five manila folders, each containing an application, résumé, and a brief background check that Elaine had purchased from an Internet research company. Each folder was labeled with the name of the applicant. Hyrum held the folders in front of him at arm's length and smiled.

"You are incredibly efficient," he said. "If you could also clean teeth, I could throw these away and save the salary."

"If I could clean teeth, you wouldn't be able to *afford* my salary," she said with a shake of her head.

Hyrum walked through his new office. He stopped to drink in the high-tech look of the digital panoramic X-ray machine. He ran his hand along the soft leather of one of the three new dental chairs, each in its own complete examination room. Then he wandered out into the waiting room bathed in soft lighting with comfortable contemporary furniture.

The reception desk was topped with rose-colored granite, and the walls were decorated with prints of important works of art by Monet, Renoir, and Pissarro. He tiptoed around on the new carpet. It looked perfect. It smelled perfect. He couldn't imagine a better start for his practice.

Hyrum began to flip through the manila folders and stopped at a name that looked familiar. Michelle Ackerman. Where had he seen that name before? Then the memory exploded in his brain and took him from the height of elation into a pit of despair. His thoughts were instantly transported to a police station in Bangor, Maine, more than twenty-six years ago, when his name was Hyrum Bookman, not Hyrum Green. He could see himself as an arrogant young man sitting on a police station bench with his hands folded in his lap. He could hear the old bench squeak with each movement as he had rocked back and forth, waiting. He heard his own impatient voice: "How the fuck long is this going to take?"

The shadows on the frosted glass of the detective's office door grew larger as two men walked toward it, and then finally the door opened.

"Just ask her," Max Bookman was saying. "I spoke to her mother yesterday. She told me that the girl lied. My son never touched her. She made it up because he paid no attention to her. Go ahead, ask her mother. You'll see."

Hyrum jumped to his feet as his father and the police officer approached. "That's right," he said. "I never touched her."

Max Bookman stared at his son with a look that Hyrum knew only too well. He stopped talking and sat back down.

Detective Plumb motioned to the bench. "Sit here with your son, Mr. Bookman, and we'll see if she's going to press charges."

Man and boy sat on the squeaky bench and waited.

"It wasn't my fault. She's been chasing me around all year. I finally gave her a break and took her out."

"Not another word until we're out of here," Max Bookman said.

Detective Plumb shifted his weight from foot to foot, trying to talk into the telephone, but not getting a chance to finish a single sentence. "I see—but—I see." He hung up the phone and looked out his office door at the two men on the bench. He motioned them back into the room.

"You stay here," Max said as he squeezed Hyrum's thigh. "I'll handle this."

Later, as they drove out of the city, Max said to his son, "You're a lucky boy.""I knew she would cover for me," Hyrum said. "She likes me. I knew she really didn't mean no. She just didn't want to give it up too easily."

"Listen, you little shit! If it was up to her, you'd be in a jail cell right now. You're seventeen years old. You would be tried as an adult. Do you know what a conviction for a sex crime would do to your chances of getting into a good college? Your plans for a career would be over right now. It was her mother who made her recant her story. And if she had taken her daughter to the doctor to be examined, you would really be in deep crap."

Hyrum remembered looking confused. "Why didn't she?" he had asked.

"I took care of it," his father told him. "That's all you need to know."

At that point, a drop of perspiration had fallen from his brow and splattered on the manila folder in his hand, shocking him back to that day. A day that had begun as a great day, but now he recalled as the start of a nightmare from which he could not awaken.

Michelle Ackerman was that young girl that Hyrum had violated as a teenager. The girl whose mother made her say she lied. That Hyrum never forced her. Hyrum never knew if his father, who was very influential in Bangor, had threatened Mrs. Ackerman, or simply bought her off. Either way, Hyrum was off the hook. Now Michelle had found him, and the price for her silence was a job with a pay scale far above that of any dental hygienist in the area.

"How much would it take to make this go away?" he had asked her. "My practice is new, but I can probably get what you need in about six months."

He remembered her laugh; it was shrill and cold. "You're not getting rid of me that easily," she said. "You ruined my life. Not just because of what you did, but because your father coerced my mother into forcing me to lie about it. We didn't speak for years, and she died before we ever made our peace."

Hyrum hired Michelle Ackerman. She proved to be a competent worker, but she demanded additional payment, off the books, each month to maintain her silence.

Now Hyrum slapped the arm of the chair again, then composed himself, checked his reflection again to ensure the right amount of sadness, and went to tell his staff of the tragic news.

***

Peirce stood in the corridor for a moment considering—or maybe dreading—his next move. Then he turned, took a deep breath, and walked toward Dr. Ruth Klein's office. A doorstop was holding the outer door to her waiting room open, and the inner door to her office was open as well. Peirce was about to knock, or shout—he doubted that she was in a session with a patient while the doors were held open—when he realized that he could see Ruth's reflection in the mirror of the open closet door in her inner office. She was standing before several easels and writing on large charts of some sort. The writing was backward in the reflected image, but he could make out some of the words: *Who Killed Sylvia Radcliffe?* There was writing under the printed title, but he couldn't decipher her scrawl through the mirror. *Doctors*, he thought, and then knocked.

Ruth glimpsed into the mirror on the closet door and saw Lieutenant Peirce standing in the waiting room doorway. She was thankful for the warning. She might not have felt quite as thankful if she had realized that the mirror worked both ways.

Ruth pulled each of the whiteboards from its easel and placed them in a stack facing the wall. Next she flattened the three easels and stuffed them behind her desk. "Come in," she called as she threw the marking pen into her purse.

"Lieutenant Peirce, how nice to see you." She offered her hand. Sam Peirce had come in contact with many private citizens who believed that they could solve crimes better than the police. Most tired of the fruitless pursuit and set aside the delusion quickly, but Peirce could see that this interloper might be persistent enough to be a challenge to his patience.

"What brings you here on a Saturday, Lieutenant? Has there been a break in the Sylvia Radcliffe murder?"

"Not unless you've broken the case." He walked to the wall and turned one of the whiteboards around, revealing its title.

Being caught in the act was not a new situation for Ruth. As a child her record was flawless. The first time she smoked a cigarette, her father smelled it on her breath. The first time she raided her father's liquor cabinet, she vomited the evidence on the living room floor. And the first time she shared her answers to a history exam with a friend, her friend copied every answer word for word, including the essay question—that resulted in a week's suspension from school and being grounded for a month.

It was time to come clean. Maybe Peirce would be interested in her theory.

"Actually, I'm not here about Sylvia Radcliffe. Did you know Dr. Green's dental hygienist, Michelle Ackerman?"

Ruth discontinued mentally planning the explanation of her theory of Sylvia's murder. "I met her occasionally in the corridor. She was usually leaving as I arrived. You said *did* I know her. Has something happened to her?"

Peirce remembered the last time he tried to give Ruth bad news gently, and how her impatience made it all but impossible to break the news without her interrupting. He decided the direct approach was best.

"She was murdered about three weeks ago."

Ruth digested the news silently for a moment and then asked, "What do we know so far?"

"*We*—don't know anything," he said. "*We* are not investigating this case. *I* am investigating these murders, and *you* need to stay out of my way."

"There's no need to be rude, Lieutenant. I'm just trying to help. I have a theory."

"*I* have a theory," said Sam Peirce, "and that's the one that counts."

"Have you ever thought about working on your anger management?" asked Dr. Klein. "I could recommend someone if you're not comfortable working with me, but actually I'm a specialist in the field."

"Thank you, Dr. Klein. I'm sure you're great at dealing with anger. It's probably the cornerstone of your career. You seem to cause enough of it to keep you busy forever."

Ruth lowered her chin and uncrossed her arms, realizing she was being defensive and argumentative.

"I guess I have been stepping on your toes. Somehow we always seem to push each other's buttons. I should know better."

Ruth's feelings were usually kept under strict control, but the recent loss of a patient had worn her defenses thin. She was a professional in the field of other people's emotions, and here she was, losing control of her own. It was embarrassing. Ruth reached into her purse, pulled out a tissue, and began to dab at her eyes. Her stare was locked on Sam Peirce's face.

For the last several years, Ruth's priorities had been to raise her daughter and to build her career. Being a single parent had taken a great deal of her time, leaving little for personal relationships with anyone. Most of her interaction was with her patients. Even if she were allowed to date a patient, she wouldn't. They all had serious problems, and she wouldn't want to add them to her own.

Ruth hadn't been with a man for longer than she could remember, and although Lieutenant Peirce was exasperating, short-tempered, and on occasion condescending, there was something in his manner that caused her to feel comfortable with him and to almost enjoy these minor altercations. She was even slightly aroused by his forcefulness and bravado.

This makes no sense, she thought. *I don't even know this man. How could I feel so sure that under all the bluster lies a sensitive, caring individual?* She felt vulnerable and looked for reassurance in the big man's face.

Peirce began to smile. Ruth wiped her nose with the tissue and returned the smile. Peirce's smile became wider. Ruth felt her face begin to flush. She reached into her purse for a second tissue and patted the perspiration that had formed on her forehead. Her pulse was becoming rapid; she breathed deeply to calm herself. Peirce's smile became broader still. Ruth widened her own smile, waiting for Peirce to say or do something to ease the sexual tension she was feeling. Peirce's smile broke into a chuckle. He lifted his finger and pointed at her, releasing a loud, hearty laugh.

Ruth's eyebrows came together, and her face formed a scowl. All Ruth's feelings of sensuality and desire quickly reverted to anger.

"You are the most insensitive, brutish lout I have ever met," she said. She picked up her glass paperweight and threw it at Sam Peirce's midsection. Sam caught the solid glass sphere in one hand while still pointing at her with his other. He tried to speak, but his laughter was so hard and his breath so short that he couldn't get any words out. His face was bright scarlet as he walked up to Ruth, grabbed her by the shoulders, and turned her to the mirror on the closet door. Through laughter and halting speech, he managed to say, "You threw an open marker in your purse. Your tissues are full of ink."

***

"Is it coming off?" Ruth asked.

"Hold still before I poke out your eye." Sam carefully wiped at the last black ring under Ruth's left eye with a cotton ball.

"It's not permanent ink, is it?" she said.

"Yes, it is. You're going to have to live the rest of your life as a panda."

"Very funny." She punched him in the shoulder.

"Hey, watch out! This is delicate work." Sam put down the cotton ball and admired her clean face. "Not bad," he said.

Ruth looked at her face in the mirror. The ink was gone, replaced by a bright-pink hue. She wasn't sure whether her rosy complexion was the result of the cleaning or a blush caused by his touch.

"I'm sorry for coming on so strong," Peirce said. "I understand that you were trying to help."

"That's OK. I shouldn't have told Dr. Green that I was helping with the investigation, or at least I should have told him that my involvement was unofficial." Sam Peirce nodded his acceptance of her apology.

"So, Lieutenant, let me tell you my theory of the crime."

Now Peirce was ready to tear into her again. To let her know once and for all that he didn't need her help. That he didn't want her help. He leaned over, placing his face within inches of hers. He looked directly into her bright-green eyes and paused a moment. Then he said, "All right, tell me what you think happened."

Ruth jumped up out of her chair, almost bumping foreheads as she ran to the easels lying on the floor and began to set them up. Peirce placed his hand on her wrist. "Just tell me."

Ruth felt the warmth of his hand travel up her arm. She could feel the beat of his heart in his grip, or maybe it was her heart.

"Tell you what?" she asked.

"Your theory of the crime," Peirce said, sounding a bit confused.

"Oh, yes," she said. "I think Dr. Green knows more about Sylvia's death than he's told you. Dr. Green and Sylvia were having an affair."

"I never asked him about Sylvia Radcliffe," he said. "I didn't know he knew her."

"There, I've helped already," Ruth said. "I have irrefutable evidence that they were having an affair."

"Irrefutable, huh? Show me your evidence."

"I can't. It falls under—"

"Doctor-patient privilege." Peirce finished the sentence for her.

Ruth rolled her eyes. "Sorry."

"Well, it doesn't matter," he said. "Let me tell you my theory of the crime."

Ruth sat up in her chair, clasped her hands in her lap, and stared into his eyes.

Peirce suddenly felt uncomfortable making eye contact with Ruth. He turned and paced around the office as he spoke.

"Mortimer Banks was an ex-convict who, we believe, has been burglarizing homes in this area for more than a year. We know Banks broke into Sylvia's house and stole a flash drive that Sylvia had hidden in her bedroom."

"Yes, you told me about the drive, but you didn't tell me what information was on it."

"The drive contained a database of customers who had purchased expensive jewelry from Stanton's. Banks must have gotten access to the database and used it to plan the robberies. I believe that Sylvia discovered Banks was using her database, and he killed her to keep her quiet."

"But how would Banks have gotten access to the list in the first place? He stole the flash drive after Sylvia was dead."

"Hold on, I was getting to that," Sam said. "It turns out that Mortimer Banks was Henrietta Radcliffe's, Sylvia's mother's, boyfriend."

"So you think Sylvia's mother somehow copied the information or gave Banks access to Sylvia's computer," Ruth interrupted.

"Well, yes, that's one way it could have happened," Sam said.

"And," Ruth continued, "Mortimer Banks murdered his girlfriend's daughter because he was afraid she might find out about the burglaries?"

"When you say it that way, it does sound a little farfetched."

"No, no, that sounds like a good theory," Ruth said. "Why don't you pick up Banks and 'sweat' him until he talks. Oh, I'm sorry, I forgot—he's dead."

"You're right, we can't question him, but we found some of the stolen jewelry, and he had the flash drive and a stocking mask in his pocket."

"So you can prove he was a burglar, but you can't prove he was a murderer."

"Not so fast," Peirce said. "We can't prove he killed Sylvia, but we have evidence that he killed Michelle Ackerman, Dr. Green's dental hygienist."

Ruth looked puzzled.

"I know it sounds a little unlikely, but we believe that Ms. Ackerman was killed when she discovered Mortimer Banks burglarizing her home. Let me explain…"

Sam Peirce folded his arms across his chest and began to tell Ruth all the details associated with the break-in and murder at Michelle Ackerman's house. He wasn't sure why he was telling her. Maybe he felt guilty for having yelled at her, or maybe he just got caught up in the moment and wanted to please her in some way.

Sam told her about the police burglary unit trying to catch the local jewel thief with no success. The burglar never seemed to leave any evidence behind. The crime scene was always free of fingerprints or fibers or anything that would give them a clue to his identity. The burglary detectives were sure that the thief vacuumed the crime scene before he left.

"After the murder, though, he slipped up," Sam explained. "We found not only hairs with roots attached, making DNA analysis possible, but he also left a plastic card he used to jimmy the door. It contained fingerprints clear enough for a positive identification."

"Wait, wait. Are you telling me that he never left any evidence behind during more than a year of burglaries? That he was very careful, and then, when he commits a murder, a really big crime, he gets sloppy?"

"It certainly looks that way," Peirce said.

Sam went on. Now Ruth was hanging on every word Sam uttered. He strutted around the office, explaining how Sylvia's death was very violent. It was the act of someone who knew and hated her for some reason, and Michelle's death had come from a single blow. The murder was probably unplanned, the result of a burglary gone wrong. They were two murders for different reasons, but both committed by the same criminal.

Halfway through his interpretation of the evidence, Ruth's eyes glazed over. She wasn't buying any of it. Ruth had her own thoughts about who killed Sylvia Radcliffe, and she wasn't about to give up investigating just because Lieutenant Peirce didn't agree with her.

In her mind, there were three possible killers, and Peirce hadn't even begun to investigate the other two. She had mixed feelings about the possible guilt of Franklin, but she couldn't see how Lieutenant Peirce could ignore the facts.

"What about Franklin Jameson?" she asked. "He knew all the details of Sylvia's murder, details that for the most part were unpublished. His weekly appointment followed Sylvia's appointment, so he could easily have met her or at least seen her in the building. Franklin was a patient of Dr. Green's for years; I would expect that Michelle Ackerman cleaned his teeth on many occasions. He knew both of the victims. He made the 911 call. You arrested him, for God's sake. How can you ignore all these facts?"

"Franklin told us he made the 911 call. That was why we arrested him. I think he claimed to make the call because he wanted to prove that he knew more than he really did. A voiceprint of the 911 call was too muffled to definitively conclude that the voice on the call belonged to Franklin. He claimed he had a premonition. He didn't say he killed anyone, and we don't have any evidence that he did."

"Isn't his claim to have made the 911 call a confession?"

"First, I don't believe him. Second, he made the claim before he was read his Miranda rights. We couldn't use it if we wanted to. We released him this morning."

"You just put him back on the street?" she asked rhetorically. "He needs psychiatric care."

"He's your patient," Peirce said. "*You* convince him that he's a nut. That's not my job."

Ruth looked at Sam Peirce through squinting eyes, her red complexion no longer a question of a skin irritation or a blush. Now it was clearly flushed from anger.

"What about Hyrum Green? Sylvia was his lover, and Michelle was his employee. He was involved in some way with both murdered women. He could have had a reason to kill both of them. Don't you want to find out exactly what his involvement was?"

Sam rubbed his forehead and closed his eyes for a moment. Ruth rocked in her seat, waiting for his answer. Sam opened his eyes and was just about to speak when he noticed a shadow on the wall across the corridor. Someone was standing in the hall just outside Ruth's waiting room. Ruth turned to see what he was staring at. Sam sprang forward just as the shadow disappeared from the wall. Ruth marveled at how fast his two-hundred-pound bulk could move. He ran with catlike speed, but not fast enough to catch the eavesdropper.

Ruth hurried to join Sam in the hall. "Where does that door go?" he asked, pointing at the door to the basement.

Not again, Ruth thought. "It's the basement," she whispered. "Two weeks ago someone tried to attack me in that basement. I barely got away. I thought it might have been the killer. Maybe he thinks Sylvia told me something that might identify him."

"And you reported this to the police," Sam said. Ruth looked at the floor and folded her arms across her chest.

"I wasn't sure; I thought it might just have been my imagination."

"Stay in your office and lock the door," Peirce said. "I'm going to find your imagination."

The door to the basement swung wide open. Sam quickly stuck his head through the door and then just as quickly withdrew it. He slipped into the stairwell and flattened out against the wall as he listened to footsteps receding into the boiler room. He heard two loud pops as the eavesdropper ran through the boiler room, smashing the light bulbs in the low ceiling as he ran. The light coming from the open boiler-room door went out. When Sam reached the boiler room, he heard footsteps from somewhere in the darkened basement. He eased himself into the room.

Sam waited, staring into the darkness. His eyes should adjust soon. In the movies, the detective always reached into his pocket for a flashlight when he chased someone into a dark space. *Not a bad habit to adopt in real life*, he thought.

Sam crept along the wall, moving ever deeper into the room. Now he could make out a figure standing against a row of steam pipes. *Come just a little closer*, he thought. He readied himself for the attack. Perspiration dripped from his brow. The salty sweat burned his eyes, but he remained focused on his target. The shadowy figure slowly approached, slightly hunched over and moving close to the wall. *One more step*, Sam said to himself. Now Sam knew he hadn't identified himself as a police officer before beginning his pursuit, but Ruth said she had been accosted in this building, and since this person ran, Sam felt he had probable cause to tackle the bastard. He leaped from the wall and wrapped his arms around the suspect. The force of his attack caused them both to topple over. Sam held on tight to keep the suspect under control. The suspect began to scream, "Sam, help, he's got me!"

Sam could hear the door at the far end of the basement slam and the sound of footsteps on the stairs.

"Help, he's got me!" Ruth screamed.

"No, I've got you," Sam said. "He's gone, thanks to you. I told you to lock yourself in your office."

Sam rolled off Ruth and began to help her to her feet.

"Are you OK?" he asked.

"I'm fine, Sam," Ruth said. "Did you see his face? I came down the front stairs to try to head him off, but he must have gotten past me."

"That was very brave, but very stupid, Dr. Klein."

"Ruth," she said. "You've humiliated me in my office with sarcasm about my efforts to help with the investigation. You washed ink off my face, you tackled me and threw me to the floor, and now you've called me stupid. Don't you think it's about time we were on a first-name basis?"

"OK, Ruth, I didn't see him. Did you?"

"No, but I know who it wasn't. It wasn't Mortimer Banks."

There was no connection between Mortimer Banks and Michelle Ackerman that Ruth could see. True, he may have known Sylvia Radcliffe, and he may have believed she was a threat to him. That could explain her murder, but choosing Michelle's home to rob and then killing her when she stumbled onto the scene was just too much coincidence for Ruth to accept.

The person who shared a relationship with both women was Dr. Hyrum Green. Whether the relationship was just business remained to be seen, and Ruth was anxious to find out the truth.

Part 4

A vacation is what you take
when you can no longer take
what you've been taking.
—Earl Wilson

27

The rabbit ran left and then right, using his agile hind legs and swift maneuverability to affect his escape. Fear caused his heartbeat to be almost a buzz as his tiny feet fought for purchase on the smooth black surface. He cut to the right and stopped short, trying to make his pursuer overshoot and not recover until the little fellow was well off the road and into the thicket. A roar filled his long ears. It wasn't going to work. His pursuer wasn't dodging or weaving in response to his maneuver—just barreling forward directly at him. All seemed lost for the little fellow. He tucked his head down and squeezed his eyes shut, waiting for the jaws of the predator to close around his neck and shake the life from his body. Then came a loud screech and a dark shadow, and a foul-smelling wind that rumpled his fur passed over him, leaving him unscathed.

Ruth put out her hand to brace Emma as the car decelerated under heavy braking. Emma opened her eyes and lurched forward to the limit of her seat belt. She grabbed Ruth's restraining hand and hugged it to her chest.

"What happened?" she said in a startled but groggy voice.

"That's the third animal that tried to commit suicide in the last hour. Maybe they know something about the future that we don't."

"Yeah, they know that there's no television at this cabin," Emma said.

"I think we can survive without mind-numbing reality shows and totally depressing news for a few days," Ruth said over her daughter's objections.

Emma frowned and settled back into her seat and to her nap. This was the first week away from home that Ruth and Emma had taken for longer than either could remember. The big SUV accelerated back to highway speed as Ruth scanned left and right, waiting for the next depressed creature to choose to end it all rather than make an appointment for therapy.

"Turn left in three-quarters of a mile onto Destiny Road," said American Jill, the voice on Ruth's GPS. Ruth thought about turning back to the city. Being forced to leave while Sylvia Radcliffe's murderer was still at large was making her angry, but Lieutenant Peirce had made it clear that the case was closed and he wouldn't reopen it in spite of her convincing argument. At least *she* was sure her argument was convincing. She thought about Peirce's reaction to her theory of the crime. Was he exercising his authority as a police officer by dismissing her opinion, or was he simply protecting his ego as the knowledgeable male in charge? After all, what did she know about human interaction and motivation for hostility? She was only a trained psychologist with a doctoral degree in clinical theories and interventions.

"Turn now!" Jill said as Destiny Road passed to the left. "Recalculating!" Ruth kept driving and waited. "Recalculating!" Ruth drummed her fingers on the steering wheel.

"Turn left in two miles," Jill said after a very long moment. Ruth was relieved to finally hear the revised directions to the cabin, but she sensed a slight condescending tone in Jill's voice.

***

The road degraded into a dirt-and-stone path not more than one lane wide, which jostled Emma awake. The evening sun shone through the trees at a low angle, turning the fall foliage to gold. Emma raised her hand to block the glare. "How soon will we be at the cabin?" she asked.

"I'm not sure," Ruth said, tapping on the GPS screen with her index finger. "Jill went to sleep a while ago. I think we're on our own for the rest of the trip."

Ruth had rented the cabin by responding to an ad placed on the bulletin board in her office building. It was an old hunting cabin, but the real estate broker said it had recently been remodeled and had all the comforts of a resort, including a hot tub and a screened-in patio. There was even a lake with a sand beach that was within walking distance.

The road curved up a long hill and eventually ended in a clearing surrounded by oak and maple trees almost bare of their leaves. Rough stones and pebbles gave the illusion of a parking lot sculpted out of the forest. Ruth sat looking at the log barrier signifying the end of the parking area and hopefully the end of their journey. Off in the distance, down a path lined with mountain laurel and wild fern, a light shone through a large plate-glass window. Either this was their cabin or some local resident was getting two overnight guests.

The sun set quickly as they removed their suitcases from the back of the SUV and dragged the roll-aboard cases over the rough stone path. The cabin was more than Ruth had hoped for. Large picture windows had been installed, updating the old Appalachian-style hunting cabin to a contemporary log home. Smoke was rising in soft curls from the gray stacked-stone chimney towering high above the roofline. A flagstone walk bordered by a hedgerow on each side led to natural stone steps and a long covered wooden porch. Emma dropped her suitcase at the base of the steps and ran to the oak porch swing suspended from the ceiling by heavy ropes. The swing creaked and groaned as it responded to the young girl's effort to pump it forward. "Can I sleep out here?" she asked.

Ruth stood at the front door and swatted a mosquito from her fore-arm. "No," she said. A note taped to the door read: *Dr. Klein, I made a fire to welcome you. I trust my directions helped you get here without incident. Enjoy your vacation. Clair, Northwest Realty.*

"Emma, get your bag. Let's see what the inside of this place looks like," Ruth said as she pulled the note from the door.

Ruth had been told that the cabin had "rustic charms," but the interior far exceeded her expectations. The fire glowed, projecting a shimmering yellow cast on the overstuffed furniture as the shadows danced about the room with the flickering of the flame. The hearth was made of thick gray slate protruding from a smooth river-rock fireplace supporting a rough-hewn oak mantel. On the wall over the mantel, a well-polished double-barrel shotgun was suspended on a rack made of short deer antlers.

Ruth lifted the hammerless shotgun from the wall and pushed the lever on the stock to break the action and ensure that there were no shells in the weapon. She raised the shotgun and peered into the barrels through the breach to inspect their condition and then snapped the action closed and set the safety. The ease and confidence with which Ruth inspected the gun shocked her young daughter.

"Where did you learn how to do that?"

"When I was born. I think Grandpa Joe really wanted a son," Ruth said as she slowly turned the shotgun in her hands. "He seemed happy enough. I mean, I'm sure he loved me, but I think he wanted someone to hunt and fish with and to play ball on Saturdays. Most of his friends had sons in Little League, and I guess he felt left out. Once Grandma Ellen was gone, and he had to raise me all by himself, I guess he reverted to what he knew best. He asked Aunt June to help out with the things a girl should know that he wasn't comfortable with…"

"You mean like about boys and stuff," Emma said with a slight giggle.

"No, I was just about your age." Ruth tussled Emma's hair. "Boys were off the menu for at least another few years." Emma looked at the floor and frowned.

"Soon enough, sweetheart, soon enough." Ruth placed the shotgun back on the deer-antler gun rack. She sat on the couch and clasped her hands in her lap. "I'm sure it wasn't easy for him, trying to raise a young girl all alone. He spent a lot of time with me, even if it was while hunting—"

"You mean you actually killed animals," Emma said.

"Not if I could help it. He would say, 'How come you're Annie Oakley on the target range, but you can't hit a deer as big as a horse just fifty feet away?' I wanted to please him. I don't know why I always missed."

While Ruth was talking, Emma sat in the chair across from the couch, put on a pair of her mother's glasses, picked up a notepad from the coffee table, and began to take notes. "Why do *you* think you couldn't hit the deer?" Emma said. "Is it possible that in spite of your desire to please

your father, your own personal code of ethics wouldn't allow you—"
Emma's analysis was cut short by a pillow from the couch striking her in
the face.

"OK, Miss Freud, I think our session is over."

***

A muffled creak signaled the failure of the deadbolt lock as it yielded to
the pry bar. The door slowly opened, and the masked figure focused a
flashlight toward the desk and file cabinet. A small amount of jimmying
with a wood chisel, and the file cabinet was breached. A beam of light
entered the window from the street and flashed across the pictures of
Sigmund Freud and Carl Jung, sending the burglar diving to the floor
before it became apparent that the light was the result of a car passing
through the parking lot on its way to the local McDonald's.

The spot of light moved from folder to folder, illuminating the name
on each tab in turn. When it reached the name *Jameson, Franklin*, the
folder was extracted and placed on the desk. The beam then continued
its mission until it settled on *Radcliffe, Sylvia*.

Next the desk drawer surrendered to the chisel. A paper desk calendar
lay at the top of the drawer. The burglar tore off the current month's
calendar sheet and stuffed it into one of the two selected folders. He
then rolled the folders into a tube and absent-mindedly tapped the tube
of data on various objects in the office while exploring the remainder of
the room.

Another set of car headlights illuminated the office; this time they
didn't pass across the wall but stayed focused on the picture of Freud.
Sigmund seemed to glow with an alternating red and blue cast, causing
the burglar to once more dive for the floor and crawl to the window.
There, his worst fears were realized. A Pennsylvania State Police car sat
in the parking lot, its headlights and colored roof lights bouncing off the
side of the building. The burglar stashed the rolled files in his jacket and
ran to the door before the trooper was out of his car.

***

Lieutenant Peirce took his Sig Sauer P226 in its abbreviated leather holster from his top desk drawer and fitted it into the waistband of his trousers. He pulled on the side of his belt and noticed how loosely the holster fit. As of this morning, he had lost eighteen pounds. He tightened his belt two notches, slightly bunching the waistband of his trousers to ensure that the holster would stay secure.

"It's about time you had that suit tailored," Holloway said from the doorway of Peirce's office. "Either that, or a box of doughnuts will fix the problem."

"C'mon in," said Peirce. "Have a carrot."

"No thanks, I've had my limit for the day. I just heard a call come in for a silent alarm in an office building near Church Street."

"I'm sure robbery will take care of it. We're homicide, remember?"

"Well, I just thought you might be interested since it's that tall lady-shrink's office."

"Dr. Klein?" asked Peirce.

"That's the one."

Ten minutes later Peirce was pulling into the parking lot of 29 Office Park Place. The burglary could have been random, but he doubted it. Dr. Klein had been nosing around, trying to get more information about the Sylvia Radcliffe murder. Maybe she struck a nerve with someone— someone besides him.

The state trooper who had responded to the silent alarm met Peirce at the door.

"The office was empty when I got here, Lieutenant. I guess he got what he wanted and left."

"Any clue as to what was taken?" Peirce asked.

"It looks like he may have taken some files from the file drawer. We won't know which files until the doctor comes in and checks them out," the trooper said. "We left several messages for her, but so far she hasn't called in."

Peirce furrowed his brow. It seemed unusual that a doctor wouldn't pick up her calls promptly, but then Dr. Klein wasn't your usual doctor. Peirce walked around Ruth Klein's office, inspecting the premises for any clues the state police might have missed. He dialed Dr. Klein's office number and waited for the answering service to respond. He questioned the operator at length as to the whereabouts of Dr. Klein but could get no answer other than "the doctor is not in." Sam thought about the last time they spoke. He had reprimanded her for interfering in his investigation and told her to "butt out" of his business. He'd suggested she take a vacation. Peirce had a gnawing feeling in the pit of his stomach that something wasn't right. Could she have, for once, taken his request seriously and left town? Maybe, but why wasn't she answering her calls? He needed to find her, and he needed to find her soon.

***

Ruth lifted Emma's head from her lap and moved to one side as she gently placed the sleeping child to rest on the sofa. A kiss on the forehead and an adjustment of the patchwork quilt covering Emma, and Ruth was off to check for messages from her service. She pushed the second button on the keypad of her cell phone and waited for the familiar voice to ask for her access code. She tapped her foot, then stopped and tiptoed to the door and stepped out onto the porch. She dialed again. "Damn," she said. "Has everyone taken a long weekend?" Ruth studied the phone's screen and noticed not a single bar of signal strength. She held the phone up as high as she could and began to walk away from the porch, turning the cell phone from side to side and occasionally shaking it just to make sure it was paying attention. The forest was uncommonly still. A beam of moonlight cast fingers of shadow from bare tree branches that beckoned her to the hill at the end of the path.

Ruth thought that the top of the hill might be the best place to find at least a few measly bars of signal strength. She walked along in the shadows, following the beam of moonlight that illuminated the crest of the hill. A sound, like the crack of a twig, caused her to stop and listen. Nothing. She felt a slight breeze begin to blow. It made faint moaning sounds as it passed through the branches of the trees and rustled the ferns along the path. *Maybe it's time to go back to the cabin and check for messages tomorrow,* she thought.

Ruth never liked to give in to any emotion, particularly fear, and it was a beautiful night. There probably wasn't another soul—other than Emma—within ten miles, and you never knew when there might be an important message from a patient. She decided that she would continue. If she still couldn't get a signal at the top of the hill, she would go back and quit for the night.

Another sound. She stopped and listened. This time it was the faint rumble of distant thunder. Ruth looked at the moon and saw wisps of dark clouds pass below it, obscuring its lower half. She picked up her pace; she might not have much time. As Ruth walked toward the hill, the clouds increased. Now the moon was blinking in and out of view, sending the forest into total darkness each time a cloud passed. Soon Ruth only occasionally glimpsed the moon between the total eclipses caused by the ever-increasing banks of clouds. "OK, I think that's enough for tonight," she said out loud.

The forest was now extremely dark. Ruth turned to face the way she had come and waited for the next passing cloud to allow the moon to reveal the direction of the path. The rumbles of thunder were getting louder. Ruth held up her phone and pushed any button to light the screen, thinking it might afford a little bit of light. Suddenly something struck her head and became tangled in her hair. She heard a rustling sound and felt something rough scratching against her shoulder. She shrieked and threw up her arms to protect her head. Her hands struck only leaves from a low tree branch, but the force of her protective action caused her to lose her grip on her phone, sending it into the low brush. "Crap!" she cried. Ruth knew that within a very short time the screen on the phone would go black and her hope of finding it would be gone. She dropped to her knees and waved her arms at the bushes, searching for the light of the screen. A flash of light just a few feet away guided her in the right direction just before the light extinguished.

Ruth crawled through the brush, feeling the ground, in the last known direction of the light. She jumped as she touched something soft that slithered away. Her heart was pounding in her chest and her breath was coming in gasps, but she kept moving forward. Luck was with her. As her hand bumped the phone, the screen again lit up. She grabbed the phone and scrambled to her feet. "That was fun," she said in a quivering voice. Now it was time to get out of these woods and back to the cabin. Ruth turned to her left and then to her right. During the mishap with the phone, she had lost her orientation. The night was now completely dark, and the forest began to take on an eerie feel. The path had melted into the surrounding darkness, and nothing looked familiar.

A bolt of lightning startled her as it lit the sky. This time the thunder was only five or six seconds away. The storm was approaching fast. Ruth waited for the next lightning bolt. This time she would be ready to make a decision and choose a direction while the flash of light lasted. "Come on, come on," she said as she waited. The sound of the thunder had come from in front of her as she walked away from the cabin. She decided that she would turn so that the lightning and the sound of the thunder were at her back. That should get her home. "Come on, come on—there!" she cried as a bright moment of daylight flashed directly in front of her. "Damn, I'm going the wrong way," she swore. As she turned, she thought she saw the silhouette of a person standing about twenty feet away just before the darkness returned. A second bolt of lightning and an almost instantaneous clap of thunder caused her to close her eyes and cover her ears. Ruth opened her eyes and looked in the direction of the apparition just before the lightning flash abated. The figure was gone. *It probably was never there at all,* she thought. She had studied the human mind long enough to know how fear could cause the imagination to invent all kinds of boogeymen. *It was probably just a tree branch blowing in the wind.*

With her phone now safely tucked away in her pocket and her arms outstretched in front of her, Ruth began to walk in the direction she now believed would lead her out of this predicament. She did, however, turn more than once to look over her shoulder. Ruth thought, *If I get back safely, I'll never...* She caught herself. A foxhole mentality was not going to solve this problem. No one ever did what he or she promised during a stressful moment. *Next I'll probably turn to religion,* she mused. Five minutes and several flashes of lightning later, Ruth could make out the shape of a car—her car—and beyond was the light of the cabin window. Ruth breathed a sigh of relief as she pushed into the clearing of the parking area. "Well, that could have been a lot worse," she said just before the sky opened with a torrential downpour. Amid high-pitched cries, shrill screams, and an assortment of colorful profanity, Ruth half-ran, half-stumbled to the porch of the cabin.

Emma awoke and opened her eyes to the sight of her mother standing in the doorway, mud caked on her knees and arms and several wet leaves plastered to her dripping hair. A small puddle of rainwater slowly grew around her feet.

"What happened?" Emma cried as she sat up and then kneeled on the couch.

"Nothing, nothing at all. I went for a walk, and it started to rain. Nothing to be concerned about," Ruth said in a matter-of-fact way as she walked toward the bathroom, her shoes making a squishing sound with each step.

28

S am parked his car in Alicia Goodman's driveway and bounded into the kitchen, ready for whatever treat Alicia had prepared for dinner. Alicia wasn't the world's best cook by a long shot, but three months of grazing on carrots and sprouts for lunch had caused him to look forward to any kind of cooked meal with some sort of meat or fish. Sam sat on one of the wooden kitchen stools, closed his eyes, and inhaled deeply, preparing to guess what lay in wait within the oven. The smell wasn't immediately recognizable, but it seemed fruity, maybe a citrus sauce on a roast chicken, or an Asian plum sauce for baby back ribs. He loosened his tie and called out for Alicia. *Must be upstairs making herself beautiful,* he thought. The red light on the telephone answering machine caught his attention. He pushed the button.

"Sorry, I had to run out. There was an emergency at the hospital. I'll probably be home late. There's a salad in the fridge for your dinner. I hope you don't mind the smell; I had the kitchen stools varnished today. See you when I see you," said Alicia's voice.

Sam peeled himself off the stool and sniffed the tacky varnish. Maybe he could pour some of it on his salad. He sighed and walked up the stairs to change out of his suit. He held his sticky trousers in front of him. "Well, that's one pair that won't need to be altered." Sam threw on the pair of jeans and a sweatshirt that he kept at Alicia's house for just such emergencies and hurried down the stairs. The only thing that would save this evening now was a visit to the Colonel.

Nights like this were generally beneficial to Sam, in spite of the calorie count. He thought very clearly while he was dining alone; extra-crispy chicken and mashed potatoes with gravy and biscuits were all he needed to solve any difficult case.

Minutes later, Sam was sitting at a table in the center of the restaurant, carefully pulling the extra-crispy chicken skin from each of the two chicken thighs and placing the skin in a pile on a paper plate. He opened the mashed potatoes and moved the container of gravy off to the left of the plate of skin.

Sam still felt uncomfortable about the burglary of Ruth Klein's office. True, it could have been coincidence that a burglar chose her office to rob right in the middle of a murder case involving one of her patients, but Sam didn't believe in coincidences. He cut a piece of chicken from the bone with the little plastic knife and fork and popped it into his mouth. Sam snapped the button on the top of his pen and laid out the facts he was pondering on a sheet a paper. As he wrote, he unconsciously picked up and nibbled on a chicken bone from his plate.

First, he thought, it was *possible* that the murderer of Sylvia Radcliffe could still be at large. That's what Ruth Klein thought anyway. He extracted a heaping spoonful of mashed potatoes from the Styrofoam container and swallowed it without chewing. Sam still thought Mortimer Banks was the killer of both Michelle Ackerman and Sylvia Radcliffe. He had evidence to support Banks's involvement in the Ackerman murder, but there really wasn't any hard proof he killed Sylvia Radcliffe. He began to wonder if he wasn't being a little hasty closing the case. He feared he might have been reacting to Ruth's meddling rather than fairly evaluating the facts. He mindlessly reached into his plate and bit the flesh from the remaining chicken thigh, groped at the stack of napkins, and wiped his mouth with several at once.

Second, there had been two incidents involving Dr. Klein. Someone had attempted to intimidate her by chasing her through the basement of her office building, and now someone apparently was trying to find out how much she knew about the murders by looting her files. The remains of the container of mashed potatoes bit the dust. Little by little it was beginning to look as though someone thought Ruth Klein might know more about the murderer than she did. More importantly, that belief may have put her in danger. This epiphany caused Sam to pound the table and whisper, "That bastard." A diner sitting near him, startled by the table pounding, dropped his chicken wing into his coffee with a splash. "Sorry," Sam said, and tossed a wrinkled stack of napkins, some used, onto the man's table. Sam really needed to find Ruth Klein before she became victim number three.

Sam jumped up from his table and started toward the door. Just before reaching the exit, he turned and looked back at the plates, cup, and napkins littering his now-abandoned table. He was anxious to get back to his office, but leaving the table as it was would not be appropriate. Sam walked back to the table amid stares from other patrons, who now smiled at his decision to return. He acknowledged their smiles and casually chose a piece of chicken skin, dipped it in the cup of gravy, and savored its flavor. With a devilish smile on his face, he picked up the plate of skin and the cup of gravy and ran for the door.

***

Sam turned the corner into the police precinct parking lot at high speed and slammed on his brakes, skidding to a stop just inches behind a car parked in his reserved parking space. He pounded on the steering wheel, cursed, and wrote down the license plate number of the car. Then he parked in a visitor's space. Normally he would have had the offending vehicle ticketed and impounded, but he had work to do and little time to do it.

Sam climbed the steps two at a time and burst through the door from the stairwell into the second-floor homicide division squad room. Sam's office door was slightly ajar. He pushed on the door, and there at his desk, surrounded by white cardboard Chinese takeout containers, was his loyal assistant, Holloway. He was leaning back in Peirce's chair holding a blue report folder, his feet resting on the edge of the desk, exposing his orange-and-yellow argyle socks.

Holloway jumped to his feet as Sam entered the room. "I'm sorry, boss. I thought you punched out for the night." He glanced at the desk and began to wipe a streak of duck sauce from Sam's desk blotter with his napkin.

"So this is what you do when I'm not here," Peirce said. "I expect my office, a lieutenant's office, to be treated with respect. That isn't your car in my parking space, is it?" Peirce walked slowly around the desk, his brow furrowed.

"I thought you were gone for the night. What can I say? I'm sorry." Holloway looked like a puppy with a rolled-up newspaper being waved at his nose.

"Well, you're going to have to pay for taking this kind of liberty with a superior officer's parking space and office." Peirce placed both hands on the desk and took a deep breath. "This is going to cost you," he said. "Now which of these containers is General Tso's chicken?"

Holloway immediately reached into the oil-stained bag on the corner of the desk and handed Lieutenant Peirce a pair of chopsticks and a napkin, and then pointed at the first container on his right.

People who knew Peirce and Holloway were well aware that this sort of preliminary banter usually proved to be the foreplay to a productive session of evidence evaluation and strategy building. It always seemed to precede a breakthrough leading to progress in solving an important case. With the preliminaries over, Peirce and Holloway settled down to review Michelle Ackerman's murder.

"There are a few things about the murder scene that bother me," said Peirce. He waved his arm at Holloway, who immediately moved around to the front of the desk, taking his egg roll with him. Peirce leaned back in his desk chair, grabbing the container of General Tso's chicken, and scratched his head with his chopsticks before continuing.

"I'm not sure we have the right perp," he said.

Holloway made a garbled sound, then chewed his egg roll very rapidly and swallowed. "You closed the case; shouldn't we be working on the next case on the board?" He pointed to the six-foot-wide whiteboard mounted on the wall behind Peirce's desk. The column on the left side of the board, labeled *open cases*, contained a list of murder victims' names written in red ink. The second column, the closed cases, contained names written in black ink and included the names of Michelle Ackerman and Sylvia Radcliffe.

"There are a few things about the Ackerman murder that don't add up, and if Mortimer Banks didn't kill Michelle Ackerman, then maybe he didn't kill Sylvia Radcliffe either." Sam Peirce turned his head to stare at the names on the board.

Holloway kept his eyes on Peirce and slowly reached for the container of General Tso's chicken.

"Do you see the problem with the evidence?" Peirce asked as he turned back to Holloway.

Holloway immediately redirected his hand toward the container of Kung Pao shrimp. "Well, he certainly did get sloppy, leaving fingerprints and DNA at the crime scene. He never left any evidence before."

Peirce bobbed his head in agreement and moved the General Tso's chicken closer to his side of the desk. "It's not just that he got sloppy. The fingerprints were on a card he dropped, and the hairs were in the messed-up bed. There were a ton of prints all over the house, but none of them were his."

"Except for the plastic card," Holloway said as he watched Peirce open the chicken container.

"That's right," Peirce said. "He obviously wore gloves. So why were his prints on the card to begin with? And as far as the hairs go, the bed looked slept in. The covers were messed up as though Michelle had been sleeping when she was attacked. The hairs were on the sheets inside the bed, but when the body was found, she was fully dressed and she hadn't been sexually assaulted. She was killed with a single blow to the neck with the baseball bat—"

"Ouch," said Holloway, holding his own neck.

"Even if he pushed her onto the bed while they struggled—and there were no signs on the body of a struggle—the hairs wouldn't have been *inside* the covers. I think the evidence could have been planted." Peirce stood and walked back to the whiteboard. He erased the names Michelle Ackerman and Sylvia Radcliffe from the right column on the board and rewrote them on the left side with a red marker.

Holloway stood, and as Peirce wrote the names on the board, Holloway swapped the two open containers of Chinese food. He placed two pieces of General Tso's chicken on top of the Kung Pao shrimp on Peirce's side of the desk and pulled the container of General Tso's chicken to his side.

"The officer canvassing the neighborhood after the body was discovered was told that a fancy motorcycle, a Suzuki Hayabusa—this guy knew his bikes—had been parked not far from Ackerman's house. He checked all the houses on the block, but no one in the neighborhood owns that kind of bike, nor did any of their guests—it's expensive. It was seen speeding away on the night of October 14th. The same night that a security camera at the airport caught Michel's abandoned car entering the parking lot. The ME puts the murder around the same date. Maybe we have an accomplice." Holloway used his chopsticks to fish a piece of General Tso's chicken from the container he had just purloined and stealthily popped it into his mouth.

"Let's run a check with the DMV to see how many of those Haya-whatevers are registered in this county. Maybe we'll get lucky," Peirce said as he extracted the first piece of chicken from his container. "Let's also take another run at Ackerman's boss, the dentist, and Dr. Klein's screwy patient, Jameson. As a matter of fact, let's reinterview Dr. Klein too; she may know something that could help." Peirce plucked the second piece of chicken from his container. Peirce leaned back in his chair and nodded, satisfied with the progress made this evening.

"Are you sure you aren't just looking for another reason to see that lady shrink again?" Holloway asked. "She's a fox. If you're not interested, I could give her a try."

"Didn't I just give you an assignment?" Peirce said. "Get the DMV info on that motorcycle." Peirce poked his chopsticks into his container and pulled out a spicy shrimp.

Holloway said, "I'm on it, boss." He took his container and quickly walked out of the room.

Peirce dropped the shrimp back into the container and prodded its contents in a futile attempt to find the rest of the General Tso's chicken.

Holloway sat at his desk in his cubicle stuffing the chicken into his mouth as fast as he could. He laughed to himself as he heard Sam Peirce's voice booming through the homicide squad room, "Holloway!"

29

Laura Carpenter," Holloway said. "There are only three Suzuki Hayabusa motorcycles registered in the county. One was in an accident and has been out of commission for six months. Another is owned by a restaurant—a burger joint—and it's on display in the lobby. The third one is owned by a Laura Carpenter. Not much I can find so far, other than her address—I vote for Ms. Carpenter."

"Why not the bike in the restaurant?" Peirce asked, taking the DMV report from Holloway and scanning it. "Someone could have used it, then put it back on display."

"I don't think so, boss. The motorcycle is mounted on the wall ten feet above the floor. It's registered, but the owner says it hasn't had gas in it for a year. The smell was driving away customers."

"Well, if that checks out, then Laura Carpenter is our winner. Let's pay her a visit." Peirce opened his top desk drawer and lifted out his gun in its leather shoulder holster. He had reached the end of the holes in his belt and still couldn't pull it tight enough to keep his waistband holster from slipping into his pants. A shoulder holster would have to do. "What have we got on Michelle Ackerman?"

"I got a court order and pulled her bank statements. It seems she deposited two thousand in cash on the fifteenth of each month. She didn't make enough to have that much left over from her paycheck, what with her mortgage and car payments and such. She was getting extra money from somewhere," Holloway said.

The ride across town was uneventful. Peirce drove while Holloway ate a box of Good & Plenty. The residence of Laura Carpenter was a garden apartment building with an attached single-car garage. Through the window in the garage door, Peirce could see the Suzuki Hayabusa standing in the center of the floor, sporting a black helmet with a tinted visor placed on its seat.

"Can I help you?" a man asked in a gruff and annoyed voice.

"Police," Sam Peirce said, pushing his badge with its leather folder a little closer to the man's face than was necessary.

"I'm the building manager, Jake Townsend." He backed away to put some distance between his nose and Peirce's badge. "What can I do for you?"

"We're looking for Laura Carpenter." Sam snapped his ID and badge folder closed while walking to the front door." A pile of dry leaves covered the doormat and several envelopes protruded from the overstuffed mailbox.

"You won't find her here," Jake said. "She owes me a month's rent. I've been keeping an eye out for her, but she hasn't been here for about six weeks. She was always on time with her rent. This isn't like her."

Jake reached for the chain hanging from his belt containing a large key ring. He sorted through the keys until he found the one marked 28D and walked toward the door.

"Are you allowed to just walk into her apartment without her permission?" Holloway asked.

Jake paused, letting the key drop back into the drove of others on his ring. "Oh, no, I would never do that. I thought you had a warrant or something," he said, stuffing the ring of keys, chain and all, into his overall pocket.

"No, we don't," said Holloway.

Sam Peirce shook his head in Holloway's direction.

"Mr. Townsend, you said you hadn't seen Ms. Carpenter for some time. Is it possible that she could be sick or injured inside the apartment?" Sam asked.

"No, I don't think so," Jake said, scratching his chin as he spoke.

"Is it *possible*?" Sam said, raising his eyebrows and making a not-so-subtle nodding gesture with his head.

"Oh, oh yeah, I get it. You know, I actually never saw her come out. Maybe she fell or something, and she needs help," Jake replied with a knowing grin. He reached back into his pocket, pulled out the key ring, and stood on his tiptoes to allow the key on the short chain to reach the high deadbolt lock on the apartment door. "Maybe she slipped in the shower and is unconscious..."

"We'll take it from here," Peirce said as he pushed past Jake Townsend. "You can wait outside while we make sure it's safe." Sam jerked his head, signaling Holloway to come in and close the door. The manager opened the mailbox and pulled the wedged bundle of mail out. "I'll take that," Holloway said. "We'll leave it inside for her."

The first-floor apartment in the two-story townhouse was larger than it looked from the outside. A bright-red sectional sofa on a white carpet demanded your attention as you entered the living room. Large modern art paintings of shapes Peirce couldn't recognize hung on the back wall. It wasn't his taste, but it looked like money.

The dining room table was piled high with folders and computer printouts segregated into piles with handwritten notes on them. Each note contained a full name written in capital letters. Peirce looked through the names, reading them aloud. He looked for anything that was familiar. "JAMES FARNSWORTH, ALBERTA KINSLEY, BRET KERCHIEF, HYRUM GREEN..." That one rang a bell. Peirce held up the folder. "This guy's name seems to be coming up everywhere we go."

Holloway walked to Peirce and began to read over his shoulder. Peirce turned a quarter turn to the left and said, "Why don't you see what else you could find? Look for a connection between Hyrum Green and this gal, Laura Carpenter."

Holloway again assumed the wounded puppy persona and began to search the other folders. He thumbed through several and then fumbled through his pocket for his cell phone. Holloway then tiptoed out of the room while poking in a number.

Peirce, his nose buried in the Hyrum Green folder, sat drumming his fingers on the table as he read the folder from cover to cover. He thought for a few minutes, then said, "This is almost the complete life story and financial report on the dentist. Why do you suppose

Laura Carpenter is interested in this guy? Holloway? Holloway!" he shouted.

"Right here, boss." Holloway slowly sauntered back into the room, beaming from ear to ear. "I was just checking a few things, and I found something interesting. All these names on the folders—well, all except the dentist—they were all on the flash drive that we found on Mort Banks, the one he stole from Sylvia Radcliffe's house. They're the names of robbery victims. They also all bought jewelry from Stanton's Fine Gems."

"We suspected Sylvia Radcliffe's mother or sister of feeding info to Banks about jewelry purchases and possibly helping to set up the robberies," Peirce said. "But what does this Carpenter gal have to do with it? Was she the accomplice who did the research for Banks, and if so, what was she doing at the murder scene?"

Holloway slowly pulled out a chair, sat, and put his feet up on the table. He leaned back in the chair and folded his hands behind his head. "I noticed that the name on the electric bill"—he held up the stack of mail—"was Laura S. Carpenter. I had Samuelsson check birth records. Laura S.—S stands for Sylvia, by the way—Carpenter was born to Henrietta Carpenter on June 7, 1971. That's also the DOB of Sylvia Radcliffe. I'll bet my argyle socks that Henrietta Carpenter was the maiden name of…"

"Henrietta Radcliffe," they said in unison.

"So that means that Sylvia Radcliffe, aka Laura Carpenter, was Mort's partner. And if Mortimer Banks didn't kill Michelle Ackerman, if the evidence was planted, then it was probably Sylvia Radcliffe who planted it," Peirce said.

"Maybe, boss. That would make Sylvia a suspect in Michelle Ackerman's murder. She could have killed Michelle and tried to blame it on her partner. She could have planted the evidence to cover her own crime," Holloway said.

"Or to cover for someone else," Peirce said, holding up the Hyrum Green folder.

"We still need a motive. This guy, Green, is in this thing up to his neck. Dr. Klein said she had evidence that Hyrum Green and Sylvia Radcliffe were having an affair. We've got two dead women, and this guy Green was involved in some way with both of them. Let's take another shot at him and see what turns up."

30

"Hyrum, dinner," Elaine sang out, holding a platter of neatly arranged slices of prime rib by its rim and a large wooden bowl containing a Caesar salad in her other hand. She rushed to the dining room table, racing to rest the warm plate on the trivet alongside the crystal serving dish of asparagus before the strength in her fingers gave out.

"Hyrum, it's going to get cold," she said in a more insistent tone.

She stood in front of the large teakwood dining table, checked the position of the silverware at each place setting, and fluffed the elaborately folded napkins peeking out of the water goblets.

The archway leading to the living room was only a few steps away. She leaned to see if he was coming.

Elaine untied her apron, revealing a form-fitting black sheath far too elegant for a weekday dinner at home. She placed the open bottle of merlot against her cheek to feel its temperature, then set it on a silver tray in the center of the table to breathe.

"What day is it?" Hyrum asked, causing Elaine to turn with a start.

"It's Monday of course," she said, looking mildly confused.

"No, I mean, is it my birthday, or, don't tell me it's our anniversary?"

"No, I just thought it would be nice to have a pleasant meal at home. So many things have been going wrong lately; I just thought it would be nice."

Hyrum put his arms around his wife and held her tight against his chest. He pressed the side of his face against hers. Both closed their eyes and held each other for longer than either expected. The chimes of the front doorbell broke the spell. They pulled away from each other, each turning in the opposite direction, both trying to hide the surge of emotion evident from the mist that filled their eyes.

"Who could that be?" Hyrum asked, wiping his nose with his handkerchief and then stuffing it into his back pocket. Elaine stood twisting the corner of the folded apron still in her hands.

"Lieutenant Peirce," Hyrum said as he opened the door.

"I hope I'm not interrupting anything," Peirce said. Before Hyrum could reply, he added, "I have a few questions I wanted to ask you."

"Actually, we were just about to sit down to dinner. Couldn't this wait until tomorrow?"

"I'm sorry; it will only take a few minutes. Then I'll leave you to your meal."

Hyrum glanced at Elaine, who nodded and picked up the food to take it back into the kitchen. "Ask," Hyrum said.

"Dr. Green," Peirce began, speaking in almost a whisper, "I understand that you and Sylvia Radcliffe had more than just a doctor-patient relationship." Peirce watched to see how Hyrum reacted to his statement. Hyrum stared at Peirce without uttering a sound.

"I also believe that you were paying two thousand dollars a month to Michelle Ackerman, possibly off the books, in addition to her salary. Can you tell me what that was for?"

Hyrum's face began to flush, and he balled his hands into fists. Peirce maintained an icy stare. His posture seemed relaxed, but he was prepared to react defensively if necessary.

"Lieutenant, I don't know where you get your information, but I am a happily married man. Sylvia Radcliffe was a patient, just a patient, nothing more. And Michelle Ackerman's compensation is none of your affair. Perhaps you should report me to the IRS if you think there's a problem."

He turned and looked quickly at the kitchen door, then hissed, "I don't appreciate your accusations. Now if that's all you wanted, I would like to get back to my meal." Hyrum pulled the door open and motioned for Peirce to leave. Peirce stepped farther into the room and said, "Just two more questions. Where were you on the nights of October 14 and

October 27, the nights that Michelle Ackerman and Sylvia Radcliffe were murdered?"

Hyrum's hands began to shake. Peirce held his ground, rising slightly on his toes for balance and, possibly, to appear taller—he wasn't sure which.

"Why, he was with me both of those nights," Elaine said, walking in from the dining room. Both men turned toward her. Neither had heard her enter the room.

"And you remember those dates specifically," Peirce said.

"No, Lieutenant. I remember that neither of us was out of the house alone any night in October. Home or away, we spent each night that month together. We're a close couple," she said, taking her husband's hand and intertwining their fingers. "I understand that you already arrested someone for those murders. Why are you harassing my husband?"

"We did arrest someone, but there wasn't enough evidence to hold him," Peirce said.

"Well, maybe you should be out finding that evidence rather than interrupting our dinner. Now, if you don't mind," Hyrum said, smiling for the first time since Peirce arrived. "If you're not going to arrest me, please leave."

Peirce said, "Enjoy your dinner." He turned and walked out the door.

Hyrum closed the door and walked back to the dining room, where Elaine was placing the food back on the table. "I don't know why you did that," he said, "but I'm glad you did."

Elaine sat in her chair and offered the crystal serving dish to Hyrum. "Asparagus, dear?"

Both Hyrum and Elaine ate in silence. Hyrum wondered why Elaine had lied and said they were together on those dreadful nights. Each was emblazoned in his mind. Hyrum knew exactly where he was and what he was doing when his lover, Sylvia, had died. It was the same for Michelle, someone he hated. He stared at his plate and moved his asparagus from side to side. He knew where he was on those nights, but what did Elaine know, and why did she say they were together?

Hyrum pushed his plate toward the center of the table. "I think I'm going to need a day or two to get past this. The death of a patient and an employee, and now the police questioning me, is just too much to handle. I need some time to absorb what's happened and to regain control of my emotions. Maybe I'll go to the Cape for a few days."

"Do you want me to come with you?" Elaine asked, not looking up from her plate.

"No, I'll probably be lousy company. I'll have Louise cancel my appointments for Thursday and Friday. You relax, and this will all be over in a few days."

"Whatever you say," Elaine said without looking up. She continued cutting her steak.

A confused look contorted Hyrum's face. *That was too easy*, he worried, but he said nothing.

31

Samuelsson sat in his dark-blue Ford sedan and stared into a news-paper spread open on the steering wheel. In actuality he was look-ing at a small video monitor on his lap that provided a view of the front door of Dr. Hyrum Green's office building. A yellow construc-tion hard hat placed in the back window of the sedan was not as casu-ally placed as one might have thought. It contained a video camera that provided an excellent view of anyone who entered or left the building. He occasionally looked up to check the side door directly. From this position Samuelsson could monitor all activity at both building en-trances, even though he appeared to be reading a newspaper and facing away from the front door.

Suddenly he leaned closer to the monitor. A young woman in a micro-miniskirt shimmied her way up the front stairs and entered the front door. Samuelsson snapped his head up and the monitor slid from his lap as his cell phone startled him back to the job at hand. He tapped the screen.

"Samuelsson," he croaked, clearing his throat.

"Samuelsson, Holloway—what's happening?"

"Dr. Green went into his office two hours ago, just like he did yester-day and the day before. He parks in the back lot, then walks to the front door. So far all this guy does is go to work and go home. How long does the lieutenant want me to stay with him?" Samuelsson fumbled with the monitor, trying to position it back on his lap.

"Sit tight," Holloway said and hung up the phone.

Samuelsson exhaled a long, hard breath and continued his surveil-lance, alternating between the monitor and the side door.

Minutes later a smile parted his lips. The buxom, miniskirted tempt-ress reappeared at the front door. Samuelsson held the monitor with both hands to afford the clearest view. He licked his lips as the woman turned away from the camera and bent to pick up the car keys she had dropped. When she continued to her car, Samuelsson craned his neck to catch a live view of her voluptuous locomotion—then he smiled and grudgingly returned to his monitor and his view of the side door. Two more hours, and he would be relieved.

Samuelsson looked again at the side door. Something wasn't right. He didn't know what was wrong, but he had a feeling… "No, no, no!" he cried, then tossed the video monitor onto the passenger seat and leaped from his car. He ran toward the side door. It took only a few seconds to realize what had changed. The sun cast long shadows across the parking lot. For the last hour, he had seen the shadow of Dr. Green's car protruding from behind the building as he watched the side door. Now, after he'd ogled the sexy blonde walking to her car, the shadow was gone. As he ran, he hoped that the sun had just shifted enough to eradicate the shadow.

"Shit!" he exclaimed, sliding to a stop in front of the empty parking space. Samuelsson looked left and right. Dr. Green's vehicle was gone. He bolted to the side door, threw it open, and ran down the hall toward Dr. Green's office. A paper sign taped to the door read: "The office will be closed until Monday. If you need emergency assistance…" Samuelsson ripped the sign from the door and crushed it into a ball. He dropped the paper ball to the corridor floor and ran to the front door of the building.

Across the parking lot, the young blond woman was backing her car out of her parking space. Samuelsson sprinted to the back of the car and beat on the trunk with both hands. Tires screeched as the woman slammed on her brakes to avoid backing over him.

"Police," Samuelsson said, holding his badge high in his left hand. "Please shut off your engine and step out of the car."

"I didn't do anything," she said. "You can't arrest me."

Samuelsson now looked more closely at the young woman: the tight, short skirt, ample cleavage, spike-heeled shoes, and not-too-subtle makeup. He finally realized that he was looking at a working girl.

"Who did you come to see?" Samuelsson said, trying to look intimidating.

"I didn't do anything; you can't arrest me."

"We can do this here or at the station. It's up to you."

"Look, I got a call from my service to meet a guy in the lobby of this building. He gave me fifty bucks to walk back out the front door and drop my keys. Hey, it was weird, but fifty bucks is fifty bucks. I didn't do anything wrong."

"What was the guy's name?"

"My service must know him or they wouldn't have sent me, but they told me to call him Mr. Smith. Can I go?"

"Yeah, you can go. Give me your card in case I need to see you—I mean, in case I have more questions."

"Sure, honey," she said, reaching into her blouse and pulling a business card from her bra. "Call me anytime."

Samuelsson returned to his car and dialed his cell phone. He said, "Holloway, Dr. Green is in the wind."

***

"Boss," yelled Holloway into Peirce's open office doorway. "Green skipped out on Samuelsson. He lost him."

"Call Green's office and home phones. Maybe his receptionist or his wife knows where he's gone. And try that Jameson guy. He's supposed to be a friend of Dr. Green's. Let me know what you find." Peirce swiveled his chair toward his computer monitor.

Holloway stared at the back of Peirce's head for a moment, then said, "Glad to be useful, boss."

Holloway lifted the receiver on his office cubicle phone and dialed Hyrum Green's office number.

"This is the office of Dr. Hyrum Green."

"Yes, this is Sergeant Holloway of the…"

"The office will be closed until November twenty-first. If this is an emergency, plea—" Holloway hung up the phone. "You got me," he said while running his finger down the list of names and telephone numbers scribbled on his desk blotter.

He lifted the receiver and dialed again, humming a pleasant tune as he dialed.

"This is Hyrum Green."

"Hello, Dr. Green, we've been—"

"I can't come to the phone right now but—" Holloway hung up the phone a little more forcefully. "Fool me twice, shame on me," he said, returning to the list on his desk blotter. He located the next number and stabbed it into the keypad. He waited as the phone rang four times.

"Hello, you've reached the home of Franklin Jameson."

Holloway decided, *OK, I'll leave a message.* He waited for the tone. Ten seconds later he was still waiting in silence. "Where's the fucking tone?" he bellowed.

"There is no fucking tone," Franklin replied. "I'm here; who is this?"

"Wrong number," Holloway uttered in a deep voice. "Very sorry." He hung up.

Holloway walked to Lieutenant Peirce's door. "Franklin Jameson is at home if you want to speak to him. Dr. Green is still MIA. What about the lovely Dr. Klein? Shall I try to locate her?"

"That's all right. I'll look for her," Peirce said, not meeting Holloway's eyes.

"Why did I know he was going to say that?" Holloway mumbled to himself.

***

Franklin heard the doorbell ring as he stood at the top of the stairs. At the same moment, he heard footsteps in the living room and thought he saw the shadow of someone running toward the kitchen.

"Is someone there?" he shouted. "I saw you go into the kitchen. Come out and face me like a man." He wasn't sure what he had seen, but he was sure he heard the creak of the kitchen door opening.

Franklin started down the stairs, bending to look through the balusters into the living room as he descended.

"Dennis, I know it's you. You've been following me for weeks. Why won't you talk to me?" He stepped off the landing and craned his neck to catch sight of the kitchen door, now closed, as he passed the archway. Resigned to the fact that his visitor had left, he walked to the front door.

The doorbell buzzed three times in quick succession. Peirce stood on the front porch, one hand on his hip, the other poking at the little round button.

Franklin looked through the peephole. He pulled his head back in an involuntary response as the police lieutenant thrust his badge into his view.

"It's Lieutenant Peirce, Mr. Jameson; please open the door."

"Lieutenant, I'm sorry to make you wait. What can I do for you?" Franklin asked, opening the door wide and looking left and right to see if anyone was running down the street in either direction. Lieutenant Peirce followed Franklin's glance and then looked him in the eye. Franklin broke eye contact first and motioned for Peirce to come in.

Peirce, now slightly confused by Franklin's actions, walked slowly into the foyer and followed Franklin into the living room. Franklin wasn't much of a housekeeper. Sam had assumed that most lunatics were fastidious. *That's one theory shot to hell,* he thought. Sam observed a glass and an empty plate on the coffee table, several articles of clothing tossed onto chairs, and an open newspaper lying on the sofa.

"Can I offer you something to drink, Lieutenant?" Franklin asked, beginning to straighten up. As Franklin started to lift the newspaper from the cushion, he noticed something concealed underneath. Rather than expose the veiled items, he turned to block Peirce's view and deftly tucked the documents inside the folded newspaper. Then he jogged the newspaper into an even package and placed it in a magazine rack.

"Sorry for the mess. I wasn't expecting company," Franklin said, looking around the room for any other unexpected surprises.

"This isn't a social call," Peirce said. "I have been trying to locate several people, and since you know all of them, I thought you might have some helpful information." *Fat chance,* Peirce thought.

"Have you seen Dr. Green or his wife recently?" Peirce continued, glancing up the stairs, and then walking toward the kitchen.

"They're not here. I'm home alone."

"Really, I thought I heard you calling to someone as I rang the bell."

"Yes, I was calling Dennis. He's a friend who was visiting me. I guess I didn't realize that he stepped out before you arrived," Franklin said, trying to concoct a believable story. He thought, *The best lies are those that are closest to the truth.*

"Does he have a reason to avoid the police?" Peirce asked, half-joking.

"I doubt that. He's an old friend who I hadn't seen in years. He left rather suddenly though. Maybe he has some outstanding parking tickets or overdue library books." Franklin snorted at his own joke.

"Yes, well, I'm not here about your friend," Sam said. "Would you have any idea where Dr. Green might be? Does he have a weekend or vacation home?"

Franklin opened a small drawer in the hall telephone table and immediately slammed it shut. Peirce watched as Franklin blocked his view once again with his body and carefully opened the drawer a few inches, then quickly closed it again.

"I thought I had a second phone number for Hyrum, but I guess not.

Sam, trying to decide if Franklin was hiding something or if this was just part of his deranged behavior said, "That would have been helpful."

"If you don't mind, Lieutenant, I have a few things I need to do." He moved toward the door, hoping that Peirce would follow.

Peirce meandered about the room. He picked up a small acrylic snow globe and held it to the light, squinting at the skyline of New York encased in the sphere. Next he walked toward the telephone table. Franklin rushed between Sam and the table. "I really do need to get some things done," he said, attempting to usher Peirce to the door.

Peirce made a quick about-face. "Just a few more questions and I'll let you get back to whatever it was you were doing. Have you heard from Dr. Klein in the last few days?" *Hopefully not in a dream,* Peirce thought.

"Several days ago I dreamed, had a premonition actually, that she was in the forest and she was in danger."

"Really? What can you tell me?"

Franklin's face emitted a newfound glow of enthusiasm. "She's being stalked by someone. He followed her into the mountains. I'm concerned for her safety."

"Well, I would like to find her. Was there anything in your dream, like a road sign or a map, that might disclose her location?" *I can't believe I said that,* Sam thought, but he was beginning to share Franklin's concern, and even though Franklin was a looney, you never knew.

"I don't know how I know this, but I think she's somewhere in the northern part of the state. The northern part of the state is mostly forest, isn't it?"

"Yes, that's very helpful," Sam said as he worked his way to the door. "If you hear from either Dr. Klein or Dr. Green, please call me." Sam took one last look up the stairs and walked to the front door. He descended the porch steps, grumbling something about a monumental waste of time.

* * *

Franklin closed the front door and leaned against it, breathing heavily. He checked the peephole to ensure that Lieutenant Peirce had driven away and then ran to the magazine rack.

"How could you do this to me?" he repeated several times as he unfolded the newspaper and examined the two manila file folders hidden inside: *Property of Dr. Ruth Klein—Confidential,* the files read.

Franklin noticed that the newspaper was not the current issue. It was several days old. He read the headline, "LOCAL PSYCHOLOGIST'S OFFICE BURGLARIZED, BURGLAR STILL AT LARGE."

The newspaper with the files inside was planted here to incriminate me, but by whom, he thought. *Is this an attempt by Dennis to incriminate me in the burglary? Is this how Dennis would get even with me for rejecting his friendship?*

No, he thought. *Where would Dennis have found the files, and how would he have gotten in here? And how would he know that Lieutenant Peirce would come to visit? Unless—the papers weren't intended to incriminate me at all, but were just inadvertently left on the couch. Could Dennis have done that?*

Next Franklin opened the drawer in the telephone table. Just as he thought, the folded paper in the drawer was the current month of Dr. Klein's desk calendar. Franklin ran his finger along the days of the calendar until he reached the previous week: *Vacation cabin, Northwest Realty, call to confirm.* Whoever left these papers in Franklin's house knew where Dr. Klein was vacationing. Franklin's concern for Ruth Klein's safety now became urgent. He must contact Northwest Realty, find the address of Ruth's vacation cabin, and warn her about the impending danger.

Dennis's attempts to make Franklin's life miserable were one thing, but if someone else, the murderer of Sylvia Radcliffe and Michelle Ackerman, was letting Franklin know that Ruth Klein was going to be his next victim—well, that was a call to action. He would leave at once.

32

R uth ushered her daughter out of the house for a day of shopping at the nearest small town. She made a list of needed provisions and checked her map for directions. While Emma buckled her seat belt, Ruth read aloud from the brochure left by the real estate broker: "'West Haven, a small unincorporated community, is a border town located on Pennsylvania Route 957 east of the borough of Sugar Grove.' They have an auction house, a dinner theater, a fireworks factory, and Sprinkle's Ice Cream Parlor. Sounds like everything we need."

"You can drop me off at Sprinkle's," Emma said, "and come get me when it's time to leave."

Twenty minutes later Ruth pulled her car to the side of the road and stopped just before a weathered painted sign that read: *You are now entering West Haven, Pennsylvania, Population 1,231.*

The road gently sloped down to a small village nestled among three hills. Each hill was replete with individual stands of gnarly black cherry, cracked shag sycamore, and tall, slender aspen trees, part of the Allegheny National Recreation Area.

Ruth began to wax sentimental. She placed her hand on Emma's shoulder and pointed to the oddly picturesque town in the clearing. It was like they had entered a time portal and traveled back to the eighteenth century. Victorian-style stone houses on the outskirts of the town exemplified a look of restrained elegance, a monument to a simpler time.

"You see, Emma," she said in a somber tone. "It was a time when people were satisfied with the uncomplicated joys of life. Children played on the floor with carved wooden toys. Old folks sat in rocking chairs before a crackling fire. The smell of a stew made from freshly gathered vegetables cooking in a cast-iron kettle floated on cool evening breezes."

Ruth checked her rearview mirror just before pulling away from the shoulder and noticed a silver sedan parked about one hundred yards behind her car. If she had really thought about it, she might have wondered why a car was parked in the middle of nowhere, but she didn't. Her cell phone had messages waiting for her, and she was anxious to get the latest news from the outside world. After Ruth and Emma descended the hill to the Farmington turnpike, the main street of the community of West Haven, the silver sedan inched out from the apron and maintained its distance from the two women it followed.

Raised wooden sidewalks along First Street formed a thoroughfare between picturesque boutiques and quaint country stores connecting new and old, fixtures and finery for tourists alongside essential commodities for the local folk. A cornucopia of rich odors and aromas assaulted the senses. Antique shops stacked high with distressed furniture and unique treasures wafted the faint scent of mildew onto the street each time a patron walked through the door. The all-too-sweet perfume of potpourri emanated from the Gift Shoppe, preceding one's arrival at the storefront. A few more steps, however, and shoppers were rewarded with the fragrance of fresh-baked bread and cinnamon rolls from the Love-in Oven, reminding them that breakfast had been hours ago. Small café tables in front of the bakery window invited weary shoppers to recharge with a cappuccino and a sweet roll.

A man stood on the corner handing out circulars for a performance of *The Unsinkable Molly Brown* at the Park Dinner Theater tonight at eight. His shoes were dusty and he was unshaven, but he tipped his bowler hat and smiled at each passerby as he anxiously anticipated reaching the bottom of his stack of circulars so that he could call it a day and retreat to the West Haven Saloon.

Ruth drove down the main street, looking for a familiar supermarket, maybe a Sure Save or a Wegman's, but found instead a butcher shop advertising fresh-killed chickens and a green grocer boasting heirloom tomatoes and winter squash, each store strategically located at the end of the street, out of the well-traveled tourist route and near the public parking lot.

The walkways were a river of brightly colored ski parkas and decorative shopping bags, punctuated by the occasional plaid lumberjack coat on bearded men wearing sweat-stained baseball caps with hunting licenses in plastic envelopes pinned to the crown.

Ruth and Emma spent the next hour strolling past shop windows and browsing through a used-book store. They tasted the "World-Famous Pierogi" at Rutka's Polish Deli and eventually arrived at Sprinkle's. While waiting in line before the sidewalk window, Ruth noticed a familiar reflection in the glass. It appeared to be the same silver sedan that had stopped behind them on the road. It was now on the opposite side of the street across from the ice-cream store. Ruth lifted her sunglasses and tried to catch sight of the driver, but the reflection from the window obscured the driver's features. When she turned to look directly at the car, the driver sped away. She tried to see the license plate number but could only see the first two letters, *EP*.

"Did you see that?" Ruth said to Emma, pointing in the direction of the dust cloud left by the retreating car.

"See what?"

"Nothing," Ruth said, shaking her head in an attempt to dislodge the paranoia that seemed to be creeping into her thoughts. Ruth knew how unlikely it was that someone would be following her. She knew it intellectually, but her frayed nerves were unconvinced.

"What's going on?" Emma asked. "You look worried."

"It's nothing," Ruth insisted. "I was just thinking of the chores I need to do while I'm here. Why don't you go inside and sit, have some ice cream, and I'll run some errands, make some calls, and come back for you in half an hour." She gave Emma a twenty-dollar bill, kissed her on the forehead, and marched off to the general store.

Berger's market and farm stand was a delightful change from the feigned elegance of the pretentious boutiques. The abundance of fresh fruits and vegetables on display hopefully counteracted the deleterious effects on health that would result from the plethora of deep-fried and sugary baked goods offered in the gourmet food shops and sidewalk cafés. Ruth wasn't generally a health-food enthusiast, but a desire to provide nutritious food for her growing daughter and a recent encounter with her bathroom scale were having an effect on her grocery choices. She filled her shopping cart with fresh salad greens, sweet potatoes, squash, and brussels sprouts. Ruth paused in front of a shelf lined with rhubarb and pecan pies. *Woman does not live by leafy greens alone,* she thought, and slid a pecan pie into her cart. She looked left and right to ensure that she wasn't being watched as she tipped a can of pressurized whipped cream into her basket and rushed to the check-out counter, keeping her head low and avoiding all eye contact.

Next was a stop at the butcher shop, where rib eye steaks and bacon eclipsed any pretense of dietary concern. Then she was off to the car in the municipal parking lot to secure her booty in a Styrofoam cooler and finally listen to her phone messages.

The first message was from her answering service. "Sorry to bother you on vacation, Dr. Klein. All patient inquiries have been redirected to Dr. Schultz as you instructed, but you have a few personal messages." The operator went on to list her messages. The first was from Lieutenant Peirce. It was only seven words: "Sam Peirce, please call and be careful." *How sweet of him to check on me. He probably misses our lively exchanges,* she mused with a slight blush. The second message was from Sophia. She simply said, "Somebody rob your office, but don't worry, they don't take much, just some files." Ruth's cheeks faded from a light blush to pale white. *Maybe Sam Peirce's call wasn't personal after all; maybe it was a warning.* The last message was from Clair at Northwest Realty. She thanked Ruth for promoting the cabin to so many friends. "I had four calls in the last two days about the cabin you're renting. They all wanted information about the area and the cabin's location. If you ever want a job in real estate…" Ruth hung up the phone.

A dark cloud moved in front of the sun. The view through Ruth's windshield changed from bright and hopeful to dark and despondent. She stared into the parking lot, her vision an unfocused blur as she pondered this new information. Was someone following her? Could the man who chased her through the basement of her office building have actually been Sylvia Radcliffe's murderer? Did the murderer believe that she had information that could expose him? Was she being followed right now? Ruth's vision began to clear as her consciousness returned to the present moment. When her eyes finally focused, she was looking at a car parked at the opposite side of the lot. It looked like the same car she had noticed twice before.

Ruth sprang from her car and strode across the parking lot. She paused. What if someone was in the car? Should she confront him? She marshaled her courage and soldiered on. The parked car was empty. *This is insanity,* she thought. *Get control of yourself. There must be hundreds of silver sedans that look just like this one. It's a common color and a common style of car.* She was about to chastise herself for her ill-considered fear when she had one more thought. She walked to the back of the sedan and looked at the license plate. EP23JL—it started with *EP.* This was the car that had sped away from the ice-cream shop and probably the same car that was parked behind her on the highway. She turned three hundred and sixty degrees, looking for the driver. She was alone. At least he was no longer following her. She began to walk back to her car, then paused. She looked toward the main street of town. "Emma!"

Ruth ran across the parking lot and took the two steps to the raised wooden sidewalk in one stride. She bumped the shoulder of a shopper who turned, but Ruth was already at the door of Sprinkle's before the woman could express her anger.

Ruth's eyes scanned the tables, then she rushed to the cashier. She shouted, "Excuse me" as she cut in front of the line of patrons. Leaning on the counter with both hands, Ruth said, "Did you see a young girl in a blue coat leave the store?"

"Yes, I think so. She was with a man; her father, maybe? They went toward the bookstore. I suppose kids can be a real handful at that age," he said with a smile.

"What do you mean?" Ruth said.

"Nothing really," the cashier said. "She didn't want to go, and he practically had to drag her out."

Ruth turned and ran out of the store, chanting "Emma, Emma" in a strained, guttural tone.

Through the window of the bookstore, Ruth could see a man standing with his back to her, his open coat blocking her view of the child in front of him. His hands were on the child's shoulders, restraining her. Ruth grabbed the door handle and yanked the door open. "Emma!" she shouted.

"Mom," came the reply, but it came from the wrong direction, from behind Ruth. She turned to see Emma standing on the sidewalk, holding a small shopping bag. Ruth turned back to the man and the child, who were now staring at her in bewilderment. "I'm sorry," she said. "I thought you were someone else."

Ruth turned again, held Emma close, and scolded her. "Why did you leave the ice-cream shop? I was afraid..." She paused. "You might have gotten lost."

"How could I get lost? The town's only five blocks long."

***

Now Ruth had a decision to make. She could pack up her belongings and her daughter and run back to the city, where she could hide among familiar objects and supportive people, or stay and stand up against whoever was following her.

She now had no doubt that she was being followed. This was not her overactive imagination causing concern. She was not jumping at shadows. An assault on her office was the final proof she needed to convince her of her vulnerability and that the threat was indeed real.

"Wait one minute, Emma," Ruth said as she stopped at the rack of travel and weekly event brochures. "I want to see what's happening in this lovely town this week."

Ruth pulled out several pamphlets and circulars advertising local events for the coming week. She also selected a bus schedule covering most of the state and carefully slipped it into her pocket. Now she had two more tasks to perform to complete her plan.

A few minutes later, before they drove out of town, Ruth stopped in front of Bert's Sporting Goods store. She told Emma to wait in the car. Ruth locked the doors and looked up and down the street to ensure that the silver car was nowhere in sight. She rushed to the hunting section of the store and bought two boxes of twelve-gauge shotgun shells and a handheld compass. After leaving the check-out counter, she removed the shells from their boxes and distributed them between her jacket pockets and her purse. She made a three-minute cell phone call and returned to the car with the compass in her hand.

"Maybe this will help me take walks in the woods without getting lost." She hoped that Emma would believe that the purchase of the compass was the reason for the stop.

"I'll be happy if it helps us find our way back to the cabin," Emma said. "I don't think the gal in the GPS wants to talk to you anymore."

"Very funny," Ruth said, feeling confident that she had just committed the perfect crime.

***

The sun was low in the late afternoon sky. Ruth sat in the wooden swing on the porch sipping a glass of red wine. The rhythmic creak of the thick ropes supporting the swing was the only sound disturbing the silence. She gently rocked back and forth, then stopped. Ruth noticed that not a leaf on a tree or a blade of grass on the ground was moving. The world had come to a complete stop. *It was so quiet.* She mused, *What if the world has really stopped, and everyone else has disappeared?* What if she were the only person left on a silent planet? It was peaceful. She felt warm and safe for the first time today, but suddenly she was lonely.

In the sky, high overhead, a turkey vulture circled, searching for game or carrion, its wings spread wide and motionless. It banked to the left and lost altitude, then turned right and suddenly rose on a column of warm air. The bird seemed to use no energy at all, its altitude dependent solely on air currents. Its only decision was to turn left or right. If it chose the direction of a thermal, it was rewarded by a boost in altitude, ensuring that it would stay aloft for a little longer. But if it chose wrong—if it chose dead air—it would lose altitude, sending it lower, closer to the ground, shortening its flight, and lessening its chances to find food. Of course it could always take matters into its own hands, or in this case, its wings, and flap to gain altitude, but that would cost precious energy, energy not easily replaced. *Life is like the flight of that bird*, Ruth thought. *You choose a direction, left or right, and hope the wind is kind to you. If you choose correctly you flourish, but if you choose wrong—make a mistake—you must double your efforts or pay the consequences.*

Now Ruth could remain motionless and wait for a kind breeze or lucky turn to provide the thermal that would keep her aloft, or she could take matters into her own hands.

"Time to flap your wings," she said aloud and walked into the house.

***

"Why do I have to go home?" Emma asked, looking at her suitcase, half-filled with her clothes, lying on her bed. She watched as Ruth emptied the dresser, carefully packing her belongings. "Mom, why do I have to go home?" she repeated.

"You have school on Monday. I made arrangements with Sophia to meet you at the bus terminal, and she's going to stay with you for a few days until I get back."

"But you said I could miss a few days of school, and why aren't you coming back with me?"

"I changed my mind. You shouldn't miss school, but I have no patients until Thursday, and I'm going to take advantage of that opportunity to catch up on some paperwork."

"So you just want to get rid of me for a few days."

"No, honey, not at all. I'll miss you terribly, but I could use some time to organize my thoughts. I know I haven't said much about it, but losing a patient has been difficult. Sylvia Radcliffe was in my office once a week for the last three years. Our relationship was one of business rather than personal, but it still feels like I lost a friend. I need a little time to grieve," Ruth said, hoping she was convincing enough to keep Emma from knowing her real purpose—to send Emma away from any danger from the stalker who was pursuing her, so she could possibly confront him and put an end to her fears for her family's safety.

"I'm sorry. I guess I didn't think about how her death might have affected you." Emma wrapped her arms around her mother and hugged her close. Slight feelings of guilt began to rise up and invade Ruth's firm convictions to send Emma home, but she quickly brushed them away in favor of her overpowering maternal instincts. Emma would be safe with Sofia, and Ruth would find an answer to the question of who was harassing her. She might even determine who the murderer was. The police had closed the case, but the murderer was obviously still at large. She needed to act. At first she had pursued the case so that justice would be done for Sylvia, but now it had become personal. Her life and, more importantly, the life of her child may hang in the balance. She would stick with the plan.

33

Peirce carefully maneuvered his car out of the city past the crowded strip malls, each sporting multiple check-cashing stores and lottery kiosks, past the rows of dilapidated single-family homes with multiple satellite dish antennas sprouting from almost every window, and past the discount stores selling everything, including the soul of the neighborhood, for only ninety-nine cents.

He grimaced and pointed his car at the rolling hills and the open skies of the Endless Mountains. He pulled a cigarette from his pack and placed it in his mouth. Almost immediately, he plucked it from his lips and stared at it. This did not fit his mood. He crushed the cigarette between his fingers and held his palm outside the window, grinding the tobacco in his fist and giving up its debris to the wind.

The suburban neighborhoods soon gave way to sprawling dairy farms, then rolling hills, and finally tracts of forest land. The evening air had turned cool, and Sam raised his collar and rolled up the window. He settled back in his seat and took in a deep breath of air laced with pine scent. Pine scent? *Why is the smell stronger with the window closed?* He scanned the windshield. Hanging from the rearview mirror was an air freshener Alicia had hung in an effort to sanitize his car the last time she had ridden with him. Peirce ripped the pine-tree-shaped piece of plastic with its artificial chemical scent from the mirror and threw it out the window. He rolled up the window and inhaled deeply a second time. The smell of stale cigarettes and cold coffee slowly began to reassert itself. Now this was his car.

In the last forty-eight hours since he had interviewed Dr. Green, a lot had changed. He had reopened the Sylvia Radcliffe and Michelle

Ackerman murder cases, much to the chagrin of his captain, and was now off to find Ruth Klein, much to the chagrin of his girlfriend. Why? Well, because Dr. Klein might be in danger, and he was a police officer sworn to serve the public. Even he wasn't sure he believed that one. The truth of the matter was he didn't know why he was driving to find Ruth Klein. He could have called the local police department and asked them to check on her. He could have sent Holloway or Samuelsson, although Samuelsson was not in his good graces right now. For some reason, a reason for which he was probably not even aware, he wanted to do it himself. For better or worse, he was going north to find Ruth Klein and her daughter.

Locating Ruth had not been an easy task. If his Spanish had been a little better, he might have avoided some of the pitfalls. He recalled his earlier conversation:

"Dr. Klein residence," the woman's voice said.

"This is Lieutenant Peirce of the county police department."

"Wrong number," the woman said with a pronounced Latino accent just before she hung up the phone.

He redialed. The phone rang four times before he heard Ruth's voice telling him to leave a message, or if this was a patient emergency to call her service number.

Peirce spoke after the tone. "Please, por favor, I'm trying to locate Dr. Klein. *Donde está el Dr. Klein? Es muy importante. No soy con el INS.*"

The housekeeper picked up the phone.

"So Ruth hires illegal aliens," he said, only half-covering his phone with his hand.

"El doctor y señorita Emma no oyen. Ellos van de vacaciones. No esté de vuelta hasta la próxima semana." The words came in rapid succession.

"Whoa, wait, wait, my Spanish is not that good," Peirce said. The population of Spanish-speaking citizens had increased fivefold in his precinct in the last few years, and Sam was struggling to remember anything he could from the three years of Spanish he had taken in high school.

"Then why don't we speak English?" the woman said, clearly annoyed at his assumption that she possessed limited language skills. "And I was born in Philadelphia, for your information."

After that embarrassing moment, and a profuse apology, Sam learned the name and phone number of the real estate broker who had rented the cabin to Ruth.

The broker was halfway through her sales pitch before Sam could explain that he was interested in Ruth, not the cabin, although he did not explain it in exactly those words.

"You're the fourth person today who has called about that cabin," she boasted. "Our advertising must be better than I thought."

That was disturbing, Sam thought. This entire day was one misunderstanding after another. It began this morning as he packed for the trip.

Peirce had placed a blue shirt facedown on his bed and carefully folded the sleeves over to the back of the shirt. He then folded the bottom of the shirt one-third of the way up and folded the sides in thirds over the back. He looked at the oddly shaped parcel he had created, grabbed it by one corner, and flung it into his suitcase. "Screw it," he said, "I'm sure the hotel will have an iron." From that point packing had become a matter of tossing the remaining clothes that he had taken from his closet and dresser drawers into the valise. He balled his socks into a tight package, held it over his head, and tossed it in the direction of the bed.

"He shoots, he scores," Alicia said, standing in the doorway of Sam's bedroom and watching the socks land in the valise for two points.

Sam, now slightly red-faced, took the remaining socks and underwear in his arms, walked them to the suitcase, and dumped them in. He looked at Alicia for a moment, then hurried to his closet and retrieved his jogging suit and running shoes.

"Are you sure you'll have time to run while you're away?" Alicia said.

"Every day—it will be my top priority."

"You're such a liar," she said, "but at least the extra weight of carrying them in your suitcase will give you some exercise."

Sam kissed her on the forehead, then patted her on the rump as he walked by.

"I should be gone for only a day or two. I just need to make sure that Dr. Klein is safe."

"Why would—Dr. Klein, is it—not be safe?" Alicia asked. "Who is he, anyway?"

"She—Dr. Klein is a she." The second the words left Sam's lips, he knew he was in for a long discussion. He decided, probably in vain, to preempt her objections by explaining his concern.

"Dr. Klein was the psychologist of a recent murder victim," Sam said as small beads of sweat began to form on his brow. "I have been trying to locate our prime murder suspects, but they seem to all have left town. I'm concerned that the murderer may think…"

Alicia stood with her arms folded across her chest, listening.

"The murderer may think that the victim told Ruth, er, Dr. Klein…"

Alicia looked at Sam through squinting eyes.

"Told Dr. Klein something that might incriminate him," Sam finished, feeling as though he had just incriminated himself. "Dr. Klein is at a cabin north of here where there is no cell phone service."

A small crease formed between Alicia's eyebrows, and she pursed her lips.

"So I'm going there to make sure she's all right, because no one has heard from her. Not that I usually hear from her. I mean, we speak about the case, because the victim was her patient—"

"You already said that," Alicia interrupted.

"I did, didn't I? Well, anyway someone had been stalking her, and when I tried to catch him in her basement, I tried to tackle him, but I tackled her by mistake and…Oh hell, Alicia, there's nothing going on." Sam held his arms out with his palms up.

"I never said there was," Alicia said. She turned and walked out of the bedroom.

Sam took his off-duty automatic from his top dresser drawer, checked that it was unloaded, and placed it in the suitcase along with two boxes of ammunition, two extra fifteen-round magazines, and a pair of handcuffs. "Maybe I should shoot myself right now and get it over quickly," Sam mumbled to himself as he closed the suitcase and followed Alicia out of the room.

***

Sam adjusted the visor to shield his eyes as he drove into the setting sun. He blinked and raised his eyebrows, trying to stifle a yawn. The coffee in the Styrofoam cup set in the car's console had been cold for at least half an hour, and his stomach was beginning to make noises that drowned out the sound of the car's engine. Sam reached into the bag of carrot sticks thoughtfully provided by Alicia and bit off a chunk as though it were the head of the murderer he was pursuing. He looked longingly at a burger joint that flashed by on the opposite side of the highway: "Finger Lick'in Ribs with the best slaw in the Appalachian Mountains."

Sam turned onto Destiny Road. The farther he traveled, the narrower the road became. He stopped at a fork in the road. A tall sycamore tree stood dead center, its branches pointing in both directions. To the left, an arrow with the words *Lake Front Road* beckoned. Sam had read the brochure boasting of a sand beach within walking distance of the cabin. He chose the lakefront road. The road continued to narrow. This couldn't be right. Sam pulled the map from the car's console and began to unfold it with his right hand. He placed it on the steering wheel and reached up to turn on the courtesy light above the windshield. A small piece of paper on which he had written the directions to the cabin fell out of the map and floated to the floor. Sam reached down to retrieve the paper. A sudden movement on the road ahead of him caused Sam to cut the wheel sharply to the left, sending his car off the narrow road and into a shallow ditch, narrowly missing a large opossum waddling across the road ridden by a full family of offspring.

Sam shifted into reverse and gently pressed the gas pedal to back out of the ditch. The front wheel spun, but the car stayed in place. He slipped the lever into drive and tried to move forward to rock the car out, but again the wheel just spun. After two more tries back and forth, each with more pressure on the gas pedal, and faster spinning of the tires, Sam decided it was futile. Some rescue mission this was turning out to be. *He* would now need to be rescued. Sam took his AAA card from his wallet and poked his cell phone to bring up the keypad. A message ran across the screen: *No service available.*

"That's just perfect," he said. On the opposite side of the road, the opossum sat with her brood, obviously explaining how no good turn goes unpunished. An object lesson Sam himself was beginning to believe. He shook his fist in the air in her direction. It was time to get out and walk. Well, he did tell Alicia he would exercise while he was away—he hadn't meant it, though.

Just a few yards farther down the road, Sam parted the fronds of a large wild fern and caught a glimpse of a body of water. He pushed his way through the bushes to the wide sand beach. The sun was sinking fast into the water. The red cast against the clouds was quickly turning to gray, and soon would be black. Sam rushed back to his car and changed into his jogging pants and running shoes. He strapped on his shoulder holster and pulled his sport coat over his shirt. He stuffed two extra ammunition magazines and his handcuffs into his inside pocket and headed back to the beach. The cabin was purported to be within walking distance of Chapman Lake. The real estate broker had said that Chapman Lake was a sixty-five-acre oasis of recreational facilities adjacent to state game lands and the Allegheny National Forest. Sam was obviously on the forest side of the lake, since there were no facilities of any kind in sight. He walked north along the bank, hoping to see a cabin or some other indication of civilization before losing what was left of the light.

34

The path from the parking lot to the cabin seemed longer somehow. Ruth stood very still beside her car, cocked her head, and listened for any unnatural sound or sudden movement. Everything looked so different now that she was alone. The last rays of the sun cast odd shadows on the path. They moved suspiciously with a life of their own, not at all like low-hanging tree branches simply dancing in the wind. She studied every detail of the surrounding forest, looking for anything abnormal. Any sign that someone might be looming in the bushes. Feeling more vulnerable than she could ever remember, but satisfied that she was probably alone, Ruth hurried, almost ran, to the cabin.

Emma was gone. Together, they had driven to West Haven before noon. Ruth monitored her rearview mirror almost to distraction looking for the silver car that she was sure would be following her. She believed that she had seen it on several occasions laying back, trying not to cause suspicion, yet always, relentlessly following. The bus from Lowell was scheduled to leave for Wilkes-Barre at four o'clock. After a light lunch and much complaining from Emma, Ruth hurried to the bus stop just minutes before departure and settled her daughter into a window seat directly behind the driver. She kissed Emma good-bye and phoned Sophia to confirm Emma's arrival time at Wilkes-Barre. The bus driver, a jovial man in his fifties, smiled and assured Ruth that he would keep an eye on his most valuable charge. He turned and winked at Emma before he flopped into the driver's seat, waved at Ruth, and closed the bus door.

Ruth waited to see that no last-minute passengers boarded the bus. Satisfied that her daughter would be safer at home with Sophia than remaining here where some nut was stalking her, Ruth returned to her car. Now that Emma was on her way home, Ruth could get on with the remainder of her plan. She drove back toward the cabin. "There you are, you persistent bastard," she quipped as she recognized the silver car following at a distance. Although the stalker's car had been a source of fear and frustration, Ruth was now happy to see it. As long as the silver car was still following her, she knew Emma would be safely away from danger.

An hour later, as she rushed up the stone steps to the cabin, she noticed what appeared to be mud on the porch near the front door. Had the mud been there when they left this morning? Had Emma tracked mud onto the porch? Ruth peeked through the window next to the door. Everything seemed to be the way she left it.

Ruth entered the cabin and immediately retrieved the shotgun from the rack over the fireplace. With shaking hands, she pulled two twelve-gauge shotgun shells from her pocket and fumbled them into the breach. Yesterday, Ruth had hidden the rest of the shells in the sugar tin in the kitchen, but these two had never left her pocket. These two were her insurance against someone breaking in and finding her stash of ammunition. She snapped the action closed, checked that the safety was set, and looked around the room. Traces of the same mud tracked on the porch were present on the rug near the front door. Had it been there all along? Ruth cursed her lack of scrutiny before leaving that morning. Had she simply failed to notice details of the room prior to leaving? Could someone have been in the cabin while she was gone, or was the dirt just the result of her poor housekeeping skills? Probably the latter, but she wasn't taking any chances. She worked her way through each room, bobbing her head into and out of the doorway before entering, just as she had seen on so many police television shows. She checked the sugar tin. The shells were still there.

Next Ruth checked each of the windows and found that they had no locks. She thought for a minute, then ran to the kitchen and returned with a fistful of forks and two pots. Ruth slightly lifted each of the two living room windows, placed the tips of the fork tines on the windowsill, and closed the window, suspending the forks by the tips of their tines. Next she placed a pot on the floor below the forks at each of the two living room windows and closed the curtains. Her plan was that if someone lifted the window from the outside, the forks would fall into the pot and warn her. *I guess watching all those reruns of* MacGyver *episodes with Emma was worth something after all. And they say television isn't educational.*

Once Ruth was sure that the cabin was clear and safe, and that all windows except the bedroom window were rigged with her makeshift alarm, she shut off all the lights except for one in her bedroom. She pulled down the shade and closed the curtains so that some light shone through the window to the outside, but one could not see in. Now she sat in the darkened living room on the overstuffed tan chair with the shotgun across her lap. The trap was set.

The acrid smell of ash from the burned-out embers in the fireplace caused her to stifle a sneeze. She held her breath until the urge passed. Here she would sit and wait. Here she would make her stand, metaphorically.

Who was stalking her? Her money was on Hyrum Green. She had been over all the facts as she knew them a hundred times and always came to the same conclusion. He was involved in some way with each of the murder victims and had been present in the building when she was chased through the basement of her office building. That wasn't exactly hard evidence, but it was enough for now. She would wait and see…*Wait and see what?* Suddenly her throat was dry. The collar of her blouse was too tight. It was hard to breathe. *What am I doing?*

You're a psychologist, a woman of science, not a vigilante. Her palms began to sweat. The shotgun was heavy on her lap. She felt slightly dizzy. This was insane. It was time to stop this nonsense and go home.

Ruth placed the shotgun against the wall next to the chair and began to rise. A creaking sound coming from the front porch stopped her in a half-standing, half-crouching position. Frozen in place, she listened. Another creaking sound from the front porch. Someone was definitely outside. Ruth dropped to one knee in front of the chair and reached for the shotgun. Her breath came fast and unevenly. She crawled across the rug, then rose to her feet but kept her head low as she crept into the kitchen. Ruth felt her way along the kitchen counter until she found the large sugar tin next to the stove. Why hadn't she taken more shotgun shells before? She reached into the tin and grabbed a handful of shells and slipped them into her pocket. Now she crawled to the kitchen door, dragging the gun by its barrel. She reached up to feel around for the doorknob. Ruth tried to turn the knob, but the gun oil from the barrel of the shotgun caused her hand to slip, not giving her purchase on the knob. She reached in her pocket and pulled out her handkerchief. Several rounds of shotgun shells, each coated with sugar granules, spilled onto the floor. Ruth froze, waiting to see if her clumsiness had betrayed her to the prowler. An additional creak from the front porch assured her that he was still out front. Using her handkerchief, Ruth quietly turned the knob and slipped out through the kitchen door. The cool night air striking the perspiration on her neck sent chills down her spine; it was an icy slap on the back that helped focus her wit and resolve. *I can do this.* The kitchen door exited onto a small deck that connected to the porch at the front of the cabin. Ruth slipped off her shoes and moved toward the porch, hoping the intruder couldn't hear her teeth chattering or her knees knocking.

On the front porch, a figure of a man was hunched over under the living room window. Ruth turned the corner of the cabin, took two steps, and placed the barrel of the shotgun against the man's backside. "Don't move," she said in as deep a voice as she could muster. In an instant, the man rolled to his left, slapped at the barrel of the shotgun, and knocked it from her hands. It skittered across the decking and came to rest on the stone steps. In almost the same motion, the man drew an automatic handgun from inside his jacket and shouted, "Police, freeze!"

Ruth threw her hands in the air and in a high-pitched voice squeaked, "Don't shoot!"

"Dr. Klein?" Sam said, quickly lowering his gun as he sat up on the porch.

"Ruth," she replied, standing over him. "Remember? We're on a first-name basis. I could have shot you," she said. "What were you doing on the porch?"

"I was cleaning the mud from my shoes before ringing the doorbell. And don't worry—you wouldn't have shot me."

"You think not? If you hadn't ripped the gun out of my hands so fast, you would be dead."

"I don't think so."

"You're pretty smug for a man who almost died. I could easily have pulled the trigger. Do you think I haven't the nerve?"

"You wouldn't have shot me."

"Why, because I'm a woman?"

"No." Sam lifted the shotgun and pointed to the breach. "Because you forgot to release the safety."

"Oh, well, come inside. What are you doing here, anyway?"

"I was wor…trying to locate you to tell you about a break-in at your office. No one had heard from you for days—and by the way, why is that?"

Ruth explained about the lack of cell phone service in the area and that she had not gone into town for the first three days. "You were trying to locate me?" she repeated with a coy smile.

"Yes," Sam said, avoiding eye contact. "Certain aspects of the Sylvia Radcliffe murder case have changed." He fidgeted with his gun. "I think we need to have a discussion."

Ruth burned with excitement. "Come in, come in, and tell me all about it. I'll make coffee."

***

Sam stood in the living room while Ruth disappeared into the kitchen. Several magazines were fanned out on the coffee table, including *Bipolar Disorder Resource*, *Human Nature Review*, *The National Psychologist*, and *In-Mind*, among others. Sam picked up a copy of *Psychology Today* and thumbed through the first few pages; it was the only magazine he recognized from the newsstand near the precinct. A loud clatter emanated from the kitchen, followed by the rattling of metal pans, the slamming of cabinet doors, and finally the shattering of glass.

"A cold drink will do," Sam said. "That is, if there are any glasses left when you finish."

"You're going to get coffee," came the voice from the kitchen, "even if you have to drink it from a jelly jar, smartass."

Sam dropped the magazine back onto the table and chuckled. "I'm sure your coffee will be wonderful."

Ruth nodded with a satisfied smile as she carefully swept the broken pieces of a glass bowl into a corner. *I'll deal with this later,* she thought. The water kettle began to whistle. Ruth spooned twelve tablespoons of coffee into her French press and lifted the kettle from the stove. "Pot holder, pot holder, pot holder," she rapidly cried as she dropped the kettle back onto the stove, making a loud clanking noise and splashing water onto the burner, extinguishing the flame. "Goddamn it," she yelled. "Sorry, Sam, I'm going to have to work on my anger-management skills."

"Don't worry about it," Sam said. "The instinctive, natural way to express anger is to respond aggressively. Anger is a natural, adaptive response to threats; it inspires powerful, often aggressive feelings and behaviors, which allow us to fight and to defend ourselves when we are attacked. A certain amount of anger, therefore, is necessary for our survival."

Ruth looked perplexed as she poked her head out of the partially open kitchen door. In the center of the living room, Sam stood reading aloud from an article in *Human Nature Review.* He looked up, saw Ruth, and began to laugh.

Ruth shook her head. "How about stirring up the fire, Sigmund? The coffee will be ready in a minute."

A half hour later, Sam and Ruth were deeply involved in Sam's most recent theory of the crime. The case had been reopened, and Hyrum Green was now a person of interest. "Do you like him for the murders?" Ruth asked.

"Do I *like* him?" Sam asked. "I think you've been watching too much television, but Dr. Green did elude our stakeout and disappeared. He certainly is moving up on the list."

"What about Franklin—are you satisfied that he couldn't have committed the crimes?"

"Not totally," Sam said, pouring a second cup of coffee for Ruth and himself. "He knows things about the crimes, like the shape and location of Sylvia's tattoo, but he doesn't seem to have the strength or physical capability to have killed her. She was very fit, according to the medical examiner, and put up quite a struggle. I think we're looking for someone stronger than Franklin, or at least someone without his disability."

Sam stood and walked to the living room window. He parted the drapes, lifted the shade, and observed the makeshift silverware window alarm; then he looked at the shotgun, and finally at Ruth.

"What are you doing here alone?" Sam asked. "I thought you were vacationing with your daughter."

"I sent her home. She has school tomorrow."

"Why didn't you go with her? You know, it's possible that the murderer could come looking for you." He stepped into the bedroom and noticed that the bedroom window did not have a fork alarm.

"Oh, I guess I didn't think of that," Ruth said, turning to watch him investigate.

"Wait a minute," Sam said, striding back into the room. "You stayed here hoping to catch the murderer. Do you have reason to believe he's here? Have you seen someone suspicious near the cabin?"

"Just you," Ruth said, still not meeting his eyes.

"You were ready; you were lying in wait for the killer. You have alarms on all the windows except for the bedroom." He opened the living room window and watched the fork fall into the pot with a loud clatter. "Do you have a death wish?"

"Oh, it works," Ruth said involuntarily, then immediately wiped the smile from her face. "Ah, no, I just happened to take that old shotgun off the rack on the fireplace mantel when I heard a noise outside. I didn't even know if the gun was loaded."

"And I guess those aren't shotgun shells bulging out of your pockets," Sam said, pointing at the stuffed pockets of her slacks and sweater.

"Look, Sam, I have been afraid that someone may have followed me up here since the day I arrived. I tried to call you, but I was told you were away on assignment. I sent Emma home to keep her out of harm's way. I can't live in fear. I'd rather fight."

"That sounds noble, but foolish. You can't catch this man. He's killed at least two women already. You're not a detective, you're a…a…"

"A woman?" Ruth said, standing to face him.

"I was going to say a psychologist, but you certainly are a woman." The sides of Sam's mouth turned up ever so slightly into a smile.

Ruth softened her stare. She actually felt that he was paying her a compliment. "Well, I was scared. I thought someone might be following me, and I didn't know what else to do."

"I know what to do," Sam said, placing the shotgun back on the gun rack. "You and I are going into West Haven. We'll have dinner and stay at a hotel for the night. I have a room booked." He paused. "And I'm sure they will have another." Now Sam avoided Ruth's eyes. "Then tomorrow, in the daylight, we'll come back and pack your things and go home."

Ruth usually had difficulty taking orders, but he was right. She swallowed her pride and said, "Give me a minute to get my toothbrush and a change of clothes."

Sam and Ruth walked along the path to the clearing that served as a parking lot for the cabin. "Where's your car?" Ruth asked.

"I don't know."

"You lost your car, Detective?" Ruth chided.

"I can find it tomorrow while you pack." Sam walked to Ruth's car with his head held high, his demeanor indicating that there was nothing at all unusual about losing one's car.

Sam stopped so abruptly that Ruth walked into him. He held his arm out to steady her. He looked left and right, searching the area. He held his finger to his lips and listened. "What's wrong?" Ruth whispered. Sam reached under his jacket with his right hand and closed his fingers around the butt of his Sig Sauer P226. With his left hand, he pointed to Ruth's car. All four tires were flat, the metal wheels pressing deeply into the deflated rubber sidewalls.

A crunch of gravel on the narrow road and twin beams of light sweeping around a turn preceded a car slowly driving to the parking area. Sam held his automatic at his side and slightly behind his back as he pulled Ruth behind her car. The glare from the headlights now obscured the oncoming car and its driver. The vehicle pulled behind Ruth's car and stopped.

Ruth and Sam stood bathed in a circle of light, momentarily blinded by the glare of the headlights. "Stay here and keep low," he said, motioning to a spot in front of her car. Sam slowly walked toward the now stationary maroon Mercedes. He tried to block some of the glare with his left hand, holding his gun on his right side at the ready.

"Police," Sam shouted. "Shut off your headlights and step out of the car."

The headlights went out. The possibility of seeing the driver was now negated by the tinted windshield. With a click, the door began to open. Sam stopped short. Again Ruth, not anticipating his sudden stop, walked into his back. "You're going to get us both killed," Sam whispered without turning his head. "Didn't I say to stay put?"

"I didn't want to be alone," Ruth said, also whispering. "And besides, I recognize the car. It's Dr. Green."

"You don't know that," Sam said. "Thousands of people could have the same make and color car as Dr. Green."

"Yes, but how many of those people have a vanity plate on the front bumper saying DDS-NO1? That's Hyrum's car, Sherlock; I see it in the parking lot all the time," Ruth hissed.

"Even more reason to be cautious," Sam whispered, now turning to look at Ruth out of the corner of his eye while still watching the door of the car. "He's our primary murder suspect."

"You said he was just a person of interest twenty minutes ago," Ruth said, stepping alongside Sam.

"Well, I just upgraded him," Sam said, turning toward Ruth and slightly raising the volume and intensity of his whisper. "He's wanted for questioning." Sam's right hand now pointed his gun at the car door to keep the driver in check while they spoke.

"Maybe you'd like to just shoot him, and then you can question him later," Ruth said in full voice.

"Maybe I should arrest you for interfering with a murder investigation," Sam shouted.

"Interfering? I'm just offering some psychological reasoning instead of your usual brute force. Who told you that Mortimer Banks was not the killer and you should reopen the case? Who told you that you had the wrong man when you arrested Franklin? Who said—"

"Excuse me," came a quavering voice from within the car. "If you're finished arguing, I'd like to get out of the car now. Could you please lower your gun, Lieutenant?"

Sam and Ruth were now staring into each other's eyes. They stared for a long moment, eyes locked. All expression drained from their faces. Sam exhaled loudly and walked to the car door. "What are you doing here, Dr. Green?"

"Am I under arrest?" Hyrum said. "I was concerned about Dr. Klein, and I came here to see that she was all right. There's no law against that, is there?"

Sam lowered his gun to his side and opened the driver's door of the Mercedes. "Please step out of the car, Dr. Green."

"First tell me what I've done."

Sam placed his pistol back in its holster under his left arm and stepped back from the car door. He didn't have any conclusive evidence that Hyrum had committed any crime, but he felt a good deal of skepticism about Hyrum's stated reason for his visit. "No, you're not under arrest, Dr. Green, but I do have a few questions I would like to ask you about the murders of Sylvia Radcliffe and Michelle Ackerman."

"And if I don't want to answer your questions?"

"Well, that's your right. If you don't want to talk to me, you can leave. But once you're back in the city, I will bring you in for questioning as a material witness. Now we can talk here informally, or I can have two officers come to your office next week and bring you in. I personally would want to avoid that kind of embarrassment."

"I have nothing to hide. Can we talk inside? It's been a long drive, and I would like to use your restroom."

Sam extended his arm toward the cabin, and Hyrum began to walk in a hurried fashion in front of Ruth and Sam.

Sam whispered to Ruth. "You see, I can use psychology as well as brute force to change someone's mind."

"You mean that not-so-veiled threat was an attempt at psychology?" Ruth laughed.

"There's just no satisfying you, is there?" Sam said as he stormed away, following Hyrum.

35

Heat from the crackling fire in the open hearth flooded the living room. Sam had directed Hyrum to sit in the wooden rocking chair he'd positioned in front of the fireplace. Hyrum, still wearing his jacket, was feeling the effects of his close proximity to the flames. Beads of perspiration had formed on his forehead and were now dripping down his face. Sam stood alongside, leaning his elbow on the mantel, watching Hyrum mop his brow. He waited until Hyrum displayed just the right amount of discomfort before he began his questioning. Right on cue, Ruth rose from the couch and headed toward the kitchen.

"I'll make some fresh coffee."

Sam watched her disappear into the next room. "Paper cups will do, if you have them." A loud clatter from the kitchen and the banging of cabinet doors satisfied Sam that she had heard.

"None for me," Hyrum said. He was ready.

Sam now went into his interrogation mode. "Tell me about your relationship with Sylvia Radcliffe."

"She was a patient. I saw her four, maybe five times for dental work. That's all."

"I know that you and Sylvia were having an affair, Doctor. I could prove it in court, but I don't think it will do much good for your dental practice or for your marriage if I do."

"There's no need to threaten me, Lieutenant. Yes, I admit Sylvia and I were close, but I had nothing to do with her death. As a matter of fact, I was out of town the night she was killed. And I can prove it."

Sam smiled and paced in front of Hyrum's chair. "Yes, that's right; your wife said you both were together on that night."

Ruth stepped out of the kitchen and watched Hyrum closely, looking for any sign, gesture, or behavioral tic that might help determine his truthfulness. Hyrum sat tall in the wooden chair, looking around the room.

Sam had been less than honest about claiming he could prove that Hyrum and Sylvia were having an affair, but the ruse paid off.

"Where exactly were you that night?" Sam asked, calling Hyrum's bluff.

Hyrum looked directly into Sam's accusing blue eyes. "I was in New York, one hundred and twenty miles away. I have the hotel receipt, a parking receipt from the garage, and a citation for speeding that one of your comrades-in-arms presented to me. I'm sure, if you check, you will find witnesses to prove my whereabouts."

Ruth watched Sam take this crushing blow with grace and dignity. He spoke with no discernible emotion. "And of course your wife was with you all night. Isn't that what she said?"

Ruth focused on Hyrum's eyes. When he answered the question about his whereabouts on that evening, he had shifted his eyes toward the upper left, a sign that he was recalling memories of the past, but now he was directing his eyes toward the upper right. It was a sign that he was creating images. Ruth was sure that his next statement was going to be a lie.

"Yes, of course, she was with me all night."

Ruth stood in the doorway to the living room, holding a tray containing a carafe of coffee and three cups. She caught Sam's eye and slowly shook her head from side to side. Sam looked confused at first, but then nodded. He moved into the center of the room, directly in front of the fireplace.

Sam decided that an accusation might shake Hyrum's alibi loose. He beat down his desire to grab Hyrum and shake the truth out of him and instead calmly declared, "So you ensured that you had a strong alibi while your accomplice committed the murder. If you forced your wife to lie for you, let me remind you that she could be considered an accessory, and she would be prosecuted to the full extent of the law."

Hyrum reached across to the sofa. He seized a pillow by its corner and pulled it onto his lap, holding it as a barrier between himself and Sam Peirce. "Leave Elaine out of this. She had nothing to do with these murders," he yelled.

Ruth again caught Sam's eye and shook her head.

Sam paused and then changed the subject. "Were you meeting someone here, your accomplice perhaps?"

Hyrum sat back in his chair and looked at the ceiling.

"Were you meeting the person in the silver car who has been following me for two days?" Ruth asked.

"Someone has been following you in a silver car?" Sam said, walking across the room to Ruth.

"It's a long story. I'll tell you about it later."

"Tell me about it now," Sam insisted.

"It's nothing. It's probably the same person who was chasing me through the woods the first night."

"Who was chasing you through the woods?" Sam and Hyrum said together and then looked at each other.

"I don't know; I never got a good look at him."

"Him?" said Hyrum.

"Who were you coming here to meet?" Sam asked. He turned, stood behind Hyrum, and placed his hands on the back of Hyrum's chair.

"No one—I drove up here to make sure Dr. Klein was all right," he said over his shoulder. "The police officers who stopped to ask if I had seen anything unusual the night of the break-in at Dr. Klein's office told me that they had not been able to contact her. I was concerned."

"How did you know she was here?" Sam asked. "It took the police several days to discover she had come to this cabin."

"It wasn't so difficult," Hyrum said. Sam's eyebrows rose at the remark. He tilted Hyrum's chair back and looked over the back so that they were face-to-face. Hyrum gripped the arms of the chair to keep from sliding back on the seat. "A flier from the real estate broker was pinned to the bulletin board in the lobby. I thought Dr. Klein might have seen it. So, on a hunch I called the broker. She gave me the location of the cabin." "Did you tell the broker you were looking for Dr. Klein?"

Sam locked eyes with Hyrum Green. "Or did you pretend that you were interested in renting the cabin, pretending that Ruth, Dr. Klein"—he nodded to Ruth as he corrected himself—"recommended you call?"

"Look, Lieutenant, I thought Dr. Klein…Ruth…was alone here. I thought maybe you could use some company," he said, turning to Ruth again as he spoke. Ruth shook her head and instinctively stepped back a few steps.

"I didn't know that the two of you were"—Hyrum paused—"*together.*"

"We're *not* together," Sam said, releasing the back of the rocking chair, which caused Hyrum to pitch forward. "I'm here on police business."

"That was a fast reply," Ruth said, folding her arms across her chest. "I thought you drove here because you were worried about me."

"Well, yes," Sam said, turning toward Ruth. Sam tried to determine how he could explain this without hurting her feelings yet maintain a strictly business relationship. "I was concerned that you weren't answering your calls. I thought the murderer might have followed you up here."

Ruth took two steps closer to Sam. "I can take care of myself. I had a plan. I was ready for all contingencies."

"*Really,*" Sam replied. "Were you going to shoot your attacker with the safety still set on your shotgun?"

"You're not going to let that go, are you?"

"You would have gotten yourself killed," Sam yelled.

"Yes, and you already have two dead bodies," Ruth said. "I guess a third dead body would make the department look bad."

"If you two are busy, I can come back later," Hyrum said.

"Shut up!" Sam and Ruth said in unison.

Hyrum mopped the sweat from his forehead with his handkerchief, stood, and stepped away from the fire. "I came up here thinking Dr. Klein might be lonely. I made a mistake. If you're going to arrest me, do it. If not, I'll leave you to your discussion of *police business.* I didn't know that you liked each other."

"We don't like each other." The moment the words left her mouth, she wanted to take them back.

Now Sam looked hurt. He folded his arms across his chest.

"What I mean is we're here because we're working together on this case—or should I say we're both working on the case, not necessarily together."

"*I'm* working on this case," Sam said. "*You* are..." Sam stopped as Hyrum walked to the window. Another pair of headlights in the parking area was illuminating the path leading to the cabin. The car stopped beside Hyrum's Mercedes and extinguished its headlights. Sam stepped alongside Hyrum and lifted the curtain for a better look. The driver of the car remained inside the vehicle, shrouded in darkness. "Who is it?" Sam asked Hyrum.

"How should I know? Maybe you have guests," Hyrum said, not looking at Sam. Sam removed his gun from his shoulder holster and motioned for Hyrum to step out onto the porch. At first Sam wanted to use Hyrum as a shield to protect himself from Hyrum's accomplice, but what if it wasn't Hyrum's accomplice? What if Hyrum was innocent and the real murderer shot Hyrum while in Sam's custody? Sam decided they would all be safer if Sam went alone. He removed the pair of handcuffs from his waistband and placed one end on Hyrum's wrist, pulled the wrist around the pillar supporting the porch roof, and fastened the other end of the cuffs to Hyrum's other wrist. Then he began to creep toward the parking lot.

"Don't shoot her," Hyrum yelled. "I'm sure she's unarmed. Elaine! Run!"

Sam looked confused at first. Then he began to run toward the parked car. "Step out of the car," he called, "and let me see your hands."

"Please," Elaine Green cried, "I wasn't trying to help him escape. I was just trying to protect Dr. Klein."

"From whom?" Ruth asked, suddenly appearing behind Sam.

"Will you stop doing that?" he said, turning toward her.

Ruth walked to the rear of the vehicle and looked at the license plate.

"This is the car that has been following me." Ruth turned toward the porch of the cabin. Hyrum had slumped into a sitting position, hugging the pillar and quietly sobbing. "You were protecting me from your husband, weren't you?" Ruth said.

Elaine Green stepped out of the car and began to run to Hyrum. Sam caught her by the wrist and pulled her back. Her other arm reached out into empty space toward her husband.

"Don't hurt her," Hyrum shouted, not having heard any of the recent conversation. "She didn't mean to kill them. I'm sure it was an accident. It was my fault anyway. If I hadn't cheated, she would never have done it."

Elaine stopped pulling against Sam's grip. She turned to Ruth. "Done what?" she asked.

"Kill Sylvia Radcliffe, your husband's lover."

Elaine now turned to Lieutenant Peirce. "I didn't kill Sylvia Radcliffe. I knew they were lovers, but I didn't kill her. I thought Hyrum did."

"No, he didn't," Ruth interjected, bringing Elaine's attention back to her. "He has a strong alibi for the night of the murder."

"Well, so do I," Elaine said. "Who told you I killed Sylvia?"

"Actually no one, but your husband implied—"

"Can I get a word in here?" Sam shouted. "Let's all walk quietly to the cabin and continue this discussion inside."

***

By eight o'clock that evening, Elaine Green had offered her alibi for the night of Sylvia's murder. She assured them that the nine women present at her book club meeting would satisfy the need for proof of her where-abouts. She even began, much to Sam's annoyance, to describe the novel that had been the subject of the meeting.

They both explained how Michelle Ackerman had been black-mailing Hyrum, another fact that Elaine Green had known for quite some time. Neither of the pair had thought the other was involved in *that* murder since they were in fact together on that night and could prove it to Sam. Besides, no evidence existed to tie either one of them to Michelle's murder. Several cups of coffee later, Dr. and Mrs. Green were free to leave, both glad to know his or her spouse was not a killer, yet concerned that each thought the other might have been.

Sam and Ruth stood on the porch and watched the two cars drive away. "What a trusting couple," Sam said.

"Did you see her face when she realized that her husband thought she was capable of murder?" Ruth asked.

"Couple that with his philandering, and I would expect Mrs. Green to be visiting her lawyer as soon as she gets back." Sam laughed. He placed his hand on Ruth's shoulder, then immediately dropped it to his side and began to talk about the weather. Ruth smiled as he babbled on about the possibility of snow in the next few days.

Sam knew that Ruth's car was disabled with four flat tires. He knew that he should have arranged to either borrow a car from the Greens or secure a ride from them to the nearest town that had a motel for himself and Dr. Klein, but he still thought he could find his own car with a modicum of effort. Or maybe, for some masochistic reason, he wanted to spend more time alone with Ruth.

Ruth, on the other hand, remembered full well that they had no means of leaving the cabin tonight. She told herself that she should bring this fact to Sam's attention before the Greens left, but she just couldn't seem to get the words out.

"I'm going to find my car so we can drive to West Haven and check into a hotel," Sam said, raising the collar on his jacket.

"You'll never find your car in the dark. Why don't we stay here tonight? I'm sure I can whip up something to eat, and I have a bottle of wine I brought from home."

Sam thought about the invitation. He hadn't had dinner, and a glass of wine after this exasperating evening sounded good, but he didn't want to sound too anxious.

"Maybe I should look for the car tonight. I think it was somewhere near the lake. That's not too far, is it?"

Ruth responded a little too quickly. "You're going to leave me alone with a tire-slashing killer out in the woods."

"I thought you had a plan, you were prepared, and you had all the contingencies covered."

"I do, I mean I did, but I would probably forget to release the safety if I were attacked." She chortled.

"OK, I give up." Sam sighed.

"How did you know that Hyrum didn't cut your tires?" Sam asked.
"He didn't, but how did you know?"

"When he stepped out of his car, his shoes were clean. There's mud all around my car. I've been tracking it into the house for the last three days."

"That was a very astute observation. You may be of some value to this case yet."

"Thank you for the compliment. Keep it up, and I may not burn your steak."

Sam walked out to the woodpile and gathered several logs in his arms. He wondered if staying the night was a good idea. Ruth always seemed to push his buttons. Well, he wouldn't let her get to him tonight—although, he began to wonder if anger was the emotion he needed to control. Slightly confused, he shook the thoughts out of his mind and carried the logs to the fireplace.

Ruth was waiting with two glasses of wine and some sort of soft cheese and crackers on a plate. The smell of steaks sizzling under the broiler wafted into the living room. Ruth asked how Sam liked his steak cooked. He said rare. Ruth jumped from the couch, ran to the kitchen, and shouted, "Too late, how about medium rare?"

"Medium rare is fine," Sam said.

After dinner they sat on the shag rug in front of the fire, their backs against the base of the sofa. Ruth's knees were pulled up to her chest. Sam sprawled with his feet facing the hearth. They watched the tongues of flame lick the sides of the fireplace andirons, and both jumped closer together when a loud pop from a crackling log startled them.

"What caused you to become a police officer?" Ruth finally asked. "Was it something you always wanted to do?"

Sam took a long pull from his wineglass and filled both glasses again before answering. "I don't think I ever thought about what I wanted to do. After high school I had no money for college, and I had no job. Then one day I talked to an army recruiter. He told me about the opportunities to get an education in the service and to build a career. To do something I could be proud of rather than settle for a factory job. I didn't really believe him, but I guess I was bored and ready to get out of that small town." Ruth tucked her feet under her and turned in Sam's direction, slowly sipping her wine.

He continued, "They sent me to schools for several different military jobs, but I guess I had no mind to concentrate on schoolwork, and I was flunking out of every class I took. I had an attitude back then—"

"As opposed to now," Ruth interrupted. "I'm sorry, please go on."

"I had an attitude back then." He paused and looked at her. "And I got into more than my share of fights. I thought they were going to throw me out, but they decided I might be useful as an MP. I joined the military police and found that police work was something I could do well. At first I was a bit of a hard-ass—sorry—but after a while I got all hung up on the 'protect and serve' part of the job. I felt I was finally doing something useful. After I got out of the army, I joined the Philadelphia Police Department and attended Penn State at night until I earned a degree. I worked my way through the ranks and eventually made lieutenant. It's been twenty years, but I still feel a great deal of satisfaction when I get a bad guy off the street."

"That's wonderful. It's not easy to decide what you want to do with your life. I envy people who find their place."

"Are you kidding? You're a doctor, for Christ's sake. You have an incredibly useful profession. You help people. They come to you, and you solve their problems; you help them put their lives back together."

Ruth placed her hand on Sam's shoulder; he stiffened slightly. "Thank you for saying that. Sometimes I wonder if I'm doing anyone any good. I do believe I was making some headway with Sylvia Radcliffe just before she died. In our last few sessions, she really opened up to me. She began to bare her soul."

"I guess it can be frustrating," Sam said, "to hear her problems, to offer her suggestions, and then have her not listen."

Ruth sat up a little taller. "I don't understand, not listen to what?"

"Well, when Sylvia told you that she and Mort Banks were burglarizing homes for more than a year, I'm sure you advised her to turn herself in."

"What?" Ruth cried. "Sylvia was in a burglary ring? Oh God! I didn't know anything about her. I knew it—I'm a fraud. I'm nothing but a fraud." Ruth placed her glass on the floor behind her, pulled a tissue out of her pocket, and began to dab at her eyes. "I thought we had a break-through because she told me about her childhood, but I knew nothing about her life."

Sam leaned forward and pulled Ruth close to him. "That's not true. You were making progress. I'll bet that within a few weeks, she would have told you everything, or maybe she just didn't want to put you on the spot. She may have been just trying to protect your relationship."

"You really think so?" Ruth placed her head on Sam's broad shoulder.

Now Sam was caught a little off guard, but he rose to his knees and placed a reassuring arm around her waist and pulled her close. He could feel her breasts heaving against his chest as her breathing became more rapid. He felt a quickening of her heartbeat, or was that his?

Maybe it was the wine, maybe it was the sexual tension that had accumulated over weeks of taunts and jibes. The attraction had been there from the beginning; it just had been channeled into other areas. Now their defenses were down. The warm glow of the fire was no match for the fire within. Sam pulled her to the floor and leaned over her body. They gazed into each other's eyes for a moment, and then kissed. At first it was just a brushing of the lips. A delicate touch as Ruth softly nibbled his lower lip, then a release of passion as their mouths opened and came together. The kiss was long and deep as Sam settled on top of her, making contact with the full length of her body.

**

A screech owl in a pine tree shouted at the car parked on the side of the road. He moved his head from side to side, watching the human in the car. Then he leaped into flight when the man lifted his head from the steering wheel and stretched his arms.

Franklin blinked his eyes and rubbed his neck, trying to get the kinks out. He wondered how long he had slept. He had left home just after Lieutenant Peirce had paid him a visit. Just after Franklin found Dr.

Klein's stolen patient files and her calendar conspicuously placed on his sofa and in his telephone stand. The burglar who robbed Dr. Klein's office obviously had been in his home.

Why would the burglar leave the stolen files in his living room? The files gave the burglar, or maybe he was the murderer, enough information to discover where Dr. Klein was vacationing, just as Franklin had. Franklin thumbed through the file folders and examined the single page from Dr. Klein's calendar and tossed them onto the passenger seat. "Shit," he cried. All of a sudden it had become very clear. He was being set up.

Franklin started the engine of his car and pulled back onto the road, tires spinning and gravel spitting into the air. He chastised himself for not seeing it before: the murderer was after Dr. Klein. By leaving the files in Franklin's house, he knew that Franklin would put two and two together and assume that the murderer now knew where to find Dr. Klein. Franklin watched the speedometer rise…seventy, eighty miles per hour.

Then another thought struck him. He was playing right into the murderer's hands. He was going to the cabin where the murderer may have already killed Dr. Klein. Now he was about to show up at the murder scene with the stolen files in his car. Franklin pressed hard on the brake and skidded to a stop at the side of the road. If Dr. Klein had been murdered, and he was caught here with the stolen files, he would have a tough time proving his innocence. Then he thought, *What if he hasn't killed her yet? Maybe there is still time.* He stomped on the accelerator again, satisfied that even a chance to save Ruth Klein's life was worth the risk of being a suspect for her murder if he were too late.

The person who had broken into his house and left the files must be the murderer—but who? For weeks he had seen a man who looked to him as Dennis would at this age. A man who always disappeared into the shadows when Franklin tried to talk to him. A man always just out of reach. Could Dennis be behind the killings and the burglary? And was Dennis trying to blame it all on him? Had Dennis's anger toward him grown out of all proportion with the passing of time? Was he now exacting his revenge for being abandoned so many years ago? *No, the punishment would be far greater than the crime. No one in his right mind...*

Franklin turned onto Destiny Road and slowly proceeded up the narrow gravel lane. He shut off his headlights and continued with only fog lights. Up ahead he could see a parked car. He turned off his ignition and let his car roll in neutral. It managed to roll about ten feet from the parked car. Now it became clear—he was too late. Dr. Klein's car had four flat tires. The murderer was already here. He must have disabled her car so she couldn't get away. Franklin hesitated before stepping into the mud of the parking area. He looked at his shoes, but since they were already covered with mud it didn't matter. He stepped from the car, his cane in his hand, and began to walk to the cabin. The dim light from the fireplace flickered through the window, guiding him down the path to the front door.

Franklin carefully negotiated the front stone steps and stepped onto the wooden porch, being careful not to let his cane click against the floorboards. He flattened out against the wall and made his way to the window. The flames in the hearth were the only light in the cabin. Franklin searched the room, looking for any sign of life. He was too late. The sofa was blocking his view, but he could see a pair of feet, a woman's feet, Dr. Klein's feet, extending past its end. On the floor next to her naked foot was a dark-red pool of liquid seeping into the rug—blood.

Franklin squeezed his eyes shut. Could this be another dream? What was it Dr. Klein had told him to do? *Press your thumb into your palm. If your thumb penetrates your palm, you are not awake.* His palm was solid. This was no dream. He looked through the window again. The feet seemed to be moving slightly. She was alive. Then suddenly he saw a figure. The back of a shirtless man and part of his head rose above the sofa and fell back again behind it, hovering over his victim. *What is he doing to her?* Franklin had to save her. Dr. Klein was one of the few people in his life who had tried to help him. Now it was his turn to help her.

Franklin worked his way to the door and carefully tried the doorknob. It turned. He pushed the door open and raised his cane over his head. "Leave her alone," he yelled.

Sam Peirce immediately rolled to the left and reached for his shoulder holster hanging on the side of the rocking chair. "Stay down, I've got him," he yelled to Ruth.

Ruth looked up while pulling her blouse closed and yelled, "Franklin, what are you doing here? Sam, wait; it's Franklin."

Franklin suddenly realized his mistake. He could now see that the red liquid on the rug was the result of a carelessly placed glass of red wine and that he had entered the cabin at a very inopportune moment.

"I'm sorry," he cried. "I thought you were being attacked."

Ruth checked to see that her body was adequately covered and said, "Easy, Sam; Franklin thought he was saving me."

"I don't care. I'm going to shoot him anyway," Sam said, pulling his automatic from its holster.

Franklin squatted close to the floor and covered his head with his hands. Sam placed his gun back in its holster and sighed. "Don't you ever knock?"

An hour later Franklin was still apologizing for his mistake, Ruth was trying to pretend that she was not completely humiliated, and Sam still wanted to shoot Franklin.

***

"I'm here because I thought you were in trouble. I thought someone might be trying to hurt you," Franklin said again, following Ruth into the kitchen as she scraped the dinner dishes and stacked them in the sink.

"You saw it all in another dream, right?" Sam said, leaning against the doorway.

"Let it go, Sam," Ruth said, giving Sam a stern look. "Franklin, what made you think I was in danger?" Sam folded his arms and stared at Franklin, waiting for an answer.

"Can I tell you in private?" Franklin asked. "I'm afraid that anything I say right now might get me arrested—or shot."

Sam threw his hands in the air. "If you have any evidence of anyone trying to—"

"Sam," Ruth interrupted, "I'm his doctor; if he wants to speak to me in private, he should have that opportunity. Now it's very late, Franklin—do you have a place to stay for the night?"

"Well…" Franklin began.

"OK, then," Ruth said. "We'll all stay here for tonight, and in the morning Franklin and I will have a therapy session before we leave for home. We have two bedrooms. Sam and I will each take one, and there is a folding bed we can open in the living room for you, Franklin."

Sam's stare was somewhere between utter disappointment and rage. Then he took a deep breath. "Franklin will take the second bedroom; I'll sleep out here to ensure that everyone is safe."

"Thank you, Sam," Ruth said. "I'm sorry, but it's been a long day. I think we're all very tired and should get some sleep." Ruth smiled a faint smile and disappeared into her bedroom.

Franklin opened the door to the second bedroom and said, "Thank you, Lieutenant, for letting me stay."

Sam Peirce nodded. "Stay in your room until tomorrow."

Franklin was about to ask why when the lieutenant looked directly into his eyes and gently tapped the Sig Sauer automatic, now tucked in his belt.

"Right," Franklin said and closed the door.

36

Now it was Ruth who had difficulty sleeping. Every time she closed her eyes, Sam's face would appear, his rugged, handsome face with his strong angular jaw and cleft chin. When they first met, she had seen him as an overweight, doughnut-eating caricature of a police officer, but last night he was different. The changes that had taken place in the last few months must have happened slowly, evading her eye. For one thing, he seemed happier—that is, when he wasn't threatening to shoot someone. And his body had changed as well. She hadn't noticed the difference until last night when she helped pull his sweatshirt off over his head. His shoulders were broad and his stomach was hard and flat. *When did he lose all that weight?* she wondered. *Could he have changed, lost that weight, because of me?*

Ruth closed her eyes and reflected on their time in front of the fire. It had been so long since she had been that close to a man's naked chest. Without thinking, she had reached out and touched him. Her impulse had been to pull her hand away as soon as he looked at it, to pretend it was an accident, a careless slip, but he had placed his hand over hers and pressed it against his skin. She knew she should have pulled away, but she hadn't wanted to. She had felt the warmth travel from his chest through her hand and spread to the core of her body. When he laid her down and leaned over her, supporting himself on his elbows to lessen his weight on her, she had relaxed her legs to let his knees rest on the carpet between them. She closed her eyes and savored the memory of his bare chest pressing against her breasts.

Last evening she was sure she was ready. Five years without a man was a long time. It was unreasonable to think that she should have resisted. Why deny herself this one night of pleasure, one moment of fantasy in an all-too-real world? Then his hand had moved down her side until it slipped just an inch or two beneath the waistband of her slacks. His fingers and palm were slightly rough, but warm, as he caressed her. She had closed her eyes and felt a flush that began at his hand and slowly grew until it encompassed her entire body.

She had been sure it was going to happen. She wanted it to happen, but instead of lying back, giving herself to him unconditionally, she had stiffened; she was frightened. She grasped his hand and held it. He pressed his forehead to hers and lowered his lips to her neck. His two-day growth of beard brushed her face, and his breath warmed her neck. She was consumed by both passion and fear.

Maybe it was his beard, maybe it was nervousness or a feeling of insecurity because she hadn't done this in so long, but she had begun to panic—she panicked, and she began to laugh. Sam had looked up and questioned her laughter with a stare.

"I'm sorry. I was just thinking of something funny," she whispered, hoping she hadn't spoiled the moment.

"What?" he asked.

"No, I can't," Ruth had said, hoping he wouldn't pursue the point.

"Yes, you can—what is it?"

Now Ruth needed to come up with something funny that would still maintain the erotic mood. But what?

"It was nothing," she had said. "I was just wondering if you were really glad to be with me or..."

"Or what?" Sam asked, perplexed.

"Or if that was a gun in your pocket." The line from an old Mae West movie had come to her at the last minute, and she blurted it out, hoping the joke might ease the tension. She had waited as Sam looked her in the eye. *Oh God,* she had thought. *He's going to think I'm nuts.* But he hadn't.

She wondered what the rest of the night would have been like if Franklin hadn't busted in and broken the spell. His intrusion had been embarrassing for her and probably frustrating for Sam. She wasn't sure how far they would have gone. She had felt sheltered and impervious to harm when she was in his arms, but she was frightened by him as well.

Again she closed her eyes to try to sleep, and again she saw Sam's face. This time he was smiling. A smile that seemed to radiate warmth and caring yet also contained an air of recklessness and daring that concerned her. Was he too confident? Was she too easy? Ruth buried her face in her pillow and tried to pretend that she and Sam had only spoken last night, and never touched. What did she know about this man, other than the fact that they could barely say ten words to each other without a pejorative outcome? He was strong and dedicated, or was he just headstrong and enthusiastic? Were they really interested in each other, or were they both just caught up in the tension and excitement of this murder case? Ruth wondered if her attraction to Sam wasn't transference of emotion. An escape from the pain of losing a patient to a gruesome death coupled with the appreciation and excitement generated by the prospect of Sam solving the murder. Or was it just the fact that Sam was the first man that had gotten under her skin since her divorce? Was she really attracted to him, or had the celibacy of the last five years finally caught up with her? Her body wanted this man. She hungered for the feel of his touch, the warmth of his skin against hers, but her mind told her that this relationship was going to be a problem. Things were moving too fast. And what of Emma—she had never even met Sam Peirce. No, she would have to slam on the brakes. They would have to wait until the case was over and the passion of the moment had passed, for a time when their lives were more settled and decisions could be made based on true emotion rather than just physical desire.

When she lifted her head, the room was aglow with sunlight. Had she slept, or had morning crept into her room while she agonized over flashbacks of the previous night? No matter, this was going to be a difficult day, and lying here in bed, warm and comfortable as it may be, would not help her find the solution to her problems.

***

A shaft of sunlight peeked through the heavy drapes of the semidark living room and fell across Sam Peirce's face. He sat up and ran his hand over the stubble of beard on his cheek, then combed his fingers through his hair. The cot on which he had spent the night was low to the floor, making standing a more arduous task than he had bargained for. A nagging ache in his lower back kept him from standing straight. He slowly massaged the offending area to unwind the muscle cramps that more than hinted at many years of abusing his body.

"Coffee?" Ruth called from just outside the kitchen door.

"About a gallon," Sam said, taking his gun from under the pillow and placing it back in the holster hanging from the rocking chair.

He walked across the room, straightening his posture and adding buoyancy to each step as he approached Ruth. He placed his hands on her shoulders and leaned toward her. Ruth held the tray of coffee between them and turned, breaking his hold, and placed the coffee on the table.

"Is it something I did?" he asked.

Before Ruth could answer, the door to the second bedroom squeaked open several inches. A clenched hand passed through the narrow opening and knocked on the doorframe. "Is it all right to come out?" Franklin asked.

"No!" shouted Lieutenant Peirce.

"Yes!" countered Ruth, flashing Sam a disapproving stare. "We'll talk later," she whispered.

Franklin entered the room, leaning heavily on his cane. Morning seemed to be a difficult time for everyone.

Franklin hung his cane on the back of his chair and unfolded his napkin. Sam watched with increasing concern as Franklin performed his morning ritual. He prepared the silverware next to his plate by carefully polishing his fork and spoon with his napkin before setting them down precisely parallel to each other on the table. He moved his coffee cup from the four o'clock to the two o'clock position, measured a three-finger-width distance from the end of the table and adjusted his plate. He smiled and nodded to Sam. Sam leaned over and whispered, "Don't get too excited. I don't think she's much of a cook."

"I can hear you," came a reply from the kitchen.

"So, have any dreams lately?" Sam asked, his voice barely louder than a whisper.

"Sam, be nice," echoed from the kitchen over the sound of a blender.

"How does she do that?" Sam asked.

Within minutes Ruth reappeared, carrying two frying pans. One contained a runny cheese frittata, and the second was filled with strips resembling tree bark. Sam was prepared to give Franklin five-to-one odds that the charred, oil-soaked, shriveled substance had started its journey to the table as bacon.

All three ate in silence. Ruth and Sam occasionally looked at each other and immediately returned their gaze to their plates of food. Franklin, feeling increasingly uncomfortable as the interloper, spoke first.

"I was surprised to see you here last night, Lieutenant. You must have used your siren and raced all the way to arrive ahead of me. I left within a half hour of your visit to my house."

Sam looked confused. "Franklin, I visited you on Saturday. I drove up here on Sunday. I didn't leave for almost twenty-four hours after I saw you."

"But that's impossible. I left Saturday afternoon and got here last night, Saturday night."

"Franklin, today is Monday," Ruth said, looking at Franklin and then at Sam.

Franklin stared at his plate, then closed his eyes. "Dr. Klein, I think we need to talk."

"You think?" Sam said, laughing. Ruth stared at Sam. A stare that clearly communicated the message: *Stop being an ass.*

"Why don't the two of you talk while I look at the tires on your car?" Sam said to protect his pride. "Maybe they weren't slashed. Maybe someone just let the air out."

"I have an air pump in the trunk of my car." Franklin reached into his pocket for his car keys and passed them to Sam.

"You know, you could have told me about the pump last night," Sam said, sliding his chair back from the table. He looked at the half-full plate of food. "I'll go now and see if I can get us out of here soon."

"You had better," Ruth replied. "If you don't, I'll cook lunch."

***

Ruth reached into her briefcase and extracted her notepad. She closed the shades to sequester them from the outside world, took a deep breath, and sat in the wooden rocking chair, pen in hand. It was time for another session with Franklin.

Ruth was beginning to feel that Franklin's problems were almost too numerous to count, but she decided to deal with the major issues first, issues that would prevent Franklin from living a normal life. He complained of a sleep disorder. That would be the logical place to start. Sleep deprivation could be the root cause of several of his other symptoms: delusions, anxiety, hallucinations, and lost time. All of which he seemed to have presented recently.

Ruth wrote *Focus* on her notepad in an attempt to concentrate on Franklin's issues. She was still rattled by his interruption last night. She and Sam had been caught in a compromising position. How does a patient trust and look for advice from his doctor after watching her grab at her clothing to cover her naked body? Would that *display*— she cringed at the mental image—on the cabin floor be the picture Franklin saw each time he looked at her? *Is he picturing me naked right now?* She could feel her face turning red. But it was time to put away her fears and don a professional persona. Franklin had come here because he was concerned about her. That was a constructive reaction to recent events, but Ruth would not let that gesture, that act of kindness, distract her from her observation of the aberrant behavior he had displayed over the last few months. Franklin needed psychological care and treatment. It was time to uncover the cause of his debilitating symptoms.

Franklin fluffed the cushion and poked the pillows before sitting on the couch. She watched him attempt to improve his comfort by adjusting his position in the seat. He seemed to be having difficulty choosing just the right spot on the couch. Ruth was careful not to show her frustration as she waited for him to settle in.

"Have you ever had the feeling that you were being watched, Dr. Klein?" Franklin volunteered.

"Have you?" Ruth replied, wondering what precipitated the question.

"Often," Franklin said.

"Were you being watched?" she asked. "Did you hear or see someone watching you, or was it just a feeling?"

Franklin's stare seemed to pass through her, his eyes either unfocussed or focused on an empty space somewhere in the center of the room. It was an uncomfortable stare. Ruth shifted in her seat.

He began. "It's nothing tangible, nothing you could put your finger on, but you know someone or something is there, a presence within your personal space that causes an uneasy feeling, a feeling of impending danger."

Ruth's concern elevated as she studied Franklin's face. His expression had become more somber. She could swear that his voice changed. It became slightly deeper. His speech mannerisms and even his vocabulary seemed slightly altered. It wasn't that he never used words like impending danger before—he had. As a matter of fact, his vocabulary was quite extensive, but somehow his voice inflection and tone seemed alien to everything she knew about him. Not that she thought she knew much.

"Your pulse quickens, and your body stiffens. Your muscles tense, your limbs begin to tremble, and a very surreal fear of dying fills your mind and crowds out all other thoughts." He leaned forward as he spoke, causing Ruth to straighten in her chair.

Was he talking about the night she was lost in the forest, or was this simply a fluke, a meshing of his fears with hers?

"When have you felt this way?" she asked, trying to shake off her acutely uneasy feeling and the taste of bile rising in the back of her throat. Was he frightening her, or was it her cooking?

"Felt what way?" Franklin asked, his voice returning to its normal tonal range and meter.

Ruth now recognized the Franklin who was familiar to her, but she still felt uneasy, slightly confused.

"When did you fear dying?"

"In my dreams, Doctor; very often in my dreams."

***

The sun was bright, the wind had stopped, and the forest gave off an earthy smell of fresh morning dew. Sam crunched along the gravel path to Franklin's silver Toyota. The air pump was in the trunk. It was a combination air pump and battery charger—a handy device. He decided he would buy one for his own car; that was, if he ever found his car. Sam walked around Ruth's Ford, inspecting the tires. He noticed that there were no caps on any of the valve stems. Could be someone removed them and then let the air out of all the tires. Either that, or Ruth's skill at maintaining her car rivaled her skill in the kitchen. That wasn't fair. Sam reprimanded himself for belittling Ruth's cooking. So she couldn't cook. She was well educated, attractive, feisty, and seemed to have good deductive reasoning skills. Although he had criticized her, and threatened to arrest her for interfering with his investigation, he had to admit that she was probably right about Mortimer Banks not being the killer. She would have made a good detective. Well, she certainly would have made a better detective than a cook.

The gravel in the parking area was damp and interspersed with puddles of mud, so Sam looked for something to kneel on while he filled the tires with air. His overnight bag was still in his lost car. He may be in these clothes for a while. He was wearing the sweat pants Alicia had bought for him, and he didn't want to ruin them. Alicia! He had forgotten all about her. They had been drifting apart lately, and this weekend certainly wasn't improving that situation. He was going to have to make some important decisions when he returned home.

Sam looked in the window of Franklin's car, hoping to find a newspaper to use to protect his trousers. No joy there, but there were some papers showing under the passenger seat. They looked like they were sticking out of a file folder.

***

"Franklin, what happened between Lieutenant Peirce's visit to your house on Saturday and your arrival here on Sunday night? You seemed to be confused about the amount of time that had passed."

Franklin shook his head and held up his hands, signaling that either nothing happened, or that he didn't want to talk about it. "I must have fallen asleep while parked in my car. I haven't slept much lately; I just lost track of time." He withdrew from the conversation by folding his arms across his chest and slowly rocking forward and back on the couch.

Ruth decided to try a different approach. "You said you came here because you thought I was in danger, and I really appreciate your concern. Can you tell me what caused you to have that belief?"

"First, you have to promise that you won't tell Lieutenant Peirce what I'm about to say. If he knew, he would probably arrest me again, and I can't spend another night in jail. Strange things happen there."

Ruth wondered what strange things he was talking about, but decided to save that question until later. "You know I can't tell anyone what is said in our sessions. Not unless you tell me that you're going to break the law."

"No, it's nothing like that. OK, here goes. Someone broke into my house the day Lieutenant Peirce came to see me."

"Did you tell Sam, I mean the lieutenant, about the break-in?"

"No, I couldn't. You see, whoever broke into my house tried to implicate me in the murder of your patient Sylvia, Sylvia…"

"Radcliffe?" Ruth said, placing her notepad and pen on the floor next to her chair. She folded her hands in her lap and leaned forward.

"Someone, the burglar who stole files from your office, hid them in my house. I'm sure he was hoping that Lieutenant Peirce would find the files and arrest me for the break-in at your office and probably for the murder of Sylvia what's-her-name."

"Radcliffe," Ruth said. "But who do you think put the files in your house?"

"Well, it wasn't just the files. I also found a page from your calendar, indicating where you were spending your vacation. You see, whoever stole the papers from your office knew where you were. I had to come here to stop him."

"And who did you come here to stop? Could it be your friend, Dennis?"

"He *was* there, and he is angry with me, but he wouldn't go that far. At least the Dennis I knew before wouldn't."

"But he was in your house the day the files appeared and you didn't see anyone else in your house, did you?"

"Well, I actually didn't see Dennis either," Franklin said. "I heard someone run out the back door, and since Dennis has been stalking me, trying to make me feel guilty, I assumed it was him. But maybe it wasn't. Maybe it was the person who killed Sylvia...Sylvia..."

Radcliffe, Ruth screamed in her mind, but said nothing.

A click of the doorknob and the squeak of the front door opening caused both Franklin and Ruth to look in that direction.

"We're not finished, Sam. You'll need to stay out a little longer," Ruth said.

"I don't think so," Sam said, holding up the stolen files.

***

"He's been following me for the last month. At first I wasn't sure whether he was real or a dream, but those papers are real, and I guess so is he," Franklin said.

"So is who?" asked Sam.

"Dennis," Franklin said. "I think he put the papers in my living room to incriminate me."

Sam looked at Ruth and asked, "What the hell is he talking about?"

Ruth touched Franklin's shoulder. "I can't say anything unless you give me permission."

"Will someone tell me what's going on?" Sam shouted.

"I need to lie down," Franklin said. He got up and headed toward the bedroom. "You can tell him whatever you like." Franklin closed the door behind him.

Ruth took Sam's hand and led him to the sofa. Sam went along quietly, alternately looking at Ruth and the closing bedroom door.

"Franklin has been complaining at each of our last three sessions that an old friend, someone he had had a falling out with years ago, was stalking him but had not confronted him."

"What does that have to do with the burglary or the murder case?"

"I'm not sure. There are things about their relationship that I still don't know, but something happened years ago that made Franklin feel very guilty and fear that Dennis was going to exact some sort of revenge on him."

"And you think that breaking into your office, stealing these files, and planting them in Franklin's house is that revenge?" Sam said, shaking the papers in his hand as he spoke.

"Possibly," Ruth said. "At first I thought Franklin was imagining that Dennis was following him out of guilt for rejecting Dennis's friendship in the past. But what if Franklin isn't imagining anything? What if Dennis has held a grudge for all this time and has finally figured a way to ruin Franklin's life?"

"You think he murdered someone—no, two people—because he wanted to blame the deaths on Franklin? Isn't that a little extreme, even for someone dealing with a nut like Franklin?"

"It does seem extreme, but there is a lot we don't know about their relationship, and we know almost nothing about Dennis." Ruth grabbed Sam's hand again and yanked him up from the sofa. "Come with me. I have an idea." She led him to Franklin's bedroom. Ruth knocked on the door, then entered before Franklin said to come in.

Franklin was standing with his back to the closet door. "I was about to get undressed," he said.

"We'll leave you alone in a minute; I just have a few questions."

Franklin walked to the bed and sat.

"Franklin, what does your ex-wife, Myra, look like?" Ruth asked as she sat next to him on the bed. Franklin began to smile. "She's quite attractive: long black hair, a very pretty face, and quite a good figure."

"Big breasts?" Sam said.

"*Sam*," Ruth scolded.

"No, I need to know. Does she have big breasts?"

"I think what the lieutenant wants to know is, does she resemble the woman who was killed in your dream, and then in real life, Sylvia Radcliffe?"

Franklin stood up. "I guess she does. I hadn't thought of that, but how does that matter?"

"I'll get to that in a minute," Sam said. "Now tell me—"

"Sam, I was questioning Franklin," Ruth said, popping up from her seat on the bed.

"Shush!" Sam said. "Now tell me about Michelle Ackerman. How well did you know her?"

"She cleaned my teeth several times. I met her once in a shopping mall, and we had coffee together. I was thinking of asking her out, but the next time I went to the dentist, she wasn't there. I guess she was dead."

"Did you see Dennis stalking you around the same time you met Michelle for coffee?"

"I didn't see him, but I guess he could have seen me. What are you trying to say?"

"Wait," Sam said. "Did you ever meet Sylvia Radcliffe?"

"No," Ruth interrupted. "He never met Sylvia."

"Well, yes, actually I did. I met her at a bar across the street from your office."

Sam was pacing back and forth across the room. He reached out for Ruth's shoulder and pushed her back down to her seat on the bed. "And did you happen to see Dennis on that evening anywhere near that bar?"

Franklin thought for a moment. "Yes, I did."

"Did Dennis know your ex-wife, what was her name…?"

"Myra," Ruth and Franklin said at the same time.

"Myra," Sam repeated. "Did he know her?"

"He hated her," Franklin said.

"She was the cause of the problems between Franklin and Dennis," Ruth added.

"You knew this and you didn't tell me? No, that's right, the doctor-patient thing," Sam said. "Well, I think this Dennis character just made the suspect list for both murders." Sam pushed Franklin back down onto his seat on the bed next to Ruth. "Is it possible that this Dennis character killed both Sylvia and Michelle to get even with you because he saw you with both women and was eliminating anyone to whom you might be attracted? He may even have mistaken Sylvia for Myra. After all, he probably hadn't seen Myra for many years. That might explain the violence with which he murdered her."

"I don't believe this," Franklin said. "I'm not going to listen to any more of this. Please leave; I'm tired."

Sam and Ruth returned to the living room. "It makes sense," Sam said. "The violence of Sylvia's murder, Michelle's death, the stolen files…" Sam paused.

"What?" Ruth said.

"You are probably the only other woman who is close to Franklin. Dennis was probably the person who chased you through the basement of your office and was eavesdropping at your door. I think we should get back to the city and find this guy before he comes looking for you. I'll get my car and be back in an hour. As soon as we can get a cell phone signal, I'll call and put out an APB on this guy. Hopefully he's still in the city."

37

S am grumbled as he set out to find his car. It had to be somewhere
near the shore of the lake. Now, which shore of the lake was the question. He thought he would start by traveling down the south shore since
the lake was north of the highway. After walking for several minutes, Sam
stopped to reconnoiter and catch his breath. The path he had chosen was
strewn with rocks and fallen branches. It didn't look familiar, but it had
been dark when he abandoned his car and walked to the cabin. He had
found the lake just a short distance from the point at which he had driven
into the ditch. He had then followed the lakeshore for what had seemed
like half an hour, but had probably been only a few minutes. Eventually
he had spotted a small point of light, the glow from the cabin window,
off in the distance. Of course, in the daylight he had no idea how far away
that point of light had been. If he was lucky, he would be able to retrace
his steps, find his car, and he and Ruth would be out of here before lunch.
Sam rubbed his protesting belly. With Ruth doing the cooking, he had
little fear of overeating. The work he had done to lose weight was safe.

He didn't like the idea of leaving Ruth alone in the cabin with
Franklin. She had been sitting in the rocking chair going over her
notes when he left. Trying to make heads or tails out of that fruitcake
of a patient should keep her busy for quite some time. They had
been up for only three hours this morning, and the guy had already
gone back to his room to take a nap. *Well, with his bad leg, he must tire
easily.* A murderer was still on the loose, possibly in this area, and
Sam knew that Franklin wouldn't be much help to Ruth in an emergency. He wasn't a small man. He was taller than Sam and seemed

reasonably well built, but with his disability he would be no match for the suspect Sam was after. Sylvia Radcliffe had been killed by someone both strong and athletic. She was very fit and the evidence at the crime scene indicated that she'd put up a valiant fight, but in the end was overpowered by brute force. No, she wouldn't have been protected by someone with Franklin's disability. He couldn't run, nor did he have full strength in his left arm. He would be useless in an emergency.

Ruth, however, could take care of herself. She had gotten the drop on Sam on the porch the night before. He actually was lucky she hadn't removed the safety from the shotgun. An accidental finger on the trigger, and that night would have ended very differently. *Well, that was a mistake she wouldn't make again,* he thought. Ruth was a handful all right, but there were a lot of things about her that Sam liked. A thought struck him: Ruth was the second doctor he was attracted to. He stopped short. This was the first time he had admitted to himself that he was attracted to her. Last night he had let the passion of the moment dictate his actions, but now after some time had passed, he realized that, in spite of their disagreements, her meddling, and his need to be in charge, which she totally disregarded, he liked her. He enjoyed their time together in spite of the exasperation he felt at almost every encounter. Dating doctors could have its benefits. Alicia could help him stay physically healthy while Ruth, a psychologist, could help him find peace of mind. Of course, if he kept leading both of them on, Alicia would probably poison him and Ruth would drive him fucking nuts. That was worth a laugh, but now it was time to get back to the business of finding his car.

Within ten minutes he was at the lake. An abandoned osprey nest testified to the fact that fall was coming to a close and winter was quickly approaching. Sam remembered reading about osprey in the magazine section of the Sunday paper. He read how they flew south separately, wintered on their own, and then met up at the old nesting site the following summer. They mated for life, but knew the value of separate vacations. Not a bad deal. He buttoned his jacket and raised his collar. Flying south sounded like a good idea right now.

Sam worked his way along the shoreline looking for the spot in the woods from which he had emerged after abandoning his car. The soft sand of the beach made it rough going. Three months ago he would have been forced to stop often to rest. Now, almost twenty pounds lighter, he was confident that he could slog through this sand in record time.

"Sure, *you* have no problem walking on this crap," he said to a wood duck waddling along. "*Your* shoes aren't full of sand."

The sun was still low in the sky and the day still cool, yet his effort was making him perspire. He unbuttoned his jacket. Sam felt a little foolish searching the lakefront for his abandoned car while a killer was still on the loose.

Losing one's car was not the action of a responsible police officer, and the duck that walked alongside and occasionally quacked remarks to remind him of his mistake did little to salve his wounded ego. The faster he found the car and got back to the cabin, back where he could protect Ruth and her lunatic patient, the better he would feel.

He decided to skirt the end of the woods where the ground was harder and the travel easier. A glint of light caught his eye. It was a reflection from not far into the woods that could be sunlight bouncing off his windshield. He stood on tiptoes to breach the low bushes and get a better look.

Next, several things happened at once. While stretching to catch sight of his car, Sam was startled by a sharp pain in his left side just below his arm. He rocked back as though reeling from a blow. He clutched at the pain, confused. He had had several episodes of angina in the past, but that pain was different—milder, and more centered in his chest. This was like being struck by a baseball bat. A crushing blow penetrating deep inside him. He stumbled backward, trying to regain his balance.

Had he brought his nitroglycerine pills with him to the cabin? No, he remembered, they were in the glove compartment of his car, a car that may be only a few yards away in the woods. He dropped to one knee, clutching the left side of his chest with both hands. His breathing was rapid and shallow, and he felt a burning, an intense burning in his side. He was suddenly aware of a sound. Not a sound that he was hearing right now. Right now he heard only a buzzing in his ears, white noise that drowned out all other sound. No, the other noise had happened before. It had been like an explosion that started his ears ringing just as he'd first felt the pain. Sam could see the bushes in front of him begin to part. Someone was coming out of the woods. Help was coming, a Samaritan to fetch his pills and rescue him in his time of need.

Then the momentary shock of the pain started to subside, and his intellect began to resurface. He detected the smell of carbide on the wind. Sam looked at his hands, still pressed against his chest. Blood was seeping through his fingers. This wasn't a Samaritan coming to his rescue; it was a gunman coming to finish what he had started. Sam forced himself to release his right hand from the wound now seeping blood through his jacket and snapped his automatic from its holster. He aimed at the moving bushes and fired three shots in rapid succession.

***

Ruth wondered whether she should wake Franklin or let him sleep until Sam returned. Franklin had refused to believe his lifelong friend could have committed these crimes. The longer they'd spoken, the more depressed Franklin had become, and he finally settled in his room to rest, his limp becoming even more pronounced as he became upset.

This episode would probably negate any progress they had made since he became Ruth's patient. Their session today was the first day he had spoken of lost time, although it didn't sound like it was a new experience for him. *And what was that discussion of a fear of dying about? His whole demeanor had changed during that discourse.* Ruth was now convinced that something in his past, something he had not yet told her, held the key to his falling-out with Dennis, and it was manifesting itself as a sleep disorder. There had to be some event in his past that triggered his anxiety, obsessive thoughts, and compulsive acts. Each time she felt that she was nearing a palpable diagnosis, his symptoms would change. Some vital piece of information was missing, and now that they had a prime suspect for the murders, she could again dedicate their sessions to finding it.

Ruth placed her notepad on the floor and closed her eyes in an attempt to clear her mind. The living room was quiet. Only crackling and an occasional pop from the burning logs in the fireplace broke the silence. Sam had brought in the logs and lit the fire before he left to find his car. The room was now warm and pleasant, and although she had work to do, and she had decided to keep her distance from Sam until they had time to talk and work some things out, she missed him. She hadn't noticed how blue his eyes were until the glow of the fireplace had danced across them as he looked down at her while they lay on the floor. She hadn't realized how much she missed the touch of a man's hand on her skin. Strong, slightly rough hands that tickled when they touched her cheek and sent quivers from that cheek down the length of her body. His touch excited yet calmed her at the same time. Her shoulders and hips seemed to melt into the floor while her toes curled uncontrollably. Now she began to fantasize about the weeks to come. She was contemplating asking Sam to her house for Christmas dinner, or maybe Christmas dinner out. No, she couldn't ask him to take her out to dinner. A catered dinner—that was it! She would ask him to Christmas dinner and have the dinner catered.

A report from a firearm not far away startled her and caused her to turn in the direction of the lake, even though there was no window on that wall of the cabin. Ruth jumped to her feet. It could have been a hunter shooting a deer. There were probably game lands nearby, but she had an unnerved feeling, a feeling of dread. Something was terribly wrong.

***

Sam lay on the ground behind a fallen log. He had dragged himself there with much effort and was now watching the bushes for any movement. He mustered all the concentration he could and periodically fired a shot in the direction from which he believed the bullet that struck him had come. Sam's mind was hazy, but he still had hope for survival. His best chance was to keep his assailant at bay as long as his ammunition lasted. He hoped that the gunshots would also attract help from anyone in the area, preferably a police officer or a game warden, but anyone with a gun would do.

Sam lay on his belly, one hand pressed against his wound and the other holding his gun braced on the fallen log. He lowered his head to wipe the perspiration from his forehead onto his sleeve. A rustle of leaves and shaking branches to his right drew his fire. Sam fired a single round. He had lost count of the number of shots he had fired. His only chance was to conserve his ammunition and hope his assailant ran out first. A puff of dust flying into the air and a loud pop from his antagonist's gun made Sam roll to the right and fire. The slide on Sam's Sig Sauer P226 flew back as it ejected the empty casing but stayed back in a locked position as smoke rose from the empty chamber. He was out of ammo.

Sam pressed the magazine catch with his thumb to release the empty mag. It popped out of the handle and bounced off the log, disappearing into the weeds and sand. He grunted and removed his left hand from his wound. Sam propped himself on his right elbow as he attempted to fish out a full magazine from his jacket pocket. His fingers were wet and sticky with blood, and he fumbled to orient the mag in his hand, to find the right grip so that he could pull it from his pocket and drive it into his automatic with a single motion, a move he had performed so often that it was second nature to him, like tying his shoes. But he was disoriented. Numbness in his arm betrayed his reflexes. The mag felt alien to him. The shooter was moving around him, trying to find an unprotected angle. Sam shifted his position, now parallel to the log and as close to the ground as possible. Slowly, a hand holding a small silver revolver poked out of a bush not fifteen feet away. The gun leveled on Sam, pointing at his midsection. Sam tried to rip the magazine from his pocket—but it was caught in the fabric and slipped from his grip. There would be no second chance. Sam lowered his head, closed his eyes, and waited for the fatal shot. The hand holding the silver handgun pulled back the hammer and slowly began to squeeze the trigger.

A shot rang out. Sam's body jerked at the sound. He waited to feel the pain of the second wound. *Maybe you don't feel the one that kills you.* Then he realized that the sound of the weapon was different. It wasn't the sound of a small caliber handgun; it was a shotgun.

There was movement in the bushes. Someone was running fast, just inside the tree line. Then a second shotgun blast exploded a large swath of branches where the movement in the bushes had been. Sam looked in the direction of the second shot. Standing to his left, feet planted firmly in the ground, shotgun braced squarely against her shoulder, stood Ruth, smoke still rising from both barrels of the old twelve-gauge.

Ruth broke the action on the shotgun, ejected the two casings, loaded two more shells into the breach, and flipped the breach shut with a snap.

"Did you recognize him?" Sam groaned.

"No, he was wearing a hood. He was still running after my second shot, but I may have wounded him." She crouched down next to Sam and helped him prop himself up against the log.

"Am I going to live?" he asked, opening his jacket to inspect the wound.

"Wrong kind of doctor," Ruth said. "Do you think you're going to live?"

She leaned him back against the log and ripped open his shirt. She could see that the bullet had entered the latissimus dorsi just below the armpit and exited through the back. She pressed her hand against his ribs and pushed.

"Hey!" He groaned. "Have a little pity."

Ruth smiled. "If I remember my biology well enough, you're going to be fine. It looks like it just went through muscle and maybe creased a rib. I don't think it damaged any organs, and the wound is already starting to clot." She helped him off with his jacket and shirt and tore the shirt into strips. She wadded up two pieces of the shirt and placed them over both the entry and exit wounds, then tied them in place with the long strips.

"You did that like a pro," Sam said. "They teach that in shrink school?"

"No," Ruth said, "they teach biology and first aid, but not enough to treat gunshot wounds. This is my first time."

"Then we're even," Sam said. "Over twenty years a cop and this is my first time too."

"Now where is that car of yours?" Ruth asked. "We need to find a hospital."

***

Ruth held the shotgun at the ready, poised to fire at anything that moved as she left the clearing, walking in the direction of the splash of bright light reflected from the car windshield.

Sam tried to call to her to check her progress and to confirm that she was all right, but each time he attempted to shout, his ribs complained louder than his voice. The ringing in his ears had subsided, and he could now hear the lapping of the water on the lakeshore. The sun warmed him, or maybe it was a fever coming on. *Ruth's pretty good in an emergency. She even remembered to release the safety from the shotgun this time.* He laughed, and then grabbed his ribs. Sam was in pain, but not enough pain to outweigh the humiliation he felt. He had been saved by the woman he'd come here to protect. There would be no way he could quash her involvement in this murder case now.

Seconds later he heard a car engine start. Sam had contended that his car was hopelessly mired in a ditch and only a tow truck could extricate it. He argued that they should leave it, retrieve his belongings, and walk back to the cabin. Ruth's car, tires now inflated, and Franklin's car, if the nut hadn't run off by now, were available to drive to the hospital. Ruth would hear none of it. He was not fit to walk, and she would deliver his car to him.

"You can't do it," Sam had said, holding his side as he spoke.

"I can't?" Ruth had countered as she parted the bushes with her shotgun barrel and disappeared into the foliage.

The roar of the car engine grew louder, along with an uneven amalgam of squeaks, thuds, and the sound of splintering branches and scraping metal.

The trees and bushes at the edge of the clearing seemed to shake as small branches cracked and leaves erupted into the air. A short silence, and then the car burst through onto the lakefront, coming to rest in the sand. Twigs and pinecones were embedded in its grill, mud painted its

325

side one-third of the way up its doors, and a plastic headlight housing dangled over the bumper by a pair of red and black wires.

Ruth rushed from the driver's seat to help Sam traverse the four or five yards to the passenger door. Sam had an opportunity to inspect the damage as he leaned on her shoulder for support. He made a mental note: *In future discussions with Ruth, use the word "can't" sparingly.*

38

By the time Ruth pulled up to the emergency entrance of Lowell General Hospital, steam was rising from the hood of Sam's car and the transmission wasn't totally cooperating with the controls. Sam wasn't totally cooperating either. He groused about needing a hospital at all.

"Just give me a few bandages and some pain-killers, and I'll go back out and catch this guy," he said to the triage nurse. But Sam wasn't going anywhere. Local police were called in by the ER doctor, as was required by law with all gunshot wounds, and after X-rays were taken and various tubes attached to his body, Sam was given a sedative to relax him while the doctors decided if surgery would be necessary. Ruth tried to fill out some of the information on the admission papers, but she wasn't too helpful. She didn't know his address or any details about his insurance or even if he had a middle name. She was, however, able to direct the hospital administrator to Sam's office for further information.

Sheriff Thompson, the overweight, tobacco-chewing, red-faced leader of the Lowell County Police Department was less than sympathetic. "I'm tired of these city cops coming up here to my jurisdiction without a how-do-you-do and shootin' up my county. We have procedures for investigating in Lowell County, and those procedures start by asking permission," he said to Ruth, pausing after every few words to spit a black viscous liquid into a paper cup he held just below his chin.

"Sheriff Thompson," Ruth said, trying not to gag, "Lieutenant Peirce was on vacation. He was staying with me when he was accosted." A little white lie might help smooth things over, she thought. "There is a gunman out there on the loose; don't you think we should be talking about that?"

"OK, lady, don't get your panties all in a bunch, I'll take care of it. Let's start with your name. Miss?"

"It's *Dr.* Klein," Ruth said, biting her lower lip to keep from snapping back. "Dr. Ruth Klein."

Ruth spent several torturous minutes with the sheriff, explaining all she knew about the incident, which wasn't much. She postulated that the gunman could have been a suspect in an investigation Lieutenant Peirce was leading, but she had no evidence to support that assumption. She had the name of a suspect, Dennis Cleaver, but knew little else about him. Sheriff Thompson said he would have someone stop by the lake to look around, but the gunman was probably miles away by now, and this Dennis character was no more than a name on a piece of paper to him.

"If that boy is from your county, get your lieutenant's people to find him. I'll send someone by the hospital later to talk to your boyfriend when the docs are through with him, but there ain't much else I can do. Most times these things are just hunting accidents. Some good ole boy thought your lieutenant was a deer, and then he hightailed it when he seen what he done. I'll get back to the lieutenant if I hear anything. You have a good day now."

Ruth, for one of the few times in her life, was unable to speak as Sheriff Thompson tipped his hat, smiled, threw his quarter-filled, foul-smelling paper cup in a trash barrel, tucked another chaw between his cheek and gum, and walked down the hall.

The hospital was quite modern for a small country facility. All the equipment and the furnishings seemed new. The floors were buffed to a glaring shine, and the walls were painted a pleasant shade of green. On the wall in Sam's private room hung a whiteboard with the name *Martha Gonzales, RN* scrawled across the center in dry-erase green marker.

"He's still asleep," the nurse said while flicking her finger against the air lock on the IV tube to check to see if the drip was still running. The patient monitor was beeping in a steady rhythm, one beep for every precious beat of Sam's heart. Ruth looked at the presentation on the screen, trying to remember if a blood oxygen level of ninety-six was normal.

"He's doing very well. You're the woman who brought him in, right?" Martha said.

"Yes, I'm Ruth—Dr. Ruth Klein."

"His vital signs are solid as a rock," said Martha. "He's OK, but you look like you could use some help. Have you looked in the mirror lately?" In the excitement, and her concern for Sam's condition, she hadn't noticed the damage that her clothing had sustained. There were blood-stains on the front of her blouse where she had wiped her hands after bandaging Sam's chest, and her elbow was beginning to poke through a small tear in her sleeve, probably sustained while thrashing through the woods from the cabin to the lake. She had a smudge of dirt and blood on her cheek. Martha stepped forward and delicately removed a torn piece of a leaf from Ruth's hair.

"You can clean up in the bathroom if you like," she said, pointing toward an open door near the corner of Sam's room. "I can get you some scrubs to wear until you get a chance to go home to change, Doctor."

"No, I'm not a medical doctor, Martha; I'm a psychologist."

"That's OK, Dr. Klein, we won't hold that against you. Take the scrubs; you'll be more comfortable."

An hour later Ruth was sitting next to Sam's hospital bed. The wound had been a clean through-and-through shot. There were no bullet frag-ments or foreign material to remove, so surgery would not be necessary. Sam had been given a unit of blood and was heavily sedated. He would probably sleep through the night.

Sam's cell phone on the nightstand began to vibrate. At first Ruth decided not to answer it, but each vibration brought the phone closer to the end of the table, and by the fourth ring, Ruth snatched it up just before it went over the edge.

"Hello, Lieutenant Peirce's phone, Dr. Klein speaking."

"Dr. Klein, this is Sergeant Holloway. How's the boss?"

"He's sleeping; the doctors say he is going to be fine. Do you know the details of what happened?"

"Ah yeah, he called me before they put him out. We put out an APB on Dennis Cleaver, but we really don't have any information to go on. Anything you know that can help?"

"Not really, but I know someone who may be able to provide some information. I'll see what I can find out."

"Should I come up?" Holloway asked.

"I don't think that will be necessary. I'll make arrangements to stay until he's released, and I'll bring him home."

"You don't have to do that, Dr. Klein. I called his…ah…cardiologist, and I think Dr. Goodman is on the way right now. Should be there in a couple of hours."

"That's a surprise, a cardiologist coming all the way up here to see a patient. Lieutenant Peirce seems to have a lot of people who care about him."

"Yeah, maybe too many," Holloway said.

***

It was time to get organized. Ruth retrieved Sam's overnight bag from the trunk of his car, removed his sweatshirt to wear against the cold, and placed the bag in the closet of Sam's hospital room. Ruth took his car to a local garage to see how much of it was salvageable. The damage she'd inflicted to the body was superficial. A small hole in the radiator was repairable, and although the transmission was slipping, the mechanic swore that it would get them back to the city as long as they topped off the transmission fluid occasionally.

Ruth then checked in with Sofia and spoke to Emma. Neither one was happy about her decision to stay a few more days, but she didn't see an alternative.

Next on the list was an attempt to find information about Dennis Cleaver. At twenty minutes to five, Ruth walked into the Lowell County Public Library. She sat at a computer terminal and began a search for any information on a Dennis Cleaver born in Binghamton, New York, between 1967 and 1970. That seemed like a wide enough range. She found a website that boasted free birth records from the New York State Archives. She found a birth record for a Dennis Cleaver in Binghamton, New York, although she was required to submit a credit card before beginning the "free trial." *Hmm, they don't tell you that part when you start to search.* It didn't give much information, but at least she now had his parents' names.

Next she decided to search the Binghamton newspapers for the article about the boating accident that Franklin had described in one of their sessions. It had been a lightning strike, she recalled. The accident had occurred when Franklin and Dennis were nineteen years old. Her hope was that the newspaper had printed a picture of the boys, an image that Dennis might still resemble.

"We're closing, ma'am," the male librarian said. "I'm sorry, but you'll have to come back tomorrow."

"Could I stay online for just a little longer? I ordered a copy of a newspaper article. I've already paid for it, but I'm afraid someone in Binghamton is searching the archives and probably won't send it for at least another half hour. It's very important." Ruth realized that she was batting her eyelashes at the young man, hoping to convince him to let her stay. She was so close.

"I'm sorry, ma'am but I have to lock the doors by five fifteen, and everyone has to be out."

"Is there any way I could convince you to let me stay until my article comes in?" Ruth asked. She would go no further than a smile and maybe a cup of coffee with the young man. That was her limit. She didn't like using feminine wiles to get her way but this was an emergency.

"Well, I can't let you stay, but maybe I can leave this computer on and print the file for you in the morning when I open for the day."

"And what would you want in return?" she asked with a coy smile.

"Twenty bucks ought to do it," he said.

"Twenty-five, and you deliver it to room two-seventeen at the hospital by nine a.m."

"Deal."

Time really flies when you're having fun; it also runs out when you have a limited amount, fun or not. The sun was setting, and a sudden surge of dizziness reminded Ruth that she hadn't eaten since breakfast. Breakfast...Ruth knew she wasn't much of a cook, but that breakfast had been enough to turn off any man. What could Sam possibly like about her that could make up for her shortcomings? What qualities did she possess that could overcome being so domestically challenged? *Maybe after that inedible breakfast, he recognized that I had no redeeming qualities at all and shot himself,* she mused. *The story of a gunman hiding in the woods was probably just a subterfuge, an attempt on his part to protect my ego.*

39

The ceiling fan slowly rotated, turned by the breeze blowing through the open window. Franklin pulled the patchwork quilt from the bed and wrapped it around his shoulders. He was shivering. The afternoon sun was low in the sky, and the temperature was dropping. The room heater did little good with the window wide open. He thought he might have had another dream, but he couldn't remember the details. Someone was running, and there had been loud explosions. It was all fuzzy, and he felt lightheaded.

Franklin looked at his watch. Five fifteen. How could they have let him sleep all day? Slowly the events of the morning came back to him. He had argued with Dr. Klein and Lieutenant Peirce. They had accused Dennis of being a murderer. He was still angry about that, but there was something else. It was there, in the back of his mind, but he just couldn't get the image to gel.

Frustrated, Franklin pulled the quilt tighter and rose to his feet. The sudden force of his rising made his head spin and put too much pressure on his weak leg. It collapsed, sending him staggering forward. He reached for his cane with his right hand, but the quilt restricted his movement and his fingers fumbled on the shaft. Although he finally caught the stick and planted it firmly on the floor, his body was already past the tipping point. He didn't have the strength to arrest his fall. Falls like this seemed to happen in slow motion, and although he could see what was coming next, he couldn't lift his arm in time to protect himself. His head struck the corner of the dresser, sending a spray of blood from his eyebrow onto the lampshade. He spun as he collapsed and landed flat on the floor. He felt a sharp ache in the middle of his back; it ached terribly.

Franklin lifted himself, trying to determine how badly he was hurt. A splash of cold water on his eyebrow and a look in the mirror told him that although blood ran freely—cuts on eyebrows seemed to do that— the cut wasn't deep. He wadded up a piece of toilet tissue and pressed it to his forehead until the bleeding stopped. Then he found a small plastic bandage in the bathroom medicine cabinet and finished the repair. It stung, but he thought the bandage gave his face character. He twisted his body in front of the mirror to view his back. He had decided to sleep in his shirt to help fend off the cold. *A mistake*, he thought. He had a spot of blood on the back of his shirt. *Must have rolled in some blood from my eyebrow when I fell.* Franklin changed his shirt and brought the soiled one into the kitchen to soak it in cold water.

"Anyone home?" Franklin called as he walked into the living room. Something had happened here. "Hello?" he shouted. A metal kitchen canister half full of sugar was on its side on the counter; its cover was bent on the floor. In the sugar he saw the brass casing and part of the paper tube of a shotgun shell. He hobbled back to the living room and looked at the empty shotgun rack over the fireplace. The rocking chair was lying on its side in the middle of the room. Something was terribly wrong. He hoped that nothing had happened to Dr. Klein and the lieutenant. He also hoped that whatever had happened had nothing to do with Dennis. Then he saw it. It was lying on the table next to a half-filled bowl of cereal and a spoon. It was a handgun, a silver Taurus .38 special stainless steel revolver. The same kind of gun that Hyrum had convinced him to buy for self-protection. The same kind of a gun that Franklin kept in his own nightstand next to his bed. It was *his* gun.

Franklin dropped his stained shirt on the back of a chair and picked up the gun. He smelled the end of the barrel. He pushed the knurled lever to release the cylinder and dumped the brass cartridge cases out onto the table. All five were empty; all five had been fired. Confusion, shock, horror, fear—which emotion first? Something bad had happened, but what?

Franklin drove his car down the narrow road back to the highway. His attention was divided between the road and the signal-strength indicator on his cell phone placed on the passenger seat. After turning onto the highway and driving about a mile, the meter registered three bars. That was enough. He braked heavily and pulled partially off the road onto the shoulder. The driver of the car behind him blasted his horn and swerved to avoid Franklin's Toyota.

"Fucking idiot," the driver yelled.

Franklin waved his hand in dismissal of the exasperated driver as he searched the contact list on his cell phone to find a number for the Luzerne County Police Station. The only number he could find was that of Lieutenant Peirce.

"County police, Lieutenant Peirce's office, Sergeant Holloway speaking."

"Sergeant, this is Franklin Jameson. I'm afraid something terrible may have happened to the lieutenant and Dr. Klein."

"Mr. Jameson, I'm glad you called. I just spoke with Lieutenant Peirce. He was hoping that you could give us some additional information about Dennis Cleaver. We were hoping you could tell us where we might find him."

"Is the lieutenant all right? Is Dr. Klein all right?" Franklin said, asking the second question before allowing time for Holloway to answer the first.

Holloway attempted to answer all Franklin's questions in one rambling utterance. "Lieutenant Peirce has been wounded in the line of duty. Dr. Klein found the lieutenant near the lake and managed to drive him to the hospital, but she never saw the gunman. Dr. Klein is with the lieutenant at Lowell County Hospital."

Then it was Holloway's turn to get answers. "Now where can I find Dennis Cleaver?" Holloway realized that he had raised his voice. He composed himself. "I'm sorry, Mr. Jameson," he said, remembering that Franklin was not a very stable personality. "You seem to be the only person who knows the suspect. We could use your help."

Franklin took the empty gun from his pocket. Now it was clear. Dennis must have followed him to the cabin and attempted to kill the lieutenant and Dr. Klein. Somehow they had escaped. But why leave the empty gun at the cabin? Then the second wave of clarity arrived. The gun that shot the lieutenant was in Franklin's possession and had his fingerprints on it, and it was probably safe to assume that his were the only prints on it now.

"Mr. Jameson, are you still there? We really need your help to find Dennis Cleaver."

"Yes, yes, I understand. I'm driving to the hospital as we speak. I'll be glad to tell all I know when I arrive." Franklin ended the call before Holloway could reply. He needed to get to the hospital. He was being set up by someone who used to be his best friend, and although he refused to admit it, he knew why. He needed to talk to Dr. Klein before the police questioned him.

***

Ruth sat next to the hospital bed and removed Sam's sweatshirt from her shoulders. The top from the pair of green scrubs was comfortable enough, but she still wore her own slacks. She had tried on the scrub bottoms, but her height had turned them into pedal pushers or some sort of baggy capri pants. The room was warm, and she could see small beads of perspiration on Sam's forehead. She took a tissue from the box on the nightstand and wiped his brow. She tried to dry his face, but the stubble of his three-day growth of beard caused the tissue to flake and leave dots of paper on his cheek. Ruth leaned over him and gently blew the bits of paper away. She inhaled and drank in his scent. The faint musky redolence of his skin was intoxicating. Maybe it was his pheromones working overtime, but Ruth couldn't help herself. She closed her eyes and pressed her lips to his forehead. Footsteps entering the room catapulted her out of the moment.

"How is he doing, Doctor?" came a voice from the doorway.

"Fine. He seems a little warm," Ruth said, wondering how much this person had seen.

"I'm Dr. Goodman, Alicia Goodman. I'm Lieutenant Peirce's cardiologist. I understand that in spite of his wound, he hasn't exhibited any signs of a cardiac event."

"Yes, that's what I understand," she said. "I'm Dr. Ruth Klein; I'm not—"

"I spoke to Dr. Bradshaw, the attending, right after I was notified of the shooting by the lieutenant's aide, Sergeant Holloway. Are you Dr. Bradshaw's relief?"

"No, I brought Sam—Lieutenant Peirce—into the hospital after he was shot."

"Well, he was fortunate to be found by a physician."

"I'm not a medical doctor. You see, Sam—Lieutenant Peirce—stayed at my cabin last night. When he was shot this morning, I drove him here."

"Oh, I see. You're *that* Dr. Klein. You're the psychologist he came up here to find. Something about a possible threat on your life?"

"Well, I guess…"

"And he stayed with you last night?"

"How do you know about me?"

"He told me. I'm not just Sam's cardiologist; we've been dating for a year."

"I didn't know that he—you both—were in a relationship."

"Obviously," Alicia Goodman said.

"No, it was all very innocent. Lieutenant Peirce only stayed because my car had four flat tires, and he couldn't find his car, and—"

"Dr. Klein," Franklin said, rushing into the room. "I woke up, and you and the lieutenant were gone. I called the lieutenant's office, and they told me he had been shot. How is he?"

"He's in satisfactory condition," Alicia Goodman said. "It sounds like you had a house full last night, Dr. Klein."

"Oh, I wasn't an invited guest," Franklin said. "I'm afraid I barged in and caught them right in the middle of—"

"Franklin is a patient of mine," Ruth interrupted. "He has a vivid imagination. Franklin, why don't we step outside so that the doctor can examine her patient?"

"That's a good idea," Alicia said. "And, Doctor, we only use our lips on a patient's forehead to check for fever in pediatrics."

Ruth took Franklin by the arm and quickly led him out of the room.

Before leaving the hospital, Ruth asked for a sheet of paper and a pen at the information desk. She stared at the blank sheet for several minutes before writing a short note. Ruth then folded the paper in thirds, addressed it to Sam Peirce, and asked that it be delivered to room 217.

Ruth didn't speak for a long time on the drive back to the cabin. Franklin rattled on about how frightened he had been for her safety after awakening and finding no one at home.

"I have something very important to discuss with you. I need to talk. I need to tell you what happened."

"Not now," Ruth said. "I have a few problems of my own."

All Ruth wanted to do now was go home. She was happy to get a ride back to the cabin from Franklin, but the ride wasn't free. Somewhere in the background she could hear him still whining about some pernicious event that had left him devastated. Ruth opened the window to let cold air blow on her face. The sound of the wind subjugated his words and allowed her to escape into the muffled din. *Sam was dating his cardiologist.* That was now apparent to her. *Does he have a thing for doctors?* He never said he was available, but he never said he wasn't. How could she be such a fool? The answer to the question she had asked herself this morning—was she being too easy—was suddenly obvious. *Well, that ends now.*

The buzz in her ears slowly began to resolve into words. Franklin was still speaking. His pitch was high and the cadence of his words rapid.

"They're going to arrest me again, and I can't go back to jail. He was my friend; how could he do this to me?"

"Wait," Ruth said. "I don't know what you're talking about. Try to calm down, and we can discuss this over a cup of coffee in a few minutes when we get back."

40

Ruth could hear the *click, click* of Franklin's cane on the hardwood floor of the cabin as he paced while Ruth made coffee. She really wanted to pack up and go home. Her pleasant little sabbatical had turned into four days of fear, danger, a little romance, and now a major disappointment. Well, she still had Emma. Emma hadn't been happy about Ruth's decision to send her home alone. Ruth would have to make that up to her in some way. *It would probably take a gift of a car to offset this parenting blunder,* she mused, knowing that Emma would never hold a grudge. She was a sweet child. She would never even think of extortion in exchange for love. It was Ruth's own guilt that made her feel that a gift was even necessary. No, she would go home, and all would be normal and loving between her and Emma. Ruth would be totally and unconditionally forgiven. She believed that, but she would have a fifty-dollar bill ready just in case. And she still had her career, which reminded her that Franklin was waiting in the next room.

She steeled herself to the task and walked into the living room. Her parenting skills may have disappointed her daughter, and the man she chose to be with for the first time in five years may have experienced enough disappointment to prefer another relationship, but she wasn't going to disappoint Franklin. She would help him reveal the deep-seated reason for his neurosis if she had to beat it out of him.

When Ruth returned to the living room with the coffee, Franklin was sitting on a dining chair with his cane resting across his knees.

"What happened to your eye?" Ruth asked. She had noticed the Band-Aid on his eyebrow at the hospital but had been too distressed, or maybe too self-absorbed, to comment. Now she felt guilty.

"I fell getting out of bed and hit my eyebrow on the dresser. It looks worse than it feels. It's my back that's killing me. I found some aspirin in the medicine cabinet. It seems to be helping." Ruth picked up the spotted shirt from the back of the chair.

"I was going to soak that in cold water," Franklin said. "I must have rolled in some blood from my eye when I fell."

"That's not all," Ruth said as she examined the shirt. "You must have ripped it as well."

"Leave it. I'll probably throw it away. It's an old shirt. I have more important things to talk about. I think you were right about Dennis."

"How so?" Ruth said, swinging into therapy mode.

"I understand that you saved Lieutenant Peirce from being killed. Did you see who shot him?" Franklin dumped three spoons of sugar into his coffee and stirred it.

"No, I'm afraid I didn't see him," Ruth said, suddenly feeling proud. She had acted quite bravely, and she may very well have saved his life. Not that he'd recognized her bravery. She tried to recall if he even said thanks. Of course, a lot was happening at once, and he probably planned to thank her at the hospital had she not left in a hurry when his girlfriend…Ruth shook her head to clear her mind and get back to the business at hand.

"You said you were sure that Dennis could never be violent. What changed your mind?"

"I never said he couldn't be violent; I've seen him violent. I said I didn't think he would kill anyone."

"Can you remember a time when you saw Dennis act violently?" Ruth asked, pushing her coffee cup to one side and picking up her pen and notepad.

Franklin took a deep breath and closed his eyes. Soon he was back in Binghamton, walking home from school with his show-and-tell project. Ruth watched him cup his hands and hold them out over the table as though he were holding a great treasure.

"I was twelve years old, and the project I built was a Green Lantern power battery. I made it from an old kerosene lamp and a flashlight. I had sent away for a genuine Green Lantern power ring. It cost three cereal box tops and two dollars and fifty cents. It was just one week's allowance, but it took a month to eat the cereal."

Ruth looked confused. Franklin explained, "The Green Lantern is a comic book superhero. He gets his super powers from his ring and the light from his lantern, a green lantern. It charges his ring with power. Well, anyway, I made this lantern, like I said, out of a kerosene lamp and a flashlight. When I held the ring against the lantern, the flashlight battery in the lantern would charge a little battery in the ring, and the stone would glow green for a while."

Ruth nodded. She didn't really understand how the ring worked, but she didn't think that was the important part of the story.

"My presentation at school went fairly well," Franklin said. "It took two tries for the ring to glow. Some of the other kids laughed, but Mrs. Shultz, my teacher, said it was the most creative of all the projects and gave me the class prize, a snow globe with the skyline of Manhattan Island inside. It had been sitting on her desk ever since her weekend in New York City during the Thanksgiving holiday. I was really excited."

Ruth looked at Franklin, and she could imagine how his twelve-year-old face must have beamed with pride. She put down her notepad and leaned back in her chair.

"I tucked the glass globe carefully into my backpack. I could picture it on my bookcase in my room, right up there on a shelf with the lantern and the ring. I guess I was pretty impressed with myself."

"You had a right to be proud," Ruth said. "It was a monument to your intellect; a trophy for a job well done."

"I wouldn't go that far," Franklin said. "Well, I was feeling good, that was, until I walked past the alley next to the pharmacy, and someone grabbed my shoulder from behind. My memory gets a little sketchy here. It all happened so fast that it seemed like flashes of light, a strobe creating images on a storyboard. I still see them that way in my mind, pictures flipping past my eyes."

Ruth loved the metaphor. Franklin had emotional problems, maybe even mental illness, but his mind was creative and his storytelling very expressive.

"I know I was attacked by boys from school. I remember them shouting…*Weirdo*…*Freak*…" A mist came over Franklin's eyes. Ruth reached out to touch his hand, but he pulled it away and began to speak louder.

"Someone slapped the lantern out of my hand. I tried to hold on to my backpack, but I couldn't. One of the boys, the biggest one, took the snow globe from my bag and held it in the air." Franklin reached up high above his head with one hand.

"I tried to get it back, but the other boys were hanging on me, holding me down. I pleaded with him not to smash it on the ground. He just laughed at me and raised it even higher."

"Franklin?" Ruth said, trying to get his attention. His voice was quavering and his hand was starting to shake.

"I looked at the globe for what I thought was the last time. He cocked his arm to throw it, and then…"

"Then what?" Ruth said, teetering on the edge of the fate of the snow globe.

"Then another hand grabbed the globe. I recognized the yellow plaid jacket and the gray hood from his sweatshirt; it was Dennis. Then one of the other boys fell on me, and all I could see were flashes of images interrupted by darkness, images of Dennis kicking the boy who had taken the globe, and the other boys standing by, just staring in awe at the savagery of his attack. I think they were too afraid to intervene. My view was blocked by the boy who fell on top of me, but I could hear the boy's grunts and cries as Dennis beat him."

Ruth marveled again at the imagery evoked by his words.

"Then I was free. Two of the boys grabbed the one on the ground and dragged him away. I had never seen this side of Dennis. He stood with his arm raised high and shrieked something unintelligible as he held the snow globe over his head in triumph."

Franklin now stood, making a sound that seemed savage if not a little high-pitched, and waved the sugar bowl over his head.

Ruth exhaled a long breath. A breath she had held for the last two minutes.

"Dennis's actions may have been violent, but they were also heroic," Ruth said.

"Yeah, he was a good friend to me," Franklin said, "but I wouldn't want to be on his bad side."

"Were there many people on his bad side?" Ruth asked.

"Yeah, Myra for one. I think he really hated her and, now, maybe me."

"What makes you think he hates you?" Ruth asked. "You told me he was upset because you spent more time with Myra than you did with him, but that's to be expected. Girlfriends take precedence over buddies. You still saw each other, just not as much."

"Well, that's not exactly what happened," Franklin said, taking his cane from the back of his chair and beginning to pace back and forth across the living room. "You see, the story I told you about the fishing trip, the day of the accident, that's not exactly the way it ended."

Ruth stood. "You lied to me?"

"Not exactly," Franklin said, now facing Ruth while leaning on his cane. "Most of it happened just the way I said: the storm, the lightning strike, Dennis swimming to shore. The part that I didn't tell you was that we argued just before the storm. It was a terrible fight. He said that Myra was no good for me, she was a controlling bitch, and I was stupid to stay with her. He said I would never find a friend like him again, and I would be sorry if I let him go." Franklin ran his fingers through his hair. "That's when I told him that if it was a choice between Myra and him, I chose Myra. He was a good friend, but I didn't feel the same *way* about him as he did me." Franklin cast his eyes down to the floor.

"I see," said Ruth.

"Well, I think he was about to say something else when the lightning struck. I don't know, but he looked really strange."

"He still saved your life. Even after you rejected him, he didn't stop caring about you."

"Well, that was another part of the story I changed. You see, Dennis swam toward shore, but he didn't come back for me. It was a fisherman who lived near the lake who came out in his boat with the police."

"Did Dennis ever tell you why he didn't come back?"

"No. I remember seeing him standing on the road as they loaded me into the ambulance. I tried to reach out to him, but he just stood there. He never came to the hospital, and by the time I was well enough to come home, he was gone. I didn't hear from him or see him again until I saw him outside your office just a few months ago."

Now Ruth would have to change her strategy. She had thought that Dennis might eventually become an ally. Someone who could help solve Franklin's problems by absolving his guilt. Now she knew that Dennis was the cause of his emotional problems. Whether justified or not, Franklin's feelings of guilt toward Dennis would not be erased by Dennis's forgiveness. If she and Sam were correct, Dennis was a dangerous criminal, and absolution for Franklin was probably the last thing on his mind.

"Franklin, what happened this morning that upset you so?"

"I think you and Lieutenant Peirce were right, although I didn't want to admit it. I think Dennis killed Sylvia Radcliffe and Michelle Ackerman. I think he left the stolen files and your calendar in my house to lure me here, and then he shot the lieutenant. Maybe he planned to kill you too, but somehow you escaped."

"Why do you think he would want to hurt me?" Ruth asked. "And if he had been successful, how would that implicate you?"

Franklin reached into his pocket and withdrew the silver revolver. Ruth slid her chair back from the table. "Franklin, where did you get that?"

"It was here." He placed it on the table in the spot where he had found it. "He left it here while I was asleep. He's trying to incriminate me. You see, it's my gun, and all this is my fault."

"I don't understand. Why is it your fault?" Ruth asked. She reached across the table and took the revolver. She released the cylinder, noted that it was empty, and placed it back on the table.

"I made a terrible mistake. Dennis was right about Myra. She never really loved me, at least not the way he did. He was a powerful friend, but now he's just as powerful an enemy. He said I would be sorry for abandoning him, and now I know what he meant. He plans to have me spend the rest of my life in prison."

"You said that Dennis was in your house and left the stolen files the day Sam—Lieutenant Peirce—came to visit. Was that the last time you saw him?"

"Well, as I said, I didn't actually see him that day. I heard someone in the house when Lieutenant Peirce rang the bell, and I assumed it was Dennis. He had been following me for weeks. If it was him, he must have slipped out the kitchen door before I let the lieutenant in."

"Franklin, when was the last time you actually saw Dennis?"

"It has been a while. He was sitting at the bus stop outside your office weeks ago. I wasn't sure it was him, so I didn't tell you at the time."

"Did you talk to him?"

"I did," Franklin said, now beginning to sob. "I tried to apologize, to say how sorry I was for not being there for him all these years, but he didn't answer me; he didn't even look at me. He just turned and walked away."

Ruth placed her hand on Franklin's shoulder. This time he didn't pull away.

Later Ruth wrote notes from the session into Franklin's file:

Franklin feels crippling guilt because of the way he treated Dennis more than twenty-five years ago. This guilt seems grossly out of proportion to the circumstances, and Dennis's violent reaction to Franklin seems out of proportion as well. There is more to this story than has been told.

Ruth knew that the only chance Franklin had to overcome this guilt was to face it head on, and he probably wouldn't be able to accomplish that until Dennis was caught.

41

One hundred and fifty feet away from the cabin where Ruth Klein was in bed, a man carefully opened the door to her SUV. He wrinkled his nose at the acrid smell of smoke from the chimney intermingled with gusts of wind blowing from the north. He reached in, quickly turned off the interior dome light, and released the hood. "Shit," he whispered as the small service light under the hood made him visible. That is, he feared he would be visible if someone was looking during the few seconds it took him to twist the bulb from its socket. He now had to complete his task with only the light from the full moon. He worked quickly. He removed the cap from the master brake cylinder and placed a long, inch-thick branch into the fluid reservoir. Next he pulled on the stick, using it as a pry bar to snap the reservoir from its mount, and dumped its fluid.

Under her down comforter and blanket, Ruth lay awake in her bed and listened to the wind whistle through the half-inch space between the open window and the sill beneath. Ruth always slept with the window open, even on the coldest nights. It had been a point of disagreement between Ruth and her ex-husband, Tom. It was just one of a list of differences too numerous to recall that eventually became more important than the relationship. She wondered if Sam slept with his window open or closed. She was about to bet on open when a small pinpoint of light became visible through the window for just a few seconds.

Ruth rose from her bed and slipped her thick red-and-orange terrycloth robe over her nightgown. Then a movement outside caught her eye. At first she thought it was bushes blowing in the wind. She took her glasses from the dresser and tried to focus on the moving shadow in the distance. It looked like someone was crouching next to the cars in the parking lot, but she couldn't be sure. Ruth put on her slippers and rushed to the front door. She flipped on the porch light and stepped to the railing at the edge of the porch. No, the parking area looked deserted. Her car sat facing down the hill, just as she had left it, ready to drive back to the city in the morning. She was really getting jumpy. She thought of waking Franklin, but since she was treating him for a sleep disorder, it didn't seem prudent to interrupt his rest. It was probably just her imagination. Tree branches swaying in the wind could have altered the reflection of the moon bouncing off her car. She could have easily mistaken the reflection for a light.

Ruth walked back into the house and began to heat a pot of water on the stove to make a cup of tea. She knotted the belt of her robe around her waist. The wind now howled through the trees outside and light snow was beginning to fall. *That's all I need,* she thought, *a few more days of being cooped up here, and I'll need a therapist of my own.* She rubbed the soft collar of her robe against her cheek, remembering the morning last Christmas when Emma had given it to her. Emma said she had saved part of her allowance for months to buy the present, but Ruth was sure that Emma had asked her grandfather to help supplement her funds. Too bad he didn't help her choose the color. She missed Emma. Tomorrow morning she would go home and try to be a better parent.

Ruth went to the cupboard and opened the tin marked "teabags," only to find that it was empty. A thought struck her. She quietly walked to Franklin's room, carefully turned the doorknob, and opened the door just a crack. Through the opening she could see his cane leaning up against the wall next to the bed and the outline of Franklin's body under the patchwork quilt and a double layer of blankets. Ruth gently closed the door and went back to the kitchen. Then a second thought struck her, and she returned to the living room. The empty revolver was still sitting on the dining table. Ruth placed it in the pocket of her robe. It was empty, she knew that, but maybe the killer wouldn't be certain, and she could use it to her advantage. That was, of course, if someone was really out there and this wasn't all her imagination. She went back to the front door and opened it.

Ruth's mind flashed back to the grade-B horror movies she watched as a teenager. The beautiful young heroine in the movie would hear a noise or see a movement in the dark, outside her window. Ruth was familiar with the scene that came next. It was the part of the movie where the shapely young heroine would do something very foolish. Ruth thought of herself as this heroine—well, maybe not quite as young or as shapely as the gal in the B movie, but a heroine no less.

It's a dark night, and the violent killer is hiding somewhere in the woods outside the cabin. Our heroine hears a noise and decides—a bad decision, by the way—to go out and investigate. The audience cringes in their seats. Shouts of "No" and "Stupid bitch, he's going to kill you" leap from their lips. Ruth remembered that these movies didn't attract the most sophisticated patrons. *But the heroine goes out anyway. Poorly armed and barely dressed, she tempts fate in a way no rational person would.* Ruth knew how the movie always ended. The heroine's curiosity to know if the danger was real or imagined was overpowering. Her best judgment aside, she walks out the door.

Next was the part of the movie where the murderer split the young woman's head with an ax, or drove a two-foot-long sword through her back and out her rib cage. *Why does she do it?* Ruth thought. *Why doesn't she just lock the door, barricade it with furniture, and wait to be rescued?* Of course, that assumed someone was coming to rescue her. Ruth knew, in her case, that no knight in shining armor, no cavalry or sheriff's posse, was on the way. She was not only on her own, but she felt responsible to protect Franklin as well; he was a patient still under her care.

Ruth knew she should stay indoors until morning when the forest would be bathed in light and her ears filled with the sounds of songbirds rather than the eerie moan of the wind and the sudden rustle of bushes that caused her heart to leap. The murmur of the forest sounds began to mimic the frightening background music of the remembered movie, a dirge punctuated by the loud throbbing of a heartbeat, her breath catching in her throat, that heartbeat becoming faster with each step.

She tried to analyze her state of mind. She realized that there was a certain added vulnerability one feels when in a dangerous situation and not wearing underwear under one's nightgown. Was it a gender thing, or would a man in pajamas feel the same? She wondered if there was any research on the subject or if it would make an interesting topic for a paper on gender-related fear.

Ruth was through the door, down the porch steps, and halfway to the parking lot before she again focused on her current situation. She stopped, reached into her pocket, and positioned the gun in her hand. Psychological research would have to wait until she was sure that that ax wasn't about to cleave her head in half and that the sword wouldn't suddenly erupt from her chest.

Ruth stood on the gravel path in her slippers, feeling the sharp stones pressing through the soft soles. She limped the rest of the way to her car. Maybe she could sit and rub her feet for a few minutes before heading back to the cabin. She relaxed her grip on the revolver and opened the car door. The first thing she noticed was that the dome light didn't come on. She backed away immediately and opened the rear door. Empty. Well, no one was hiding in the car. The bulb in the dome light could have burned out. She reached up and flicked the switch at its base. The light came on. Curious, but it didn't seem that suspicious. She could have bumped the switch while unloading the car, or Sam might have shut it off for some reason while he was filling the tires with air.

Her feet really hurt. She sat on the driver's seat, feet out the door, and crossed her leg to massage her right foot. She pressed her fingers into the ball of her foot and rubbed her thumb on the base of each toe in succession. She closed her eyes and was lost in the fantasy pleasure of someone else's warm hands rubbing her aching toes, someone with large, strong hands that could manipulate her feet so hard that it almost hurt, rubbing the arch of her foot and squeezing each toe, then moving up her ankle to—

A cracking sound of a breaking twig caused her to pry her eyes open in time to see a man in a hooded jacket running full speed with his head down toward her car. Ruth swung her legs into the car. It was too late to reach for the wide-open door to pull it closed. He was too close. She began to crawl over the console to exit from the passenger side. She swung the passenger door open and was about to dive out when his hands caught her right foot. That same foot that she'd imagined in a man's strong hands was now being clawed at and restrained in a most unpleasant way. Ruth held the side of the seat with both hands and kicked at his head several times in quick succession. Her kicks hit their mark. She could feel the flesh of his face and the firm bridge of his nose against the heel of her left foot. His head snapped back, and by the third kick, her right foot was free. She tumbled out of the car and slammed the door. The fierceness of her kicks, or maybe it was the slamming door striking his head as he tried to follow her out of the car, seemed to disorient him. He paused, stunned. Now it was time to run.

Each step on the sharp-edged gravel was extremely painful and cut into her already tender feet. The hooded man was still for a moment, then started to stir. The cabin was too far down the stony path. She chose to run into the woods instead. The soft pine needles on the forest floor afforded both comfort to her feet and an opportunity to move without making much noise.

Ruth watched from her hiding place beneath a wide pine tree. The hooded man in the plaid jacket rubbed his head and looked toward the cabin. Ruth ducked down. He exited the car and stood still, apparently listening and wondering if she had gone back to the cabin or into the woods. Ruth didn't believe in psychic powers or any form of extrasensory perception, but while she hugged the ground, cringing, she found herself trying to will the man into not finding her.

After a long and frightening moment of indecision—frightening for Ruth, that is—he began to walk toward the cabin. At first she felt relieved. She could run back to the car, get the magnetic key box out from under the fender well, and drive off the mountain. However, assuming the hooded man was Dennis, she would be leaving Franklin at the mercy of a man who now appeared to be his sworn enemy.

Ruth quickly formulated a plan. She would wait until he was almost at the cabin, then make a dash for the key and start the car. She would hesitate after the car was started, hoping that he would run after her. She would then try to lead him away from the cabin. She could blow the horn to wake Franklin. Once awake and hopefully warned, he would at least have a chance to defend himself.

The hooded man was approaching the porch. She could see his silhouette in the light from the full moon filtering through the trees. It was time to act. Ruth rushed to the fender well of her car, dropped to her knees, and reached inside. She felt around for the magnetic box. "Shit, shit, shit," she whispered. Could it have fallen off on the road? *Why did I trust a freaking magnet with such an important job?* Technology never was her friend. By now, the man was at the base of the porch; time was running out for Franklin. No wait, it was in the left fender well that she had hidden the key, the driver's side. She quickly clambered around the car on all fours and felt inside the wheel well for the box. Finally, the box was hers. She slid out the key and climbed into the driver's seat. Through the rearview mirror, she could see a rectangle of light; the front door was open. Ruth pressed on the horn in quick, short beeps. Her purpose was twofold: to attract Dennis away from the cabin and to alert Franklin to the danger.

She watched the rectangle of light in the mirror. At first she was confused. It appeared that the light from the door blinked. Then it became clear. The fleeting darkness was the body of the killer as he passed through the doorway, heading toward her car at a full run. Ruth placed the key in the ignition. She had a momentary fear that he might have disabled her car earlier. She wiped the perspiration from her brow with the back of a muddy hand. If she had any religious beliefs at all, this would be the time to pray. Ruth closed her eyes and made a low moaning sound as she twisted the key, then a loud yes when the engine started. *I guess he's not that smart after all*, she thought.

Suddenly a new plan took shape in her mind. She would start down the hill just far enough ahead of him to make him believe he could catch her if he kept running at full speed. Then, when he was close, she would hit the brakes, throw the transmission into reverse, and floor the gas pedal. He would be running downhill as fast as he could and hopefully not be able to stop before she could paste him to the back of the vehicle.

Ruth tried to judge his speed and distance and started down the hill. She planned her speed well, and he was gaining enough ground to keep him interested but not enough to catch her. She said aloud, "Now, you bastard," and slammed on the brake. The pedal fell to the floor and stayed there. Ruth tried to pump the pedal, but all she was doing was mashing it against the floorboard. She grabbed the shift lever and tried to throw the transmission in reverse. It made a loud clanking sound but only rolled faster down the hill. Ruth focused on steering the car down the narrow, winding path, gaining speed with each second. *The parking brake, where was the parking brake?* She glanced quickly at the console to locate the handle. She looked up to see the road turn sharply to the right. A turn much sharper than she could accomplish at this speed. The big SUV veered off the road into the trees. There was the sound of breaking glass and tearing metal, and then the bone-jarring eruption of the airbag crashing into her face and upper body. Then there was quiet and darkness.

At first there was no sensation at all. No awareness of temperature. No light, just a silent black void, a moment of sensory deprivation. Then she noticed a flow of small droplets running down her upper lip and into her mouth. They felt warm and tasted metallic. Soon the pain told her what the droplets were. The air bag had protected her face from hitting the steering wheel or the windshield but at the cost of her nose.

She could feel someone tamping down the air in the airbag and pulling at her robe, trying to yank her out onto the ground. He had reached the car. She couldn't see, but that wouldn't lessen her resistance. She swung her arms and kicked her feet at this man who was responsible for her condition. He had taken a reasonably sophisticated, affluent woman of science, and degraded her to a base human being, fighting for her very life. She was in pain and bleeding, but she wasn't beaten. He stopped suddenly and let her go. Maybe she had hurt him. She hoped she had. Then, just as suddenly, two hands were back, reaching around her waist, trying to pull her from the car. She lashed out again. She would not yield.

"Hold on, hold on, lady, I'm trying to help you," said a voice. "I'm one of the good guys." Ruth's waving arms knocked Trooper Sullivan's hat from his head, exposing an extremely close buzz cut, a haircut common among law enforcement, particularly in the state police. When this was over, she would have to find out if there was some advantage to the haircut, or if it was just a way to mask a receding hairline.

"There was a man trying to kill me; he was here."

"Man in a hood? He was right here at your side, but he ran off when I climbed through that fallen tree blocking the road. He ran back up the hill. Is he the one who shot that downstate lieutenant yesterday?"

Trooper Sullivan looked in the car to find something to wipe the blood from Ruth's eyes and nose. He reached in his back pocket and snapped his handkerchief open. "It's clean," he said. "Mildred laundered it just last night."

Ruth jerked her head back as he began to wipe the blood from her eyes and nose.

"Is it broken?" she asked.

"I don't think so. It's straight, and I'm sure it'll be just as pretty as before once we stop the bleeding and the swelling goes down. I think we should still get you to the hospital though, and make sure nothing else is broken."

"No," she shouted. "There's a patient of mine in the cabin. He's disabled, and that man is going to hurt him. I'm fine—go help Franklin." Ruth pressed the handkerchief to her nose and almost pushed the officer toward the cabin.

Trooper Sullivan looked uphill at the winding, narrow road. He put his hand on his service weapon. "You stay right here and don't move till I get back." He touched his belt where his radio usually hung. The clip that secured it to his belt was there, but the radio was not.

He took a step toward the fallen tree. If he returned to his car and called in his situation and location, backup would be there in a matter of minutes. That tree, however, had been a challenge to climb over the first time, and he wasn't sure his suspect would wait for him to call in before hurting someone else. No, he was going to do this alone. He patted Ruth on the shoulder, removed his automatic from its holster, and cautiously started up the hill. Ruth watched him, illuminated by the first light of dawn, disappear around the turn in the road.

***

Trooper Sullivan was a barrel-chested man with large biceps and heavily muscled thighs. He spent hours each week in the gym toning his body and building his endurance by running five miles three times a week. He was proud of his physical conditioning and trudged up the hill toward the cabin like a locomotive under full steam—arms swinging at his sides and legs, making powerful strides over the rough terrain. When he reached Franklin's car in the parking area, he ducked down behind it to assess his best approach to the cabin. He hugged the tree line next to the path until he reached the clearing and then ran the last few steps to the porch.

The door to the cabin was open. Trooper Sullivan flattened himself against the cabin wall next to the door, then peeked through the window into the living room. The room was dark. The sun was not yet high enough to illuminate the living room. Sullivan removed his flashlight from his belt and held it under his gun hand as he darted through the door and crouched behind the sofa. He methodically cleared the room as he had done so many times in his career, first the living room, then the kitchen. The hall closet and the back hall all proved empty. Next he grasped one of the bedroom doors and swung it wide, pointing his gun at each corner of the room in turn.

He suddenly pointed his gun at the ceiling. A man was sitting on the bed, staring at his cane on the bedroom floor. The man's face was bloodied, and one eye was half-closed. He was reaching out with one foot, trying to drag his cane within reach. The police officer locked eyes with Franklin and saw Franklin's eyes shift toward the open bathroom door. Trooper Sullivan nodded, put his finger to his lips, and then silently approached the bathroom. He stood against the wall next to the door and signaled Franklin with his hand to get down. He hesitated for a moment, but when Franklin didn't move, he held his automatic in both hands, entered the bathroom, and dropped to one knee. The room was empty. As he stood, he heard a distinctive sound come from the bedroom behind him. The sound caused him to freeze in his tracks. It was a sound that every police officer who's seen action fears, the *click* from the hammer of a revolver being cocked.

42

"G ood to see you among the living," Martha said. Now that the pain-killers were wearing off, the gauze pad and the bandages fastening it to Sam's chest itched. He tried to reach his left side with his right hand, but the tube delivering the saline drip and antibiotic wasn't long enough to make the trip. He winced and shifted his position in the bed to create more slack in the tube. It wasn't enough. Sam lifted the sheet and tried to focus his eyes on his bandaged chest, trying to will the itch to stop.

"It took a pretty heavy dose of sedative to put you out; how well did you sleep?" the nurse asked.

"How long did I sleep is a better question. What time is it?" Sam asked, wriggling back and forth, hoping the weight of his blanket might scratch the itch. This was going to drive him crazy.

"You slept through the night. It's almost seven in the morning. I have breakfast for you. It's scrambled eggs and bacon, hot coffee, buttered biscuits, and a fruit tart. Let's sit you up while it's all hot."

It had been almost twenty-four hours since Sam had eaten. His last meal was memorable, but far from satisfying. "Bring it on," he said, the itch now totally forgotten. He scooted up in the bed, snapped his napkin open, and draped it over the bandage encircling his chest.

"There was a woman here with me last night. Do you know where she is?"

Martha looked down and made a sound that was half laugh and half snort. "Do you mean the woman who brought you in yesterday, or the one that chased her away?"

"Sam, you're up," Alicia said, entering the room holding a tray from the cafeteria. "You can take that breakfast tray back, nurse. I brought his breakfast."

Alicia pressed the up button on the bed to elevate Sam into a semisitting position and slid the overbed table in front of him. She removed the hot breakfast tray Martha had delivered and handed it back to her. Then she slid the tray she had specially ordered for Sam into position and lifted the stainless steel plate covers.

"It's organic oatmeal, dry five-grain toast, and a sliced kiwi. Enjoy."

***

"I think I'm ready to get out of here," Sam said as he pushed the overbed table to the side. "Has anyone seen my overnight bag, or my car, or my gun?"

"Your bag is in the closet," Martha said. "Dr. Klein put it in there. I don't know anything about your car or a gun."

"Well, where's Dr. Klein?"

"She left last night just after I arrived," Alicia said. "She was with a man. He had a limp and used a cane. I think he was going to drive her back to wherever she was staying."

"She left with Franklin?" Sam said, swinging his feet over the edge of the bed.

"You don't have to worry about her; she has a man to protect her," Alicia said. "You're injured. She's not your responsibility any longer."

"Alicia, you don't understand. There's a killer still out there, and Franklin wouldn't be much help in an emergency. He's one of her nutty patients."

"Are you sure she's in danger? The sheriff seemed to think that you were shot accidentally by a hunter who ran away rather than own up to his carelessness."

"A hunter using a handgun and shooting from the cover of the trees? I don't think so. This case has narrowed down to one suspect, a guy named Dennis Clever. We haven't figured out his motive yet, but he killed two women that we know of, and he tried to kill me." Sam pulled the rolling stand holding the IV bag close to him and used it for support to stand.

"Where do you think you're going?" Alicia said. "You're here for at least another twenty-four hours."

"Listen to the pretty lady," Sheriff Thompson said, hiking up his trousers as he entered the room. "I had my deputies, the auxiliary police and, by God, even the volunteer firemen sweep those woods yesterday for three miles. Your guy is gone, if he ever existed."

Sam raised an eyebrow, but caught himself before commenting.

"What about a car, or a blood trail at the scene? Dr. Klein thought she might have hit the man who shot me while he ran."

"No car. No blood, except for yours—a mess of blood by the lake." He laughed. "I should charge your county for the cleanup." Sam's face started to redden.

"I'm just funnin' with ya. Your friends are OK. There's nobody up there for miles. You get back in bed and get well. We'll keep an eye on the roads in and out of those woods. Oh, by the way, Mavis at the front desk asked me to give you this note." Sheriff Thompson pulled a folded piece of paper from his back pocket. "The red-haired gal left it for you last night." He ambled over to Sam and handed him Ruth's note. Looks like you're a popular guy." He smiled and tipped his hat to Alicia and Martha as he left.

Alicia sat Sam back down on the bed. "I'm sure Dr. Klein and Franklin can take care of themselves. Besides, the sheriff said he sent some men to search the woods and found no one. Your suspect has probably left the state by now. Let's get you back in bed; you need your rest."

Sam sat on the edge of the bed and opened the note.

Dear Sam,

I spoke to your doctor before I left the hospital. He assured me that you're doing fine and will be up and around within twenty-four hours. You're receiving excellent care, particularly since your cardiologist arrived. Your car is being repaired at the garage indicated on the enclosed card. It will be ready tomorrow afternoon. Let me know the cost of the repairs, and I'll send a check to reimburse you for the damage I did. Unfortunately, I can't reimburse you for the damage I may have done to your relationship with Dr. Goodman. That will be up to you. Thank you for driving here to come to my aid. I'm sorry for a lot of things. I'm sorry I damaged your car. I'm sorry for the terrible meals you were forced to eat, and most of all I'm sorry you were hurt. What I'm not sorry for is the evening we spent together, even if it meant more to me than it did to you. I won't complicate your life any longer, and I'll stop interfering with your work. I have my practice and should focus my energy on my patients. Franklin is taking me back to the cabin. I can now concentrate on his problems and hopefully be of some help to him before we return home. Heal well, and stay safe.

Ruth

Sam swung his legs back onto the bed. He folded the letter and placed it under his pillow.

While Sam was reading the letter, Alicia had walked to his closet to keep busy arranging his clothes. She turned to look at him every few seconds to note his expression. She aligned his shoes evenly on the closet floor and picked up his sweatshirt from the chair to place it on a hanger. Alicia raised the sweatshirt to her face and noticed a light scent, a scent that she knew was too feminine to be Sam's. She hung the shirt on a hanger and turned to Sam.

"Do we need to talk?" she asked.

Sam looked out the large plate-glass window at the bare trees bending in the wind. The few remaining leaves were fighting to hold their grip on the moving branches. He was silent for a long time and then said, "I think it's going to snow."

Alicia watched his face until he turned and met her eyes. "We can talk when we get home," he said.

***

"I don't care who is in the room. I was told to deliver this newspaper clipping to room two-seventeen and collect twenty-five dollars."

"Sir," said Martha, blocking the doorway, "if you don't have the name of the person you're delivering that envelope to, who do you think is going to give you twenty-five bucks?"

"She didn't give me a name. She just said if I brought this article here this morning, I would get twenty-five dollars, and I'm not leaving without it."

"Nurse," Sam called out while holding his ribs. "Let him in."

The librarian skirted around Martha's girth and eased through the door, trying to keep as much distance as he could between the angry nurse and himself.

"Who told you to bring that here?" Sam asked.

"She was a lady doctor, I guess. She was wearing one of those green doctor shirts under a gray sweatshirt jacket."

Alicia took Sam's sweatshirt jacket from its hanger. It was part of the sweat suit she had given to Sam to encourage him to exercise. She held it again to her nose to confirm her suspicion and then dropped it to the floor of the locker.

Sam stood at the side of his bed and took the IV stand in his hand. "Hold on," he said. "I'll get your money."

"Wait." Alicia reached in her pocket and handed several bills to the librarian. "You get back in bed," she said to Sam, and opened the envelope.

"It's just an old newspaper article from 1988. It's about two boys in a fishing boat on a lake in upstate New York who were hit by lightning."

"Does it have a picture of the boys?" Sam asked.

"No, I'm afraid it doesn't," Alicia replied, "just an account of the accident." She read on, then said, "Two boys were fishing on a lake and their boat was struck by lightning, Franklin Jameson and Dennis Cleaver. Is that the same Franklin who took Dr. Klein back to her cabin?"

"Yeah, I guess that was how he lost the full use of his leg. What about the other boy, Dennis Cleaver? Does it say anything that might help us? Any reference to family, where he lived, anything we could use to find him?"

"Sure, it says exactly where he is." Sam stood as Alicia began to read a portion of the article aloud:

A fisherman, Maxwell Trendle, who had seen the young men leave the pier hours before the freak thunderstorm arrived, called police, who accompanied him on a search for the small boat. They found Franklin Jameson in a portion of the boat that was still floating. Apparently the boat had been severely damaged by a bolt of lightning. Young Jameson, suffering from shock and burns, was taken to General Hospital. The body of the other boy, Dennis Cleaver, washed up on the far shore Tuesday morning. Jameson said that Cleaver had left the disabled boat to swim for help. Police believe that Cleaver, an excellent swimmer, was disoriented by the storm and swam in the wrong direction.

Sam took the article from Alicia and quickly read: "Services for Dennis Cleaver will be held at the Christ Methodist Church on Saturday, and he will be laid to rest in Griswold Cemetery."

Sam threw down the article. "Son of a bitch," he said. "He was right under our nose all the time." A loud electronic tone sounded as Sam disconnected the wire leads from the electrodes stuck to his chest and held out his arm with the IV needle to Alicia.

"Sam, what are you doing?" she yelled.

"Either you take it out, or I will," he said. Alicia stared as Sam peeled the plastic tape from his arm and pulled out the needle.

"Wait," she said. She tore open a sterile pad, swabbed his arm, and placed a folded piece of gauze and tape over the puncture.

Sam was half-dressed before Alicia could present a cogent argument for not leaving the hospital. She knew it was a losing battle, but she tried anyway. Sam handed her his car keys. "My car won't be ready until later this afternoon. I'll need yours."

"I don't understand. If Dennis is dead, what did you mean when you said he was right under your nose all the time?"

"Franklin said he had been seeing Dennis for the last three months. If Dennis is dead, then Franklin is nuttier than we thought."

"Nutty enough to be the killer?" Alicia asked.

"I think so."

Alicia handed him her car keys. "Go. I'll call the sheriff and tell him what happened. Be careful," she said and leaned toward Sam to kiss him good-bye.

"Thank you," Sam said and kissed her on the forehead.

43

7:00 a.m.

R uth was sitting on the running board of her car, tilting her head back and holding Trooper Sullivan's handkerchief to her nose when she heard the gunshot. At first she cheered, "He got him." Then she felt embarrassed by her reaction. The death or injury of anyone, even a criminal, was reprehensible. She was angry and in pain from her injuries, but she felt that was no reason to delight in her attacker being shot. *Well, maybe just a little.*

Ruth stood and rummaged under the front seat for her slippers. Her hand barely fit under the bent seat frame, and one of the slippers was wedged between the seat and the console. She yanked it loose, tearing the front tip. An open-toe slipper was better than none.

Ruth retied her belt and smoothed out her robe. Trooper Sullivan would be back soon and she would have to face the arrival of more police, but hopefully no reporters. Ruth checked her nose in the side-view mirror. The bleeding had stopped. She licked the corner of the handkerchief and wiped the dried blood from her upper lip. This was not a face anyone would be pleased to see on the evening news. She stuffed the handkerchief into her robe pocket and suddenly realized that the revolver was no longer there. Had she lost it in the accident? She scoured the floor of the car and the area around and under it. Nothing. Dennis must have taken it when they struggled while she was in a semi-conscious state. He had been pulling on her robe, though at the time she had assumed that he was just trying to force her from the car. The question that now concerned her was, assuming Dennis had again taken possession of the gun, did he also have ammunition? The revolver had been stolen from Franklin's home; why shouldn't she assume that he had also stolen more than just the five bullets that were originally in it? Now more questions began to flash across her mind like the cars of an express train streaking through a local subway station.

Did the police officer shoot Dennis? Did Dennis shoot the police officer? Did either one of them shoot Franklin?

The fallen tree lying between the ravine and the rock outcropping on the other side of the road made the police car inaccessible unless one climbed through the dense branches. She had neither the strength nor the appropriate apparel to make such a climb. Besides, it would take too long. She needed to go to the cabin and try to help, whatever the current situation.

The sun filtered through the trees as it crested the horizon. Chickadees and nuthatches sounded their familiar calls, and chipmunks and squirrels scurried about their morning collection of nuts and acorns. None paid attention to the bedraggled woman in the torn, bloody robe and one open- and one closed-toe slipper who limped up the hill.

***

7:20 a.m.

The bell rang, and the capital letter "P" illuminated above the stainless steel door of the hospital elevator just before it slid open. A man carrying a bouquet of flowers in a white ceramic vase stepped to the side and extended his arm in front of his wife to shield her from the man rushing out the door while snapping a full fifteen-round magazine into the grip of his Sig Sauer P226. The woman gasped when she saw the weapon and tried to blend into the wall behind her husband. Sam tucked his gun into the waistband of his trousers without acknowledging the couple and rushed into the parking lot.

He held Alicia's key over his head and pushed the button marked "open" until flashing lights and a single tone from the horn alerted him to her car's location. Sam slid into the driver's seat of the metallic-red BMW. His knees were jammed against the steering wheel, and he groped at the side of the seat for the controls. Smoke rose from the spinning tires until they made purchase with the garage floor and launched the BMW into a fishtailing dash for the exit.

Sam knew he was in a difficult situation. He knew his duty; it was clear. Ruth was in danger from what now appeared to be a lunatic that Sam had had in custody and then released. If anyone else was hurt by this man, Sam would feel personally responsible. True, he didn't have all the evidence he had needed to hold him for more than twenty-four hours, but his "police sense," that instinct that he had developed in twenty years of chasing criminals, should have alerted him to the possibility that Franklin was his man. He had pursued suspects in the past purely on the strength of his instincts and had eventually gotten the evidence needed to put the perpetrators away. He had had much less of a personal stake in those cases than he did in this one. If Ruth were killed or injured, he could never forgive himself.

The red BMW roared out of town and headed north on Route 62, then slid through exit 5 to Route 69 toward Russell. Fifteen minutes later he saw the *Finger Lick'in Ribs* sign on the right and knew that Destiny Road was no more than fifty yards ahead. He had expected, but did not see, a police car parked somewhere in the bushes, posted by Sheriff Thompson to monitor the traffic in and out of the small lane leading ultimately to the cabin.

Sam turned into Destiny Lane. He slowed to what he thought was a reasonable speed for the terrain but continued to bounce over rocks, branches, and uneven gravel, knowing it would probably cost six months' pay to repair Alicia's BMW, even if he just dented a fender. At the fork in the road, he chose the branch to the right. The last time he had driven this road, he chose the Lake Front fork and had ended up in a ditch. He hoped there were no more decisions to make before the cabin appeared.

Up ahead the state police car that he had expected to see at the forest entrance sat at an angle across a road that was blocked by a massive fallen tree. The BMW slid to a stop, and Sam assessed the situation. The colored roof lights of the police car were flashing, and the driver's door was open. Sam stopped and squatted behind the open door of the BMW and began to reconnoiter. Several broken small branches of the felled tree indicated to Sam that someone had climbed over the downed tree to gain access to the continuation of the road. He assumed a crouching position with his gun held in both hands and approached the police car. When he felt comfortable that the area was secure and the trooper was nowhere to be found, he inspected the fallen tree. Through its branches he saw Ruth's empty car, with its crumpled front and sideswiped doors, lying at an angle against the splintered stump of the tree.

The police car radio crackled, then the voice of the dispatcher sounded.

"Four-two-three Lima, report. Sullivan, where are you?"

Sam entered the police car and clicked the mike button.

"Dispatch, this is Lieutenant Sam Peirce, shield number five-two-nine-seven. I just found your unit, car four-two-three, abandoned on Destiny Lane off Route Sixty-Nine near Russell. There is a tree blocking the road and a disabled car on the other side of the tree. I'm going to investigate and look for your officer, over."

"Shield five-two-nine-seven, is the trooper's X-unit in the vehicle?" Sam looked around the console and dashboard of the police car and spotted the handheld radio. He heard another blast of static and then the dispatcher's voice. Sam released the talk button on the car radio, placed the earphone from the X-unit in his ear, and pressed the talk button.

"I have the unit, dispatch."

"Switch to channel three and stay at the vehicle until backup arrives. They're fifteen to twenty minutes out." Sam switched the radio to standby, placed it in his pocket, and began to climb through the branches to Ruth's car.

Sam made his way through the tangle of branches, snapping many of them out of frustration as he approached the SUV. He gritted his teeth when a broken twig poked him in his ribs. The earphone connected to the radio in his pocket hissed, but he had no intention of answering it or waiting for backup. Twenty minutes could be the difference between life or death for the trooper and for Ruth.

In Ruth's SUV he found the deflated air bag stained with blood and began to feel sick to his stomach. He knew it wasn't the blood that upset him. He had seen hundreds of wrecks in his career, many with crushed, lifeless bodies embedded in the twisted metal. No, it wasn't the sight of blood that upset him; it was the fact that he knew to whom the blood had belonged.

***

When Ruth arrived at the cabin, she was met by an eerie silence. The heavy oak door was ajar. Ruth called, "Hello, Trooper Sullivan? Franklin?" Ruth picked up the blood-stained shirt that Franklin had left on the chair. He had intended to soak it so that the stain wouldn't set. She hoped this stain would be the worst of Franklin's problems.

The door to Franklin's bedroom was open, and she rushed to the threshold. Using the doorframe to obscure her body, she leaned and tilted her head into the room.

On the far side, Trooper Sullivan was sitting in a chair, bound and gagged by strips of duct tape.

His head was hanging forward and he was slumped over, restrained from falling to the floor by the tape that bound him. Ruth could clearly see a bullet hole in his shirt in the center of his chest. She didn't need her biology training to tell her that the bullet had been aimed at his heart, and its aim had been true. She rushed to the trooper and placed her hand over the wound. It was dry. Ruth could feel the gnarly fabric of the Kevlar vest under his shirt and the stiffness of the steel plates suspended within. Ruth placed her hand on his neck and found the carotid artery. She felt a pulse. The force of the bullet must have knocked the wind out of him and rendered him unconscious. Next Ruth looked at Franklin, who was still sitting on the bed. On the floor in front of him was Dennis's hooded jacket. There was a small blood-stain in the center of the back of the jacket. He must have been struck by some of the BBs from her shotgun blast as he ran through the woods after shooting Sam.

Franklin looked as though he had been beaten about the face. His eye was beginning to swell, and he sniffed and wiped the blood from his nose on his sleeve.

"Franklin, are you all right? What did he do to you?" Ruth asked.

"Dennis," Franklin said as he pulled the revolver from behind his back and pointed it at her. "I'm Dennis, and it was you who did this to me."

His voice was sharp and lower in tone than Franklin's usual slightly whiny pitch. It was a voice she remembered hearing before. It was just days ago when he spoke of his fear of death. Ruth looked at the shirt in her hands. The bloodstain on the back of the shirt matched the location of the stain on Dennis's jacket. She spread the shirt in her hands and now noticed two small holes from the BBs. In a flash Ruth began to process much of the information she had gathered from her sessions with Franklin but had been too distracted by Sam Peirce's shooting to form a diagnosis. No one—no one that she knew of, that is—had spoken with or seen Dennis other than Franklin. Ruth had been pursued by a hooded man she assumed to be Dennis, and Sam had been shot by the same hooded figure, but the hooded man and Franklin were never seen at the same time. Ruth chastised herself for not seeing it sooner. The insomnia, the personality shifts, complaints of lost time, and now assuming a totally different persona—they were all symptoms of dissociative identity disorder. Franklin had multiple personalities, at least two anyway. How could she have missed it?

"Where is Franklin?" Ruth said. "I'd like to speak with him."

"He's here, but you can't talk to him. He'll be back in time to take the blame for everything that happens here. The policeman here saw Franklin shoot him. When he wakes up and finds you dead, he'll be the witness who puts Franklin at the scene and in possession of the murder weapon."

"But why? Franklin is your best friend." Ruth thought that by appealing to his sense of loyalty and love for Franklin, he might let him reappear. "I know you loved Franklin, and I'm sure he loved you."

"Wrong," Dennis shouted. "I loved him, but he never returned my love. He abandoned me for the first girl that came along. I didn't mind him wanting to be with a woman, but he didn't have to ignore me, to end our friendship over her, to choose her over me, to reject me completely. I gave my life for him." Dennis began to shake, and his features seemed to change. Ruth tried to process his last raging statement. *Dennis is dead?*

Ruth was standing several feet away from Trooper Sullivan's chair, looking across the room at Franklin, who was sitting on the edge of the bed aiming his revolver squarely at her chest. Ruth noticed movement in the mirror behind and to the right of Franklin. It was a reflection of the window to Ruth's left. Ruth glanced directly at the window and saw Sam outside, crouched at the corner of the sill. He was raising a short-barreled riot gun and aiming it at Franklin. He saw Ruth's eyes flit in his direction, and he signaled her with his hand to back away and give him a clean shot at Franklin.

Now Ruth could have moved closer to the trooper and both would have been out of Sam's line of fire, but Ruth felt that she was making progress and enough people had been hurt and killed. She stepped to her right, causing Franklin to turn slightly in her direction. This now placed the window and Sam's shotgun at Franklin's back but put Ruth directly in line with the blast. Shotguns fire hundreds of small BBs from within every shell, and the BBs expand in an ever-wider spray as they leave the muzzle of the shotgun. Ruth knew that Sam would not fire at Franklin because the spray of shot would be wide enough for much of it to pass either around or through Franklin and bring Ruth down as well.

"Franklin," she said, "I know that Dennis is dead, and I know you must feel guilty for rejecting his friendship, but whatever the circumstances of his death, I'm sure it wasn't your fault."

"He's not going to talk to you," the deeper Dennis voice said. "He took away my life, and I'm going to take away his. I'll make sure he suffers for the rest of his days for deserting me."

Sam put down the shotgun and drew his Sig P226 automatic. At this range, with a single bullet he could fire a kill shot that would end Franklin's life without any messy scattershot to cause collateral damage to Ruth. Ruth saw him raise the pistol and continued to call Franklin out.

"Franklin, it's your guilt talking," she said in a loud voice. As she spoke, attracting Franklin's or Dennis's attention, whoever he was at the moment, she walked forward and placed herself between Franklin and the window. Her body now blocked Sam's shot and also blocked Franklin's view of Sam.

Sam cursed under his breath. *Do you want to die?* he thought.

"Franklin, I understand you feel that Dennis hates you and wants to hurt you and anyone you care about, but before it's too late, tell me why. I can help you through this; just tell me why."

Franklin's voice returned to its normal higher pitch. "It's my fault that he drowned. I was a terrible friend, and he died trying to save my life. He had to hate me just before he died; he had to swear he would get even if he could."

Sam touched the earpiece from the police radio and pressed it to his ear as he heard: "This is Sniper One at the back of the house. I have a clear shot at the target through the bathroom window. Please authorize the shot." Sam thought for a moment. He looked back at Ruth, and although the gun was still aimed at her, she and Franklin were talking.

"This is Sniper One. I say again, do I have a green light to fire?"

Sam held the radio close to his lips and said, "Abort, Sniper One, do not fire."

Franklin heard Sam's whisper and leaned to the right to see where the sound had come from, and Ruth immediately snatched the gun from his hand. Franklin looked at the trooper tied in the chair and then at Ruth holding the revolver pointed at the ceiling. He said, "Dr. Klein, you look terrible. What happened?"

Two police officers in riot gear burst through the bedroom door and lifted Franklin to his feet. He looked confused. They cuffed his hands behind his back.

"You're going to be OK, Franklin. I'll make sure you're taken care of," Ruth said.

Sam ran into the room, took the revolver from her hand, and handed it to one of the officers leading Franklin out of the room.

He placed a hand on each of Ruth's shoulders. "You're a crazy woman," he said, but he was smiling when he said it. He put his arms around her and held her close. Sam groaned as Ruth's body pressed against his bruised ribs, and Ruth cringed as his cheek brushed against her swollen nose, but neither pulled away.

Epilogue

Ruth and Sam sat across from each other in a corner booth of the Bluebird Diner on Airport Road in Hazleton, Pennsylvania. The swelling of Ruth's nose had diminished; it was almost back to its normal size. Only a small Band-Aid across its bridge and a slight darkening around her eyes remained as evidence of the events two weeks ago. Emma had carefully administered makeup to compensate for the dark rings.

"You have a natural talent," Ruth said, pleased with her daughter's effort. The sight of Ruth's injuries caused Emma to forget her displeasure at having to leave the cabin and return home early. Ruth knew she would be forgiven but slipped the fifty-dollar bill into Emma's allowance envelope anyway.

Sam, on the other hand, showed no outward signs of the gunshot wound he had received. He moved gingerly and seemed in perfect health, although he did occasionally protect his bruised ribs with his left arm if anyone walked close to him.

"Have you seen your patient since he tried to kill you?" Sam asked, opening a packet of sugar and then placing it on his saucer instead of pouring it into his coffee.

"I saw him last week. Dr. Thornhill, a psychiatrist, has taken over the case. Franklin will get good care at Cedarcrest. They have the facilities to manage his illness," Ruth said, winding the wrapper from her straw around her finger.

"I still don't understand what made him go nuts like that. I've dealt with my share of murderers and violent criminals. I have to admit, I didn't see this one coming. Franklin never seemed to be violent," Sam said.

"Guilt," Ruth said. "Guilt is a powerful emotional force. Franklin had done something that he considered unforgivable when he was just nineteen years old; he abandoned Dennis, his best friend."

"A lot of guys choose to spend time with their girlfriends rather than their buddies. Isn't that the way we're built?"

"It's more complicated than that, Sam. I think Dennis loved Franklin more deeply than just as a friend, and although Franklin may not have felt the same, he understood how much he'd hurt Dennis. Then Dennis died trying to save Franklin's life, and the guilt became more than he could bear. To repress the guilt, his conscious mind shut out the fact that Dennis was dead."

"Well, it sounds like he lived with the guilt for over twenty years. What finally set him off?"

"He looked reasonably normal. He seemed to function in society, but he was a time bomb. As long as he had Myra, he believed there was a greater good that he had accomplished, but when Myra divorced him, that rationalization fell apart." Ruth pulled her chair closer to the table and leaned forward.

"Franklin has a very creative mind. He always did. I think that his extreme feelings of guilt caused him to believe that he was the cause of Dennis's death and that he should be punished. He brought Dennis back to life as an alter ego. The illness is called dissociative identity disorder. It's what we used to call a split personality. He always spoke of Dennis as his avenging angel, someone who righted the wrongs perpetrated against him. But this time it was Dennis's death that needed to be avenged."

"So Franklin was trying to hurt himself when he killed those women?"

"Franklin believed that he should go to prison for life or worse to atone for his sins against Dennis. I think Sylvia Radcliffe and Michelle Ackerman just happened to be in the wrong place at the wrong time. Sylvia was killed because she reminded him of Myra. His alter ego, Dennis, hated Myra. She was the cause of Franklin hurting him."

"What about Michelle Ackerman? She cleaned his teeth, for Christ's sake. Why would he kill her?"

"Franklin was interested in Michelle. He was planning to ask her out. His illness caused him to believe that he should be denied any happiness, so Dennis took her away from him. These were people in Franklin's life that he either liked or he had romantic thoughts about. As Dennis, he committed the murders, and as Franklin, he would pay the price for them. Somehow in his twisted psyche, Dennis was getting even with him, and once they were even, once Franklin was convicted and sentenced, he would be absolved of Dennis's death."

Sam shook his head. "I doubt any court would try him for murder. Even I can see that he isn't competent to stand trial. Will he ever get out of the nuthouse?"

"Mental hospital," Ruth corrected. "I don't know. I'm going to see him this evening; would you like to come?"

"Um, well, this evening?"

"It's all right, Sam. I'm sure you have better things to do. How is Alicia?" Ruth asked, collecting her handbag and her briefcase and sliding back her chair.

"She's fine," Sam said. "She decided to close her father's practice and find a job in research. It was what she always wanted to do. She was offered a job at Stanford University in California."

"Do you think you could be a West Coast cop?" Ruth asked, fidgeting with the check.

"Nah," Sam said. "I couldn't handle bean sprouts and watercress sandwiches. I'm more of a Philly cheesesteak kind of a guy." He reached over and took the check from her hand. "Why don't you stay with me for one more cup of coffee?"

***

An orderly opened the door and nodded to Ruth. Several of the paperback books that she had previously brought to Franklin were scattered on the floor below the bookshelf. Ruth picked up the books and arranged them on the shelf before crossing the room to Franklin.

A large man in a white coat and white trousers stood, arms folded, next to Franklin's chair. Ruth handed Franklin the new book she had brought.

It was a paperback copy of the latest Stephen King novel. Ruth chose not to ask about the scattered books. Franklin was no longer her patient. She had no authority to treat him, but Ruth still felt a responsibility to help him adjust to hospital life if she could. Franklin now spent much of his time reading, that is, when he wasn't in a therapy session or in physical rehabilitation. His ability to walk without a cane only appeared when his alter ego, Dennis, was in control. As Dennis, he could run and showed no weakness in his limbs. As Franklin, his disabilities were as real to him today as they had been for the last twenty-five years.

The symptoms of DID were clear to her, but there was still something unique about him. He seemed to possess some special trait, a peculiarity that she needed to better understand. Her visits were as a friend, but she had an ulterior motive for visiting him. There were still questions for which she needed answers. For example: How did he know about the tattoo on Sylvia's hip before he killed her as Dennis? How could he describe the burglary at Sylvia's home weeks before the flash drive was stolen? And how did he know that she believed she was being stalked in the forest? He had been a hundred miles away at the time. She wanted to ask these and more questions, but Dr. Thornhill had asked that the topic be avoided for now. She would wait. There was no rush.

"Franklin, is there anything else I can bring to you on my next visit?"

"Yes," he said. "I need a telephone, my cell phone."

"I'm sorry, but your doctor doesn't feel that you're ready to make calls. You need to rest and avoid any stress."

"Well, then will you make a call for me? It's very important."

"I'm not sure that I can, Franklin. Who is it you want me to call?"

"The airport, the Wilkes-Barre airport," he said.

"Franklin, who do you want to talk with at the airport?"

"Security, Dr. Klein. I need to warn them. In two weeks a plane will explode on takeoff. You have to tell them. I know it. I saw it in my dream."

Acknowledgments

To Officer David Saponieri, one of New York's finest, for helping me understand how a detective thinks, his choice of weapons, and methods for cleaning powdered sugar from a uniform.

To Peggy Samson who encouraged me to refine my ramblings into an edited work.

To Beryl Byman, Nancy Saponieri and Lisa Caviglia for patiently reading early drafts of the manuscript and propping up my ego enough to see it through to completion.

To my wife Ada, whose support, encouragement, recommendations, and ability to amuse herself during my long writing sessions made this book possible. You are my life, my past, my future, my muse and my wings. Thank you.

16318551R00226

Made in the USA
San Bernardino, CA
28 October 2014